# Between
# Two
# Moons

# Between Two Moons

*a novel*

Aisha Abdel Gawad

DOUBLEDAY
New York

Jacket illustration by Raphaelle Macaron
Jacket design by Emily Mahon
Book design by Cassandra J. Pappas

Library of Congress Cataloging-in-Publication Data
Names: Abdel Gawad, Aisha, author.
Title: Between two moons : a novel / Aisha Abdel Gawad.
Description: First edition. | New York : Doubleday, [2023]
Identifiers: LCCN 2022030656 (print) | LCCN 2022030657 (ebook) |
ISBN 9780385548618 (hardcover) | ISBN 9780593467824 (trade paperback) |
ISBN 9780385548625 (ebook)
Subjects: LCSH: Muslims—New York (State)—New York—Fiction. |
Brooklyn (New York, N.Y.)—Fiction. | LCGFT: Domestic fiction. | Novels.
Classification: LCC PS3601.B423 B48 2023 (print) | LCC PS3601.B423 (ebook) |
DDC 813/.6—dc23/eng/20220712
LC record available at https://lccn.loc.gov/2022030656
LC ebook record available at https://lccn.loc.gov/2022030657

MANUFACTURED IN THE UNITED STATES OF AMERICA

1   3   5   7   9   10   8   6   4   2

First Edition

*for Kelly and Natalia,*
*whose hands I am always reaching for*

The Hour has drawn near and the moon was split in two.

—THE HOLY QUR'AN, 54:1

# Part I

Eat and drink until you can tell a white thread from a black one in the light of the coming dawn.

—2:187

W E WOKE THAT MORNING, the first day of what would be a very
hot Ramadan in June, to find the police raiding Abu Jamal's
café. A dozen men, dressed more like construction workers than cops,
loaded boxes of Nescafé instant coffee and Lipton tea into vans. They
carried away glass shisha pipes the size of small children, and dumped
mismatched cups and saucers into a large bin of shattered porcelain.
Some led dogs on leashes—big majestic German shepherds and one
runty beagle, who sniffed furiously around all the tables.

I might have slept through it. I might have woken up a few hours
later to find Abu Jamal's café closed, to be replaced a few months later
with another Arab business—a falafel stand or a travel agency specializing in trips to Mecca. But Baba woke me up.

"Wake up, ya binti," he said as he pushed our bedroom window
open, the one that led out onto the apartment's fire escape. "Shoofi!
They arrest that stupid Libyan."

He climbed out onto the fire escape in his ratty old galabiya with his
black hair sticking straight up. In the bed across from mine, my twin
sister, Lina, put a pillow over her face and groaned.

"Hurry up, Amira," Baba called to me. "Come see." He sounded
gleeful. He leaned against the railing and peered down to the street

below to get a closer look. Baba didn't like Abu Jamal, not since they got into a big argument over whose dictator was worse, Egypt's or Libya's. It escalated until Abu Jamal accused Egyptians of turning everyone into religious nuts. "Look at your wife!" he'd said. And that's when Baba slammed his hand down on one of the plastic folding tables, right in the middle of Abu Jamal's café, and shattered a plate filled with discarded olive pits. "It was just a plate," Baba said when he returned home later that night. But that didn't matter—ever since then, Baba had been banned. He was now forced to walk another three blocks to the next-nearest shisha café, and for that, he just couldn't find it in him to forgive the stupid Libyan.

I pulled on a sweatshirt of Lina's that she'd left lying on the floor and flipped the hood over my head to cover my hair before I stepped out onto the fire escape next to Baba. The approaching dawn spread like a great purple bruise over New York, but the café was illuminated by a streetlight as if by an interrogator's lamp. The men with their dogs were milling in and out, talking into radios, and taking photographs. They were moving so fast—I wanted to call down to them, ask them to slow down, so that I could make sense of what I was seeing. Across the street, Imam Ghozzi, who volunteered as the custodian of the Islamic Center of Bay Ridge, swept dust and bits of trash off the sidewalk in front of the mosque as if nothing unusual were happening.

"What do you think he did?" I asked Baba.

"He probably steal money from little babies," Baba said.

"It looks like they're sniffing for bombs or drugs or something," I said.

Baba blinked rapidly three times, like he does when he can't hear. "Bombs? No, it's nothing like that." He took a step back from the fire escape.

I heard a rustling behind us and turned to find Mama standing at the window with her arms crossed. Her face was pink and glowing, and I could tell it was freshly scrubbed for prayer. She was wearing a long gray abaya and a white prayer veil.

"What's going on out here?" she asked.

"Shoofi! ya Maryam," Baba said, "they are arresting the stupid Libyan! Come and see."

"Shame on you, Kareem," Mama said. "You want to bring bad luck on us like that?"

Mama's God was a capricious one. He could turn on you on a dime. You had to be careful.

"No, no, Amira and me just out here praying that God forgive the stupid Libyan's sins," Baba said, grinning at me.

Mama snorted and then leaned down to wake Lina. She removed the pillow from over Lina's face, and the lacy edges of her prayer veil brushed Lina's cheek. Lina swatted it away like a fly. "Sabah al-khair, ya gamila," she said.

"Come and eat," she told us. "It's almost dawn."

Bay Ridge was about to fast for a whole month of fifteen-hour days. We would be one dry mouth, one rumbling belly, one pounding head. Mothers would wake at least an hour before dawn to make the suhoor meal, to scramble eggs and basturma in skillets. And when the children and the husbands finally woke up, usually with only a few minutes to spare, the mothers would stuff the mixture into pita halves so their families could eat more quickly, in time to perform wudu and pray with the sun. It was your last chance to eat and drink and smoke and fuck and curse and gossip and think unkind thoughts until the sun set again in the evening.

Baba shuffled after Mama like a bad dog. Lina stood up and yawned, letting out a long moan. Mama made us a breakfast of hard-boiled eggs, mashed fava beans, and sliced tomatoes. We sat around the kitchen table, shoveling food sleepily into our mouths, letting bits of egg dribble down our chins. After we'd eaten, Mama stood sentry over us and watched as we each downed three full glasses of water.

"I'm going back to bed," Lina said after she'd finished.

"Haram, ya binti," Mama said and grabbed the collar of her Wu-Tang T-shirt.

The sun was creeping up the horizon and we still needed to pray Fajr. Mama dragged the coffee table to the corner of the living room to clear space for the four of us to pray all lined up. Then she brought us a basket of delicate white prayer scarves with edges like doilies. Lina and I each slipped one on, and then Mama pointed to the bathroom. We zombie-shuffled over to it, purposefully knocking into each other as we went.

Lina and I stood side by side in front of the bathroom sink. Silently, we washed ourselves with cold New York City tap water. We were efficient and thorough. In the name of God, state your intent to perform wudu. Wash both hands up to the wrists. Rinse your mouth three times. Clean your nostrils, breathing in water and blowing it out three times. Rinse your face three times. Wash your arms up to the elbows three times. Slick your hair back like an Italian mobster, once. Wash your ears. Wash your feet. Do you feel cleansed? Are you ready?

After we had performed wudu, Mama wanted Baba, our patriarch, to stand in front and lead us in prayers, but he was annoyed about being late to the shop. Baba didn't like to pray—sometimes, when he was feeling nostalgic about the old days in the old country, he would tell me about the time he was eighteen and he stormed out of his village masjid back in Egypt.

"That stupid imam, he tell me man come from ball of clay and clot of blood, and I tell him, What, are you stupid? Man, he come from monkey, not clay! So I leave and I go home and I tell my mama, Mama, I'm not praying anymore. And ever since that day, I never pray again."

Except, of course, he did pray again. Countless times. But I think I know what he meant. He meant that he never really felt it again, never again believed that it would help him ace a test or publish the poems he wrote in the margins of his school notebooks. He prayed now like a man following orders, like a man too tired to put up a fight.

The clock on the mantel chimed. It was like a cuckoo clock, except instead of birds it opened to reveal a tiny golden Ka'ba that spun and played a recording of a famous muezzin from Egypt reciting the call to prayer. A robotic voice told us that prayer is better than sleep. There are no minarets in Brooklyn. God's name does not echo across the buildings. There is nothing but a clock on the wall.

Baba was persuaded to stand in front of us, his womenfolk, and lead prayers. But he rushed through all his rakat, touching his forehead to the carpet for only a moment before standing up again. The rest of us were only halfway through when we heard the door close behind him.

When we had finished, Lina and I squeezed together in her bed. I tried to close my eyes and determine whether I felt any different on the first day of the holy month. The month when, a zillion years ago, the Prophet Muhammad received his first revelations up on that mountaintop. He thought he was just a poor illiterate orphan escaping to the mountain to rest his mind. But then the Angel Jibrail came down, and—bam—all of a sudden he was a prophet, *the* prophet.

For some that summer, the next thirty days would be filled with prayers and reflections and recitations. Bodies and minds would be purified. But for the rest of us, it would be thirty days of waiting for the sun to set so we could eat and drink without incurring the judgment of all the collective mothers and grandmothers and aunties of Bay Ridge, who with one wagging finger and one cluck of the tongue could banish us into a prison of guilt.

The waiting. Every Ramadan, people waited for Lina to change. To be struck with the spirit of Islam, to ditch her cutoffs and halter tops for a nice, modest abaya. To hang out after prayers with the good Muslim girls at the Starbucks on 3rd instead of drinking with the Mexicans in Sunset Park. And every Ramadan, Lina waited for people to go ahead and give up on her.

Baba waited for Mama to mellow, to hang up her abayas, put down her Qur'an, and become once again the quietly irreverent girl he had married.

Mama waited for us, her husband and daughters, to believe as we ought to.

They both waited for Sami, their boy, their firstborn, to come back to them.

I waited for something without a name. A jolt, a tingling, a filling up.

Ordinarily, I didn't care much about Ramadan. But that summer, with our high-school graduation only days away, it felt momentous. Suddenly the things around me—tables, books, clouds—were imbued with meaning that I was supposed to be able to decipher but couldn't.

In September, I would go to college, and I was sure that by then I would be different. I would push and the world would stumble in response.

Lying next to Lina that first morning, I closed my eyes and tried to imagine the woman I was destined to become. I saw a glimmer of my own future arm, thinner, with a figure-eight tattoo curling around my wrist. I smiled to myself, but then I realized that I had stolen this wrist off the girl who served us pizza yesterday after school. It was her tattoo, her skin, her body. I had plagiarized my own imaginings of myself. So, eyes closed, I kept waiting for knowledge to strike me like an arrow in the heart.

These are the normal kinds of waiting that fill the long, dry-mouthed days of Ramadan. But this Ramadan, this particularly long and hot Ramadan, there was another kind of waiting that we all shared. It kept everyone in Bay Ridge strung together on a long, tenuous thread, knocking into one another like prayer beads.

We were waiting for the men with dogs to return.

Outside, Abu Jamal's café sat abandoned, wrapped in yellow police tape. Across the street, Baba led a calf around the corner, to the alley behind his butcher shop, where he would drag a very sharp knife across the skin of its throat while muttering verses from the Qur'an. Some-one from one of the mosques had brought it to him, because there's no better way to kick off the holy month than with a sacrificial slaugh-ter. He'd have to do it quickly and quietly and be sure to mop up all the blood afterward; otherwise, the Health Department would be back with another citation.

We could hear the calf mewing gently. Lina leaned out the window and called down to Baba. "Baba," she said, "don't do it!"

Baba smiled up at her and called back, "Close your eyes, ya Lina, look away." And as he said it, he moved his own hand over the calf's eyes so it wouldn't have to see what was coming next.

It was seven hours into the first day of Ramadan, and we were as hungry as shit. Our girl Reina kept offering us sticks of Juicy Fruit gum because our stomachs were rumbling so loudly.

"Nah, homie," Lina said, pushing the pack back toward Reina.

"Not even gum?" Reina asked.

"Not even water," I said.

Lina and I had been friends with Reina since elementary school, but every year she still asked all the same questions. We were chilling on a bench near the playground in Owl's Head Park. Lina kept shifting around, pulling one leg up to her chest and stretching the other out across the sidewalk, trying on different poses for the boys at the basketball courts, like some kind of mannequin. We were graduating from Fort Hamilton High School in two days, but classes for the seniors had already finished, and everyone was out, clustered around various benches, listening to music on their phones, a cacophony of tinny techno beats and muffled rappers. We were listening to Ol' Dirty Bastard on Lina's phone, because she was going through what she called her "OG" phase.

"And I thought Lent was bad," Reina said.

"Lent is for pussies," Lina said. "Muslims are hard."

"Yeah, so hard they be blowing up shit." Reina made an explosion with her fist.

"At least we don't go around with cocaine up our assholes—right, Roo?"

Lina looked at me for backup. This was a game we usually loved to play with Reina—sometimes it was a competition over whose people were the most fucked up or sometimes the least fucked up—but, today, I wasn't paying any attention.

I was thinking about our brother again. Usually, I was pretty good at limiting my thoughts of him to once a month. Once my brain hit that quota, it shut down that lobe for another month, and Sami was again banished. But he was up for another parole hearing, and I kept seeing his face on other people's bodies as they walked around Bay Ridge. While Reina and Lina argued, I was looking across the street at a mural of schoolchildren holding hands in a circle and imagining his face painted onto all their sweet multicultural cartoon heads. A dozen cartoon Samis holding hands. And earlier that morning, during suhoor, I saw him holding a baseball mitt on the back of a Cheerios box. Sami didn't even like baseball. Or at least he never used to. I didn't know what he liked or didn't like anymore.

"Amira?" Lina said, elbowing me.

I wondered what they did for Ramadan in prison. Did some disgruntled guard have to deliver meals on trays at four in the morning to all the Muslim inmates? Or did they get to leave their cells and shuffle sleepily to the cafeteria before dawn? Or did none of this happen, did the prison just make them wait for regular breakfast with all the other inmates? If so, how did they break their fast? With a single dried date, like the Prophet Muhammad? Or with water and a slice of white bread? In Guantanamo, they were force-feeding the prisoners, sliding bloody tubes down their throats during the fasting hours, choking them with life, because what was the difference between Ramadan and a hunger strike? Is that what was happening to Sami in that turreted prison upstate while I sat on a bench in Owl's Head Park listening to my own stomach growl?

Lina placed a palm on my forehead. "You all right?" she asked.

I nodded. "Just wondering what happened to that Libyan guy," I said.

"I heard they shipped his ass straight to Guantanamo," Reina said.

"I heard he was in for embezzlement and tax evasion," Lina said. "He *was* always talking about the Maserati he had back in Tripoli."

For the next half-hour, Lina and Reina made up crazier and crazier reasons for the Libyan's arrest.

"He traded in exotic jellyfish," Lina said.

"He sold his semen on eBay," Reina said.

"He raped a shisha pipe," Lina said.

"He raped a camel," Reina said.

I left Lina and Reina at the park and walked over to the local community center, where I worked as a part-time receptionist. It was the sort of place you find at the heart of immigrant communities all over New York—nondescript storefront buildings that still wear hauntings of their former lives as churches or hair salons or travel agencies, or, in our case, a gynecologist's office. The Center, as everyone in Bay Ridge called it, because its real name was too long and too Arab—it was actually called the Muhammad Ibrahim Abdulraziq Center for Arab-American Community Life—was where everyone came when they needed help applying for a green card, or deciphering a parking ticket, or paying an electricity bill, or learning English. People came to gossip, to trade recipes, to drop their kids off while they went to the grocery store, to complain about employers, landlords, wives, husbands, children.

When I got to the Center to start my shift, I could hear a woman moaning and hiccupping from a back office. "The Libyan's wife," someone whispered to me when I arrived. The caseworkers were making calls, but all they could find out was that he was being held in an undisclosed location, on various undisclosed charges. That was all the police would tell them. There was some code, some law, that made it okay not to tell us anything. The caseworkers were all huddling in the back, calling the ACLU and Legal Aid and trying to triage something that was already way out of their league. I heard them say something about Homeland Security and the Patriot Act, and I knew that the Libyan was in deep, ineffable, and labyrinthine shit.

I sat down at my desk, with one of its legs held up by cinder blocks, and listened as the wife's sobs slowed to a sporadic choke. My job was mostly to get clients to sign in on the waiting list. Most of them didn't, because lines are a uniquely Western invention. But today the lobby was quiet, almost empty, as if people were staying away either out of respect for Um Jamal or out of fear that they might catch what she had.

I had been working at the Center since I was fifteen. I told myself it was to help Baba with the groceries and the utility bill, but really it was so Lina and I could impulse-shop at the CVS down the street, lunge at neon nail polish and bags of chips. Lina could never hold down a steady job—she had picked up the odd babysitting gig and had one time dressed up like a giant cell phone and passed out flyers in front of a MetroPCS store, but that was it.

The Center was across the street from our apartment on 5th Avenue and 72nd Street. Sometimes, if I stood out on the fire escape and craned my neck around the corner, I could see inside the lobby to get an idea of what kind of day we would have. If I could see men chain-smoking out-side and children leaping off the waiting-room chairs, I knew it would be one of those deep-breaths, count-to-ten days. Days when old men yelled at me for not letting them skip the line, and when old women brought me Britney Spears perfume sets from CVS as bribes. Arabs at the Center were always waiting for something—*My mother needs an operation, My cousin needs asylum, I can't read my phone bill, I can't read at all, Teach me English, Get me food stamps, Don't send me to the soup kitchen, soup kitchens are shameful, I need a job, I need unemployment, Do allergies count for disability, Tourist visa, Marriage visa, Green card, Green card, Green card.*

I had only been there for about an hour when Lina pushed open the front door.

"What's good?" she said as she walked immediately over to the window-unit air conditioner and stuck her face into the cold blast.

There were only two women and a toddler in the lobby when Lina arrived. One lady who apparently cared nothing for Ramadan—most people at least pretend to fast—was cracking sunflower seeds between her teeth and spitting the shells onto the carpet. The other lady was clucking her tongue with every seed spat. The baby was making eerie Shrek-like noises and seemed not to belong to either woman. He was running around the room and hitting me on the shin with a flopping banana peel.

"Everyone's trying to figure out what's going on with the Libyan," I said to Lina when she came to sit down on the floor next to my desk.

"Hmm," Lina said, chipping the nail polish off her big toe. She didn't care. She had probably already forgotten all about the stupid Libyan.

"I mean, it's crazy, no one even knows what he's being charged with," I said, in spite of, or perhaps because of, her overwhelming indifference. The truth was that the whole thing was starting to freak me the fuck out.

"I thought Reina and I already settled that," Lina said finally, dust-ing the chipped nail polish off her fingertips. "He was breeding mutant donkeys."

My head began to pound. My mouth was dry, and my stomach had given up its rumbling. I had gotten up to rummage through the first-aid kit for some aspirin when I remembered that I couldn't take any. Because the office was gifted to the Center by a wealthy Arab gynecologist, most of the rooms had small random sinks or metal tables with floral cloths draped over them to cover the old flaking stirrups. Cabinets full of syringes and ten-year-old Pap smear kits along with Post-it notes and ballpoint pens. I found the aspirin next to a pink plastic replica of a uterus and decided to put the pills in my pocket until sunset.

When I returned to the lobby, Lina was coloring a page from a coloring book we'd left out for the kids of our clients. It was one of those dollar-store booklets with the knockoff Mickey Mouse pictures. She scribbled silently for a few minutes, and I put my head down on the cool surface of my desk. Then I heard her rip a page from the book. She folded it carefully, like a middle-school note, and handed it up to me. She had drawn a large red boner on Mickey and a speech bubble that said, *I met a boy.*

"Ya Allah," I groaned.

She rolled her eyes.

"Tell me," I said.

"Not if you're going to be judgy about it," she said.

"I won't," I said.

"You will," she said. But then she started telling me anyway.

"I met him at that party I went to with Reina a few weeks back. Remember her cousin's stepsister's birthday party?"

Sometimes Reina and Lina went to parties without me, because I didn't drink and they said I was a buzzkill.

"I thought you said all the guys there were fat and old," I said.

"They were," she said. "Except Andres. All the food at the party had pork in it, even the rice. So Andres took me to McDonald's and got me French fries and a McFlurry."

"How romantic," I said.

"Shut up," she said. "That's not even the important part."

One of the caseworkers came out from the back to check the clipboard. She called the name at the top of the list, and the woman with the sunflower seeds got up and followed her to an office in the back. I checked her name off the list and motioned for Lina to continue.

"He runs a nightclub in Manhattan, and he knows all these big people in the fashion industry and stuff. And he said that I have real potential."

"Potential for what?" I asked.

"Modeling," she said.

"Modeling?" I said.

"Modeling," Lina said.

"Isn't that just what guys say when they want to sleep with you? You should be a model?"

"Except this is for real," she said. "He's booking an appointment for me to meet with a photographer and get head shots done."

"Really? When?" I asked.

"We're texting about it right now," she said. She shoved her phone in my face but took it away before I could read anything.

I felt a little jealous, of course. I was used to Lina's being the beautiful one, and I generally didn't mind. We were twins, but not identical. She was taller and thinner and darker, with wavy black hair that fell around her shoulders like she was in a hair commercial. I was shorter and paler, and my hair frizzed in corkscrews around my face. I was proud to be her sister and best friend in the whole world. But her beauty had never taken her out of Bay Ridge before. I was going to college in the fall, but that didn't really count. I would be commuting, and I always pictured Lina there, waiting for me when I got home. But, lately, she had been leaving me behind more and more. And I didn't even know I'd been left behind until after the fact, when she came back from a date or a party or shopping with "friends." I was starting to feel like a little sister from whom Lina was gently trying to shake herself free.

Lina waited with me until my shift ended. More women had filed in as my shift wore on. I walked out past all them still sitting with their half-filled forms on their laps. Some of them called out to me—"Ya Amira," "Ya habibti," "Ya aroosa," "Ya hilwa," "Ya gamila"—but I just kept on walking through the doors. I suddenly felt a desperate need to get far away from there—from the mothers with their beseeching glances and their prayers, from the overworked caseworkers and the disgruntled, humiliated men sitting across desks from them.

Outside the Center, Lina sighed impatiently and said, "Let's get the fuck out of here." I looked through the windows at the mothers straining over their incomprehensible forms, sliding their drugstore eyeglasses up and down their noses, as if the problem was that they just weren't seeing things right. "Yes," I said. "Let's."

It was all I wanted in the world, my greatest, best-nourished, and most tender dream: to get out. To change my name and dye my hair, to become someone bold and careless. I wanted brand new. I wanted unrecognizable, untrackable, untraceable. But there was another desire, one I did not want to acknowledge, that was holding me back. And that was the desire not to abandon my tribe, not to be disloyal, not to be like *them*—those people, out there in the world, who didn't know us and despised us.

This was the cycle we had fallen into. Lina and I separated, floated away from each other, groping the boundaries of Bay Ridge for an escape hatch. And then, when slapped with the cruel indifference of the world, especially to solitary female bodies seeking discovery like long-forgotten satellites drifting through space, we'd crash back into each other.

When we got the call, I was wandering around Baba's butcher shop. It was the second day of Ramadan, and Mama had sent me down from our apartment upstairs to get some groceries. She was mad at him for something, as usual.

I followed the sound of Baba's muttering into the back room. He was reciting poetry. I stopped to listen to the melodious Arabic trilling from his mouth: "Don't cry for Layla and don't rejoice over Hind, / Instead, drink to the rose from a rosy red wine."

He was taking a boning knife to a massive beef shank, slicing into the flesh like it was butter. "Don't let Mama hear you reciting that poem," I said. I was not worried about startling him, because Baba was born with a butcher knife in his hand. He laughed a little. "Did I ever tell you why I name the shop Abu Nuwas Halal Meats?" he asked.

"Yes," I said. "Many times. Thousands."

"The whole story?" he said.

"Yes, Baba."

He ignored me and said, "The Arabs, they always worry too much for who is doing what. This lady has too-short skirt and that man too-long hair. But we love our poets. We grow up learning al-Mutanabbi and Imru al-Qays. We are very proud of our poets."

"Yes, I know, Baba," I said.

"But these Arabs," he gestured with the knife in front of him, "they do not know that their beloved poets wrote about drinking wine and kissing boys. So, when I open the shop, I decide to name it Abu Nuwas, who was the worst of all the poets, always singing about boys' pretty bottoms and the sweet taste of wine, and it is my secret joke."

He laughed hard, resting his free hand on his belly and leaving a spot of blood.

"I've come to get some groceries for Mama. She's really mad at you," I said. "What did you do?"

He waved his hand in the air and said, "I make it better later."

I left him to his disassembling and started collecting Mama's supplies: a package of pita bread, three lemons, green olives, and a jar of tahina. Baba had a few shelves where he stocked condiments and other pantry items in addition to meat. When I came back, he was grinding up some fresh trim for me. I used to love to watch him put whole chunks of meat into the top of the grinder and see them slither out the other end in curled ribbons. But now it made me feel sick, so I walked to the far end of the shop and stuck my face into the open barrel of cumin seeds and took a deep breath in.

While Baba was wrapping the beef neatly in a wax-paper parcel, his cell phone rang. He answered on the Bluetooth that was almost always clipped to his ear.

"Abu Nuwas Halal Meats," he answered. He dropped the parcel on the counter, and suddenly his face got pale.

"Bolice," he whispered to me, pointing at the phone, but that's not what he meant—what he meant was that someone from Sami's lawyer's office was calling. He often got the two confused—the police and Sami's lawyer. Until maybe two years earlier, we would often get calls from this lawyer—a small bald man who didn't even have an e-mail address, or at least not one he shared with us, and insisted on writing everything by hand. *Sami's been moved to a different facility . . . He's doing a week in solitary . . . He's in the medical ward because of a fight.* But over the last couple years, these calls had been rare. If it wasn't for the giant photograph of Sami hanging in the living room, you might even be able to forget he had ever lived with us in the apartment. It looked like the portraits of Gaddafi people used to hang in their living rooms so they wouldn't be accused of betraying the Supreme Guide. No one would ever be able to accuse Mama of forgetting her firstborn, her son.

Baba motioned frantically for a pen, so I reached behind the counter and got him one, along with a scrap of old receipt paper. As he wrote, I could see the receipt paper growing red from the oily blood on his fingers. He was saying, "Okay, okay . . . Yes, sir, we will be ready . . . Okay, great. Yes."

When the call ended, he stared into the receipt paper for a long time. I could feel myself starting to sweat.

He looked up at me with tears in his eyes. He's dead, I thought. But Baba started to laugh in great heaves. Then he was hiccupping, and I thought he might choke, so I patted his back until he calmed down enough to tell me the news. "Good behavior," he kept saying between gasps. "The lawyer, he say Good Behavior." He pronounced it slowly, breaking up all the syllables, adding new ones. *Good Be-hav-i-or.*

He wouldn't say anything more until we were upstairs with Mama, who forgot all about her vow to be angry at Baba for whatever it was that he had done once she saw his face. "What is it?" she asked. "It's Sami, isn't it?"

"Yes," Baba said, smiling like a drunk. "He is coming home. The lawyer says it is because Sami has Good Be-hav-i-or."

It was like this was the most unbelievable part of the story—not that the State of New York was releasing him after only six of his eight years served, but that that they were rewarding him for this thing called good behavior that no one knew Sami was even capable of.

"When?" Mama asked. She was clutching me, leaning on me. Her fingernails dug into my arm like I was a prop for support.

When Baba spoke next, I felt as if a skyscraper collapsed in my guts. "Two weeks," he said.

The lawyer, in one of his handwritten notes, had gotten the date of the parole hearing wrong. It wasn't approaching; it had already happened. And Sami won.

My mother shrieked like a predator bird. She slapped my body and hers. But I was frozen. Time stopped. The collapsing feeling had now become an eye in my stomach, opening and closing very slowly.

I guess I had only ever considered the possibility of parole abstractly. When these sorts of things came up, they only served to remind me that I had a brother—that he was real and I hadn't made him up. It's not that I had never imagined him getting out, but in my head, it was always years from now, like twenty or thirty years from now, and he would be impossibly old and shriveled, and I would be living somewhere very far away—I would have a closet full of expensive professional trousers in shades of black and gray and navy, and I would take exotic vacations and send money to my parents back in Bay Ridge. His life would never touch mine.

As much as I didn't want to admit it, I was afraid of him. It wasn't just that he brought what felt like enemies into our lives—petty gangsters and drug dealers, police officers, lawyers, probation officers, judges. It wasn't just that I had always felt that my parents loved him more precisely because of the trauma he caused them. It was all of that, but it was also this feeling that, out of all the people Sami loved and hated, he loved and hated me the most. It was like he was practicing something on me—some essential skill he would need in order to become a man. Like I was the whetstone of his future. The duller I was, the sharper he could be. And yet his attention on me made me feel spotlighted, suspended in blinding light. He practiced a different trick on Lina—he ignored her. He made her invisible. And now? Look at us. Lina, the girl lighting herself on fire like a flare, an emergency you couldn't put out. Me, trying to make myself small, smooth, something you wouldn't notice if you stepped on it.

Baba gathered me toward him. He put his hand on my back and whispered, "Don't be worried, habibti." I didn't like that he could read my face so easily.

I looked over at my mother, who had sunk down into the couch, her body slumped against the cushions like a pile of laundry. She also was too easy to read—the ecstatic hope brimming in her watery green eyes made me sad and scared for her. Unlike Baba, she had a tendency to say exactly what she was feeling. Baba had three modes: laughing at his own jokes, complaining about the stupidity of his fellow human beings, especially other Arabs, and silence. Not inscrutable silence— not the type of silence that smothered layers of complicated feelings—it was just empty quiet, as if he shut off for hours at a time. Mama liked to label and announce her feelings: "I am angry with you" or "That was funny" or "I'm confused" or "That makes me sad." When I was a child, this habit of hers comforted me because I always felt I knew where she stood, that there would never be any surprises. But as a teenager, I was beginning to see these proclamations as dams built up to stanch the flow of the real thing that was swelling and churning somewhere inside of her, something that I could not see.

I looked at the heap of my mother on the sofa, her body hidden in the folds of her abaya.

"I can't believe it," she said. And I knew that Sami would break her heart with a glance, with the flick of his hand, or with the shake of his head.

I hadn't laid eyes on him in years. When they had the money to take Baba's old Tercel for an oil change and fill it up with a tank of gas, Mama and Baba would make the drive upstate to see him. But I never went with them, and they had stopped asking a long time ago. I stayed in Bay Ridge with Lina and the rest of the Arabs, stayed where, even with the spies that lurked in our mosques and restaurants waiting to ship our brown asses to Guantanamo, it felt safer.

.  .  .

Lina and I were seventeen, the same age Sami was when he disappeared into that prison upstate. Now he was twenty-three, which felt impossible. How could anyone grow in that place?

Sometimes kids at school who heard about him from their parents would ask us what he had gone in for. Our answers depended on our moods, on the day of the week, on who we were trying to impress or frighten: Murder, assault, bank robbery. He was a commander of a fearsome drug cartel, he dealt heroin to preschoolers, he kidnapped the daughter of Goldman Sachs (we assumed that was the first and last name of one very rich man) and held her for ransom.

But the truth was, Lina and I actually didn't know. He had always been getting into trouble, had been locked up in juvie countless times before. For our whole childhood, he was in and out of one institution after another. We lost track after that first time, when he mooned the bus driver and got arrested (that was when Sami found out he was brown; before that, he just thought he was Ferris Bueller). Things really shifted after he came home with his first two tattoos scrawled onto his biceps and his hand. That's when we started to hear words like "burglary" and "assault," when the whole family would be made to blink at probation officers sitting across from us in the living room. This time, though, it had not been a few weeks or a couple months in County, but eight years in State.

It had something to do with a car. Maybe a dime bag in the glove compartment, maybe an unregistered handgun. Was the car stolen? Who was in the car with him, and where were they going? The only detail that ever really filtered down to us was that of an olive-green Jaguar. For years, we'd look out for one. Sometimes we would see a Jaguar gliding down the street and, in between a pocket of shadow and sunlight, we'd think it was the one. But then it always turned out to be slate gray or hunter green.

It was probably all quite ordinary. But we could never see Sami as ordinary. His delinquency, his coldness, his anger—these were all almost supernatural to us, beyond comprehension. Because, in truth, it was easier to think of him as special, even if he was especially bad, than to admit that he was no different from so many other brown boys.

No, Sami was special. The car was an olive-green Jaguar. His crime? Unknowable.


I left Mama and Baba in the apartment. They were calling everyone they knew; phones were ringing from Brooklyn to Egypt. I could imagine my female relatives in Alexandria shrieking and thanking Allah and saying how they had never understood how something like this could happen in America in the first place. And our neighbors in Brooklyn would all congratulate Mama and Baba and say what a fine young man Sami had always been and how they were sure he was innocent. And then they'd hang up and raise their eyebrows to one another. "Did you hear that the criminal Emam boy is coming home?" they would say.

Lina was out somewhere. It suddenly felt imperative that I not be home when she got back. I had this vision of myself sitting on my hands, waiting to tell her the terrible news. I wanted to be gone when she found out. I wanted her to wonder where I was, to wait for *me* to return. The only problem was that I had nowhere to go. I thought I might go to the Center even though I didn't have a shift, but then I remembered that it would be closed: everyone was at some kind of vigil or protest for Abu Jamal. They had figured out where he was being held—at a jail in Lower Manhattan. I didn't like the idea of going to a jail. I wanted to go someplace where I could forget. A movie theater or a street fair. A submarine or a rocket ship. But I found myself walking to the train anyway.

Forty minutes later, I was standing in the shadow of the Metropolitan Correctional Center, a deceptively sprawling building made up of conjoined rectangles, like a tower built by a child. The protest was bigger than I thought it would be, but also more boring. It wasn't just a few caseworkers from the Center holding signs. There were people from other organizations there, too. From the ACLU, some South Asian nonprofit, the Yemeni Business Owners' Association. There were white people and Black people, Asians and Arabs. But they were all just kind of standing around across the street. The police had barricades set up around the jail so no one could actually go near it. The protesters seemed to be patiently taking turns speaking into a microphone. There was a woman in hijab talking about solitary confinement. I drifted closer to the crowd, although I wasn't really paying attention. I was gazing up at the building, watching it unfold like an accordion around the block, when I felt this tickle in my ear. A voice, a hiss of warm breath. So close I could smell his deodorant, the same kind Baba used.

"Do you think he can see you?" a man whispered into my ear. He was standing behind me, leaning down. I jumped and whipped around.

"Sorry, sorry," he said, and put his hands out in front of him, as if trying to soothe an aggrieved cat. "I didn't mean to scare you. I just noticed you looking up at the windows." He gestured to the MCC building.

He was younger than I first thought. The smell of Baba's deodorant had thrown me off. He was maybe late twenties, although how good a judge is a seventeen-year-old of age? He had dark-brown skin and a neatly trimmed black beard. Traditional, I thought. Religious. But then I noticed the little man-bun at the back of his head. His hands were still outstretched toward me. His fingers were long, his nails clean. He was handsome in a hajji kind of way. I didn't know how he could have gotten this close to me without my noticing. Someone else was at the mic now, talking about access to unmonitored legal representation. Across the street, the MCC building was briefly black in shadow.

"Who?" I asked.

"What?" he said.

"Do I think who can see me?"

I scanned the people around me, over to the police looking bored at the barricades, to the polite protesters a few feet away. I didn't like feeling watched.

"Abu Jamal," he said, making his voice soft, as if in respect for the disappeared. "I thought maybe you were looking up at the window hoping he could see you."

"Oh," I said, feeling a flush of shame up my neck. I hadn't been thinking of Abu Jamal at all. I had entirely forgotten that he was the very reason we were all gathered here, that he had been taken, and that we were all supposed to be desperately worried. I had been thinking about my own brother, in his own prison, about to be set free.

"Well, he can't. See you. See those windows?" He pointed, and I turned back around to face the prison. He was at least a foot taller than me. I caught a whiff of his breath. Cinnamon. I squinted up.

"Just for show," he said. "Just to make those of us standing down here on the street feel better. So we'll walk on by. Go about our day. But if you're one of the poor souls in there? You don't see natural light. For *years*."

"How do you know?" I asked, turning away from the building, because suddenly I couldn't bear to look at it anymore. He was leaning down close to me again. I wondered if this was something very tall people learned to do. But then I heard someone calling my name.

"Amira! Amira! There you are!" I stepped away from the man, feeling acutely aware of how close we had been. I scanned the crowd. Finally, I spotted Laila, the lead caseworker at the Center, breaking through a cluster of people and approaching me. She grabbed me by the wrist and started tugging me away. I didn't dare look back at the man.

"We need you to run and find somewhere to make more copies," she said. She was breathless.

"More copies of what?" I asked.

"The flyers!" she said, exasperated now. "We ran out. And people will be leaving their offices soon for their lunch breaks. Yalla, find somewhere to make copies, please, ya habibti."

I wanted to tell her that I wasn't even working today, that I wasn't even supposed to be here. I could have told her about my brother coming home. But, instead, I just took the one slightly damp and wrinkled flyer she held out to me and went in search of a place to make copies.

There were a lot of make-your-own-salad places on this block. I passed by three Starbucks and two smoothie places. Weaving around people on the sidewalk, I searched my phone for a place to make copies. I walked seven blocks to a big box store that sold office supplies. But when I got there, it was closed, out of business. Through the smeared window, I could see an abandoned copy machine, sitting plugged into nothing in the middle of the carpet. I tried the next place that came up on my phone, another ten blocks away. I had looked up to figure out which way was east when I saw him, the guy with the hajji beard and the man bun. He was standing on the other side of the street, just watching me. He nodded when we locked eyes. I glanced away quickly and felt my arms go prickly. I started walking, not even sure if I was going in the right direction. Even though I kept my eyes down, I knew that, if I looked over, there he'd be, keeping pace with me on the other side of the street, his bun bobbing up and down gently with each step. I had to stop at an intersection, and caught a glimpse of him in my peripheral vision, jogging lightly across the street toward me. I raised my phone toward my face, pretended to study the screen. There was an opening in the traffic, and I hustled to cross the street. I could hear his footsteps behind me now, could see his shadow stretching out in front of me. He was all around me. What did he want? A different kind of girl would whip around now and ask him that. Lina would. But I was the sort of girl who convinced herself that a man wasn't following her when he definitely was. I glanced down at my phone and realized I was walking away from the other copy place. But I couldn't turn around now.

"Sister," he called.

I kept walking. There were beads of sweat forming above my eyebrows.

"Hey, sister," he called again.

I'd been followed by all sorts of men before. Fat ones, skinny ones. Arabs and Muslims and Orthodox Jews. Black and white, Latino, men in expensive-looking suits and homeless men pushing shopping carts. That was girlhood in New York City. But this guy was different. The way he had started talking to me *before* he started following me. I didn't know why this felt scarier—a breach of the rules. A thought occurred to me, but I quickly brushed it away. The same thought that occurred to lots of Muslims whenever someone new appeared at the masjid. Especially if that person was friendly. Especially if that person tried to talk to you. For Arabs, this learned suspicion was a particularly unnatural habit, overriding generations of cultural training to seek out strangers, to invade their privacy instantly, to take them home to your mother and feed them the food that made you. We made jokes about it when we met new people: "What do you think? FBI or NYPD?"

Maybe, I thought. But no. Of course not. How ridiculous. No one cared that much about what I thought. I wasn't a sheikh or a community leader. I was just Amira Emam, Muslim but not *Muslim*. Don't flatter yourself, I thought. You're not that important. Maybe he's not even following you. Maybe he's not even talking to you.

"Sister Amira," he said, louder this time, over the rumble of a passing bus. He was speed-walking to catch up to me, gaining on me, flanking my right side. I looked around for somewhere to go, a store to dash into.

"Hey," he yelled this time, tapping me on the shoulder.

"What?" I finally said, stopping so suddenly that he passed right by me. He stumbled a little and then turned around to face me.

"Don't you need to make copies?" he said.

The paper flyer was crumpled in my left fist; I had been squeezing it. He pointed over my shoulder.

"You just passed a copy place. I've been trying to get your attention. It's right there."

I turned and followed his finger to a small storefront next to a massive deli with neon lights. I squinted at the lettering over the door. "Business World," it read. "Printing. Fax. Internet."

"Oh," I said.

"Did you not hear me?" he asked.

"Sort of. I guess. Um, thanks," I said, and started walking toward the Business World.

"I'll help you," he said. "I told Laila I'd help her pass out the flyers, and we really need them ASAP."

He started walking beside me again. I was sweating so much that my scarf was starting to slip back away from my hairline. I pulled it forward and tried to wipe my forehead without his noticing.

"You know Laila?" I asked.

"A little. We just met when we started organizing this vigil. I'm Faraj."

"Amira," I said.

What an idiot. What a vain, conceited idiot I was. He was not trying to hit on me or to spy on me. He was trying to help me hurry up and make the fucking copies already.

At Business World, he held the door and let me go in first. A strand of hair had come loose from his bun in the chase. A little bell rang as we entered. There was a man sitting behind a desk, but he didn't even look up. Faraj said something to him in Urdu, and the man waved his hand toward a copy machine.

"Now, let's see, how do we work this thing?" he asked. He tucked the errant hair behind his ear and started pressing buttons at random.

"Like this," I said, smoothing the crumpled flyer out on the scanner. "How many do you think? Fifty?"

"More like two hundred," he said.

I punched in the number and hit the green "start" button.

"Wow," he said. "You're good at this."

"I make a lot of copies at my job. It's sort of my passion," I said.

"Really?" he asked.

"No," I said.

He laughed then, and I smiled into my shoulder. He had a girly laugh, a sweet, small giggle.

"You work at the ACACL?" he asked, using the acronym for the Center that no one ever used.

I nodded. The machine was spitting out copies.

"That's really cool. You working for your community and everything."

I didn't tell him that all I did was make copies and ask people to sign in on a wait list. I didn't tell him that I hadn't even planned on being at the vigil today, and that I had barely thought of Abu Jamal since he had been taken. I picked up a fresh, hot copy from the stack and turned it over to read it.

"Defend the Constitution!" it said in big black letters at the top. "MCC is Guantanamo in NYC!" Then a list of demands in a smaller font below. I scanned through the list. Things like daily access to fresh air and exercise, access to family visits and regular legal services, pen and paper so prisoners could write and receive letters, the end of solitary confinement, the end of indefinite detention. I could feel Faraj watching me.

"You know the worst thing they do there?" he asked me.

I shook my head. "What?"

"So they keep the guys locked up in solitary, right?"

I nodded like I knew.

"But without a trial date, sometimes without ever being charged. For years, you're alone in there, wondering what they're going to do to you. So, when they eventually get around to going to court, you're so messed up in the head, so desperate to get out of there, you plead guilty to whatever they say you did."

The machine spat out the last of the copies, and Faraj reached over to take the stack.

"We should get back," he said.

I wished I had something to do with my hands, so I grabbed the wrinkled original from the scanner and held it tightly. Faraj spoke to the man in Urdu again and then counted out some cash and handed it to him. He opened the door for me, and I stepped outside.

As we walked back toward the protest, Faraj tried to hand people flyers. "Stop abuses at MCC," he said, thrusting papers in their unwilling hands.

The prison expanded as we approached. I could hear a muffled voice from the loudspeaker. They were still at it, still droning on about prisoner rights as office workers shuttled past.

"How do you know what it's like in there?" I asked. I nodded up at the prison.

"My brother was in there." His voice was like a shrug, casting off this bit of biographical data like it was nothing.

"In *there*?"

He nodded.

I wanted to shout, "My brother's in prison, too!" But then I was embarrassed. It wasn't exactly the type of thing you wanted to have in common with someone. Plus, my brother was in a regular prison with regular abuses. He wasn't here—in Guantanamo in NYC. I wanted to ask him what happened to his brother. I wanted to ask him if he had ever been inside. But we were approaching the crowd. Laila had spotted us. She was weaving through people to get to us.

"Hey," he said suddenly, turning toward me, "can I have your number? I'd like to hang out with you sometime. I think you're cool."

I stared at him. No one had ever asked me out before. I'd been hit on, groped, followed, flirted with. But never formally asked out. Like on a date. Like in the olden days. He misunderstood my delay.

"Sorry," he said. "I didn't mean to offend you." He gestured vaguely toward my hijab. He thought I was one of *those* girls. I had thought the same thing when I saw his beard.

"Give me your phone," I said. Laila was calling out to us. I turned away so she wouldn't see and punched in my number.

He grinned.

"Yalla, you got them or what?" Laila said, panting a little as she reached us. Faraj handed her the stack, and they rushed back toward the center of the protest. I stayed where I was, on the outskirts, and watched as they disappeared into the crowd. I could see Faraj's bun bobbing over the tops of people's heads. I stayed until I lost sight of him.

At the entrance to the train headed back to Brooklyn, someone handed me a flyer. "Defend the Constitution!" it said. I took it, folded it neatly, and tucked it into my pocket, next to the original, crumpled one. In my other pocket, my phone kept buzzing—five missed calls from Lina. So she knew about Sami. But she didn't know about this. Not yet.

On the walk home from the train, I stopped at a deli and bought a pack of gum. Cinnamon. After the sun set that evening, I'd pop a piece in my mouth. It would be spicy and sweet and make my tongue tingle.

The view out my bedroom window that night: a perfect snapshot of 5th Avenue, a sniper's view. Napoli Bakery four blocks to the south, Ruben's Laundromat five to the north, the borders of our Arabland lit up like a burning carnival in the night.

The last time Sami was free in Bay Ridge, I was a girl. Now I was a woman, and I should have been able to throw reins around the snarling beast of fear. I had to make myself. Before he appeared and filled up all the space in our little world.

A BU JAMAL HAD A WINDOW, but the glass was frosted. Sometimes the light coming into his cell was blue, sometimes it was gray or white, and occasionally it was yellow. But with the fluorescent lights always on overhead, he couldn't tell what time of day it was. In the beginning, he associated yellow with morning and blue with night. But the yellow light trickled into his cell so infrequently that he began to wonder if it was ever daytime outside. Maybe mornings had gone extinct since he had entered the colorless walls of the Metropolitan Correctional Center.

Sometimes he stood under the frosted glass and pretended he could see outside. Over there, tourists swarming near the Manhattan end of the Brooklyn Bridge. Down below, office workers ordering chicken and rice for lunch from the halal carts. If he looked to the left, he imagined break dancers performing in a circle in Foley Square.

They kept him in a small solitary cell in 10-South. It sounded like the name of a bar or restaurant—the type of place that had a rooftop deck and served twenty-dollar cocktails. *10-South is gonna be LIT tonight. Go to our Web site to see how ladies can get in FREE!* For one hour each day, he was moved from his cell to a metal indoor cage for his allotted exercise time. At first, he refused to do anything inside that cage except sit. What did they want him to do? Pace like an animal, like a lion at the circus? But then, after weeks or months—he wasn't sure—he felt his muscles begin to atrophy. He stood up one day when the guards came to get him to move him to the cage, and one of his legs simply gave out on him, collapsed beneath him like ribbon. After that, he started using his one hour of exercise time. Push-ups. Jumping jacks. Squats.

The walls of his cell were metal, and sometimes, depending on the color of the light coming from the frosted glass, he could catch distorted reflections of himself in the walls, like being surrounded by funhouse mirrors. The walls heated up like an oven in the summer and chilled like an icebox in the winter. Sometimes the Abu Jamal in the cell would talk to the Abu Jamals in the walls. Sometimes the Abu Jamal in the cell would talk to the camera always trained on him, but the walls and the camera never talked back. Sometimes he closed his eyes and held his own hand, pretended his left hand was someone else's—anyone else's. Sometimes he'd stand and swing his clasped hands as if he and the someone else were taking a leisurely stroll down the street. He had read that psychologists call this kind of prolonged isolation "sensory deprivation." But Abu Jamal did not feel deprived of his senses. He felt overwhelmed by them. The only person allowed to visit him was his lawyer, but even those visits were sometimes denied, for no apparent reason. When he was permitted to see his lawyer, he'd get so excited just to use his voice and know it was being heard by someone other than himself, by someone other than the guards. To have someone use his name. They were separated by a metal mesh barrier so he couldn't touch the lawyer, which crushed him anew each time. He longed to be touched. He longed to feel skin that wasn't his own.

THE NEXT DAY, I was waiting for Lina outside of Fort Hamilton High School because she wanted to trade in the cap and gown they gave her for one that "doesn't make me look fat." She wanted one that she could cinch in at the waist, one with slits up the thigh, or at least a V-neck. We were graduating from high school later that afternoon.

Leaning against one of the brick walls of the school, I yanked on my hijab, which was caught in my hoop earring. I was annoyed at Lina. She was always making me wait for her while she went and did something ridiculous and pointless just so she could continuously remind people how bad and crazy and sexy she was. In my irritation, I pulled too hard and almost ripped the earring right through my earlobe. Then I looked up and saw him.

It was my brother, standing under the awning of a Western Union across the street. He chugged furiously from a large can of iced tea and stared at me. My ear throbbed, and I knew that if he came over I would say the absolutely wrong thing and that I would never be able to take it back, that it would define this next phase of our relationship until he disappeared or died or got locked up again. I would say something like *Hi* or *You're back* or *How are you? I am fine,* and then he would think that I was his little sister. But I wasn't his little sister anymore. I was Amira. I was me.

It wasn't him, the boy with the tea. Didn't even look like him. Way too young. Darker skin, straighter hair. I blinked and couldn't understand how I had ever thought it was Sami. You need to practice, I told myself. You need to prepare.

"Sorry," Lina said as she jogged toward me from the school entrance. "Mrs. Lipschy was getting on my ass. She gave me some lecture on inappropriate clothing and self-respect and presenting myself for the world to judge. Can you believe that shit? Amira?"

I stared at the silhouette of the boy's back as he walked away. The sun was shining so that I had to squint to make him out, his gleaming body moving away from me.

"What? Oh yeah, Mrs. Lipschy," I said.

"So—tell me more about your future husband," Lina said, because we were pretending the Sami thing wasn't real. Lina had tried talking to me about it the previous night, when I got home from the protest. But I didn't want to talk about Sami, so I told her about Faraj instead. Lina played along.

"He's not my future husband. I'll probably never hear from him," I said.

"He's totally your future husband," she said. "You said he's older, so he's probably tired of hooking up with white girls and ready to wife a good Muslima."

I laughed, but I also felt a little rush of panic. How many girls had Faraj hooked up with? I'd never hooked up with anyone before.

"How old are we talking about, anyway?" Lina continued. "And exactly how did you meet again? He came up and started hitting on you? How? Where?" she asked as we walked away from the school that, despite being the center of our lives for the past four years, had been largely indifferent to us. She wanted specifics—she wanted to know exactly what he said and where I was standing and was I facing north or south?

"Um, well," I said, "it started at the protest, and then we sort of walked together to the copy place."

"So what did he say to you at the protest?" she asked.

"Nothing, really," I said. I didn't know how to characterize our first encounter at the prison, and I didn't want to try. Lina would say it was weird and she'd ruin the whole memory for me.

"So how did you walk together if you hadn't spoken yet?"

"Well, we didn't exactly walk together. He sort of walked behind me and then we started talking later."

"So you're telling me he *followed* you to the copy place?" Lina said. "Like a stalker?"

"It wasn't like that," I said, but feebly, knowing that I had already ruined my own story, and would never be able to retell it better.

"I'm never gonna leave you alone again," she said, reaching for my hand as proof. "Look what happens when I'm not with you—you hang out with random crazies."

"So it's crazy for anyone to like me?"

She looked at me long and hard, her gray-green eyes open wide. She had Mama's eyes. I had Baba's eyes—as brown and wide as a cow's. Sami had his own eyes—narrow and hazel.

"Boys check you out all the time," she said. "You just don't see it, because you're one of the humble beautiful girls. Not like me. I'm another breed—the cocky beautiful girl. Boys always like your type better." Then she proceeded to list all the boys who had ever, in my life, checked out my ass or boobs or legs.

"Sixth grade," she said. "That kid Santiago who played the clarinet . . ."

I clamped a hand over her mouth and we walked home, the exact same graduation gown Lina had tried to exchange tucked under her arm.


Later that day, Lina and I sat side by side on the soccer field, sweating in our itchy robes in the ninety-degree heat—me with the gold Honors sash draped over my shoulder, Lina in her undecorated C-average robe. While the valedictorian made her speech, I looked around the crowd. It was easy to spot the Muslims. All the others had big bottles of water perched next to them. And all the Muslims looked like they were about to faint.

They started reading names, and when they got to "C," I zoned out. With all of Bay Ridge sitting above and around us in the bleachers, I was thinking about what it would be like to have Sami home again, sitting among them. It wasn't supposed to be this way. He wasn't supposed to get out until after Lina and I were already grown and studying abroad in Italy, riding on the backs of Vespas, clinging to the waists of muscular Italian men as they navigated tight, cobblestoned corners, not even caring when the wind lifted the edges of our skirts up.

I was still in Italy when they got to the letter "E," and Lina had to give me a gentle shove to snap me out of it.

When they called my name, I walked up and shook hands with a bunch of administrators who had never known anything about me except who my brother was. The vice-principal who got my brother thrown in jail for selling marked-up loosies after school held my hand like it was a grenade and pretended not to be surprised by the gold sash around my shoulders.

When I got back to my seat, I scanned the crowd for my people. I spotted Baba almost right away—standing on the bleachers to my left in a flowing white galabiya, like he had a donkey and a bundle of mangoes waiting for him on the sidelines. He held the phone out in front of him, snapping photos. The two of them stood side by side—Baba in his white galabiya, Mama in her black abaya. I hollowed out a space between them for Sami. I closed my eyes, and a few seconds later felt Lina's body sink back down next to me.


After Maghrib prayers that night, we had a sad sort of party. Baba propped open the door to the apartment so the neighbors could come and go as they pleased. Mama reheated the meat and rice and stuffed vegetables that she had prepared earlier that morning. She tied two balloons to a leg of the kitchen table, and everyone had to bat them out of the way if they wanted to refill their plates.

Lina and I sat on the floor of the living room, ceding all the proper seats to the adults like the good girls we mostly were, eating giant slices of white sheet cake with a photo of us screened onto it. Lina was eating my face and I was eating hers. We answered questions obediently when asked—questions like "What will you study?" and "What profession have you chosen?" Baba instructed us to answer any Arabs who asked with "medicine" and "doctor" respectively.

The adults lingered in the living room for ages, drinking tea and shouting over the television that was blaring Egyptian soap operas. They spoke about Sami mostly. They were planning out his entire life for him. He must work, they all agreed, he must complete his studies, he must pray and attend masjid regularly. He must stay here, in Bay Ridge, with the Arabs, and avoid bad influences elsewhere. He must live at home, with his mother and father, so they could feed him and watch over him. He must, he must, he must.

Lina and I lay on our sides, discarded paper plates smeared with frosting next to us, and made up new plotlines for the soap opera. We were whispering to each other in English, but no one was paying enough attention to us to hear or be offended anyway.

"I love you, Salma," Lina whispered to me as a man with a thick black mustache and an entire bottle's worth of hair gel poured onto his head reached out to a beautiful, overly made-up woman in leopard-print pants. "I really do, but I never expected to fall in love with my donkey."

The woman whipped her dyed, honey-colored hair around and glared at the man. "Just tell me one thing, Ibrahim," I whispered to Lina. "Can the donkey love you more than I do, can the donkey cook for you the way I do? Can the donkey ever hope to please you as much as I do?"

Behind us, someone was lecturing Baba. "It is vital that he have a schedule. Keep him busy. Get him work and make sure he prays all five prayers. This will remind him of God and keep him on the right path. Enroll him in college classes. He can study medicine, or perhaps go to pharmacy school."

Ibrahim and Salma were kissing now, and I wondered what it would feel like to have that great bushy mustache tickling your lips. A whiny violin screeched over them as they embraced.

"Do you want to talk about it?" Lina asked me, resting her palm gently on my back.

"Not really," I said. "Not yet."

She nodded and got up to bring us each another slice of cake. This time, I ate my own stomach and she ate her own knees.

Mama didn't sleep that night. I heard her moving around. I listened to the clatter of dishes in the kitchen sink. I tried to go back to sleep, but I just kept thinking of her pacing the apartment alone. So I got up to see if she wanted to have a cup of tea with me and watch bad late-night television.

I cracked our bedroom door open slowly, so as not to wake Lina. It took a while for my eyes to adjust, but then I spotted Mama, floating around the living room in her nightgown. Behind her, the television flickered, casting a strange light around her. From the sofa, her husband's grumbling snores. The darkness outside told me that the sun was still far away—that we had several hours left before it was time to rise and pray. I was good at reading the dark.

I was opening my mouth to speak when I saw her slip her sandals on. I watched her tiptoe past my sleeping father, turn the dead bolt on the front door, and open it. My breath felt hot in my mouth. I could hear her walking down the stairs. I should run after her, I thought. I should call out. I should wake Baba. I should turn around and go back to bed, pull the sheets over my head.

But then I was creeping down the stairs barefoot. My hair wasn't covered, but neither was hers. I gripped the banister and carefully stepped down after her. When I got to the lobby, I placed my hands on the front door to the building. I thought I might push the door open and leap out to catch her. But instead I just stood there and peered through the thin rectangle of glass.

My mother stood on the concrete steps looking out at the street. She smoothed her nightgown, and then sat.

The darkness. There was nothing else for blocks. We had to be patient with Mama. We had to watch her gestures, decipher the meaning behind her words. Despite her tendency to name her feelings outright, those labels always felt to me a little like a defense mechanism to keep us from looking too closely. Sometimes I'd catch a flash of something in her eyes, but then it would flit away like a deer through the woods. She was like my brother in that way: like they were born with secrets they had to guard. Because they were alike in this, she always thought she could be the one to crack his silence, to unburden him. She wanted to carry his pain for him. But instead she kept losing more and more of him. Sami would return from the principal's office, or the probation office, or the county jail quieter than he was before. She knew there was an anger smothered beneath that silence, but she couldn't see its source. A rage that was itself a black marker—the color of redaction, the color you would see with a bag over your head. A rage that each day rendered him, renditioned him, that much darker.

What must it be like to have created and birthed such anger? My mother gazed into the darkness. I squinted after her, chasing her gaze. Could she see the outline of the awning over the Alpine Cinema? On Wednesday afternoons, when tickets were only five dollars, kids lined up in front of the ticket booth, waiting to see a movie about talking animals and parents who never fail to protect their children from the world. When the theater opened a few hours later, they'd switch on the lights and the old-fashioned lightbulbs that edge the marquee would flash brightly. If my mother saw the outline of the cinema, that was all she could see. She couldn't see the time Lina let a boy finger her in the alley out back. She didn't exactly let him; it was more like she did nothing to stop him. Our mother couldn't imagine Lina's body pressed up against the fire exit, the sign glowing red above her soft head. She couldn't see me, ducking into the lobby to escape a strange old man who made loud, wet kissing noises on the 5th Avenue sidewalk behind me. Or the time Lina and I were leaving the theater after seeing an afternoon showing, our eyes still adjusting to the white sun, when we saw Sami standing outside our apartment building. We waited to see what he would do—if he was coming or going. The two of us watched as he put his key into the lock and disappeared into the building's entrance. Then we turned around and walked back into darkness. Our mother couldn't see any of this, the pain of her girls, because she couldn't see her own.

I left my mother sitting on the stoop and crept back upstairs to sleep next to my sister. I did not hear her, but in the morning my mother had come back to us.

I woke in the same body, the same sweaty sheets twisted between my knees, the same wheezing fan blowing the same tired air around the same bedroom. It was bright outside—I had missed suhoor. I stumbled out to the living room to find Lina.

"What time is it?" I asked.

"Shh," Lina said, and gestured over to the sofa, where I saw our mother splayed across the cushions, her mouth open, her hair bunched under her neck, her right arm clutching a throw pillow.

"I don't think she slept at all last night," Lina said.

"How long have you been awake?" I asked her, because it felt strange for Lina to have started her day before me.

Lina shrugged. "You wouldn't wake up," she said. "I tried shaking you, but you just pushed me off and rolled over. So I got up to eat and found her sitting here, making all these lists." Lina gestured to a notepad on the coffee table.

I flipped through a few pages of the notebook—my mother's odd, round handwriting looping across six full pages. She had made lists—of Sami's favorite and least favorite foods, of clothes and toiletries he would need, of all the mosques in the area and the imams and the imams' wives and their phone numbers, of lawyers and caseworkers, of various borough parks and basketball courts, of hospitals and county jails. Toward the end, her scrawls became largely incomprehensible, written in a mother's Sanskrit, the question marks and exclamation points the only decipherable symbols.

"She say anything to you?" I asked.

"Me? No," Lina said. "She just seemed surprised when I walked into the room, like she didn't know what time it was."

Mama woke up not long after and started hammering the shit out of some chicken cutlets in the kitchen. She was in one of her moods. Lina and I were sprawled on the couch watching TV until Mama came out of the kitchen and stood pointedly over us.

"Don't you have anything to do today?" she asked.

Lina shook her head, but I got up and headed toward our room to get dressed. Lina was terrible at picking up the signs, even though she herself got into the same moods. It was hard to know what would set them off, but when they got like this, they'd pick fights over just about anything. The best thing was just to remove yourself from their field of vision.

Lina finally got the message and joined me in the bedroom. I was already dressed, but I sat on the bed and waited for her to get ready.

"Jesus, what's the matter with her?" she said, pulling on a pair of shorts, not even bothering to change her underwear.

"What do you think? Sami," I said.

It was the first time I'd spoken his name out loud since we found out he was coming home.

"I thought she was happy about that," Lina said.

I shot her a look in the mirror as she threaded hoop earrings through her earlobes. Sometimes Lina pretended not to understand things. She had done it in school and she was doing it now. Sami coming home was never going to be a cause for any single pure feeling. It would make a mess of all of us.

"What?" she said.

"Yalla," I said. I got up and walked through the living room to the front door. Mama was clearing off the table. We didn't say anything to each other. She probably had a student coming over for summer tutoring. Mama sometimes tutored kids in the neighborhood—in Arabic or French or biology. She could teach anything, really—she was that smart. She used to have a full-time job teaching Arabic and Qur'an classes at the Islamic school until people started to complain. There was some sort of dispute about something that happened way back in Egypt; whenever we asked Mama and Baba about it, they were vague.

But people couldn't deny that she was smart. And cheap. So they hired her as a private tutor to help make their children into doctors, just as long as she wasn't trying to improve their souls.

I pulled my sneakers on and waited out on the landing for Lina, just to get some distance from Mama.

We walked most of the way to Reina's apartment in silence.

"Yo, are we ever going to talk about this?" Lina said suddenly, reaching for my shoulders to stop me from walking any farther.

"What?" I said.

"You know what," she said. "Your brother's coming home, and Mama is tripping, and shit is weird."

"He's your brother, too," I said, shoving her off me gently so I could continue to walk. "And I don't know what you want me to say." I waved to a client from the Center who was pushing her baby in a stroller across the street.

"You are unbelievable," Lina said.

"What?" I said.

"You have to talk about this," she said.

"Why?" I said.

"Because it's this major, huge thing happening."

The return of the son. As if the universe was being righted now, straightened, unfrozen, smoothed out like a fitted sheet across all space and time.

"Why does it have to be major?" I said. I quickened my pace and pulled a few steps ahead of Lina. Behind me, I could hear her panting to keep up.

Reina was sitting on the front stoop of her building, waiting for us. A pigeon that looked like it had just escaped from a serial killer's basement stumbled in circles around her feet. She took one look at us and said, "Uh-oh, what's wrong with you two?"

Lina told her about Sami.

"So this is good news, right?" Reina asked. She looked from me to Lina and back to me again.

I shrugged. Lina shrugged. We sat down on the steps next to her.

"What's he like, your brother?" Reina asked. "I don't even remember him."

I thought back to one time when Baba had buckled Lina and me into the back seat of the Tercel. We were little and it was late at night. We had been asleep. I remember Baba carrying us one by one to the car, strapping us in, draping a blanket over our knees. Mama sitting next to him in the passenger seat, silent and completely still. Baba stopping once to shine a flashlight into an alley. Dumpsters with their eerie shadows. It was like we were disturbing them, the dumpsters, like we had intruded on their privacy. I don't remember where we found Sami or what he was doing or who he was with. But I do remember that we found him, because eventually I woke up and opened my eyes, and there was his strange body sitting next to me in the back seat. We always found him. Until, one day, the police found him first.

"He used to be . . ." I said, pausing, ". . . quiet."

But that wasn't quite right. *Separate?* I tried the new word out in my head. He could never stay still. We were always looking for him.

Lina said, "He was cold. Like he was empty inside."

But that's not how I remembered him, either. To me, he was always too full. Bottled up. Always on the verge of overflowing.

HE ONCE THREW a piece of the pyramids through a window. Shattered the window, and there were pyramid smithereens on the pavement below, pyramid dust blowing away down the streets of Brooklyn, pyramid pieces sticking to the bottoms of people's shoes.

It was Baba's favorite party trick—showing people this hunk of dusty yellow limestone he had pilfered from the Great Pyramid of Giza. He would offer it up to anyone who visited our apartment, especially non-Arabs. "Here," he'd say, "hold this." And he'd place the ugly rock in their palms. "Now you're carrying a pyramid! Now you are holding one of the Seven Wonders of the World!" He did this to plumbers trying to fix a broken faucet, to Sami's probation officers, to Jehovah's Witnesses who knocked on the door. It was completely illegal, of course, to take a four-thousand-year-old rock. But he justified it by saying that it had already been loose.

I have two kinds of memories of living with Sami: kid Sami and teenage Sami. My memories of kid Sami are patchy. He was six years older than us—an enormous gap when you're little. Most of the time, kid Sami ignored us. Sometimes, he tortured us—twisting our arms behind our backs, pinching us until we bruised, locking us in rooms. And, very occasionally, he played with us. We couldn't trust kid Sami—he could fly into a rage at any moment, collapsing into toddlerlike tantrums, lashing out at the nearest human or object, even at nine and ten years old. But sometimes, he invented a game so fun that we took the risk and willingly entered his world. Like the time he transformed our living room into an elaborately constructed fort that he called Sherwood Forest. He was Robin Hood and we were his fellow noble thieves, ducking into secret hiding places to dodge the sheriff of Nottingham, conducting raids from our treetop village. As New York City kids, we had never played in an actual forest before. Sami could create wonders when he wanted to, invent whole worlds that didn't exist for us. But even as we reveled in the magic of it all, even as our heads were bent close to his, squinting as we aimed our imaginary bows and arrows at enemies below, we were nervous. Something inside him could shift without warning, and we could find ourselves shoved off the sofa, knocked to the ground. I say "we," but most of the time it was me. Unless I could scrabble away fast enough, I might find myself pinned to the floor, his knee jabbing into my back, my wrist twisted behind me, until one of our parents discovered us and held his arms down so I had a chance to escape.

But teenage Sami was different. At some point, he shut himself off, turned a valve somewhere deep inside of him. He stopped speaking to us, and it was like living with a silent and terrifying stranger.

"Where are you going, ya Sami?" Baba would call out to him if he saw Sami slipping on his shoes. The only answer he would get was the slamming of the door behind him. But it didn't stop Mama and Baba from trying: *How was your day? What do you want for breakfast? Where have you been? Are you hurt? Who were you with? Are you hungry? Did you pray today? Are you warm enough? Where have you been? Will you answer me, please?*

Sometimes, Sami would grunt in reply or string together two-word answers. But often, he would just walk right by our parents as if he hadn't heard them, as if they were nothing to him. And I began to wonder what they had done to him to make him treat them this way, even though I also knew that this wasn't the right question and that things would be a lot simpler if it were.

Mama's and Baba's whole days, their whole lives, became calibrated just to elicit a response from him. Just to get him to see them, to engage with them, to be with us, even if it was only for the time it took to answer what kind of cereal he wanted from the store. Lina and I stopped trying to talk to him at all, but when he was home, we were tense, trying not to bother or annoy him, trying to make ourselves as smooth and unobtrusive as possible. Because, if we could just be still and not say the wrong thing, then maybe he would stay. And maybe he would love our parents again.

At night, I could hear Mama and Baba whispering, trading notes—what had Sami said to them today, what had he eaten, what had he watched on TV, what did they know about their son at all. They would strategize about their plan for the next day—whether they'd play it cool, let Sami come to them, or whether they'd put their foot down, insist he be home in time for dinner. It didn't matter: he would not be home for dinner. The automated calls from the school started coming in: "One or more of your children has been marked absent today. Please call the school at your earliest convenience." They must have longed for the days when they could hear his cries, run to him, hold his arms down, and whisper in his ear until the thrashing subsided, until he could no longer hurt himself or others. Now there was no body to hold, nothing to see or hear at all.

There was one day when teenage Sami did scream out, did open his mouth and release what was inside of him. But, of course, our parents weren't home. They weren't there to hear him, to hold him, to stroke his head and tell him that, no matter what he'd done or what had been done to him, he was loved. They were out looking for him.

Sami would have been seventeen, tall and skinny with ropy muscles and bad, backroom tattoos. I remember because it wasn't long before they took him and put him in a prison for adults. Lina and I were eleven, and we were alone in the apartment doing brain surgery on some walnuts—cracking the shells, carefully plucking out the nut with a pair of tweezers we had stolen from Mama's toiletry cabinet. There were bits of shell and walnut dust all over the kitchen counter. Our heads were bent low, our hands steady, when we heard the front door open. I knew it was Sami by the silence that followed. My hands froze. Lina kept operating.

We listened to the soft tread of his socked feet as he approached the kitchen. "Scalpel," Lina said, holding out her palm. But I was still frozen. His shape appeared in the door frame. He paused for a minute, took in the surgery before us, didn't say anything. He opened the fridge and took out a can of soda. It opened with a pop and a hiss. "He's bleeding out," Lina said, waving her hand in front of me. "Quick, nurse, I need the scalpel." I handed her the tweezers.

Sami stood at the window and took a long sip. Then he turned and looked at us, surveyed the room. This time, even Lina stood still.

"Why do you always have to be such freaks?" he said.

I gripped the counter and waited for more, but that was all he said. Then he walked out of the kitchen and into the living room, and the next thing we heard was a bright burst of a wail that ended with a terrific crashing noise. We ran to the doorway and saw Sami standing there, his head thrown back, mouth open, his right arm twitching ever so slightly. There was a hole in the window, shattered glass all over the living-room floor, cold air streaming in, and, though we didn't know it yet, pieces of the Great Pyramid scattered across the sidewalk on 72nd street.

Egyptians like to call our country Um al-Dunya, Mother of the World. We were the makers of civilization. We built wonders. Tombs eternal. It didn't matter that now we were poor, ruled over by bloated kings who couldn't even build a decent road, let alone one of the great wonders of the world. And there, on the streets of Bay Ridge, was the evidence of our greatness, smashed into a fine yellow dust.

We turned from the window back to Sami. But he had moved—he was by the door, hunched over, putting on his shoes. And that is the view of him I have seen more than any other: the bend of his neck, his back curved like a shell, his long fingers working at the laces.

When our parents returned home, he was gone—the wind shrieking through a hole in the window the only proof of him.

WE WERE TEENAGE GIRLS with nowhere to be and no money to spend. We stretched out on Reina's front steps, sunning ourselves and listening to music. We were golden, and we looked more beautiful than we ever had before or ever would again. It seemed a waste not to go somewhere, not to be seen. We were silent for a long time as both Reina and Lina disappeared into their phones, looking for somewhere for us to go. I knew I had nothing to contribute, so I just leaned back and enjoyed the sun on my neck.

Reina found something first. Her head snapped up triumphantly. "There's a party," she said. She showed Lina her phone, and the two of them bent over it, discussing train routes and the likelihood of cute boys as if I wasn't even there.

"I'll come," I said, trying to edge closer to them on the steps.

"Really?" Reina said. I could tell she was about to crack jokes about me being up past my bedtime, but then Lina stopped her by throwing her arms around my neck and kissing my cheek.

We went inside to Reina's apartment to freshen up, reapplying deodorant and too much makeup. Lina sent our parents a photo of us hanging out in Reina's room and told them we were going to break our fast and watch a movie at her place. When it was finally time to go, I was tired and worried there would be nothing for us to eat come sunset. Lina could tell I was getting nervous. Still, I was determined to keep up with them. I was determined to be fun and spontaneous and carefree. As we walked to the train she said, "Just don't get all Amira on me, okay?"

"Getting all Amira" was my own particular form of shyness, like a disease. It meant clamming up the moment we were around new people, or old people who were so old they'd become new again. Not cute, not endearing, not the kind of shy that made me fade into the background. Instead, it was the kind that made sure I stood out. Me staring into my Diet Coke for the length of entire parties until every last bubble, every hint of carbonation, was gone, while everyone else stared at me. When I went all Amira, Lina overcompensated. Told jokes like a court jester, lifted up her shirt and showed people the birthmark on her stomach that she swore looked just like Saddam Hussein. Tried to be the loudest, funniest, flirtiest Lina of all the Linas.

"I won't," I said defensively.

We got onto the train and lurched away from Arabland, riding into the dying sun. It was a long ride, across two boroughs. When we finally got off, we stood on a quiet corner in a residential Queens neighborhood I had never been to before. Reina led us to a small house painted bubble-gum pink. We walked up three steps—each a different-colored wooden board—to the front door. Reina knocked and knocked again. The music inside was fighting to get out. The whole house was buzzing like a spaceship about to blast off. Finally, the door opened and we were sucked inside.

It was a party—some distant relative, Reina's fourth cousin by marriage or some shit like that. But it was unlike any party I had ever been to before. Upstairs, there were the grandmothers—frying plantains and drinking bottled beer and gossiping on the plastic-covered sofas. They kissed Reina and looked at Lina and me like, Who are these Latinas who can't even speak Spanish? We served ourselves heaping plates of rice and beans from giant aluminum trays.

While Lina went around kissing everyone like they were long-lost relatives, I refilled my cup, Amira-ing hard. Just when I was running out of things to do with my hands, I felt my phone buzz in my purse. I made slow work of unzipping the bag and riffling through it. Then I retreated a few steps away from the girls. His name stared at me from the screen, and I felt my face go hot. Faraj. My thumbs were suddenly sweaty and clumsy. This was perhaps the first time a boy had ever texted me about something other than homework or Lina.

"What you up to?" his message said.

I looked around at the paper tablecloths and the soda bottles and felt the music rumbling through the soles of my shoes. "I'm at a party," I wrote back.

"You're too cool for me," he wrote.

I didn't know what to say next. I wanted to keep the flirty banter going, and I needed Lina's help. But Lina had a large cluster of girls, and even a few grandmas, huddled around her own phone, showing them photos of something apparently hilarious. My fingers froze over the screen. But then he messaged me again.

"Hey, how old are you?"

I didn't need Lina for this one. "Eighteen," I lied. "How old are you?"

"Too old for you."

Damnit. Now I definitely needed Lina. Just then I felt her glaring at me from among the many beautiful, overly made-up faces. I realized I had inched even farther away from the group and was standing in a corner by myself, facing the wall. I slipped the phone back into my bag and returned to stand awkwardly on the fringes of their girl huddle.

At some point, someone handed me a cup with a mysterious brown liquid in it. I took a large sip before I even had time to think about it. I always thought there'd be some sort of ceremony the first time I drank. The lighting of a candle, a long-winded and nonsensical toast by Lina. But instead there was just the clink of ice against my teeth and a burning in my throat.

We salsa-ed awkwardly with little girls and old women. I took my scarf off, because it was just us girls and because it was starting to slip off anyway. My hair was big and curly, tight corkscrews jutting out in a crown around my head. Lina's hair was kinkier than I had seen it in a long time, from being outside all day in the humidity. We looked more like twins than ever before. And, in fact, Reina's relatives had trouble telling us apart, which almost never happened. They gave up calling us by our names and just called us "las hermanas." I was starting to feel better. I was starting to have fun.

Then, at some point, the grandmas all sat down and turned on the television. It was some show, some Spanish comedy, they were all obsessed with. Lina sat down with them, sandwiched between two old ladies she had never met before, and began to watch. Spanish had been one of the only subjects she was good at in high school, and pretty soon she was laughing alongside the old ladies.

Reina and I went to the bathroom together. She sat on the toilet while I examined a zit on my chin, and then I sat on the toilet while she examined her eyebrows, looking for stray hairs that needed plucking. And then we both squeezed in front of the mirror, talking and messing vaguely with various parts of our faces and hair. It was rarely just the two of us—Reina and me. And when it was, we usually talked about Lina. But occasionally we talked about other things, things that we couldn't talk about with Lina around. In high school, we studied together, compared grades, quizzed each other on SAT words. And now we talked about that mythic future we had worked so hard for: college. Reina and I both believed what we had been told by our parents and our teachers all our lives: college was the master key; it would open up all doors. With college in our clutches, we would soar past our parents, and they'd smile as they watched us leave them behind in the detritus of first-generation toil. We knew a lot of children of immigrants who had gone to college, had majored in practical things like business administration, and most of them were back home, living with their parents or living a few doors down, manning the till at the family bodega. But, still, we believed. Because this was the only path that had ever been imagined for us.

We talked about the classes we were thinking of taking in the fall—me at Brooklyn College and her at City. Reina was twirling and re-twirling a strand of hair around her index finger.

"Like—don't tell anyone?—but I'm really excited to be a student in one of those huge lecture halls. The professor going on and on and everyone falling asleep in the back rows, but me sitting up front taking color-coded notes," Reina said.

I could picture Reina with her meticulously organized pencil case. She wanted to learn in a place of discipline, order, and respect, not in a place like our high school, where kids were constantly playing music from their phones and throwing chip bags over your head. I smiled at the image of her with her highlighters and multicolored pens all laid out before her.

"You're laughing at me," she said, slapping me lightly on the arm.

I shook my head, because, no, I wasn't.

"What are you excited about?" she asked.

I thought for a minute. I could picture myself sitting around a table in a small classroom, book out in front of me, cup of coffee steaming in my hand.

"Being somewhere where no one knows me," I said. "I could be really different in college. I could talk a lot, and no one would know that it's weird."

Reina smiled and nodded at me in the mirror and then continued dabbing a square of toilet paper across her sweaty face. There was a knock on the door.

"Let me in, bitches," Lina whispered on the other side.

Reina reached over and kissed my cheek before opening the door for Lina. She piled into the tiny half-bathroom with us. We reapplied lip gloss. I wrapped my hair up and put on some dangly earrings I found lying forgotten in the pocket of my bag. As the old ladies and the little girls settled into their show, Reina took us each by the hand and led us downstairs, where it was another world.

It was so dark and wet and loud that it felt like we had climbed several stories beneath the earth. There were men downstairs, drinking out of red plastic cups. There were women, too, in tiny satin rompers and denim miniskirts. They spun around in the center of the basement that had been transformed into a dance floor, and even though they were all wearing enormous heels, they looked perfectly in control.

As we walked down the stairs, all the men looked up from their drinks like we were stars hurtling down to this subterranean disco planet.

We threw back shots of something clear. And then the men took our hands and spun us around, held tight to our hips, grinded up close to our asses, pressed their sweaty cheeks against our sweaty necks. I didn't even have time to think. It was sexual but not scary. No one was trying to fuck us or trick us or kill us. It was just dancing. And maybe that doesn't seem like a big deal, but to me—it was a revelation. The music and the hands and the voices urged more—more of me, just more, just let it all out, just don't worry how you look or what we think of you or what will happen tomorrow, just dance, Mami, just move, just breathe, just be.

At some point, Lina collapsed into a chair off to the side and closed her eyes. I crouched next to her.

"Are you okay?" I shouted over the music.

She nodded. "Just have the spins."

When Lina opened her eyes again, she was smiling.

Later, when Lina started puking, I held her hair back. I would take care of her, and she would always come running back to me when she needed me. But then I felt my heart burning like a lump of charcoal in my chest and I realized I was drunk, too. When Lina was done, I took my turn heaving over the toilet. Lina rubbed my back and patted my face with a wet paper towel.

It was a baptism. There was a sheet cake with trick candles. I don't remember whose birthday it was.


Back in Bay Ridge, the night air was blessedly cool. As we passed each apartment building, I could hear snippets of Egyptian-dubbed Turkish soap operas. I heard teakettles whistling, and the crunch of phyllo dough being cut through with a serrated knife. Everyone was right where they should have been.

After saying goodbye to Reina, Lina and I stopped at Sunrise Deli and bought some stale, reheated chicken wings. Lina said we needed some food to soak up the alcohol. We sat on a bench in Leif Ericson Park, ate the chicken, and watched some boys play basketball. Cars on the Verrazano in the distance, the Styrofoam container half finished, our bellies sticking out like Baba's.

"I didn't know you could move like that," Lina said, nudging my hip with hers.

"There's lots you don't know about me," I said. But Lina just laughed.

Then I took out my phone, as if to prove it, and showed her Faraj's messages. She helped me respond to his last message about being too old for me.

"I promise I'm very mature," she wrote for me, adding a winky face.

Then she put an earbud in my ear and RZA screamed to *"bring da motherfuckin' ruckus."* I switched to Gucci Mane, because Wu-Tang reminded me of our brother. Then I took the buds out of our ears and turned the volume all the way up, the Trap God's voice warbling into the Bay Ridge dusk like I imagine grasshoppers do in the country.

*"Fuck* Bay Ridge," I said then. I stood up and started doing a little salsa move I had learned in that underworld basement. Lina threw a chicken bone at me.

"Yeah, fuck Bay Ridge," she said. "And fuck your stupid brother, too."

"Fuck *your* stupid brother," I said and threw the chicken bone back at her. We had a chicken fight then, flinging the bone back and forth. He was my brother. No, he was her brother. Mine. Hers. Mine. Hers. Mine. The bone clattered at my feet, and I let it sit there. When the wind started to pick up and the breeze from the bay made us feel like our nipples were about to fall off, we decided it was finally time to go home.

We stood outside our building and slapped our faces until we felt more sober. We chewed on the cinnamon gum I had bought after meeting Faraj and practiced walking in a straight line. When Lina fell off the curb, we decided it would be best just to go in, say as little as possible, and walk straight back into our bedroom.

"Is it going to be okay?" Lina asked as I punched in the building code on our front stoop.

"I don't know," I said. The door buzzed, and I pushed it open. We could hear at least a dozen different televisions murmuring. The stairwell smelled of hot ghee and cardamom.

"But we'll be okay," I said. "Me and you."

"How?" she whispered.

I could hear the voices of Salma and Ibrahim declaring their love. I imagined finding Mama and Baba curled up on the couch watching, a bowl of tiny sweet apricots in front of them. I didn't know what would happen to them when Sami came home. But it was different for me and Lina this time. We weren't little girls. We didn't have to wait around for Sami to do or not do anything. We could leave. We could make our own lives.

"We'll figure it out together," I said and gave her hand a little squeeze.

When we walked up the stairs to our apartment, I could hear the noises of women. Women crying, women wailing, women laughing, women yelling at children, women eating, women praying. The stairwell was clogged with people. None of this seemed strange to us yet. During Ramadan, people often stayed up late into the night, eating and visiting friends. On the landing, four children clustered around a little boy who was holding a guinea pig, its black eyes bulging out of its head. Lina lingered there a moment to run a finger gently along the creature's spine. I continued up the stairs toward our apartment, pushing past our neighbors, all my bodily juices swelling inside me like water churning in a washing machine.

It wasn't until I saw the crowds of people in our apartment that I realized what had happened. He was thin-looking, gaunt, standing there in the living room with his hands clasped in front of him. His face was sharp, sharper than I remembered, all angles, no curves, his bare scalp sloppily shaved. His skin was paler than I remembered, too.

Imam Tariq said, "Look who I found just walking down the street." He laughed and slapped Sami on the back, but Sami didn't smile.

Through the other bodies, I could make out the shape of my mother. She never stopped moving. She set a tray of tea down on the coffee table. She shooed a child off a chair so she could offer it to an older neighbor. She twisted this way and that, turning to keep her son in her line of vision at all times.

Baba was on the sofa with Imam Tariq.

"So they just let him out early?" someone asked Baba, as if Sami wasn't standing right there.

"There was a mix-up with the paperwork? The lawyer gave us the wrong release date?" Baba said everything like a question, staring up at the gaunt figure of his son for confirmation. I saw Sami's jaw move. A small, quick nod.

Mama walked over to him, touched his face, moving her fingers over his nose and eyes like she was trying to memorize his features.

"Habibi," she said, "why didn't you call? We would have come to pick you up. We were planning on being there, waiting for you. We were going to get balloons. We were going to take you to Starbucks," she said because in one of his letters he once told her that the prison coffee was undrinkable. And I knew then that this would stab at her for years—this image of him being released and finding no one there to greet him. We'd later learn that it took him eight hours to get home. They bought him a bus ticket and dropped him off at the Syracuse bus station, with forty dollars in his pocket.

My brother put his big hand on Mama's shoulder, patting it awkwardly. "It's okay, Mama. I'm home."

Just then, Lina stumbled over the last step and collided into my back. She was laughing, and suddenly the walls were spinning. Then I felt her gasp, her breath hot on my neck. "Amira," she said, too loudly, and everyone, all those Arabs, my mother, my father, and my long-lost brother, all turned to look at me. Everything went dark.

OF COURSE, our childhood was filled with locked doors, silence, and tears welling; of course, there were search parties and sirens and whole days spent coloring in the back of courtrooms, waiting to hear your brother's name. Of course, there were probation officers, home visits, a court-ordered psychiatrist at whom the whole family once blinked silently on a chenille couch. Of course. Of course, there was terror; of course, there was shame.

But there was also magic.

Once, a trip upstate before upstate came to mean prison. The closest we would ever get to camping. We thought we were on vacation, but really Mama and Baba were visiting a nearby school for wayward boys.

One of those wilderness programs where sunburned men shove boys' faces into dirt, grind boots into their backs, and call it making men of them. A judge back in Brooklyn had said it was either this or juvie. But it turned out that beatings in the woods cost money, a lot of it. So, while Mama and Baba pled their case to the program director, Sami, Lina, and I were left alone at an Econo Lodge surrounded by trees.

We were afraid of being alone with him. But Sami, perhaps sensing his last days of freedom, was a different animal up there in the cool, damp air of the Adirondacks. Once the adults had left, he turned to us, huddled on our cot in the corner of the small motel room, and said, "Let's go exploring." There was a light in his eyes and a girlish lilt in his voice. We recognized a long-lost friend in him and quietly edged off the bed.

We rambled around the woods surrounding the motel like a litter of mangy pups. Sami knew he was out of time and thus conjured more of it, pulling silky sheets of it from his sleeve. The three of us were ensconced in a green timelessness—Sami dark and lean, his boy muscles like knotted ropes, the leader of our pack; Lina, dark like him and also skinny; and me, as white as dusty cotton and round all over, always the odd one out.

In the woods, we found a strange sidewalk, overgrown with weeds and dirt, which both started from and led to nowhere. We pretended that those three squares of pavement were a lagoon we splashed around in. We weaved between trees and thorn-covered vines. "Faster," Sami would call to us, his hands clenched around our wrists, pulling. "Faster." We found a concrete tunnel in a dried-up creek bed. Mud squelching and twigs crackling beneath our city feet, we crawled inside; Sami was hunched over, his hand around Lina's wrist; Lina had her hand around my wrist. "It's a cave," he said. "Watch out for bats." Our eyes darted upward, imagining black shadows hanging above. The concrete cave was hot and dark and wet. Bits of trash whispered under our sneakers. We inched farther and farther inside.

In a wood-paneled office a few miles away, in a log cabin built by other children, our mother and father sat sweating beneath the incessant beating of a ceiling fan. A man in a ridiculous hat that made him look like he was on walkabout pushed pamphlets across a desk. He ran his finger down columns with dollar amounts and pay plans. Our father nodded constantly, which annoyed our mother. He was only half listening, doing mental math, calculating money he did not have, money it was his job to have. Mama was not listening at all. She did not like this man, in his olive-green shirt with various flaps and vents, in that stupid, wide-brimmed hat with all its grommets, the ghost of sunscreen glowing on his nose. While Baba counted, Mama looked around. A small boy had been summoned into the office to bring them bottles of water. She saw a gooey wound behind his left ear. She saw the crescents under his eyes, the dirt-crusted cuticles. She did not like the look of the hair on the director's knuckles—red and curly. In the end, when it was clear they would never be able to afford this place, Mama and Baba would get the same advice from this man as they would get from all the others—police officers, judges, neighbors, teachers—*Watch him; watch this kid like hell.* Sometimes the advice was also to beat, to deprive, or to smother with love. But it was always to watch. People seemed to believe that if you were always watching you could stall the disaster that loomed ahead of you. It was similar to the way we would all be watched in the years after the towers fell. Watch them. Never let them out of your sight. Look at them through binoculars, in grainy security footage, through the eyes of informants and undercovers, through the sights of rifles, through drones and satellites, in mosques, in restaurants, on subways, in deserts, on mountaintops, in university dining halls, at soccer matches, beauty parlors, delis, in caves, in palaces, community centers, in cells. *If you see something, say something.* Watch them. Watch him. You can avert disaster forever this way. Until that one day, that one second, when you look away. And now, years later, we wondered why Mama and Baba were wandering the apartment like two amnesiacs, their eyes lolling around, searching for Sami, trying to go back to the time when one or both of them had accidentally closed their eyes.

Back at the Econo Lodge forest, we were hovering over a discovery. We were following a scent, the scent of death, deeper and deeper into the concrete tunnel, the closest we Brooklyn kids had ever been to life unneutered by city grids and city water and city blocks with planned "green spaces." Here it was: actual nature, the decaying corpse of a deer buzzing with flies that we swatted away. Sami's gaze fixed on the black, impenetrable eye; Lina's on the unblemished brown-gray of its beautiful flank. Mine focused on the dried red pools spread out under and around the open gash. We were vultures, standing over the body of the deer, picking it apart with our eyes. Until Sami did something magical. He cupped his hands, bowed his head, and read the words of God on his palms. "Bismillah ar-rahman ar-raheem," he said. We mourned the deer like it was our mother, like we had come from its white-spotted belly.

In the distance, beyond the sidewalk lagoon and the thorn-covered vines, in the shaded asphalt ocean of the parking lot, a voice cried out. Another mother from a different time. "Sami," the voice cried. "Amira. Lina. Where are you?" We could hear the terror in her voice, could imagine her staring into the dense wall of trees, scanning the brush for signs of movement—her babies lost in all that green.

That night, at the Econo Lodge wedged into the Adirondacks, I can imagine Sami looking up at the clearest, most star-strewn sky he had ever beheld. I can imagine that in the constellations he saw the outlines of a great jagged trap looming over him. He stood in the mouth of that trap, waiting for someone to trip the wire, waiting for metal jaws to clamp down on him. All any of us—mother, father, girls—ever wanted was to be let inside, to join him in that wait, even if it meant being sealed forever in darkness.

I WOKE TO THE HANDS of my father and my brother pressed against my back—father's hands at the crook of my knees, brother's hand at the nape of my neck. They carried me like a rag doll through the mobs. I could hear the voices of women yelling contradictory instructions: *A wedge of lemon under her nose! Sprinkle her face with rose water. Just give her one quick slap across the cheek.*

They set me down on my bed. I knew that if I opened my eyes he would be there, so I kept them closed a moment longer, until Ustaz

Walid from the fourth floor made his way through the crowd of neighbors. In Tunisia, Uztaz Walid was a doctor, but now he worked as a line cook at a restaurant in SoHo. When I felt his shadow over me, I opened my eyes and squinted.

"Ahlan wa sahlan," Ustaz Walid said. "Welcome back."

He checked my pulse and my temperature and decided that I was dehydrated as a result of fasting in the heat. He ordered that I drink a full glass of water every thirty minutes, and that I stay in bed for the rest of the night. People quickly lost interest in me once they found out that I was alive. A group of women had Sami cornered and were trying to force-feed him olives. But Ustaz Walid ordered everyone out of the apartment with an authority that surprised us all.

"Let the poor girl rest," he said to them.

Once all the neighbors were gone, Mama entered my room, carrying an enormous glass of water and a little bowl filled with cold grapes.

"Get better quickly," she whispered. "I need you." She set the tray down on the nightstand table and left the room without another word.

I drank the water in five big gulps. Then I lay back down and closed my eyes. The bed buzzed. The room spun. I tried to sleep, but I was fighting a desperate urge to pee. I could hear Baba talking with Sami and Imam Tariq in the living room.

I would have to step out into the living room in order to get to the bathroom. I stalled in my room for a few minutes, wondering if there was any other way. When my bladder felt like it was about to burst, I opened the door to my room and stepped out. The men went quiet as I passed.

"Assalaamu alaykum," the imam said, his eyes glued to the floor. I didn't reply, even though I knew Mama would yell at me later. I just wanted to concentrate on putting one foot in front of the other, relieving myself, and then shutting myself away for the rest of the night, for days or weeks on end, for as long as I could possibly avoid facing him.

I made it to the bathroom and, after peeing, I considered digging a hole in the linoleum with a pair of nail clippers. When I opened the door, Baba called out to me. "Ya Amira, now you feeling better, come say hello to your brother."

Sami rose from the sofa. "Hey," he said. And then he walked toward me.

I let my brother hug me, a one-armed hug, the sort of hug one American man gives to another. He was so much smaller than I expected. Underneath his clothes, I could feel his ribs. His wrists looked like I could just reach over and snap them. His skin was sallow, and his eyes were bloodshot. But he still had all the tattoos, crawling up both arms and then down, underneath his T-shirt, on his stomach and back.

"How are you?" he said, and it was just how I feared it would be. He was asking me questions that were impossible to answer. What could I say? *Good? Okay? Alhamdulillah? Yourself?* But when I looked up at him, I could see that he didn't know what to do, either. He didn't know what to say or where to look or how to speak. The discomfort was written all over his body, across his slumping shoulders. He looked meek—like someone who had just walked into the wrong room, as if he was about to say *My bad,* turn around, and leave.

I could see Mama smiling at me from the kitchen doorway. And, behind her, I could see Lina frowning. Then the two of them came out carrying bowls of dried figs and sliced mango. They set the bowls down on the coffee table where Baba and Imam Tariq sat, and everyone was immediately made uncomfortable by Lina's long, glistening legs, the dress that barely covered the curve of her ass.

Sami looked at the floor. He was nothing like he used to be—swollen with anger. He looked like he had gotten the fight beaten and starved right out of him. Who was this meek, emaciated man? I didn't know whether to feel contempt or resentment, pity or embarrassment.

He didn't make me decide. He just said, "Good to see you," then took a pack of menthols from his jeans pocket and shook them against his palm. Then he stepped out the front door and left everyone inside to listen to the sound of his footsteps echoing in the stairwell.

Mama stood at the kitchen window watching him smoke until he threw his cigarette into the gutter and turned back inside: he couldn't leave again if someone was always watching. Baba had run out of things to say to Imam Tariq, and Lina was sulking in a corner because Mama had made her put on pants. We were silent, waiting for Sami to come back. And when he did, Imam Tariq stood and excused himself—he needed to get back to the masjid for the late-night Taraweeh prayers. Lina and I escaped to our room while they said their goodbyes.

Lina collapsed on her bed. I sat on the floor next to her and rested my cheek on the meaty part of her thigh.

"What now?" she asked.

We listened to the sounds of shuffling in the apartment. The door closing. A faucet running. Mama, Baba, and then a third set of footsteps. A phantom creaking the floorboards. We listened until it got quiet.

"This doesn't change anything," I said. "We can still . . ." I waited for Lina to jump in, to help finish my sentence. But then I heard her breath coming slow and deep. I tried halfheartedly to go to sleep, but gave up after just a few minutes.

I opened our bedroom door, just a sliver, and peered out. Nothing. I tiptoed into the hallway and craned my neck to peer into the living room, ready to retreat to the bedroom if he was out there. But it was just the two of them: Mama asleep, her head on Baba's shoulder, on the couch.

"Hi, ya banat," Baba whispered, using the plural—*girls*—as if Lina were still beside me.

"Hi, Baba," I said, and I wondered if he could ever imagine where we had gone earlier—if he could ever picture us dancing and throwing back shots.

"Sami is sleeping," Baba said, smiling so big it must have hurt. He put a finger to his lips and winked at me.

I went to the bathroom to brush my teeth, because I could still taste the alcohol from earlier. The door to Sami's room was closed—no sounds coming from inside. I was about to put on my pajamas when Baba knocked gently on our bedroom door. "You want to go on a walk?" he asked me. Lina was still fast asleep, her mouth hanging open.

"Okay," I said, nodding, because I didn't want to sleep anyway. I put a hoodie on to cover my hair. Baba had laid Mama down on the sofa and covered her with a blanket.

We walked slowly through the neighborhood. I loved the sound of his leather sandals shuffling along the sidewalk. We passed a group of women sitting in a cluster on a stoop. One of them made a lewd joke about her husband's lovemaking during Ramadan, how for the rest of the year, when he could have sex whenever he wanted, he never came to her, but now that it was forbidden during the daylight hours, he got a hard-on every time he so much as glanced at her. When they saw me and Baba approaching, they went silent. But as soon as we rounded the corner, we heard them explode into wonderful embarrassed laughter.

Their laughter faded away as we kept walking. I glanced at Baba from the side of my eye to see if he was embarrassed, too. But he made no indication that he had heard them.

We passed a house that had wind chimes hanging from the porch ceiling. They clanged loudly, as if calling hello.

"You drinked the alcohol tonight, no?" Baba asked. For a moment, I wasn't sure if he had really said it. But I looked at his face, and he had this sheepish expression, his lips puffed out slightly, his eyes shifting.

"No," I said, but then he turned and looked at me like he had rarely ever done before, and I nodded before I could stop myself.

He was quiet for too long. Finally, he spoke. "One time I had what they call a lager. It was not very nice. So, okay, you try the alcohol, but now you know that it is not nice, yes?"

"Yes," I said.

"Good," he said.

He was silent for a moment, and I could tell he was struggling with what else he should say. He was in the process of parenting, and he knew there was more he should do.

"You won't drink again?" he asked finally.

"No," I said, which felt like the truth at the time. And I knew that my truth would also be taken as Lina's truth, because our parents couldn't always disentangle us.

I was impressed he had noticed. I didn't know he could even see us sometimes. I thought he would say more, tell me about the time he'd had the lager, and try to teach me a lesson about life.

"I know it's hard," he said. "Your brother coming home. I know it's, how would you say, *weird*?"

I nodded vehemently. It *was,* how would you say, weird. I wanted him to say more about how it was weird for him, so I could say more about how it was weird for me. We had never talked about the effect Sami had on us.

We turned the corner, and suddenly we were back in front of our building. Instead of going upstairs, he unlocked the door to the shop, and I was glad, because I knew that if we went back home now our talk would be over before it had really begun. Before he turned on the light, I took a moment to smell the darkness: coriander seeds and lemon disinfectant. He turned on the light and motioned for me to sit at one of the bar stools near the deli counter. "Itfadali," he said, pulling the stool out for me like I was a fancy lady.

I watched him heat the griddle and test its temperature with a small flick of olive oil. From the refrigerator case, he took out a rack of lamb chops. He sliced between the ribs, separating the chops, and began to rub each piece gently with a nub of peeled garlic. Then he placed them on the hot grill and sprinkled them with salt and cayenne pepper. If we were in an upscale restaurant, the chef would serve us this lamb pink and bloody on the inside. But the Arabs cook their meat through, until all traces of life are eviscerated and the flesh is a dull, uniform brown, effectively killing it twice. This is the way we like it, so we can gnaw and chew and work at our food without having to remember what it once was.

When the meat was cooked through, he picked the chops straight off the grill; Baba's fingers no longer felt pain. He handed me three and kept two for himself. Together, with him holding his chop firmly between his fingers, and me tossing the hot flesh back and forth between my two burnt hands, we ate. We tore and pulled and chewed until there was nothing left but bone. I took one bite of my third and final chop and then handed the rest to Baba, who finished it off with a swift suck to the bone.

"Your brother is finally home," he said when all the bones were lying naked in front of us. My fingertips still throbbed from the heat.

I nodded. I wanted to encourage him to go on, to tell me what things would be like now.

"We need to spend time together, all of us. Family times. So you cannot be always running around with Lina, okay?"

I felt my heart sink. Outside, we had been veering toward some form of awkward truth. With the wind chimes in the dark and the Arab ladies making jokes behind us, we were approaching some essential confession about the way the precious boy made us feel, the things he did to us, the small people he made us into. But we had left all of that on the street. Now we returned to the old, familiar narrative: how to save Sami. None of the rest of us mattered anymore.

"We're not always running around," I said. *We're right here. We're always right here,* I wanted to say, but didn't.

Instead, he just started talking about Sami again.

"The lawyer, he say we need time to accentuate. No, that's not right." Baba furrowed his brow, looking for the right word.

"Acclimate?" I offered bleakly, feeling deeply and suddenly wounded.

Baba nodded gratefully. "Ac-cli-mate, yes. It is funny to think he need to acclimate to his own family. But this is what we all need, yes? To learn how to be all together again."

"I'm going to college," I reminded him.

But Baba wasn't listening to me. Instead, he said, "The lawyer say Sami need job. That parole officer will check to make sure he has good job, not in the gang anymore. But I tell him my son is Muslim now, good Muslim, that good Muslims have no gang."

He stared down at the cash register. "A job," he muttered again. "I will give him a job. And this way I can watch him. The problem is, I didn't watch him enough back then."

"Here?" I asked. In my heart, I pleaded with him not to take away my only sanctuary. When I was walking down the streets of Bay Ridge and I could see the line snaking out the door of the Arab Center, when the men in the cafés clucked their tongues at me as I passed because the shadow I cast was shameful, or when I could hear the police tape around Abu Jamal's café rustling in the wind, I could duck into the shop and hear Baba reciting poetry from the days when Arabs were kings and inventors and rulers of civilization.

"Yes," he said. "You and Mama and Lina upstairs, me and Sami downstairs. It is beautiful thinking, no?"

In his dreams, I'd always be upstairs, studying, getting straight A's in my college courses so that I could go nowhere and see nothing, so that I could stay exactly where I'd always been, silent and waiting for someone to call my name.

I left Baba in the shop. He was scribbling numbers onto old napkins, trying to figure out how much he could afford to pay Sami. I walked back upstairs to the apartment by myself. I lay on my bed and traced dollar signs into my palm until I fell asleep.

I woke up hung over, dry-mouthed, and irritable. Across the room, Lina seemed to be sleeping but poorly—drunk sleep, half-sleep. I stood and lurched over to the fan oscillating in the corner, pushing hot air around. I lifted my hair off my sweaty neck and crouched down next to it. My black curls swayed, and I felt the blood returning to my brain.

Footsteps outside our bedroom. He was there, on the other side of the door, then on the other side of the wall, in the bathroom. The pipes above and all around us groaned with rushing water. Shower sounds. I snuck out into the kitchen. Daylight. Dust motes hovering by the windows. Mama rinsing lentils. I watched her for a moment, and wondered if her body was ever still.

"Good morning, my love," she said. "I made you some breakfast." She gestured to a plate covered in plastic wrap on the counter.

"But . . ." I began. My head hurt, and it cost me too much to finish the sentence. Mama finished it for me.

"You were sick last night," she said. "You shouldn't fast today."

I couldn't tell whether Baba had told her about the drinking. Her voice revealed nothing. I took the plate and sat down at the kitchen table. Fried eggs sweating grease, potatoes flecked with paprika and cumin and turkey bacon. I felt sick to my stomach and ravenous at the same time. I stared at the plate.

"Eat," Mama said gently, without turning from the lentils.

. . .

I had never been more relieved to go to work. I spent the morning hiding in various rooms, listening for Sami's movements so I wouldn't run into him. I got ready quickly after eating, kissed Mama, and practically ran down the stairs.

The lobby of the Center was packed when I arrived. All the seats were taken, and there were a few men standing in the center of the room. It was unemployment-renewal day. I no longer felt like I had to vomit, but I was sweating and clammy and I was sure everyone would be able to take one look at me and know what I had done. But if they did, no one said anything. It was a pretty normal shift. One woman tried to set up a marriage between her niece and another woman's son. A man video-chatted with his brother in Tunis. Multiple people played Candy Crush with the volume on. I closed my eyes, tried to breathe through my headache. I checked their names off the list, salaamed and smiled as the people came and went.

I got a text from Lina: "When are you coming home? I don't want to talk to him without you."

I felt bad for her, stuck in our room, trying to avoid our brother in our small-ass apartment. But I also liked the feeling that she was waiting for me.

I got another text and thought maybe it was her again, begging me to come home. But it was from Faraj.

"Make any copies today?" he asked.

Lina would have told me to wait fifteen minutes. *Don't seem thirsty,* she would have said. My fingers hovered over the screen. But before I could decide what to write, he sent me another message: "You look bored." Immediately I looked up, and spotted him through the window. He was leaning against a streetlamp, grinning at me. My first instinct was to dive under the desk and hide. How long had he been there? Had he seen me picking at my cuticles? Was he there when the old woman in the lobby shuffled over to me and picked some lint off my shoulder? I couldn't bear to look at him again, even to confirm that he was really there. I was sure someone in the lobby would notice, would see the way

I looked at him, and would know everything. Even though there was nothing to know.

"Come outside," flashed another message.

"I can't," I wrote back. "Fifteen minutes left on my shift."

"I'll wait," he wrote.

And he did. For fifteen minutes, he stood outside the Center, with all of Bay Ridge walking and driving past, and waited for me.

When my fifteen minutes were up, I gathered my belongings and crammed them into my bag. I poked my head into the back and said goodbye to the caseworkers. One of them would have to cover the desk until the other receptionist arrived, another girl from Fort Hamilton, two years behind me in school. I tugged my scarf down over my hairline, ran my tongue over my teeth, and walked outside. *There's a boy waiting for me,* I said to myself. *There's a boy picking me up from work.* If only Lina could see me now.

Faraj raised his hand in a wave. "Surprised?" he said.

"Yes," I said. But I was eager to get moving, to walk away from the large window of the Center. They would be watching me, I knew, and wondering who this boy was, a Desi, a stranger.

Faraj picked up on my discomfort. He nodded to the window. "You know them?" he asked.

"Yes," I said.

"All of them?"

"Yes."

He laughed. "It's the same with Pakistanis—don't worry," he said. "Let's go."

He started walking, and I followed, not daring to look back at the Center. We went two blocks without talking. He walked quickly, taking big strides with those long legs of his. I felt like a little girl tagging along.

"Where are we going?" I finally asked.

"I have no idea," he said. "It's your neighborhood."

I froze in place on the sidewalk. I had no idea where to take him. I thought of Lina. Where did Lina take her boys? How did she make *a* boy into *her* boy? Besides being groped on the train, I had never had any stories of my own. I considered making something up, saying that my parents needed me to come home. But I didn't want him to think of me as a kid. Then, suddenly, he started moving again.

"Are you fasting?" he said as I jogged to keep up.

I had a belly full of breakfast, and my pores were still sweating out the alcohol from last night. I nodded, but it didn't feel like a lie. I still felt like the girl who fasted, the girl who didn't drink.

"Good girl," he said, which both flattered and annoyed me. "Come on, I'll show you something."

Without any warning, he turned into the deli on the corner. I followed after him. He walked straight to the back, to the refrigerator section. I salaamed the man behind the counter, a Yemeni who knew my father. Faraj opened one of the glass doors, letting the frosty air billow out, and browsed through the selection of sodas. I stopped a few paces behind him, not sure what to do. I had assumed he was fasting, too. If he got a drink, should I get one so he wouldn't think I was too much of a good girl? Or was he testing me, to see if I really was a good girl? The Yemeni man at the counter would see. What if he told Baba? God didn't factor into my deliberations at all.

"Come here," he said, beckoning me.

I went and stood next to him. I watched as he selected two ginger ales from the case and handed one to me.

"I'm fasting," I said again, cringing a little.

"So am I," he said. "This is something I do when I'm having a hard time getting through the whole day." He turned so he was facing me directly.

"Close your eyes," he said.

I stared at him until he closed his own eyes. Then I closed my eyes, laughing a little to smother my embarrassment.

"Open and close your mouth," he said.

I thought about the Yemeni man up front, who might be watching us on the camera. I told myself I wasn't going to do it, but then I heard Faraj's own mouth open and close. I heard the wet pop of his lips opening. I opened my mouth a very little and closed it again quickly.

"How do you feel?" he asked.

"Thirsty," I said, suddenly feeling just how dry my tongue was against the roof of my mouth.

"Now hold the soda can in both hands and bring it up to your face." He reached over and guided the can up in my hands until the top met the bottom of my chin. I flinched a little at the icy metal.

"Tip your head back and imagine you're taking a sip," he said. With his hands still around mine on the can, I tipped my head back. I listened to the liquid inside the can slosh as I dipped backward and forward again.

"Now, last thing," he said, releasing my hands. "Open and close your mouth one more time."

I did as he instructed, listening again to his own mouth popping open and smacking closed again.

"How do you feel?" he asked.

I moved my tongue around in my mouth gently. Suddenly my mouth was wet and cool inside.

"Better," I said, laughing. I opened my eyes and found him smiling at me.

He took the can of soda from me and put them both back in the case. Then he started walking toward the front of the store. I salaamed the Yemeni man again on our way out, and tried not to catch his eye.

"How did you do that?" I asked, when we were back outside. It felt ten degrees cooler outside than it had before we entered the deli.

"Mindfulness," he said, tapping a finger to his temple. "It's actually a big part of Islam, especially during Ramadan. Most people forget that. Ramadan is all about meditation and about being aware of the relationship between body and mind."

I had never heard anyone talk about Ramadan like that. Ramadan was always a chore or a test.

We started walking toward Shore Road Park, bumping into each other as we walked. His hand brushed mine, and his touch sent a searing flash of heat up my arm.

"What are you doing here anyway?" I asked.

"I came to see you," he said, and I felt my face light up. "I had a meeting at that masjid over on Sixth Avenue. And then I remembered you worked nearby."

"Oh," I said, feeling a little disappointed that he actually hadn't come to Bay Ridge just to see me. "What was your meeting about?"

"Abu Jamal," he said. He squinted his eyes at me like it was a dumb question. "One protest isn't going to free him. We have to keep going. I'm kind of like a full-time organizer."

I nodded, but I wasn't sure what he meant by "organizer." It made me think of a wedding planner or a personal assistant.

"So you get paid to, um, organize?" I asked.

"Well, no, no one pays me," he said. He started talking as if a faucet had been turned on somewhere inside of him. He told me that he worked at Enterprise, the car-rental place, as a sales associate. But that what he really wanted to do was go to law school so he could help people like his brother and Abu Jamal. He just had a few more credits to finish at Hunter, and then he was going to take the LSATs.

"I want to help Muslims," he said. "Like you do at your job." This made me feel ashamed and flattered simultaneously. I never thought about my job this way. I was just a receptionist—it could have been at a dentist's office for all it mattered to me. It was just a thing I did in high school, while I waited to go to college. And once in college, I would study something practical—what, I hadn't figured out yet—something that would make money. Not an insane amount of money—I wasn't that naïve. Just more money than my parents made. A step up the ladder. Nowhere in this plan did helping Muslims factor in.

A few blocks ahead of us, the water shimmered. A pack of cyclists whizzed by in their technicolor spandex.

"Can I ask what happened to your brother?" I said it so quietly, I wasn't sure he had heard me. For the first time in six blocks, he was quiet.

"He's in Pakistan now," he said finally. "They deported him once they finally admitted they didn't have a case against him. But before that, they kept him locked up at MCC for two years."

"What did he do?" I asked.

"He didn't *do* anything," Faraj snapped.

"Of course. I didn't mean it like that. I'm sorry," I said.

"They wanted him to be an informant, but he wouldn't do it," he said, his voice softer. "They offered him money, even citizenship. But he kept saying no. And then they got mad."

"And they deported him just for that?" I asked.

"Yep. He immigrated here when he was three, with my parents. But I was born here. They're stuck with me," he said.

We crossed the Parkway and reached the water and stood under a big leafy oak tree.

"It was probably the same sort of thing with your brother, right? Locking him away for some trivial bullshit?"

I wanted to invent some noble story of injustice. Something about racial profiling or wrong place, wrong time. But I was pretty sure Sami had done whatever they said he had. I felt my mouth dry up again, as if all the saliva had been sucked out. We had probably walked at least twenty blocks already that day. My legs felt heavy, as if there were weights tied to my feet.

"You all right?" Faraj asked. "You tired?"

I nodded.

He guided me to a nearby bench, and I sat down. I closed my eyes and tried to picture myself holding a glass of water to my lips. I imagined the ice tinkling against the glass, the cool water sliding across my tongue and down my throat. I opened my eyes.

"How do you know about my brother?" I asked.

He was standing over me, blocking the sun. He frowned.

"You told me," he said. "At the vigil."

"No, I didn't," I said.

"You did," he said. "I specifically remember it. It was right after I told you about my brother. Then you told me that your brother was also in prison and that he was getting released soon."

I closed my eyes again and tried to remember. I could see us walking back toward MCC, rows of fake windows staring down at us. I shook my head to get the building out of my mind. Maybe I had told him?

"I don't think so," I said.

"I'm pretty sure you did," he said, sounding a little annoyed. "But even if you didn't, maybe I heard it somewhere. Maybe someone at the vigil or at the meeting at the masjid mentioned it. I don't know."

We were quiet for a minute. A man rode by on a bike, blasting an old Run-DMC song.

"Is your brother some big secret or something?" he asked.

"No," I said. To my mortification, I could feel tears welling up in my eyes. I stood up from the bench to get away from him and walked over a few paces to the sea wall.

"Amira," Faraj said, putting his hands to his hair, smoothing it back. "Are you okay?"

The sun moved behind a cloud briefly, and I could see his face without having to squint against the light. He looked bewildered.

"I'm sorry," I said. I turned away quickly and walked back to the sea wall. I clenched my eyes shut and bullied the tears into retreat.

"Aren't you happy about him getting out?" he asked softly, standing next to me again.

I leaned against the metal railing of the sea wall and imagined what it would feel like to dive in. I shook my head.

"It was supposed to be my summer," I said to him. It sounded petty, like it was merely a matter of sibling rivalry, of jealousy. How to explain that I was trying to become myself, my true self, the self I was sure was there, buried somewhere deep inside, just waiting for the chance to rocket out of my body? And how could I do this when Sami was lurking in the periphery, always inching toward my center?

"I get it," he said. "I really do."

I could feel his eyes on me, but I kept my own eyes glued to the water, watching a plastic milk jug float by, my hands gripped around the railing.

He traced his fingers across my white knuckles, and I felt a shiver run up my spine.

"Can I see you again?" he whispered close to my ear.

I nodded, but had to close my eyes, because I was starting to see spots in the sunshine.

As I walked home that afternoon, I glanced at everyone I passed and wondered if any of them had seen me with a handsome older boy, not knowing what I was more afraid of: that someone *had* seen or that *nobody* had seen. I felt the ghost of his fingertips on my knuckles. I felt aware of every inch of my body, as if my insides had expanded to fill my skin better. I had a secret, and I wasn't the kind of girl who ever had a secret. It made me feel, even if just for a moment, that I could walk into our apartment right then, and even if I came face-to-face with Sami, I'd be fine. I'd be able to smile, say, "Welcome home," and then just keep walking past him, untouchable.

When I got home, I found my family bent in prayer. The coffee table had been dragged off to the side of the living room. Mama, Baba, and Sami were praying in a line. Lina was a little behind, in a line of her own. If they heard me enter, no one broke the prayer to acknowledge me. I slipped off my shoes and stood in the kitchen doorway, watching them. One by one, they stood to begin a new rakah. In prayer, Sami stood straighter, his shoulders pinned back. He didn't look as shrunken as he had the night before. In fact, I could see that he was now taller than our father. I felt a pang for Baba then—to have missed the moment when his son surpassed him. In a wave, they all bent again, hands to their knees. I didn't like seeing him there, in my living room, kneeling next to my mother. Praying for a long time, doing more rakat than was required. But then I just sort of lost myself in the watching of him. I counted how many seconds he stayed with his head pressed to the floor. I observed the near-perfect ninety-degree bend of his body, the way he placed his hands just above his kneecaps. Even as he was finally nearing the end, sitting on his feet, whispering to angels over his left shoulder and then his right, even when I knew that in a moment he would be finished, he would stand and turn and see me and maybe even speak to me, I couldn't move. He was one of *those* guys—hands exactly where they're supposed to be, praying perfectly, meticulously, the prayer itself a show. Did he have a bruise between the eyes from pressing his forehead to the prayer mat so many times—a third eye? I couldn't remember. He was getting up now, rising, folding his prayer mat, helping Mama drag the coffee table back to the center of the room. Finally, he turned. Our eyes met for less than a second, before he looked back down at the floor. And there it was—the faintest trace of it, a suggestion of a purple bruise hovering in the center of his forehead. He didn't say anything to me. He merely turned and walked quietly back to his bedroom.

I tried ignoring him. This strange roommate. This foreign-exchange student. This intruder in the living room. But I couldn't stop watching him. I spent the next twenty-four hours observing him from corners, trying never to be fully in the same room as him if I could help it. I learned a few things:

He liked his coffee black, no sugar. Also, he loved smoking now. He had started smoking young, when he was just a teenager, but he'd never *loved* smoking; he'd always just done it, joylessly, sulking as he took in the smoke and let it back out, like it was the worst chore. Now, though, he sat outside on the stoop after Maghrib prayers, smoking cigarette after cigarette, taking his time with each one. Now he pulled the stick out of the pack gingerly, tucked the pack carefully back into his pocket, lit up, and breathed in so deep and so slow that you thought his lungs might not be able to contain all that smoke, they might explode. He wasn't like everyone else, hurrying home from Maghrib prayers, rushing to dinner tables laden with food. Instead, he took his time smoking out on our front steps, smoking and smoking and smoking, while the rest of us waited hungrily because Mama wouldn't let us eat until he came inside.

He liked to watch TV on mute—CNN mostly, sometimes sports. Once, he pretended to know about soccer, the way he used to when he was little. Mama asked him about a player for Al-Ahly that he had loved as a boy. "Is he still playing?" Mama asked. And Sami, slumped on the sofa, watching the news anchor's mouth open and close silently, said without hesitation: "Yeah, and he's still their best player." Such a strange lie. I knew for a fact that the player had retired several years earlier, that he'd gotten really fat. He still showed up on Egyptian TV sometimes, like a fallen child star, commenting sadly on this or that team.

Sami had a cheap flip phone and carried it with him everywhere. I heard it buzz sometimes in his pocket, but I never saw him answer it or even look at it.

I tried to notice as much as I could as I was on my way out of spaces he was entering—diving into the bathroom as he approached in the hallway, backing out of the kitchen, peeking out from my bedroom door. But somehow the things I noticed didn't add up to him. He kept dissolving. For all his patterns and habits, his likes and dislikes, he seemed to me a person unknowable. A blank. A placeholder. The bruise on his forehead kept slipping off. Sometimes it was there—I could see the purple traces of it spreading between his eyes. And sometimes it was gone. It moved, I realized. It slipped beneath the skin, it peeked out, it blinked and opened, and then it was gone again.

At the end of his second full day home, I stepped into the living room after I heard Sami go into his room. I found Mama and Baba on the sofa, watching their show. They both looked so tired. They had been watching Sami, too, and it was exhausting.

Just then I felt Lina at my left shoulder.

"If we don't leave this apartment right now I'm going to scream," she said. And as soon as she said it, I felt it. The urge to scream. There was a party at Andres's cousin's apartment. I nodded yes.

"Back by curfew," Mama said.

"Back by curfew," Lina said.

"Be good?" Baba said.

"We'll be good," I said.

Lina waited for me by the door as I ran back to the bathroom to grab my lip gloss. On the way, I glimpsed Sami in his room, the door a crack open, sitting on the edge of his small twin bed, hunched over Baba's old laptop. I found myself frozen, watching him punch the keys with his unwieldy caveman fingers. He was frowning, his face illuminated in blue light.

He looked up then and saw me peering with one eye into his bedroom. His fingers lingered over the keyboard. He looked right at me—into my eyes and through all the chutes and ladders inside me, down and out the back of my soft neck. The look was familiar and feral. He stood up, laid the computer gently on the bed, walked over to the door, and then shut it in my face.

The party was not a party but, rather, just Andres and his cousin playing video games in a basement apartment in Sunset Park. My lips were sparkly, and Lina's hair was straightened and shiny, and we looked ridiculous. We watched the boys play video games for a while. After we had been there for about an hour, Lina scooched closer to Andres on the couch, ran her finger up and down his arm lightly. He paused the game and turned to her, and almost immediately it was like the cousin and I didn't exist. She spent most of the night straddling his lap while they made out. The cousin offered me a Smirnoff Ice, which I accepted. The cousin began playing a different game, a one-player game, and I watched him maneuver a Lamborghini around some sharp bends while I slowly sipped my drink.

Suddenly Andres lifted Lina off the couch and, without ungluing their faces, carried her to a bedroom. He kicked the door shut behind them.

"Wanna play?" the cousin asked me when they were gone.

I shook my head. "That's okay," I said.

At one point, he scooted closer to me and tried to put an arm around me, but then he needed both hands for the controller and removed it again.

At another point, as he waited for the next level of his game to load, while a pixelated babe in a yellow bikini stuck a large ribbon onto the Lamborghini on the screen, he plucked my hand from my lap—it was still cold and a little wet from holding the Smirnoff bottle—and dropped it like an arcade claw on his lap.

I felt myself turn red. "That's okay," I said, taking my hand back.

"Had to try," he shrugged.

When the game started again, he was racing in the desert. By the time the landscape had transformed into some sort of tundra, Lina appeared from the bedroom, picked her purse up off the couch, looked at me, and said, "Ready?"

We made it home before curfew.

I had a dream in which Lina was a veterinarian—she wore lilac scrubs with little dog bones all over them and sat on a gray concrete floor among all these puppies. She opened her arms to them and they clambered all over her greedily, licking her chin, her cheeks, her lips, her earlobes. In the dream, I was jealous, because it seemed a wonderful thing to be smothered with all that love. I was jealous, but I wasn't even there—I was just seeing it through a security camera. I was somewhere else, somewhere far away, watching it through a screen. And then the dream turned into another dream—we were back in the apartment, lying on Mama and Baba's bed with the air conditioning blasting. We were watching TV and eating ice cream out of bowls that were balancing precariously on top of our big, pregnant bellies.

I told Lina about the dream the next morning.

"Weird," she said.

"It made me think—you'd actually make a great vet," I said.

"I'm going to be a model," she said.

She glanced at her phone distractedly. There had been no messages since the previous night. I thought of our matching dream babies, growing fat in our bellies.

"Did he use a condom?" I whispered.

Lina nodded yes, but I didn't believe her.

"No, he didn't," I yelled, and whacked Lina hard across the arm.

She hit me back even harder. We were silent for a while, then both picked up our phones and turned away from each other, pretending to become absorbed in whatever we found in them. But Lina hated it when I was mad at her—she couldn't stand it. She was always the first to cave.

"He pulled out," she said.

"Just don't get fucking pregnant," I said. I got up and left her sitting there alone.

Lina had lost her virginity when we were sixteen, to a boy in her woodshop class who had recently emigrated from Costa Rica. They had sex in his mom's bed while she was at work. When Lina told me about it later, she was weirdly withholding. I wanted the details. I wanted to know what his left hand was doing. I wanted her to describe the exact shade of red that dotted the mother's nice cream sheets afterward. I thought if I could know it all it would be like it had happened to me, too, and then we would be the same again. I thought of God and heaven and what would happen if both Lina and I died that night in our sleep. Would we go to different places? One to heaven and one to hell? Or one to little-girl heaven and the other to grown-woman heaven? I imagined sitting on a cloud and looking through it and seeing Lina sitting on another cloud, below me. And I could see her but I couldn't talk to her, I couldn't go to her. It was like we were in adjacent soundproof glass cages. I wanted to put us back together again. My belly, her belly. My uterus, her uterus. My heart, her heart.

Out in the living room, I was alone. The building was strangely quiet, and I was frustrated and bored. I couldn't think of a single thing to do, a single place to go. I was sick of the neighborhood, of the parks, of the same boys whistling from the same tired corners, of wondering about my brother, of waiting for Lina. I was sick of fasting. I was sick of summer. *Just end already, just go,* I thought, as if summer were the thing holding me back.

I texted Faraj. "Hey," I wrote.

I waited for his reply. He didn't text back. I pretended not to care.

I left the apartment, not knowing where I was headed. I just stuffed my hair into a baseball cap and left. I hoped that Lina would hear the door close behind me and come out of our room to find me already gone.

I stood out on the steps of our building and looked left and right. All around me, the sky was a bright gray. Across the street, some kids, too young to fast, were trading licks of their Ring Pops—leaning over and licking one another's slobbery red-and-blue-jeweled knuckles. Somebody came out of Abu Nuwas, paused at the door, called back to my father. I could hear Baba laugh inside. I didn't want him to see me walking past, so I turned right.

Someone had finally taken down the police tape in front of Abu Jamal's. But the little tables and chairs that the police had kicked over were still there, tipped on their sides, lying like shrapnel on the sidewalk. I was going to cross the street, to keep a wide radius between me and wreckage, but then I saw a figure step out from under the awning over the front door.

My first thought was that it was Abu Jamal himself. That he'd been released from prison and was about to unlock the door, flip over the "closed" sign to open, and resume his life. But it wasn't Abu Jamal who got out. It was Sami. Abu Jamal would never get out. He'd get sent to a super-max in Colorado. Someone would take over the store—turn it into a tax office—and we'd forget all about him. Unless it was the middle of the night and we woke to a strange sound, the impact of boots on the pavement, a hand at the door. Then we'd gasp or swallow, recall the blurry memory of his face, blink him away, and forget all over again.

Sami stood in front of the store and squinted up at the building. Then he reached into his pocket and retrieved his phone. He flipped it open and started typing something. It took him a long time, his fingers tapping at the tiny buttons. I could tell he was getting frustrated. But, finally, he finished, put his phone back in his pocket, and started walking.

I didn't realize I was following him until he turned left at 80th and I turned left with him. He could have just turned around at any point and seen me there, half a block behind him. But he never did. He paused again near the corner of 6th Avenue, in front of a pale brick house with a white wrought-iron fence around it. There were these gaudy white lions perched atop brick columns. He started coughing, this deep, gravelly smoker's cough, and leaned against one of the lions. He coughed so loudly and for so long that I thought for sure someone would come out of the house to see what was going on. Eventually, he stopped coughing and took his phone out again. He looked up at the house, typed something in the phone, looked up again, looked down, typed. Then the phone was back in his pocket and he was moving again. This happened two more times. Once at a deli—the same one, in fact, where Faraj had held a cold can of soda to my chin. And once again at Masjid Al-Madina, the big mosque all the way over on 63rd that was way nicer than the rinky-dink Islamic Center on 5th that we went to. We had walked nearly twenty blocks, and in a series of zigzags that made no sense. We walked backward and forward again. North and then south. East and west.

Outside of the masjid, he typed into his phone again. I stood in the shadow cast by one of the large warehouses across the street and watched. The block was quiet, and I thought for sure that he'd finally see me. I was so tired of walking. My forehead was damp with sweat, and the baseball cap was chafing my skin. I closed my eyes for a second and wiped my forehead; when I opened them, he was slipping through the men's entrance of the mosque. One second later and I would have missed him entirely.

I sat on the curb for a few minutes, but he didn't come out. It was happening again: seeing things I wasn't supposed to see. It was like there was some sort of blinking tracking device beneath his skin and a transmitter beneath mine. The air between us was thick with invisible signals. I didn't want it. I would cut it out if only I could find the source of it. It would be more bearable maybe if Lina had it, too, but she didn't. It was always just me and him.

I caught my breath and stood up. Somewhere inside, my brother stood barefoot on cold white tile. He was turning a squeaky faucet and the water would run icy over him. I walked the twelve blocks home.

I told myself I wouldn't wonder what Sami had been doing on that strange walk around Bay Ridge. *Don't even think about it,* I told myself. *Don't even care.* I was feeling okay, but then I showed up at the Center the next day and, instead of having me sit at the front desk like usual, they wanted me to walk around from mosque to mosque, handing out the *What to Do When the FBI Knocks* flyers that we've handed out dozens of times before. People had been coming in and telling stories about how they had been followed by a black SUV, how they had heard a clicking on the phone, how the mailman had been acting strangely lately.

"Ever since Abu Jamal, people are . . ." Laila tapped a finger to her brain.

She thrust the stack of flyers into my hands and told me to enjoy the fresh air. It was ninety-seven degrees outside, and as humid as an armpit.

Lina came with me, I guess because she had nothing else to do. Passing out flyers to Arabs was easy. It wasn't like those poor guys I'd seen in Manhattan, trying to give away flyers to New Yorkers who would rather die than take one. No, with Arabs, all you have to do is stand still, hold out the stack of papers, and wait for them all to come to you. Arabs can't stand to be left out of anything.

We went to all the closest mosques first, gave a few flyers away in front of Abu Nuwas and Balady Foods. But we still had about half the stack left.

"What about Masjid Al-Madina?" Lina asked.

I didn't want to go back there, but I didn't want to tell her why, either. So we ended up standing outside the women's entrance of Masjid An-Noor, because the imam there had once scolded me for standing too close to the men's entrance. I caught one woman before she went inside. "Would you like one?" I asked her in Arabic. I handed her a pamphlet, and she turned it over in her hand. Then she went inside without saying anything to me. Within minutes, streams of women were coming out of the mosque. All of them were asking for a flyer. Lina and I were both mobbed by clutching hands.

When they had each gotten one, they filed back into the mosque. Lina and I leaned against the brick wall of the building, panting.

"That was intense," she said. And then: "I gotta pee." Lina went inside the mosque to use the bathroom, while I shuffled a few yards away to stand under a patch of shade.

"What was all that about?" a voice called out.

I looked up and saw a uniformed cop approaching me. He was walking alone on the rather empty street—nothing here except for the mosque and a giant warehouse with faded Chinese lettering scrawled across the side. It was strange to see a cop by himself. They usually came in pairs, like Lina and me. Except here we both were—alone.

The police officer was young and handsome. He had sweet curly black hair and blue eyes and rosy Irish cheeks. I found myself sucking in my stomach.

"Nothing," I stammered. "Just passing out some flyers."

"That's cool," he said like we were old pals. "Can I see?"

I handed him the Arabic flyer. He blinked at it. "It's for free mammograms," I said.

"You're funny," he said. Then he looked me up and down, real obvious about it. "You don't look Muslim," he said.

It was more reflex than courage that caused what happened next. I meant it objectively, with honest curiosity, more than as a challenge. I said, "What do Muslims look like?"

The pretty cop instantly turned ugly. "Now, don't go taking offense," he said, both smiling and frowning simultaneously. "It was a compliment."

And just then, with perfect comic timing, Lina came sauntering out of the masjid. She was still holding her remaining flyers, but she was mostly practicing her model walk.

"Hi," she called to me, raising her eyebrows at the cop standing next to me, like *Everything okay?*

"Don't tell me she's a Muslim, too," the cop said.

Lina stopped a few feet away from us, put one hand on her hip. "One hundred percent," she said.

The cop laughed like it was the funniest joke in the world. Then he kept walking, saying, "You girls have a nice day, now."

After that, I didn't want to hand out flyers anymore, so I left the remaining ones in a pile at the mosque's entrance and anchored them with a shoe I found lying around.

It was almost sundown, and neither of us wanted to go home. We walked aimlessly for a while, trying to think of something to do, in a single-file line on the curb, to avoid the gross water dripping from the air-conditioning units above. We had our hands out to our sides and we were balancing like gymnasts.

"We could go to Andres's club. It's called Lotus," Lina said, as if that was supposed to mean something to me.

"Maybe," I said. I didn't want to go there. I knew what would happen—she would disappear somewhere with Andres, and I would be left alone at the bar, watching the ice melt in my glass.

"Andres says I need to practice my posing," she said. She twisted this way and that, freezing in the oddest positions, her face stuck in this constipated-looking frown. I laughed, and she got mad. We walked on in silence.

My phone buzzed in my pocket, and I immediately reached for it. It was Faraj. He was "sooooo sorry" he hadn't responded earlier. His phone was acting up. He wanted to see me.

"When?" I wrote.

"How about tonight?" he responded. He invited me to iftar at his apartment. Said he was having some people over. I was impressed that he had his own place. I assumed he was like most people I knew, living with his parents until marriage. The one time I brought up the idea of living in a dorm at college, Mama and Baba had straight-up laughed in my face.

I forgot that Lina was mad at me and showed her the messages. "What do I do?" I asked. And she, feeling necessary and wise again, snatched the phone from me and began to type.

"Kinda busy now," she wrote. "Headed to a party in Manhattan."

"What are you doing?" I hissed and tried to grab the phone back from her.

"Trust me," she said, and then she sat down on the curb and began to concentrate, like she was solving complicated mathematical equations.

They wrote back and forth. He asked her—me—where the party was. She was vague. He asked if he could meet me after. She was even vaguer. He talked up his own dinner. Said there'd be cool people there, some folks he knew from Brooklyn College that he wanted to introduce me to. He sent long messages about their involvement in the BDS movement. Though this might have been a selling point for me, it was not very appealing to Lina, and she was the one with the phone.

"Is that his idea of fun? Is that what you guys do when you're together? Talk about Palestine and, like, Abu Ghraib and shit?"

I had told Lina about Faraj's surprising me outside of the Center, about our walk to Shore Road Park. I had tried to make it sound romantic, a seaside stroll. I did not tell her that I cried over Sami in front of him, or that he already knew about Sami's coming home. I had played our first meeting outside of MCC a dozen times over in my head since then. I felt certain that I'd never told Faraj about Sami, but he felt so certain that I had. Maybe I did say something accidentally, something my own memory blocked out. And who cared how he knew about it? Look at what had happened to his own brother, look at how much he cared about Abu Jamal, a man he had never even met.

"No," I said. And then, testing the word out, "He's an organizer."

Lina rolled her eyes. "What kind of food you got?" she wrote.

"Damn. You must be really hungry," he replied.

"Can you get us pad Thai?" she wrote. Baba didn't like the taste of Thai food, so Lina and I considered it a special delicacy.

"I'll see what I can do. Who's we?"

"My sister Lina," she wrote. "She is awesome, my best friend in the whole world, and she's going to be a famous supermodel one day."

This time I really did snatch the phone away from her. Faraj texted me the address, said he couldn't wait to see me soon.


Faraj lived in a five-story walk-up in Park Slope. The subway was all backed up, and by the time we got there, it was ten minutes past sunset. Lina was pissed. She seemed to blame Faraj for the fact that she wasn't already eating.

"There better be fucking pad Thai," she said as I rang the buzzer.

But I was so nervous, I didn't even think I could eat. I had never been to a boy's house before, unless it was one of Lina's boys. It felt like the scales were balancing. And instead of playing video games in some dank basement, we were going to a party with college kids who would talk about Palestine and books we'd never heard of. I didn't know where Sami was and he didn't know where I was, and it was like the universe was correcting itself.

We climbed up four flights of stairs. I was out of breath when Faraj opened the door to greet us. He briefly touched my lower back to usher us inside, and I was afraid he'd feel the sweat clinging to my shirt. He lived in a studio—a small kitchen with a breakfast bar to our left, and a combined living space and bedroom to our right. There were a few closets and a door to the bathroom near his bed. It was immaculate and sparsely furnished, and there was absolutely no one else there. I kept thinking someone might appear from the bathroom or a hidden room, but no one did, and I waited for Faraj to say something, but he just pointed proudly to some plastic containers on the kitchen counter.

"Your pad Thai, as requested," he said.

"Thank God," Lina said, pushing past him to get to the food.

Faraj didn't seem to notice her rudeness, which pleased me. Usually, boys noticed everything about her. Then they'd say something about how we didn't look like twins, and I knew what that meant. While Lina started eating directly out of one container with a plastic fork, he led me over to a leather sofa and had me sit down.

"I'll make you a plate," he said.

He returned with a plate piled way too high with noodles and a glass of murky clear liquid.

"Coconut water," he said. "Replenishes your electrolytes."

I took a sip—it tasted like feet, but I liked that he didn't break his fast with Fanta or Diet Coke, like most of the Muslims I knew. With Lina, I poisoned my body and ruined my fast with alcohol and junk food. With Faraj, I meditated and replenished my electrolytes. I took another sip of the coconut water and smiled.

Faraj handed me the plate and I speared a small piece of tofu with my fork, because I could feel him watching me.

"I mean, I know you're hungrier than that," he said.

I laughed and then took the biggest bite I could manage. It felt like

I was chewing for an hour, and the whole time Faraj was nodding and smiling.

When I finally swallowed, I looked around the apartment again and asked, "So where is everyone?"

"They had to go home," he said.

I waited for him to say more, but he didn't. He just started telling me about his day. About this customer at work who tried to return a car filled with trash and claimed it was like that when he rented it. "Literally, just bottles and crumpled-up chip bags piled up to the ceiling," he said. After work, he'd gone to the gym. I was careful not to look at him when he said that, not to scan his body under his shirt, not to trace the strong shoulders, the hint of pecs. He still worked out, even when he was fasting. My strategy had always been to move as little as possible.

"How was your day?" he asked, and it felt like we were a couple having dinner at the end of a long workday. He nudged my shoulder with his as he asked, and all my organs lit up inside me, like stars in a black sky.

I told him about handing out flyers for the Center. About the women who mobbed us like we were giving away free money, and about the cop who didn't believe we were Muslims.

"What did the flyers say?" he asked.

"Just the usual know-your-rights stuff," I said. "You don't have to open the door without a warrant, you don't have to talk without a lawyer, that kind of thing."

"Hmm," he said as if I'd said something really deep. "Does the Center often do that? Tell people not to talk to the police?"

"They don't tell people *not* to talk to the police. They just tell them what to do when the police talk to them," I said.

"Right, right," he said. "So the Center, like, helps people get away from the police?"

I choked down another sip of coconut water, and glanced over at Lina, but she kept her back stanchly to us, her head bent down low, scrolling through her phone while she ate.

"Not really, no," I said.

"I hate police," he said.

My phone buzzed. I angled away from Faraj a little to read the message. It was from Lina, sitting only a few feet away.

"He lied to us," it said.

I thought about ignoring it, about pretending she wasn't even there, but then I got afraid that she would do or say something to ruin this for me.

"How?" I wrote.

She wrote back this long tirade. "Um, where is everyone? He made it sound like some fun college party. I could be at Lotus meeting important people for my career right now."

"Go if you want," I wrote back. "I'm having fun." It felt good to think that maybe she was jealous, being the one left out for once.

"No, you're not," she wrote.

"Fuck you," I wrote. I put my phone back in my pocket so she would see that I wasn't going to talk to her anymore.

Faraj had moved closer to me on the couch while I was texting. His thigh touched mine now.

"Everything okay?" he whispered into my ear. His breath tickled my neck and I had to stifle the urge to laugh or shudder.

I nodded.

"Tell me more about your work at the Center," he said, but he was still whispering, still talking into my neck, as if we were trading the most intimate of secrets.

My phone buzzed again in my pocket. I counted to thirty, I waited. I told myself not to look, but I couldn't help myself. I thought it might be Lina sending me some advice, telling me what to do now. But that's not what she wanted to tell me.

"There's something weird about this dude," she wrote.

But what did Lina know? She was screwing some wannabe entertainment mogul in the back rooms of shitty midtown bars and the bedrooms of creepy cousins.

Faraj looked between me and Lina, and then down at the phone humming in my palm.

"Want to see the roof?" He stood so suddenly that, without his weight on the seat cushion next to me, I sort of tipped to the side. He held out a hand to pull me up without waiting for me reply.

"We're going up to the roof," Faraj called to Lina, in what was not exactly an invitation.

She wheeled around on the bar stool, gave us this little salute, and then turned back to her phone.

Faraj led me up another staircase until we reached a metal door with a sign on it: "Do not open. Alarm will sound." He pushed it open. No alarm sounded. I expected lounge furniture, potted palms, a view of Manhattan in the distance. But it was pretty bleak up there—the roof was sloped and covered in black tar paper. A few mismatched lawn chairs were clustered in a messy circle. A big, humming electrical box stood in the corner. There was a blue comforter, surprisingly clean-looking, spread out between the chairs. He sat down on the blanket and patted the place next to him. I sat down and tried to appear relaxed.

"Nice up here, huh?" he said, and I looked around and nodded.

People were laughing on the street down below. I could hear the words "picnic" and "coincidentally."

"So what are people in Bay Ridge saying about Abu Jamal?" he said.

I shrugged. "Not much. I guess people are a little freaked out, but, mostly, it's back to normal." I pulled my legs into my chest and then stretched them out again. It was hard to get comfortable.

"See? That's exactly the problem." He got up and began to pace in front of me. "And I bet the Center's not doing anything, either."

"That's not true," I said. "Aren't the lawyers working on it?"

He stopped pacing and stood directly in front of me. He shot me a look that made me feel very, very young. I scrunched my body up and hugged my knees. The sky was darkening rapidly around us. All of a sudden, the electrical box started humming so loudly that I jumped. Faraj's mouth was moving but I couldn't hear anything.

"What?" I said.

He knelt down so that his knees kissed the toes of my sneakers. Together our bodies made a W or maybe a س.

"Their laws are not for us. Don't be fooled," he said. I nodded, a promise that I wouldn't. I was pretty sure he had said something else when he was drowned out by the electrical box. I tried to replay the movement of his lips, but I couldn't.

I guess I wanted to redeem myself a little, because then I found myself telling him about that morning on the fire escape, watching cops snake through Abu Jamal's café, knocking over tables, breaking coffee cups.

"I saw the whole thing," I said. "It was right before Fajr. The sun wasn't even up yet."

Faraj sat down next to me on the blanket again. And, to my utter delight and mortification, he covered my hand with his. He was trying to comfort me, I realized. But I wasn't even sure if I needed comforting.

"They came for my brother before sunrise, too. They dragged us out of bed in our pajamas. I was twelve years old. And I thought they were going to kill us."

I flipped my hand over so that my palm pressed against his, and I squeezed.

"Does Abu Jamal have family here?" he asked.

I nodded. "A wife and a son—I think he's in middle school."

I thought back to his wife's choking sobs that morning in the Center. I wondered what kind of pajamas his son had been wearing when they came to take his father.

"All of these years, and nothing has changed. They keep doing it, because they know we won't do anything to stop them." Faraj tilted his chin down and shook his head.

"But there are people who are trying, right?" I thought about Laila at the Center. A woman with three kids she barely saw, because she was always drowning in paperwork at her desk or at the ACLU or waiting in security lines at the courthouse.

"Not hard enough," Faraj said. It was properly dark now, and Brooklyn lit up before us like a massive game of pinball. I had left my phone on his coffee table, I realized. Was Lina messaging me? Were my parents wondering where I was? I was holding the hand of a very sad boy on a rooftop in the dark.

"When it happened to us, some people tried to help at first." I had to lean closer to Faraj to hear him. The electrical box was rumbling like it was about to blast off, and some cars honked on the street down below. "But what we had was contagious, so after a while they all stopped calling." He laughed a little. I couldn't hear it, but I could see his body shudder.

"What do you mean, what you had was contagious?" I asked.

"My brother's friends, our aunts and uncles and cousins, even one of his teachers who tried to help him—they started getting stopped at airport security. FBI agents would show up at their houses, outside of their work. Once the connection became clear, they dropped out of our lives, one by one."

There had been people who stopped calling us after Sami went away. People who wouldn't acknowledge Mama and Baba on the street. But none of them got dragged off of airplanes just because they knew us.

I tried to imagine what would have happened if, instead of just watching from our windows and fire escapes when they came for Abu Jamal, all the kids I went to high school with ran outside and blocked the streets. If all the mamas and the babas held banners and staged die-ins on the sidewalk outside of MCC, put tape over their mouths. Just the thought of it made me want to laugh. The same adults who were always telling us to be grateful for what we had in this country, to behave ourselves in public, and who were mostly just so fucking tired all the time from trying to earn a living and submitting to an ever-changing and mythological set of rules—but who believed that success was surely just around the next corner if you were patient.

"They scared the fight out of them," I said. Faraj whipped his head up, but this time he looked at me like I'd said the perfect thing.

"Exactly," he said. "You know that meeting I went to the other day at that masjid in your neighborhood?"

I nodded.

"Well, there was this old imam, and when I say old, I mean ancient. And he just went on and on and wouldn't let anyone else speak. I mean, he started by talking about how, if we thought this was bad, we should have lived under the dictatorship in Tunisia. But by the end, he was telling us all about the importance of getting annual colonoscopies.

Wallahi. I think he just straight-up forgot what we were even talking about."

I laughed. And then he laughed, and our shoulders touched.

"That must have been Imam Ghozzi," I said. "He's, like, a hundred."

"It's so cool to finally meet a Muslim girl who gets it," he said. I was going to ask him what "it" was, but then he removed his hand from mine and placed it on my knee. "I never do this," he said. And before I had time to wonder—do what?—his mouth was on my face. Small, hard kisses on my cheeks and forehead, my chin, even my nose. I closed my eyes and tried to stay very still. He picked up one of my hands, which were lying like weights in my lap, and draped my arm around his neck. He kissed my mouth a few times, but there was no tongue, and I thought, *This is okay. This is how Muslims kiss.*

He pulled back and grinned at me.

"Is this okay?" I said, looking around the roof. "Can anyone see us?" But this time the buzz of the electrical box drowned me out.

"What?" he shouted. And then, before I could repeat myself, "You're so pretty." Then his face was closing down on mine again. Except now his tongue was in my mouth. He held my head in both of his hands. My mouth was filled with him, and it felt like the best thing to do was make my tongue as small and unobtrusive as possible. As we kissed, I thought about the evening as a story I could tell later. My first kiss on a rooftop. It sounded romantic, like something other girls would be jealous of.

But my mind wouldn't quiet. I didn't know how to make this story fit with the rest of him—with the protest and the mindfulness and the coconut water. Is this what he wanted from a Muslim girl? Or did he expect me to resist, to push him off, to scold him? Just like when he offered me the can of soda at the deli, I felt like I was being tested.

One hand was sliding down my arm, grazing the side of my breast. The other hand held my face. I didn't know what to do.

And then I felt Lina's shadow standing over us. I opened my eyes and looked up until I found her. Faraj pulled away quickly, wiped his mouth with his forearm.

"I need something from the drugstore," she said, holding out her hand for me.

"Okay," I said. I put my hand in hers and she pulled me up.

"Bye," I said, not looking at him.

He lifted his hand. "Bye," he said. "Nice to meet you, Lina."

Lina didn't say anything. She kept hold of my hand all the way down the four flights of stairs. Out on the street, she led me to a Duane Reade a few blocks away.

"What do you need?" I asked her as we walked through the sliding doors.

"Nothing," she said. "It was just time to go."

I nodded.

In the brightly lit aisles, we wandered around aimlessly. We kept asking each other if we were okay. We fondled tubes of lip gloss and flipped open the caps of body washes and lotions. "You okay?" Lina asked me. We read aloud the names of lipstick colors: Crave, Femme la Crème, Loudspeaker, Russian Red, Whisper, Shy Girl, Mocha Latte, Va Va Violet. "You okay?" I asked her. We sat on the ground in the magazine aisle and read celebrity tabloids—"Who Wore It Best?" and "Stars! They're Just like Us" and "Hollywood Divorce Lawyer Tells All!"

We were flipping through a story about a sitcom actor neither of us had ever heard of when Lina asked, "Do you think you're ready to go all the way?"

My head snapped up. "What?" I was stunned by the question.

"Do you want to have sex with Faraj?" she said, as if perhaps I had not understood the question. She said it softly, neutrally, like how I imagined a therapist might speak.

"That's not what was happening," I said.

"Looked like it to me," she said, closing the magazine in her lap. "Blanket on the roof . . ."

"Well, maybe that's what it looked like, but that's not how it was. Trust me," I said.

"Okay," she said.

She stood up, put the magazine back, and started wandering around the aisles again. I rose and followed her. She lifted the caps on some shampoo bottles and smelled them. I felt like I needed to defend myself.

"Really," I said. "It wasn't going to go that far. He's a Muslim."

"Muslims have sex, Amira," she said, her nose in a bottle of coconut conditioner.

I wanted to argue with her, but then I remembered his hand creeping down my side and the feeling of the hard roof under the blanket. I put a fist to my mouth, bit down on my index finger.

"Oh my God," I said, "did I almost have sex?"

Lina set the conditioner down and walked over to me. She put her hand on my shoulder.

"Did you want to?" she asked again.

"I don't know," I said, and Lina patted my shoulder.

"Yeah," she said.

We returned to the front of the store to get a cart. We wheeled it around the store, but before we could add any items, we had to discuss each product in detail, debate its merits, compare it with its neighbors, come to a consensus.

"Mango Madness or Citrus Breeze?" Lina asked, holding up two bottles of body wash.

"Mango," I said, and she dropped it into the cart.

We selected chips, candy, hand soap, dental floss, new coloring books for the Center's lobby, Post-it notes, lip gloss in shades that were too old for us, and one jar of nail polish each—a glittery, reptilian green for Lina, and an inky midnight black for me. We wheeled the cart to the front and pooled our cash.

"Seventy-four dollars," she said, looking down into the cart. "That should be enough, right?"

It was all the money we had in the world.

We purchased our carefully curated selections and walked to this playground near the subway, which was swarmed with kids even though it was getting late. There was an empty picnic table, and we spread our loot across it before sitting down. We ripped into our purchases, shaking the crumbs from the bottom of chip bags into our open mouths. I propped my phone up against a soda can so we could use the flashlight to paint our nails. When I was midway through my left hand, Lina looked up at me and said, "If you want my opinion, I think you should wait."

"To do what?" I asked.

"You know," she said, raising her eyebrows.

"Why?" I asked. "You've done it."

"But you're better than me."

I was shocked. I had never heard Lina talk about sex with any regret. Since that first time with the Costa Rican kid, she had discussed it with a detached casualness that always seemed to be a sign of great maturity, like perhaps she understood something fundamental about the world that I could never grasp.

"I am not better than you," I said, and I grabbed her wrist to show her that it was true. Her hand slipped, and she painted a long green gash down her index finger.

"Agree to disagree," she said. She wiped her finger with a crumpled wrapper. What more was there to say? Everything. Nothing. For a few minutes, I forgot about Faraj on that rooftop. I forgot about Sami and Mama and Baba at home. Even though the night hadn't turned out as I'd expected, I felt a stirring deep down inside me, like something waking up. I blew on Lina's fingers. She blew on mine.

We rushed home and arrived at the building a few minutes past curfew. We were making a game out of fake panicking, saying things to each other that neither one of us believed, things like "Oh man, we're dead," like "They're gonna kill us." In our fake hysteria, I mistyped the code to the building's front door. Then I entered it correctly, and we tumbled inside. We were running for the stairs, giggling and shushing each other, when I heard a voice. The small lobby was dark—a lightbulb had blown months earlier. I grabbed on to Lina and pulled her to a halt. There was a man in the lobby with us. He was somewhere very close to us, but I couldn't see him.

Lina pointed to a shape in the dark. The outline of a man. He was sort of shuffling around, pacing three steps and then turning around and facing the wall. He was talking.

"But I don't know anyone anymore."

He was whispering, his voice a small whine.

"Why don't you just go yourself?"

Lina pulled me toward the stairs.

"Can't I do something different?"

"Yalla, come on," Lina said. The man whipped around as if we had struck him, and it was our brother.

"Oh," he said, looking straight at me. "It's you."

Lina was two steps ahead of me on the stairs, her hand on my wrist, pulling me.

"No one," Sami said, into the phone this time. "It's just my sisters."

It felt odd to hear him talk about us so casually to strangers. Just his sisters. It made me wonder if he had talked about us in prison. If he'd told the other inmates random facts about us—whatever Mama wrote in her letters. *My sister Amira got an A on that history exam. My sister Lina brought a one-eyed cat home.* It sounded so normal, like we were regular brother and sisters. Like we had a relationship.

"No, I *am* paying attention," Sami snapped. "What do you want me to do? I live in an apartment building. There are other people here, you know."

I let Lina tug me up the stairs. Lina fished the keys out of her bag and unlocked the door. Inside, Mama and Baba were sitting on the couch, watching a news story about a bombing in Baghdad. "You're late," Mama called to us in this singsong voice, but it was clear she wasn't really mad. Baba tapped on a wristwatch he didn't wear. "Late, late, late," he echoed her. But then they turned back to the television. One of them said that the world was a terrible place.

We wandered into the kitchen. Lina inspected the contents of the refrigerator and pulled out a pitcher of qamar al-din. Moon of the religion. She poured herself a glass without offering me any. The thick apricot purée stuck to the walls of the glass as she tipped it back into her mouth.

"Who do you think Sami was talking to down there?" I asked.

"Ten bucks says it's a girl," she said, wiping her mouth with the back of her hand.

"You think? How would he have met a girl already?"

"Everyone loves a bad boy," she said. "I bet there's a line of Muslim girls just waiting to get their hands on him so they can fix him."

I scrunched up my face. It didn't make sense to me. Who would want to take Sami home to her parents? *Hey, Mom and Dad, here's this felon I want you to meet.*

"I'm telling you," Lina said, "a boy only complains like that when a girl is nagging him to do something he doesn't want to do."

I couldn't picture Sami talking to a girl, holding her hand, taking her to the mall, and carrying her bag. I couldn't picture him talking to anyone at all.

That night, late, 3:00 a.m. probably, I woke Lina completely, all the way up, just by calling her name. I was having bad dreams, although I couldn't remember what they were about.

"Tell me about Egypt," I whispered into the dark between our beds. This was something we did when we had trouble sleeping. We told stories, some real, some made up, about the homeland, Um al-Dunya. And somewhere along the way, we'd both drift off again, maybe at the exact same moment.

In the morning, back home in Bay Ridge, back in the light of day, we'd look down at our hands and see messy streaks of green and black paint. We had made blind and optimistic brushstrokes in the dark.

# Part II

By the night, when she lets fall her darkness, and by the radiant day! By Him that created the male and female, your endeavors have varied ends!

—92:1–3

I MAM GHOZZI, eighty-six years old, deaf in one ear, cataracts clouding his gray eyes, was leaving the Islamic Center after Asr prayers. It was no longer his mosque, and he still wasn't quite used to shuffling in and out of the main entrance just like any other worshipper. Back when he had the keys, he'd used the back entrance, which led to his own personal office. He'd leave his shoes there, and not have to riffle through the piles of shoes that crowded the public entrances. It was a dignified thing, to be the imam of a mosque in America. Back in Tunis, there were so many mosques and so many imams that no one paid him much mind. But here, he'd been the imam of the busiest mosque in Bay Ridge. Here, everyone knew and respected him. New immigrants always came to him first—he was like the gatekeeper of Bay Ridge—and he'd take them to the Arab Center next door to get them a caseworker, and then he'd invite them over to dinner with his wife. So it pained him when the board of directors at the masjid gently suggested that it was time for him to retire. Yes, he'd fallen asleep during a sermon, but it only happened once. And, yes, he couldn't really see or hear so well anymore, but that didn't mean he couldn't talk to people—they just had to sit a little closer, talk a little louder. He was prepared to put up a fight, but then his wife, the wisest person he knew, told him the truth, flat out, no sugar coating. "Go out with dignity," she had said. "Don't wait until you're a joke." So Imam Ghozzi ceded his position with grace, giving the keys to his office and to the back door to that young, flashy imam from New Jersey who always wore those ridiculous sneakers. But the kids—especially the teenage boys—loved Imam Tariq and came to prayers far more frequently than they ever had when Imam Ghozzi was in charge, and how could a man of God complain about that?

It took him a long time to find his slippers among the messy pile of shoes at the men's entrance. He found the right slipper but needed to enlist the help of a boy to find the left one. The boy rolled his eyes—even the cataracts couldn't hide that—but searched diligently through the pile until he found the missing shoe. Two soft leather sandals on his feet, Imam Ghozzi emerged into the brutal mid-afternoon sun and started to make his way home. His wife, Aziza, was cooking liver for supper, and his mouth watered at the thought of sunset. Distracted, he lifted the hem of his thobe just in time to avoid dragging it through a yellow stream of fresh dog urine running down the sidewalk. To let a dog relieve itself in front of a mosque—people were really unbelievable sometimes. He turned to see if he could spot the offender, squinting down the street in the sunlight. There was a man coming out of the bagel shop—he looked like the type of American who would have a dog, one of those big, slobbery beasts—but he had no dog with him today. Outside of the Italian bakery, a waiter was shaking out a checkered tablecloth. A teenage girl almost walked right into the flapping table-cloth, because she was looking at the mobile device in her hand. Imam Ghozzi sighed and turned back around to continue his walk home.

The pain was hot and deep, and the blood poured as if tipped out of a pitcher. The skin on his cheek flapped open in a red, gummy smile. What happened? The old imam clutched his face. A shadow had appeared in front of him like an evil afreet, then the pain and the blood, and then the muffled sound of footsteps running away out of his one good ear. Had he been shot? Stabbed? Punched? He wasn't sure. He staggered on the sidewalk. Somewhere next to him, a woman with a baby strapped to her torso screamed. She screamed and the baby screamed and Imam Ghozzi tried to speak, but she couldn't hear him through her cries. "Please," he said. "Please, I think I need to sit down."

I WOKE UP from a mid-afternoon nap in Brooklyn with hideous green-and-black-painted fingernails and a pit in my stomach. The sun filtered through the window in this really kind and gentle way, and I tried to lie very still and let it fall all over me. I should have been thinking about how, the night before, I maybe almost had sex on a rooftop, but I wasn't thinking about that. Instead, I was thinking of my brother in a dark stairwell, talking to someone who knew him better than we did. I closed my eyes and tried to imagine exactly where he was in that moment. I tried to access the tracking device inside of me, inside of him—I made a map of the apartment in my mind and saw a red light blinking in his bedroom. I followed the blinking light as it moved from the bedroom to the hallway to the front door. I heard the sound of keys jangling.

There was a soft knock at our door, and I froze in bed. Lina called out "Come in." But it was Mama. She was holding a Kingsborough Community College catalogue in her hands, obviously meant for Lina. Something crunched below her bare feet—a Duane Reade bag filled with the remnants of the previous night's loot. She made a disgusted face and pulled a shard of barbecue potato chip off her heel.

"This room is a disaster," she said.

"KCC is a disaster," Lina said pre-emptively, eyeing the booklet.

Mama whacked her on the elbow.

They would have gone on, an argument they had begun many times before, but then they were interrupted by the screams. A woman was screaming out on the street, a scream that started and stopped as if it were being played on a loop, the exact same length and pitch each time.

We all ran to the window and craned our heads out to see around the fire escape. I couldn't see where the screaming was coming from. But I could see a figure lying on the sidewalk, with Imam Tariq and a few others crouched over him. I could see a shock of red on the man's clean white thobe.

We went down to the street to see what had happened. Outside, the crowd around the bloody man had thickened. Sami was sitting on the stoop, tossing a pack of cigarettes softly from hand to hand. Not smoking, just tossing.

"Do you know what happened?" Mama asked him, resting her hand on the top of his head. He shook her off so gently that she might have thought her hand had dropped of its own accord.

"The old imam got slashed," Sami said, as if he were reporting the weather.

"Imam *Ghozzi*?" Mama asked.

The woman had finally stopped screaming. But the crowd across the street was talking loudly, several people shouting into cell phones.

"What do you mean, slashed?" I asked.

"What it sounds like," Sami said. "Some guy ran up to him and slashed his face open with a knife and ran away." He was still tossing the pack from hand to hand.

"You didn't *see* it, did you?" Mama asked.

Sami nodded. "Sitting right here."

The people in the crowd were gesturing wildly, pointing in different directions. Through small shifting gaps between their bodies, I could see Imam Tariq holding a towel to Imam Ghozzi's face. Both men, the young one crouched in his red Nikes and the old one lying on the pavement, were very still as the crowd moved around them. We stood and watched until an ambulance arrived.

. . .

That night, there was a police car parked outside of the mosque. Now they were here to help. They were here to investigate.

Mama and Baba had gone to visit Imam Ghozzi's wife, to bring her a casserole dish still hot from the oven. I was standing in the kitchen, plucking grape leaves from a container in the refrigerator, when I heard a strange, muffled sound of voices coming from the living room. I glided in from the kitchen, where I found Sami sitting on the sofa, his shoulders hunched over Baba's old laptop. He was watching a video. The sound was distorted through the tinny speakers. I stood behind the sofa and peered over his back. There was an animated black flag waving across the screen. The one we all knew so well, with the crude white bubble letters scrawled across the top, that misshapen white circle in the center, the whole thing as if drawn by a child. A voice crackled over the image, reciting the words written on the flag. Ten words. You could boil our whole religion down to those ten words, the only words you needed to say if you wanted to become one of us. No tricks. No ceremony. Repeat after me—ten words and the world is yours. But who would want our world? A man in a black turban and black robes, saying something in his wire-rimmed glasses. Hordes in a pickup truck, waving their AKs. The flag waved across the screen again, like a stage curtain between scenes. Some starving army marching. The pop of gunfire, white flashes, brilliant orange blooms of fire. The flag waved one final farewell, and then the video ended.

"You shouldn't be watching that stuff," I blurted out as soon as the video ended.

I expected Sami to jump at the sound of my voice behind him. I expected him to be embarrassed or defensive. But he just said, "Why?"

"Because they'll see it and get suspicious."

Now Sami turned to face me, twisting his torso around and leaning his elbows on the back of the couch. "Who's they?" he asked. I searched his face for hints of a smirk, but it was slack, and his eyes were blank.

"The police," I said, unsure if I was being played. "They watch what Muslims do online."

Sami laughed, and I felt silly. But it was true, wasn't it? Just look what had happened to Faraj's brother.

"Haven't you even been tempted to google them, all those bad Muslims out there?" he asked.

The conversation had turned somewhere. From somewhere deep inside of me, a red light pulsed. I decided just to stop, to walk away, to find Lina.

"Bad or good—doesn't matter. They already know everything about you, Amira."

He wasn't mocking me. He spoke with a strange earnestness. I could feel his eyes on my back as I walked away.

I walked past Lina in the bedroom and opened the window. I climbed out onto the fire escape and looked down at the now quiet street. Just around the corner, just out of view, was Abu Jamal's coffee shop, dark and gathering dust. At some point, Lina had climbed out the window and was standing next to me. We stood looking at the red shape on the sidewalk in front of the mosque. Lina's green-gray eyes: solemn. The wind ripping through her hair, trying to tie it in a knot around her neck.

"Let's get drunk," I said to Lina, because I had an idea. That idea was this: To lap that night up and let it churn through our veins. To fill ourselves up with it until it had nowhere to go, until it seeped back out the pores of our skin and back up our throats and out of our mouths like a car in reverse. To leave it in a puddle in a dark alley somewhere, alone and ashamed, surrounded by the most hated and depraved creatures.

"Yes," Lina said. "Let's."

On the train into Manhattan, Lina kept fussing over me. I was wearing her clothes, which made her feel both proud and possessive of my body. I kept tugging the white minidress down—it was practically glued to my wide ass, and I had already earned the appreciative grunts and glances of several men on the street. Lina spat on her palms and smoothed the frizz peeking out of my scarf around my temples. She was my mother and my twin and my lover. I swatted her hand away. Reina, who was sitting on the other side of Lina, leaned back to roll her eyes at me.

Lina stared at herself compulsively in the small compact mirror she carried in her purse. She was finally going to get those head shots taken—Andres said that the photographer was waiting for her at the nightclub. She flipped her hair this way and that, applied more lip gloss, tilted her chin down and then up; she closed her eyes and asked us if her eyeliner was symmetrical.

"You know, I had a cousin who did modeling for a little bit. She even went to L.A. and everything," Reina said as the train conductor announced something incomprehensible through the loudspeaker. The train had been lingering with the doors open at Jay Street for almost five minutes.

"What happened?" Lina asked. "Did she make it big?"

Reina shook her head. "My tia doesn't even talk about her anymore. It's like she *died*. I don't know exactly what happened, but her brother told me that she works at strip clubs now."

Lina elbowed her hard on the arm. "Why would you even tell me that right now?"

"Yo, I'm just saying be careful, is all. My cousin had the same dream, and look what happened to her," Reina said.

"Yeah, well, your cousin's an idiot," Lina said.

The train finally lurched forward, and I passed around the thermos we had brought, of vodka filched from Reina's mom's liquor cabinet and pineapple juice, a concoction we made because we thought it sounded sophisticated. It served as a peace offering, soothing all our nerves, each of us taking long, dramatic sips and then passing it to the next girl. By the time we got off the train, the sidewalks and the skyscrapers were all my friends. Everything was buzzing brightly, and I felt alive.

The bouncer guarding the door at Lotus was playing scrabble on his phone when we walked up.

"Andres is expecting us," Lina said, all bitchylike. She was thinking he would jump to his feet, nod eagerly, and throw open the doors for her. But he just nodded without taking his eyes from his phone. He called Andres and said, "Some girls outside for you," then hung up and went back to his game. By the time Andres came out, the bouncer had just played the word *"craven"* for eleven points.

Lina was annoyed that he had made us wait. "Can't you tell the bouncers who I am, so that next time they remember and just let me in?" she said as we followed Andres inside.

Andres was smooth. Once we were inside, he stopped dead in his tracks and looked Lina up and down, shaking his head like he was in awe. She did look fantastic—black hair blown out all shiny and straight, and her body poured into a black dress that barely covered her hoo-ha.

"What?" Lina pouted at him, pretending not to understand what he was looking at. Then Andres staggered toward her, hand clutching his heart, and she broke down and laughed, forgetting all about her commitment to haughty fashion-model behavior. Andres held her and dipped her back so that the tips of her hair almost dusted the floor. He kissed the tops of her breasts, as if Reina and I weren't standing right there.

The club was pretty empty. It was a weeknight, and there was a group of people sitting around the bar and a few scattered at the high-tops, but no one was dancing. When Lina and Andres finished making out and she had reapplied her lip gloss for the fiftieth time, he led us to the bar and pulled out three seats for us. He told the bartender to take care of us, and then he disappeared into the back for a while. We ordered three vodka-and-cranberries, and when the bartender set them down in front of us, she lingered.

"Thank you," Lina said, flashing her a big smile.

"You're welcome," said the bartender. "Do you want to start a tab or . . ." She trailed off, and I felt my cheeks get hot for Lina. She thought she was a star, a VIP, but no one here knew who she was. We scrounged through our purses for enough cash to pay for the drinks, piling crumpled bills onto the soggy bar.

We listened to the group next to us talk about this woman they worked with that they all hated. We stirred our drinks and bopped our heads to the weird, ambient house music. Finally, Andres returned, appearing suddenly and immediately putting his mouth on Lina's neck. She shook him off gently.

"When are we going to do that photo shoot?" she whined.

He smiled at her blankly.

"With that fashion-photographer friend of yours?" she prompted.

"Oh right, right. Billy. I think he's in Thailand or something right now," Andres said.

Lina lowered her voice and placed a hand on Andres's chest. "It's just that you promised me."

Andres was twirling a piece of her silky black hair around his index finger. He was looking at her like he wanted to dive into her mouth, and I wondered if Faraj would ever look at me like that.

"Okay, you know what? Let's do it right now," Andres said with a startling burst of energy. He pulled Lina up off her bar stool with both hands.

She laughed and tripped after him. "But I thought you said Billy was in Thailand."

He guided Lina over to a high-top where two men were sitting drinking beer and watching a baseball game playing on mute over the bar. Reina and I followed awkwardly.

"This is my man Julian," Andres said, clapping one of the men on the shoulder. "He takes amazing pictures. Show her."

Julian, without saying anything, pulled his phone out of his pocket and started scrolling through photos on his Instagram account. I peered over Lina's shoulder to see. There was a picture of the Manhattan Bridge at sunset, a picture of some brunch he had eaten, a picture of some girls dancing at this very club.

"Wow," Lina kept saying at every photo.

"My girl here is a model. Think you can take some pictures of her to help her, you know, build her portfolio?"

Julian paused at a photo of a dog sniffing a fire hydrant and looked up at Andres. "I'm not, like, a professional," he mumbled, so low that we all had to lean in to hear him. "I just take pictures of shit I see."

"Yeah, but you're really good," Andres said. "So just take some pictures of Lina. I'll get you guys another round from the bar."

Julian shrugged, set his phone on the bar, then nodded. He finally looked up and saw me and Reina lurking behind Lina.

"Who are your friends?" he asked, his eyes lingering on me. Lina introduced us. I saw Andres do a cartoon double take. He didn't recognize me.

"That's your sister?" he asked Lina. "The same one from last time?"

"Yep," she nodded proudly. "Isn't she stunning?"

"Stunning," Andres repeated blandly. But he was looking at me like he was confused, glancing from the sexy dress to the scarf and back to the sexy dress, like they didn't compute. This annoyed me. I immediately liked Julian better, because he didn't seem to care or even notice. All he saw was a pair of tits and a big ass, which he was now staring at openly.

"Do you want some pictures, too?" he asked me. I stammered and giggled like an idiot before finally declaring an almost inaudible "That's okay." He shrugged again and hopped off his stool.

He directed Lina to stand against a wall covered in black and gold brocade wallpaper—and asked Andres to move a table and chairs out of the shot. Lina sucked in and smiled.

"Don't smile," Julian muttered. "Just, like, be."

Lina's smile evaporated. Her face was momentarily blank and then puckered into a scowl. She lifted one leg so that her foot rested against the wall. Julian started taking pictures on his phone.

Then Julian asked her to climb up onto one of the platforms in the center of the empty dance floor. She pouted down at us and Julian nodded, squatting down and angling the phone up at her.

And then, without speaking, Julian started walking away. He pushed open the door and left the club. We all hustled after him. It was lighter outside than it was inside. He walked around the side of the building to some dumpsters.

He motioned for Lina to stand in between a large green dumpster and a large black one.

"Someone give her a cigarette," Julian said, waving at the air as if he had an invisible assistant. Andres patted his own pockets but came up empty. He disappeared for a second, to bum one from a bouncer, then delivered the cigarette into Lina's hands and lit it for her, stopping to kiss her mouth before moving out of the frame.

"Smoke and look off into the distance, like you're bored," Julian said.

Lina took a puff, coughed violently, recovered, took another puff, and gazed blankly out to the intersection, where some cabs were honking at nothing.

Julian took more photos out there by the dumpsters. Eventually, he stopped and scrolled through the images on his phone, nodding to himself. He looked up at Andres. "You want me to text them to you?"

"That's it?" Lina asked, the cigarette burning in her right hand.

"Don't worry, they're, like, *very* good."

Julian lingered outside with us for a few more minutes, sending the photos to Andres and Lina. He took one more look at me, a long neutral scan of my body, and then walked back inside to rejoin his friend.

"So—how was it?" Lina asked when he was gone, and her face was so open and eager—a wide, fertile Kansas plain—that not even Reina had the heart to tell her how lame the whole thing looked.

"You know, it was sexy but not too sexy," Reina said.

"Yeah," I said. "The pictures are going to make you look very versatile," parroting one of Lina's two favorite words to describe successful fashion models: "versatile" and "transcendent."

We scrolled through the photos for a long time, Lina pausing and zooming in on each one. She was euphoric, breathless, pointing out the light in this one, the angle of her neck in that one. But Andres was impatient to get back inside, because business was starting to pick up, so Lina reluctantly slipped her phone back into her purse, and we followed him inside.

The energy had shifted while we were gone. Barbacks were busy slicing limes and scooping ice. Suddenly there was a churning sound, and the place was transformed with bluish smoke. As the fog machine sent its clouds rolling over us, I felt like not even the tracking device could have recognized me under that haze.

The floors and the walls and the people vibrated with the music. Lina held my hand, and I held Reina's, and together we stepped into the blue fog. Lina hopped up onto one of the platforms and danced over us. In that outer-space spotlight, she looked like she had been painted in silver, like at any moment she would freeze in place, a gleaming statue to commemorate the victims of some obscure battle. The DJ was making foghorn noises from behind his MacBook. Lina pulled Reina up onto the platform with her. They were shouting down to me. I was seized with that summertime desire of girls: to push my body to its limits. I climbed up to join them. Lina pressed into Reina and Reina pressed into me, and together we filled each other's valleys.

But Lina's energy shifted. She was looking out over the dance floor at something I could not see. She was still, and Reina and I were left bumping awkwardly against her motionless body. Then she hopped off the platform. Reina and I were broken without her, so we hopped off, too. Lina marched, and we marched behind her. My body felt strong following in her wake. Like she was streaming rage, and Reina and I were lapping it up behind her. We stood behind Lina, who stood behind Andres and some blonde girl. We watched his hand creep down her back, settle onto the bony curve of her ass. With one eyeball, the three of us saw the hand squeeze. Lina didn't cry, she didn't run. What she did was leap onto the girl. A fistful of blond hair in one hand, the other one smacking, slicing through the air. It didn't last long. Andres reached one thick arm around Lina's midsection, yanked her away. He pulled her into him. She panted against his chest. The blonde girl's friends gathered around her as she cried like an idiot. Reina and I yelled things like *That's what you get* and *That's how we do in Brooklyn, bitch,* because this felt somehow required of us. Like the words themselves had been predetermined for us, written in ancient girl-blood on some apocryphal scroll. Andres signaled to the bouncer. He picked us both up as if we were dolls and placed us gently outside. He smiled nicely at us. He shut the door. Lina was still inside. Once we became separated, the moment was drained of all victory. We called and texted Lina, begged the bouncer for second chances. We smiled deranged serial-killer smiles at the blonde girl and her friends as they left the club. We chased them, sloppily, down Fifty-second Street, Reina and I staggering like dumb giants, the girl and her friends tottering in their stilettos as they screamed. I puked outside of some fancy office building. I imagined fashion editors stepping in it the next day on their way through the revolving doors.

We returned to our vigil outside of Lotus, and one hour and fifteen minutes later, Lina emerged from a side door. She had a hickey the size of a fist on her neck, and eyes that had been rubbed red and swollen. She sat down next to us on the curb and laid a hot cheek on my knee.

"It was supposed to be transcendent," she whispered.

"It was," I said, and it was almost true. But I wasn't talking about the photo shoot. I was talking about the moment right before Lina leapt onto the other girl, when the three of us were sharing bodies, when we were a Cyclops, the most beautiful monster.

A taxicab honked at us, and we waved it away. It was very late, and without saying anything, we all knew we would be in trouble when we got home. We were tired, our brightly made-up faces had faded and smeared, our tight dresses were covered in glitter and sweat, and our feet throbbed inside our shoes. Then I lied to them.

"We're going to run this city one day," I said to them. "The three of us together. I can feel it."

But Lina just looked at me like I had called her the worst name ever. Reina ignored me. Then the two of them just pulled each other up and started heading for the train. I had to run to catch up.

We returned home at two in the morning, dressed the way we were dressed, my breath smelling of vomit and peppermints, Lina looking like a domestic-abuse victim with that wet, purple bruise on her neck. We wanted to be stopped. What other explanation is there? We wanted someone to grab our wrists, yank us inside, order us to remove our eyeliner, and send us to bed. Maybe they would lock us indoors for the rest of the summer, and we would be forced to return to the petty amusements of little girls—nail polish and magazines, horoscopes and homemade face masks.

I dialed the code to the building and pushed the heavy metal door open, holding it for Lina. When it closed behind us, we saw him sitting on the steps, and it felt like we had traveled six years back in time. There he was—our brother. Lina gasped with fright when she saw him; I could feel the gasp on my left shoulder. But when Lina realized it was Sami, she laughed nervously and said, "What are you doing sitting in the dark like a creep?"

"Waiting for you," he said. "Where have you been?"

And then, as if reconsidering his choice of language, he asked again in Arabic: "Feyn konto?"

The floor and the ceiling shifted. I had questions, too. I was full of questions that chased one another around inside me—questions I didn't know how to ask.

The lobby was dark—the bulb still broken—but light washed down on us from the second-floor landing above. I tried to focus on the reality of my brother's body. He was sitting meekly in front of us, hands chastely resting on his knobby knees. His third eye had moved again—it was slightly to the left of where it had been that morning.

"Are Mama and Baba up?" Lina asked.

Sami shook his head. "But you know how worried they would be if they woke up and you weren't home?" he said.

That was too much for me—Sami looking out for our parents? Lecturing *us* about being gone?

"Move," I said, stepping past Sami on the stairs. I meant to bark it. I wanted it to come out as a command. But my voice cracked, and half the word was lost in my throat.

Still, Sami scrunched himself up into a smaller ball as we walked by him, pressing himself into the banister. This was all wrong. He wasn't supposed to be the one watching us.


The next morning, the world was hung over. Mama and Baba knew we had been out late, but seemed to have no idea just how late. Sami hadn't told them. We were in vague trouble, but Lina mostly talked our way out of it. A story about movie night at the youth center at the big mosque in Staten Island. About having our ride flake out and then waiting for the bus. All the details checked out. And I realized Lina had done this many times before, maybe even with me. We apologized profusely. We promised never to stay out that late again. We kissed Baba's cheeks until he blushed and Mama rolled her eyes.

Lina and I spent the morning hours scrolling through the images from her photo shoot. She zoomed in on one image, her favorite. Her hair sleek and falling straight down her back. Her expression somewhere between bored and pissed. Her eyes bright and her skin smooth.

"Your eyes really pop in that one," I said.

Lina flipped through the rest of the photos, and none of the rest of them were nearly as good as that first one. She looked uncomfortable in most of them, her body tensed, her face frozen in a pout. Finally, she got to the last photo and let out a big sigh. I thought she was about to start complaining about how cheap and unprofessional the photos looked, but when I glanced at her, she had this expression on her face like that of someone winning an award they already knew they had in the bag: fake relief, the sharp glint of triumph.

She told me that Andres had promised to feature one of her photos on the club's Web site, advertising for ladies' night. "And he's going to print them on flyers, too."

"Wow," I said.

"There are literally gonna be hundreds of little Linas floating around Manhattan."

"What if someone sees it, though?" I asked.

"That's the whole point," she said.

"No, I mean what if someone from Bay Ridge sees it," I said.

She shrugged. "They already think I'm a slut."

I wanted to disagree with her, to tell her, No, that's not true, everyone loves you.

After we looked through all the photos twice, Lina told me she had a date with Andres that night.

"I'll just tell Mama I'm babysitting," she said.

I was surprised. I thought we were stuck in Bay Ridge together. I didn't know she had made escape plans without me.

"It's not really a date if he's just inviting you to his work," I said.

She knew what I was getting at, and she didn't like it.

"This from the girl whose last date was on a dirty blanket on some roof."

The words knocked the wind out of me. Like a hundred fingers wrapped around my esophagus. "That was really fucking mean," I said.

"I know," she said, her voice suddenly small. "Sorry."

But she was right. An hour later, after Lina had sweet-talked Mama into letting her babysit, I called Faraj.

"So," I said when he answered, trying to sound teasing and mysterious, not like the girl from the rooftop, but a different girl, an abstract girl, one who floats above all rooftops everywhere. "When are you gonna take me on a date?"

I told Mama I was going to the Met, which was technically true. I also told her it was educational, and that I'd bring her back the sticker they give you at the entrance. "Because I'm thinking about taking art history," I said. Mama looked at me. "In college," I said, because that was always a magic word with Mama.

Faraj didn't offer to come pick me up, not that I would have let him anyway. On the phone, he exhaled this big comic groan when I told him the museum was in the city, all the way up near Eighty-second Street. We met at the Atlantic Avenue stop, took the train together. Holding hands even when it wasn't convenient. Faraj telling me, over the grinding steel, about his new promotion to assistant manager at Enterprise.

He put his arm around my shoulder as we walked the streets of the Upper East Side. I imagined that the wealthy women walking their tiny dogs were staring at us—this bearded terrorist-looking guy and this hijabi terrorist-looking girl out on a date in *their* neighborhood. But, really, no one stared at us. It was New York.

I almost skipped up the steps leading up to those giant columns. I had only been there once before, on a school field trip in the fifth grade. It was the classiest place I could think of—I wanted Faraj to take me somewhere that was the opposite of Lotus. Inside, the entranceway was cool and smooth with white marble. We didn't look at the museum map, but instead just wandered rooms filled with mummies and Chinese pottery. It was boring, but I didn't want to admit it. And, for the first time, Faraj didn't have much to say.

There was only one exhibit that was interesting to me—a large white room filled with bright paintings of women—brown women in drooping sarongs, lounging on floor mats, fanning themselves with palm fronds. There were sometimes lizards scuttling around on the red earth beneath their wide, flat feet. The painter was some French guy.

Faraj started to fidget. When he went in search of a bathroom, I took the opportunity to really look around. I chose one long painting that stretched across most of a wall. In it, there were clusters of women lounging in what looked like diapers among various animals—goats, chickens, feral dogs, two lumpy white cats. Two of the women were whispering in the back, away from the others. The one in the center was plucking an apple from a tree, and the other women were all glaring out of the canvas, cutting their eyes sideways in this mean, knowing sort of way. They should have been judging the girl with the apple—that had to be Hawa, right? But they weren't. They were judging me.

"Man," Faraj said, returning to my side. "Women back then sure were ugly."

I laughed like it was funny, but I felt disappointed in him. I wanted him to see something in these paintings, to teach me something new. I thought of him as so mature. But now he just seemed like any other boy.

"Okay, well, I'm done. We can go now if you want," I said.

"Alhamdulillah," he said with a laugh. He started winding his way down toward the exit, and I followed behind him.

We ended up walking through Central Park, and my faith in him was restored when he led me to a secret patch of grass behind a giant boulder.

He held my hand again as we climbed up the big rock. I slid once in my sandals, and he caught me and pulled me up. We climbed to the top of the rock and back down the other side. It *was* a particularly nice patch of grass. The leaves of a big maple tree arched over us, creating a canopy. There were daylilies, and somehow the sounds from the rest of the park and the streets beyond were muffled by the boulder. It was like a private garden where no one could see us. "It's always empty," he said. Once again, he was a man who knew things, who made ordinary things special.

He sprawled out on his back in the grass like he was about to make snow angels.

"Come and look at the clouds with me."

Lina wasn't there this time to pull me away. I hesitated. But there he was, stretched out like a star. He was the opposite of other men that I knew. The opposite of my brother. He was wide open. So I sat down next to him and looked up at the sky.

"What do you see?" he asked.

"A peacock," I said, just making up the first thing that popped into my mind.

"No, you don't," he said, laughing.

He tugged gently on my wrist. I lowered myself so that I was lying next to him. The grass felt pleasantly cool against my neck. I searched the sky for a peacock and found one, its feathers fanned out in white wisps. I took his hand and guided it, tracing the bird's beak, the top of its head, the glorious fan of feathers.

"All I see are clouds," he said.

"Not everyone has my gifts," I said. We were facing each other now, turned onto our sides.

"No, you're special," he said, and I so wanted to be what he saw in me.

He kissed me, and it was gentle and soft. His hands didn't go anywhere. One lay limp on his hip, and one held my cheek. I thought again about the story I could tell. Kissing in a secret garden in Central Park. Who wouldn't want that?

We kissed for a while, and at some point, we just stopped. I'm not sure who pulled away, but there we were, our faces an inch apart, smiling at one another. But then his face shifted. He frowned and looked away.

"Your, um . . ." he said, pointing without looking at me. "Your scarf."

My fingers traveled up to my forehead. My scarf had slipped back and was bunched at my neck. My hair had been tucked into a messy bun, but now pieces of it fell around my shoulders. I felt around and plucked a piece of grass from the back of my head.

"Oh," I said, laughing. I looked around, but no one could see us back there. We were shielded by the rock and the maple tree.

I shook the rest of my hair loose and began to regather it up into a bun at the crown of my head. Faraj sat up quickly and turned his back to me.

"It's okay," I said. "I don't mind if you see."

But Faraj didn't reply. He just rested his head on his knees, gazed down at the grass.

"So what's it been like at home with your brother around?" he asked the grass.

"Awkward," I said, holding pins between my lips.

"How so?" he asked.

I shrugged, though he couldn't see me. "Seriously, you can turn around. It's okay. You've seen more than my hair already." I thought he might laugh, but his shoulders were still. He kept his head down.

"Is he religious?" he asked.

I wrapped the scarf quickly around my head. I felt like an idiot for alluding to what we had done on that rooftop. Would he think I was a slut now? Did good girls not talk about the things they almost did? Did he want me to be good or bad?

"I guess. I mean, he prays and fasts and stuff, if that's what you mean."

"Who does he hang out with?" Faraj sat up, but he put his hands up to his temples like blinders. I tucked the ends of the fabric in at the nape of my neck.

"No one. He just hangs out at home, mostly," I said.

"*No* one?" Faraj asked, as if this were too incredible to believe.

He was annoyed at me now. Somewhere along the way, between the boulder and the lilies, our bodies in the grass, his tongue at my lips, I had made a mistake.

"I'm sorry," I said.

"Are you finally done? Can I turn around now?"

"Yes," I said.

"You're very closed off; did anyone ever tell you that?" If he had waited for me to answer, I would have said, "Yes." I might have told him about the verb Lina had invented for me—to Amira it. Amira-ed. Amira-ing. To shut down. To freeze. To become mute. To retreat. But he didn't.

"I keep trying to talk to you, to get to know you, and you won't tell me anything about yourself." He was facing me again, but not looking at me.

"I'm sorry," I said.

He stood up and brushed his hands off on his jeans. "I have to get going," he said.

"Okay," I said, rising up from the grass.

"You should be more careful next time," he said, pointing to my head. "We're in public."

"Okay," I said.

We climbed up one side of the boulder and down the other. Suddenly there were cyclists and joggers and people walking fluffy dogs. As we walked silently back to the train, I tried to keep track of the turns, but I knew I'd never be able to find the secret garden again without him.

When I got home, I gave Mama the sticker from the Met and tried to tell her about the paintings I had seen. I didn't want to be alone. I felt like, if I went to our room and Lina wasn't there, I'd cry. And I didn't like crying.

"The women were big," I said, "like as tall and thick as trees."

Mama said, "Oh?" She was flipping through a schedule of iftar meals at the Islamic Center. She was mumbling about how whoever had volunteered to provide tomorrow's meal was 99 percent likely to flake out. She kept saying that—"Ninety-nine percent, she forgets. I think I'm going to make something extra just in case."

"Mom!" I shouted, louder than I meant to.

"What?" she asked.

"I'm trying to tell you about the art I saw."

Mama shuffled the papers in front of her so that all the edges matched up and then flipped the whole stack over. "Okay," she said. "Done. I'm all ears."

I told her about the French painter and the brown, flat-footed women. About the animals and the dripping fruit trees and the lizards. About the girls who glared at me from the canvas.

"Maybe they were glaring at him," Mama said.

"Who?" I asked.

"The painter," she said. "He's there, just outside of the frame, right? With his canvas and his paintbrush, staring at them."

This hadn't occurred to me earlier, but it made me feel better. Like I could go back and see the painting again, because I was not the intruder. It also made me feel like maybe I could talk to my mother about some things.

"Did you like art when you were young?" I asked her.

"I liked a lot of things when I was young," she said.

"Like what?" I thought she might tell me about her friends when she was growing up, about boys and the music they listened to that she pretended to like. But then the azan on her phone went off, and she got up to get ready for prayer. "You coming?" she asked. I nodded, but instead of joining her, I just sat there and listened to the refrigerator hum.

W̲HILE AMIRA WAS HEADED back to Brooklyn, the other girl was just leaving it. While Amira was changing out of her street clothes into her pajamas, the other girl was waiting on a bar stool at Lotus, tapping her manicured nails to the hysterical thudding of the speakers. She drew smiley faces on the sides of discarded beer glasses. She inhaled deep breaths, sucked in her cheeks, arched her eyebrows, and took countless selfies. Andres said he was running late, but Lina had the sneaking suspicion that he was just on the other side of a wall, in his office. She checked her phone compulsively, scrolling back through their text messages, checking to see if perhaps she had gotten the time wrong.

Eventually, all the smiley faces had collapsed into puddles on the bar. She kept telling herself she should leave, go home before her mother uncovered her lie. Any second now, she would hop off her bar stool and walk out the door. She'd use the subway ride home to think of a story to tell Amira—*You'll never guess what happened. I was walking down Forty-second Street and this homeless man walked right up to me and gave me a dollar. He said he owed it to me, said I had given him a dollar a long time ago. Isn't that crazy?* Lina liked to delight. She needed to please. She would also need to think of something to tell Amira about her modeling career. Something impressive, dropped casually. Maybe someone at

IMG had seen the club flyer with her photo on it and wanted to meet her. It was a lie, but Lina believed firmly that it could be true, *would* be true. It was one of the only things she knew definitely about herself: she was beautiful. People kept telling her. Had been telling her since she was four. Chased her down streets to tell her. She couldn't go a single day without someone telling her, always as if informing her of something she didn't already know: "You're *beautiful,* you know that?" Yes, yes, she did.

Lina was just about to leave—or so she kept telling herself—when Andres finally appeared. He was with his boys; they were going bar-hopping and had stopped at Lotus first to use Andres's connection for free drinks. He wasn't even working that night. He was only the assistant manager, but Lina didn't know that. She assumed he was the owner, or a part owner, from the way he pushed open doors and snapped his fingers at the bartenders.

"Mi amor," he slurred into her neck. She spun around on her bar stool, convinced that she was really going to let him have it this time. Didn't he know that she had better things to do with her time? Didn't he know that there were hordes of boys back home in Bay Ridge who would kill to take her out? But Andres's homeboys were scattered in a semicircle in front of her. They drank up her legs and her tits and her glorious shiny hair. And Lina knew from the way they looked at her that Andres had told them about her, about the girl who was waiting for him on a bar stool at the Lotus Lounge. She knew that she did not disappoint. She knew that she was making Andres proud.

The full-time manager was in the office that night, so they fucked in the bathroom. In a stall that didn't lock. The door swung open and closed, and with her back pressed against the side of the stall and her foot braced against the toilet, she could catch glimpses of other men pissing at the urinals. It was quick, a few minutes in and out. Then he buried his face in her hair, left a wet kiss on her collarbone, and tried to leave again. He wanted to go back out with his boys, but Lina held on to his wrist with a death grip.

"Oh hell no," she said.

Andres laughed—he still found her charming. Her crazy, frenetic energy, her possessiveness, her long, hood-rat nails, the way her voice was all baby doll one minute, all violence the next. So he stayed, and they sat in a corner while his boys enjoyed free drinks at the bar. They worked on her résumé together, tapping out letters on his phone. Later, when the full-time manager went out for a cigarette break and to pull the prettiest girls from the line, they'd sneak into the office to use the computer. They sent an e-mail to a guy Andres said he knew at Ford with her résumé and some photos of Lina attached. Andres wasn't sure of the guy's e-mail, so they just sent the e-mail to info@fordmodels .com and addressed it to "Tom." She gripped the back of his chair as he clicked "send." Now, he told her, all they had to do was wait. Andres liked helping Lina with the modeling stuff at first. He thought it was a game they played. Nothing turned Lina on like fantasies of her own future.

Lina had spent plenty of time alone on that bar stool, thinking about her future. She sometimes had dry, sober thoughts about Kingsborough Community College, about beauty school, about becoming a career nanny. Over the hours spent waiting for Andres, Lina had already become a fixture at Lotus. A mascot. An evil little fairy. The bouncers, who at first found her bossy and annoying, had come to love her, brought her egg-and-cheese sandwiches from the deli next door so she could break her fast. The customers—the men, anyway—crowded around her, told her she was too beautiful to be waiting on some guy, that if she was their girl they'd never make her wait a second in her life. When she told them she was a model, they believed her. Because look at her, just look at her. What else was she made for if not for being paraded past the eyes of Americans, swathed in silk, stomping through their irises, crawling seductively up their brain stems, slithering like a Victoria's Secret Angel through their cortexes?

On this night, after Andres clicked "send" on the e-mail to Tom, she saw her future unfolding like a runway before her. It was thrilling to imagine a stranger, a stranger in an expensive suit in a glass-walled office with a receptionist sitting out front, clicking open pictures of her. He'd zoom in on her mouth, her eyes, her clavicle. Finally, the world would see her.

She was so excited about the e-mail, she kept refreshing the screen, waiting to see if there was a reply. And then, when that got frustrating, and she needed a place for the hot hope inside her, she turned from the computer and pulled Andres down to the floor with her. While he was moving on top of her, she pressed on his shoulder blades, his hips, his ass, pushing him down so that she was always on the verge of being smothered by him. She needed to contain her own breath sometimes; otherwise she might just float away. Even when the full-time manager walked into the office and started screaming at Andres, she didn't stop. She pressed and pressed until he was stuck to her, until the skin of her torso and the skin of his melted together, until he couldn't just get up and walk away without taking her with him.

As she waited for the train that night, she reminded herself to be patient. Surely, it took a while to get discovered. It was only in movies where it happened in an instant and your whole life was changed. She could wait. She crossed and uncrossed her legs on the sticky wooden bench; she was sore from the two times with Andres. When the train screeched into the station, she boarded the first car, closest to the conductor, just in case someone needed to hear her scream. She sat on the yellow plastic seat and thought of a story to tell Amira, something that would make the other girl smile.

I T WAS A FRIDAY, and the whole family went to Jummah prayers. As
we left our building and walked across the street to the masjid, I saw
some cops park their car next to a fire hydrant. Two cops got out and
went into Balady Foods. They came out a few minutes later with two
wrapped shawarmas.

There was a bottleneck at the entrance to the masjid. People were
salaaming and hugging in the doorway like they hadn't seen one another
in years, taking forever to slip off their shoes and move out of the way.
Lina and I waited outside on the steps with Baba for as long as we
could. It was always so crammed and hot upstairs in the women's section, and the air always stank of too much drugstore perfume. I watched
Sami push past the lingering crowd into the masjid. He didn't say hello
to anyone except for Imam Tariq, who stood in the doorway greeting
people. They chatted for a minute, and Sami laughed at something the
imam said. Then they both walked into the mosque together, Sami to
find a place to pray and the imam to make his way to the pulpit. Lina
and I did a quick, messy wudu and then trudged upstairs.

Mama had saved us a prime spot next to her by the little half-wall
that overlooked the men's section down below. From here, you could
actually hear the sermon, and it got a little more air than the rest of the

women's section. Imam Tariq gave a fairly standard sermon on purity of body, mind, and spirit. I wasn't really supposed to look at the men down below, but there wasn't much else to do. I kept my eyes on Sami for a while; I could only really see the top of his white kufi, and after a while, it blended in with all the other white kufis surrounding him. So next I watched the boys in the back, boys I went to high school with, some of whom had grown pathetic, patchy beards in an attempt to look more pious during Ramadan. Then I heard a door squeak open and I looked over to see a tall man sneaking in late through the side entrance. He wore a black kufi and a white thobe over his jeans. He had a real beard, full and neatly trimmed. He found a space in the back and knelt down. I elbowed Lina and gestured with my head for her to look down at the men's prayer hall.

"What?" she mouthed, peering over me to see.

"Faraj," I whispered back.

Mama looked up and glared at us.

Lina opened her eyes wide and pointed with her index finger at the ground. "Here?" she said.

"Be quiet," Mama hissed.

Imam Tariq was wrapping up the sermon, and prayers were about to begin. There was a chorus of cracking knees and rustling abayas as a sea of bodies rose to their feet. I stood with the others and took one more look down at the men, just in time to see Faraj raise his hands up to the sides of his face and then fold them at his midsection. I felt a sharp tug on my arm. Mama was yanking me away from the wall.

"State your intention," she said.

"I'm here to pray," I said.

"Are you sure?" she said.

"Yes," I said. Other women were looking at us, and I felt my cheeks burn.

"Now say it again, to God, and mean it."

Mama turned away from me and lifted her own hands up to her temples to start her prayers.

I tried to clear my heart and mind. I even shook my head a little to give myself a jolt. "God," I said to myself, "I'm here to pray now. Really." I started to pray and even recited some of the longer surahs I knew by heart, to make up for earlier. But I kept losing my place, thinking about Faraj down below, praying just a few rows behind my brother and father. Prayers finally ended, and I grabbed Lina's hand and made a beeline for the stairs.

"He didn't tell you he was coming?" she whispered as we elbowed our way downstairs.

"No," I said. I hadn't heard from him at all since our botched date.

"So what? He prays at our masjid now?"

"I don't know."

We reached the bottom of the stairs and pushed toward the exit to find our shoes. Lina yanked the prayer veil off her head, and her hair stuck out in a staticky crown around her head. We stood by the door on tiptoes, peering inside the men's section and scanning the crowd for him, but people were streaming out of the mosque now, and tut-tutting as they pushed past us.

"This is outrageous," Lina said, as if angered by a tax hike or a parking ticket. "Doesn't he know not to come here?"

I'm not sure exactly what I was afraid of. It's not that I thought Faraj would climb up the pulpit and tell all my family and neighbors what we had done. But it did feel like some sort of invasion, him coming to my mosque without asking me.

We circled around the masjid, hovering awkwardly at each door.

"This is why I don't date Muslims," Lina grumbled. "Got to keep that shit separate."

And I knew what she meant. There were our lives here in Bay Ridge, where we were Arabs, Muslims, daughters. And then there were our other lives, out there, away from all this.

At the side entrance, we watched as the boys from our high school strutted out and paused in front of us, blocking our view. They thought we were waiting for them. They stood there and smirked, waiting for us to giggle and fall at their feet, until Lina reached over and physically moved one of them out of her way.

"Move," she said. "I can't see."

But that only made it worse, because then the boys demanded to know who we were waiting for. They, too, started peering into the prayer hall.

"We're waiting for our brother," I finally blurted out to the boys. "The one who just got out of prison for stabbing a kid in the eye just because he looked at us for too long."

Lina was right there with me. "Yeah," she said. "I didn't know an eyeball could bleed so much."

The boys laughed but then scattered, leaving us alone. The mosque was finally clearing out enough so we could see inside. Old men were gathered around Imam Tariq in the front, either congratulating or correcting him on his khutbah. Another group clustered around Imam Ghozzi, who had a bandage taped to the side of his cheek. Lina tapped me.

"There," she said, pointing.

I followed her finger and saw him—he was taller than most of the other men. His black kufi bobbed above their heads. He was weaving through the thinning crowd, crossing the mosque from the back to the front. Then he stopped, turned around, scanned the room. He was looking for someone. Maybe he was trying to find me to apologize for the other day. I was torn between the urge to fling my hand up in the air and wave him over, and to duck behind Lina for cover. Faraj crossed to the other side of the mosque again, this time headed for the hallway where everyone left their shoes. He stood above a crouched figure, someone searching the pile for his shoes. I breathed in sharply and grabbed Lina's arm. Faraj tapped my brother on the shoulder. Sami looked up and then stood, a lone sneaker dangling from his fingertip.

"Oh shit," Lina said.

They were talking now. I wanted to run across the prayer hall and fling myself between them. But all I could do was watch.

"It's okay," I said. "Maybe he's just, you know, asking for directions."

"*Asking for directions?*" Lina said, louder than she meant to. Some of the folks talking to Imam Ghozzi looked over at us.

"I don't know," I said, and sank my head onto her shoulder.

Faraj was doing most of the talking. I stared at his lips, trying to make out what he was saying. Sami stood very still, one of his shoes now cradled in his arm.

"There you are," came a voice from behind us.

I jumped, and turned around to see Mama.

"Let's go," she said. "I have chores for you to do at home."

I looked back at Faraj and Sami. Sami was bent down to the floor again, looking for his other shoe. But Faraj stood above him, talking to his back.

"Yalla," a voice bellowed from the street. It was Baba, holding his arm up in the air and tapping his wrist.

Lina and I turned and followed Mama toward him.

"Anyone seen your brother?" she asked, but Lina and I didn't say anything.

"He's inside, talking to some Pakistani," Baba said.

"Don't say it like that," Mama said.

"Like what?" Baba said.

"Like *that*. Like there's something wrong with being Pakistani."

"I like Pakistanis," he said. "I like them better than Arabs."

We were crossing the street, headed home, when we heard light footsteps behind us. Sami jogged to catch up to us, both shoes on his feet. I felt my whole body tense as I waited for him to say something.

"Who were you talking to?" Mama asked.

"No one," he said. "Just some guy."

I tried to keep my face neutral, to look straight ahead, but I couldn't stop myself from glancing over at him. He wasn't looking at me. His face didn't give anything away. He could have known everything or nothing.

Back at home, Sami said he was going out for a little while. He didn't say where. I could tell Baba was annoyed—Friday afternoons were the busiest time at the shop—but he didn't say anything. Mama made us sweep and mop the floors. I sent Faraj a text—"Were you at my masjid today?" I checked compulsively for a reply, but none came.

WHEN THE BOY LEFT home that afternoon, he went to meet Imam Tariq. He could have told his parents this—they would have been thrilled to hear it. But his instinct was to withhold even the most mundane, most basic facts of his life. They were originally going to play basketball. They met at the courts, both dressed in mesh shorts and white T-shirts, the imam in fresh white kicks, Sami in faded black ones. They dribbled and passed the ball back and forth for a few minutes, before they both agreed it was too hot. They leaned against the chain-link fence and panted, trying to catch their breath, the wire cutting diamonds into their skin. The imam suggested they return to his air-conditioned apartment. Sami tried to think of a reason why he could not go—he preferred meeting his friend outdoors, in large, loud public settings, where nothing of much consequence was ever said, or could even be heard over the din of basketballs and shoes on blacktop. He didn't want to have any heart-to-hearts. But, panting against that fence, the sun bearing down on him, Sami longed for the promise of air conditioning. He couldn't help himself. He nodded yes.

He had never been inside the imam's apartment before. It was fastidiously tidy and modernly decorated. Clear Lucite chairs around a black oval dining table. An abstract painting on the wall that appeared to Sami to be nothing but blue. He was afraid to sit on or touch anything.

He was afraid to leave his oily marks on things so shiny and clean. But the imam ushered him inside and told him to sit on the sofa, a surprisingly comfortable black sectional.

Sami could hear the imam's beautiful wife talking on the phone in another room—to her sister or another very close female friend. He knew by the way she was speaking in clipped sentences, half-completed thoughts. He recognized this from listening to the girls—Amira and Lina. An exclusionary closeness that he always read as a threat—*Don't come near us,* it said, *don't try to understand us*—at the dinner table and in the living room and in the muffled sounds coming from their bedroom at night. He didn't begrudge them this. But it did make him feel alone.

His anxiety increased. He didn't want to talk to his friend, to get to know him, to learn about his childhood or his hobbies. He didn't want to hear it. And, luckily for him, the imam was also in no mood to talk. He talked all day long, for a living. He could barely walk down the street without having ten people stop him, all needing his help. He liked Sami because he was quiet and easy to be around. The imam reached down below the television and fiddled with some cables. In a moment, the screen flashed on. A computer-generated military helicopter was landing in a dusty town square next to the ruins of a toppled statue. The game zoomed in on the mustachioed stone face of the dictator, his head now severed from his body and rolling down the square. The imam handed Sami a controller.

The imam didn't need to explain the game. Sami picked it up quickly enough as they roved in their fatigues down the deserted streets, scanning their assault rifles slowly from left to right as they went. A street sign dangled from one hinge above their heads. It was swinging in the wind, but Sami could see it was written in some language that he didn't recognize and that he doubted existed—some cross between Hindi and Greek, perhaps. They played for hours, the two boys. The hot wife came out once to say hello. She was luminous: Her skin was brown and dewy. A single black curl fell out from the scarf she had hastily wrapped around her head when Sami arrived. She wore a purple velour tracksuit and slippers, and Sami thought she was the most perfect thing.

Sami unraveled a whole complex political narrative as he played. The enemy was hard to identify. Something about ultranationalist separatists and a Russian coup. Together, the boys raided villages and took shelter in abandoned homes during a firefight. Together, they died over and over again. An IED, one fatal bump in the road. A suicide bomber who ran wildly at them, waving his arms like the boogeyman.

After many hours of playing, it appeared they had completed their mission, although Sami did not know what that mission was. Surely, the city was emptier now than it had been when they arrived. They ran, their boots kicking up dust, toward the helicopter that had come back to retrieve them. Sami held on to a rope and felt himself lifted up into the air.

In the distance, beyond the square, the city was burning.

When Sami's phone started buzzing, it did not stop. It buzzed and buzzed on his hip bone, impossible to ignore.

"Want to answer that?" Imam Tariq said.

Sami shook his head, and they returned to their game. But the phone would not stop.

"I think you should answer that," Imam Tariq said.

Finally, he reached down and flicked it open. "Hello?" he asked.

He listened for a minute, nodded once slowly, and then hung up.

"Wrong number," he said to his friend. But it was time for him to go now. He said his father needed him at the shop. He slapped hands with Imam Tariq and slipped out of the apartment.

Outside, he looked left and right down 5th Avenue. He could go to the shop, where his father almost certainly did need help. He could go home to his mother, who would fuss over him endlessly. He could go back to the masjid and face God. He turned left, back to the basketball courts. It was still just as hot as it had been a few hours earlier, when he and Imam Tariq had abandoned their game. But now he wanted heat. There was only about two hours of daylight left. Everyone was at home, counting down. He was grateful for the empty stretch of black asphalt. He imagined he could see it steaming, hear it sizzling, feel it sinking beneath him, a sea of roiling tar. His fingers gripped the ball now and pounded it against the black. He loved the sound of it, that reverberation. Why couldn't more things reverberate like that when he hit them? He ran up and down the length of the court, dribbling, passing the ball under his legs, throwing it up in the air. He played himself, shooting into both nets. The sweat poured down him, and he could feel it stippling the blacktop. His body was a stoplight flickering. His breath was a fire inside of him.

He played until his body broke down, until his knee gave out on him mid-jump, faltering, falling away. He fell like a building lit up with explosives, bottom first. He landed, a pile of rubble, on the blacktop. He was a shining heap of gold.

He lay still for a long time, breathing. When he finally stood, his limbs were studded with asphalt. Slowly, he walked home.

S AMI CAME HOME later that night with presents. He didn't say anything about where he had been, and no one asked. He had a fresh
scrape down one shin, and I knew it took Mama everything not to ask
him about it. Instead of immediately slinking off to his room, he greeted
us all cheerfully and distributed the little gifts he had bought for each
of us. Little-girl ChapSticks flavored like soft drinks for me and Lina. A
*Finding Nemo* bootleg DVD for Baba. A teal polyester scarf for Mama.

Lina and I were helping Mama prepare dinner when Sami came in.
He dropped the gifts down on the kitchen table, even though we were
sitting there with knives and cutting boards and bundles of parsley. He
sat down and smiled as Mama cooed over her cheap scarf.

"What are they for?" I asked.

"What?" he said.

"The gifts," I said.

"No reason," he said.

Mama folded the scarf and gingerly draped it over a chair. "Thank
you, habibi," she said. She went back to shaping ground beef into little
footballs. She sank her hand into the bowl of meat and squeezed as if
trying to kill it all over again.

"I can help with dinner," Sami said. All three of us women looked
up at him.

His voice was deeper, steadier. He was a solid, heavy shape filling his chair. The bruise on his forehead, like the tiniest smear of ink, was just where he'd left it that morning.

"Okay," Mama said after a pause, like she wasn't quite sure this was the right answer. She set a cutting board, knife, and five tomatoes in front of him.

We probably made a pretty picture—the tattooed felon hunched over a tomato, his womenfolk leaning in to inspect his work. So the four of us sat working around the kitchen table, me with parsley that stuck to my hands, Lina crushing pistachios with a mortar and pestle, and Mama with red onions, her knife flying. The four of us dicing and slicing and crushing and chopping. And after a while, I could feel the air relaxing around us. In the living room, Tom and Jerry tried to kill each other and Baba laughed. It didn't last long, but for a little while, we, our family, felt supremely normal.

Sami was like a caveman with his first tool. "Your brother chops tomatoes at the rate of one per hour," Mama said, and it felt good to hear her joke. She tried to show him how to chop tomatoes without bruising the skin, glowing like the happiest woman in America. I couldn't even remember the last time I'd seen her smile so big or talk so easily. She was laughing at his big clumsy man-hands.

Just then, he stabbed at a tomato and the flesh exploded, the juice and seeds bursting straight at his face.

Mama went to hand him a paper towel, but then she froze, her hand about to rip a sheet away from the roll. She reached into her pocket instead and snapped a photo of Sami with her phone—quickly, at lightning speed.

"Got it," she said.

We all burst into laughter, Sami still trying to wipe tomato out of his eye with his tomato-covered hands. And the more we laughed, the funnier it got. We clutched at one another's knees, fingers, faces.

We ate dinner together, trying not to laugh every time one of us bit down on a tomato. Baba didn't know what was going on, but he was smiling and nodding like he did. Lina didn't go anywhere, and neither did Sami. Baba didn't fall asleep or go to his coffee shop, and Mama didn't go to her room. We all sat, Baba and Mama and Sami on the sofa, me and Lina twisted up on the love seat, and we watched as Nemo tried to make his way home. Baba laughed long and hard, even at the bits that were supposed to be serious. We could not laugh with him, but only because we'd already laughed enough for one day.

After the movie, Mama and Baba got ready for bed, but Sami, Lina, and I stayed by the television.

"I heard an interesting thing today," Sami said.

I was lifting a piece of bread laden with dip to my mouth and nearly choked on it. I froze, and waited for him to speak.

"Apparently, I stabbed someone in the eye defending your honor?"

Lina started coughing violently. "Oh shit," she said when she finally caught her breath. "I forgot all about that."

"Why the eye?" Sami asked.

"It was just the first thing I could think of," I said.

"It's just that the eye is so specific," he continued. "And I'd have to have really good aim."

"It was symbolic," I said. "An-eye-for-an-eye kind of thing."

"Ah." He nodded knowingly. "Of course."

Lina and I laughed, and it felt like everything was maybe okay. For a few hours, I wasn't wishing myself anywhere or anyone else.

ONCE, when we were all still children, he brought a snapping turtle home for us. A snapping turtle in Brooklyn.

We weren't scared of him yet, just beginning to feel wary. We missed him—the brother he had never been—and still held out hope that one day he'd pay attention to us, play with us, invite us into his world. So, when he came home with the turtle that day and called our names from the front door, we came running.

He set the turtle, which was hiding in its shell, down on the table. When Lina peered inside the head hole and moved to stick her finger inside, Sami swatted her hand away and said, "Careful, it'll bite your finger right off." This, of course, only delighted us more. He'd brought us something from nature, something alive and deadly.

We sat around that turtle for what felt like hours until it finally emerged, first the tail, then the tip of the nose, then all four legs. Sami told us to be very quiet so we wouldn't scare it, so we could watch it waddle across the table, searching for home again. But when it finally showed itself, we couldn't help it—we screamed, we shrieked, we pointed and cried, "There he is!" And then there he wasn't again. We turned to look at Sami, to see if he was mad or annoyed or ready to take the turtle away and leave us alone again.

But he was just smiling and shaking his head. "Let's try that again," he said. "Quiet this time. Quiet."

THE MORNING AFTER Sami brought us presents, the sky was sick-looking. Low and bloated. We were gathered around the kitchen table for suhoor, and Sami kept looking out the window. Then he grabbed a peach from a bowl and went outside to smoke his last cigarettes of the day. This had become part of our pre-dawn routine.

He was still out there when we went to do wudu in the bathroom. Lina and I were walking by his room when we heard his phone buzzing on his nightstand again.

"Who the fuck is always calling him?" I said.

"It's the secret girlfriend," Lina said like it was obvious.

"At four-thirty in the morning?"

Lina started to say something about how this was more proof that the girl was Muslim, because she was awake for suhoor, too. I doubled back and knocked lightly on his door, even though I knew he was still outside. When no one answered, I pushed open the door. The phone was still buzzing, and whoever it was would not stop. I picked it up and answered.

"Sami's not here right now," I said, my voice cracking like a twelve-year-old boy's. "Who may I ask is calling?"

Lina gasped at the doorway and smacked a hand to her open mouth. Then she started giggling, and it made me feel like I had done something really cool and bad. I kept going.

"Hello? Is anyone there? Can I take a message?" I said.

"Who is it?" Lina whispered.

But it was no one. Just silence on the other end. I hung up and placed the phone back on his nightstand.

"Damn, this room is neat," Lina said, and crept farther inside. Sami always kept his door shut, so we'd never really gotten a good look at his room since he came home. His bed was made, the denim-blue comforter smooth and straight. I lifted a corner of the blanket, convinced that underneath I would see the sheets twisted and crumpled, but they were smoothed out, too, tucked neatly under the mattress. I replaced the corner of the blanket and ran my hand along the top to get rid of any wrinkles. I lay down on his bed, my head propped up on his two thin pillows. I wanted to see what he saw when he went to bed each night. I scanned the ceilings for cracks or stains, for the smear of a dead mosquito, for cobwebs in the corners. But there was nothing, just a perfect white sky. The sliding door of his closet was open. Inside, a few wrinkled button-downs hung lifelessly from their hangers. I sat up in the bed and opened the drawer of his nightstand table. Inside, there was a pocket Qur'an and a gnawed pencil. I reached for the pencil and brought it without thinking to my own mouth. I held it clamped between my top and bottom rows of teeth. I bit down and felt the wood compress slightly. Then I put the pencil back and closed the drawer.

When I got up, there was an imprint of my body on the comforter, an Amira-shaped dent. This felt satisfying to me, and I wished that more things would bend or recoil at my touch.

Lina was opening his dresser drawers. He kept them organized, with one drawer for jeans and one for socks and one for T-shirts and one for boxers. But, really, he could have fitted most of his clothes into one drawer. In his jeans drawer, there were crumpled pamphlets he must have gotten on the subway and shoved into his pockets. *El Milagro de Cristo!* and *The Watchtower: Why Do Bad Things Happen to Good People?* There were receipts from CVS, and a couple matchbooks printed with the American flag. Lina found a neat stack of New York City subway maps pushed into one corner of the drawer. They looked like they had never been opened, their creased edges still perfectly intact.

"Does he not remember how to use the subway or something?" she asked, picking up the stack of maps. "How embarrassing."

I took one from her and opened it. Someone had circled various points on various lines in black pen. The circle over the Chambers Street stop had been traced over so many times that the paper was torn. There were others at Dekalb, Court Street, South Ferry, Christopher Street, and one way up on Ninety-sixth Street on the 6 train.

"Yo, we should really help him learn the train. He cannot be seen walking around with his nose in these maps," Lina said.

I took the whole stack from her and unfolded the next one. This one just had a big "X" marked through all of Manhattan in thick black marker. Over Staten Island, some notes in pencil, but I could only make out one word: "Albanians." The third map had a red circle around the Flatbush Avenue stop and another around the Bay Ridge Avenue stop. Someone had drawn an arrow to it in red ink and written "You Are Here" with a smiley face next to it. Some more notes were scribbled onto the East River, these ones more legible: "TV stations?" "Languages?" "Current Events?" "YouTube?" The fourth map had no markings on it whatsoever, and the fifth had only a small note scrawled into the Hudson River: "If You Say Something, See Something."

"What is this?" I whispered.

"Looks like some kind of weird art project," Lina said.

We heard the front door open and we jumped. I scrambled to fold up the maps and put them back into his drawer. We ran out of his room, and as I closed the door behind us, I turned to look at the bed, to see if my imprint was still there. But it was perfect once more, smooth and unruffled. There was no sign of me.


We sat on bar stools at the window of a Trinidadian café in East Flatbush. There were two gurgling soft-drink dispensers, one orange and one pink, and a vat of steaming oxtail soup behind the counter. We felt like we had to order something, so we got two drinks, one orange and one pink. They sat untouched in the Styrofoam cups in front of us. Lina couldn't stop nervous-talking.

"I can't believe we're doing this. So stupid," she kept saying.

Directly across the street from the café was a tiny storefront mosque called Abu Bakr Masjid. As far as we could tell, there was no women's entrance. Just one narrow doorway in the front that men were streaming into.

"How can they even all fit in there?" Lina said as we watched the men steadily approach from either side of the street.

In its past life, the building had probably been a deli or a dollar store, or perhaps some dubious medical practice—a chiropractor no one trusted.

We were waiting for something, although we didn't know what. We were watching for something, although we didn't know what. We had never been to this masjid before. It was one of dozens like it scattered across the city. The only reason we were sitting across from this one now was that I thought Sami would be there. I had watched him study a flyer posted on our masjid's bulletin board for the esteemed sheikh Abdulwhatshisface giving a talk at Abu Bakr Masjid in Flatbush. It was after Maghrib prayers, and I was waiting outside with Mama and Lina for the boys to join us. Baba had put the wrong shoes on and had to go back to retrieve his own. We were standing by the entrance, laughing, as Baba slipped off the stolen shoes, when I saw Sami standing at the bulletin board with Imam Tariq. And as we walked home, the correct shoes on Baba's feet, I heard Baba asking him about it.

"You going to see the Somali sheikh?"

"I was thinking about it, yeah," Sami said.

"Isn't it on Saturday? Very busy day at the shop, Saturdays," Baba said.

"I don't have to go. I can stay if you need the help," Sami said. But then Mama intervened, saying, But it's Sheikh Abdulwhatshisface, highly respected, all the way from Somalia by way of New Jersey, what an opportunity, couldn't Baba manage without him, etc.

"Sure, sure," Baba said, throwing up his hands to stop her. But then he grumbled the rest of the way home about how, during Ramadan, suddenly everyone was an esteemed sheikh, how it was like a traveling circus of the esteemed sheikhs making the rounds. How just once he would like someone to admit that they had never heard of Sheikh Abdulwhatshisface, and how, when it wasn't Ramadan, these guys were just regular old insurance salesmen or Dunkin' Donuts franchise owners.

So here we were. It was Saturday, and thobed men across Brooklyn were packing into this tiny mosque to see the insurance salesman. Back home in Bay Ridge, Baba was annoyed because he was working the shop alone. We were waiting for Sami.

"Why are we even doing this? So stupid," Lina said, stirring her orange drink with a straw.

I couldn't really explain why we were there. But when I listened to him talk to Baba about going to the sermon, I thought about the subway maps tucked away in his drawer. I remembered a red circle around the Flatbush Avenue stop, which was about a block away from where we sat now. I thought maybe, if we could follow him here today, we could somehow make sense of the rest of the maps. Maybe they were maps of the traveling sheikh circus, of various khutbahs at various mosques around the city. Maybe Lina was right and he really had forgotten how to ride the subway. And maybe that's what he'd been doing when I followed him around the streets of Bay Ridge: he was taking notes on his phone to help orient himself around the neighborhood. I could make it all make sense. And then I could forget about it and move on, return to the task of making myself into the woman I was destined to become.

I didn't explain any of this to Lina. I just told her I wanted to follow Sami here, and she thought it was going to be some sort of stakeout. Like a *Law & Order* episode. She thought it was going to be fun. But now we were here, and it wasn't fun.

"He's not coming," she said.

The stream of men across the street had slowed. I could picture them all inside now, the early birds sitting cross-legged on the floor, the latecomers standing shoulder to shoulder in the back. I closed my eyes and tried to access the tracking device inside of me. The one I wished I could locate under my skin and cut out with a scalpel. But today, when I wanted to feel its red light pulsing, nothing.

I got up to throw my full drink away in the trash. It splashed back at me, flecking my white T-shirt with pink dots. I was dabbing at it with a napkin when Lina shrieked, "Look!" The woman behind the counter jumped. I jumped. Lina was into it now, crouching down, trying to hide behind a napkin dispenser. I could see them from where I stood: Sami and Imam Tariq walking slowly, as if they weren't already late, Sami in a crisp, brand-new thobe I had never seen before. They were laughing, and I could see all of my brother's teeth. He looked like a different person, some strange, lighthearted, happy person. He has a friend, I thought. He's hanging out with a friend.

I approached the window so I could see them better. Imam Tariq doubled over for a second, then recovered. They were ragging on each other, the way boys do. When they arrived at the entrance to the masjid, Sami slapped Imam Tariq's arm lightly as if to say, *Enough now. Straighten up. Fix your face. The teacher's coming.* Both boys became suddenly somber. Imam Tariq adjusted his kufi and then opened the door and disappeared inside. Sami didn't immediately follow him. He was standing alone under the eaves of the building. Next to me, Lina gripped my arm.

"What's he doing?" she whispered. "Why doesn't he go in?"

I shook my head silently.

We watched Sami reach into the breast pocket of his new thobe and pull out a single cigarette. He slid it under his nose, seemed to inhale deeply, and then placed it back inside the pocket. There was someone else approaching now. Another latecomer. He was jogging lightly toward the masjid. He was very tall, and his salwar kameez was just a couple inches too short for him.

Lina kept narrating beside me: "Oh shit. Shit, shit, shit." Her grip around my wrist tightened.

I knew even from a distance that it was Faraj, but I squinted my eyes and pressed my forehead to the glass as if, by looking harder, I might find him transformed into another person, who hadn't had his hands on my body.

Sami stood at the entranceway with his hands clasped behind his back like some sort of bouncer. *Go inside,* I thought. I even made a flicking motion with my hands as if I could shoo him inside before Faraj approached. But he stood very still and just watched as Faraj jogged the last few yards toward him. *What is he doing here?*

"Why does this guy turn up everywhere?" Lina asked.

The inside of my mouth suddenly went very wet. I swallowed a large mouthful of warm saliva. "It's probably just a coincidence," I said. "There are a lot of people here to see the sheikh."

Lina shook her head. "I *told* you this guy was weird."

I willed Sami to turn around, to go inside, but he stood still. He, too, was watching Faraj approach. Just then, Lina started tapping my arm furiously.

"Look, look, look. Sami is about to fight him," she whisper-shrieked.

"What are you talking about?" I said, although I already knew.

"Look at him. That's the way he always looks right before he fights someone," Lina said.

It was true. I could see him at sixteen, about to face another kid at the park, staring down a probation officer, a teacher, enemies all. He had that look about him now—still, body tensed, mouth set. I knew that if we got closer we would see a tiny muscle in his jaw flickering.

Faraj was within striking distance now. I waited for Sami to move. Faraj slowed to a walk until he was standing right next to Sami in the entranceway. I saw his mouth moving. But still Sami did not move. I had this horrible vision of Sami latching on to Faraj's thick head of hair and slamming it into the brick wall. Faraj leaned closer to Sami, close enough to kiss. He said something into Sami's right ear. Sami nodded once, a motion so small I would try to convince myself later that it hadn't happened. One inch up and one inch down. Faraj slipped inside the door. When the door shut behind him, Sami's body relaxed. His arms hung limply at his side, his shoulders rounded forward. He looked very small then. We waited for Sami to go inside. The sermon must have been well under way by that point. But instead he turned and walked away.

SECRET

**NYPD Intelligence Division
Demographics Progress Report
Bay Ridge, Brooklyn**

July 14, 2014

**Table of Contents:**

## SECTION 1: Overview

Demographics unit examined town of Bay Ridge, Kings County, New York. Objective was to identify and document places where people of ancestries of interest congregate. Ancestries of interest may include, but are not limited to: people from the region of North Africa, the Arabian Peninsula, the Levant (Lebanon, Syria, Jordan, "Palestine"), and other regions of what is commonly called "The Middle East." Ancestries of interest may also include Somalians, Pakistanis, Sudanese, Albanians, and other countries where there is a large "Islamic" population.* This report catalogues community hubs, businesses, religious institutions, schools, restaurants, and other *locations of interest*. Examining these locations provides maximum ability to assess opinions and behaviors of people of ancestries of interest.

---

*In the 68th Precinct there are twenty-one Protestant churches, eight Roman Catholic churches, two Greek Orthodox churches, one Jewish "Center," one Eastern Orthodox church, one Coptic church, and three Islamic mosques. It should be noted that Bay Ridge is home to a diverse group of religious communities. This report does not concern itself with those other groups, and provides insight only into Islamic or "Muslim" centers of activity.

For the purposes of this report, *a location of interest* is defined as follows:

- Localized center of activity for a particular ethnic group (including but not limited to the ancestries of interest listed above). These may include: house of worship, community center, coffee shop, restaurant, grocery store, fitness center, library, clothing store, nail salon, barbershop.
- Location that ancestries of interest or persons of concern may be attracted to.
- Location that individuals may frequent to search for ethnic companionship.
- Location in which individuals may find co-conspirators for illegal actions.
- Location that has demonstrated a significant pattern of illegal activities.
- Location that can be used as a listening post.
- Popular *hangout* or meeting location for a particular ethnic group that provides a forum for listening to neighborhood *gossip* or otherwise provides an overall *feel* for the community.

**SECTION 2: Maps**

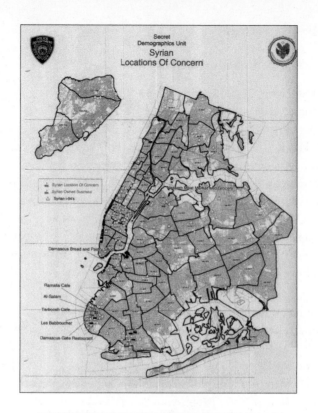

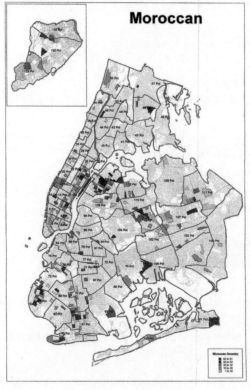

## SECTION 3: Locations of Concern

**Tunis Tea Room:** 3146 5th Avenue
  **Business:** "Traditional" "Arabic" "Café"; Serves "tea" and "coffee"
  **Owner:** The original owner of this café was a Tunisian man who was
deported back to Tunisia in 2007. New owner is an Egyptian man named
"Magdy." Also owns the "Gold Star" car service next door.
  **Information of Note:** Café is popular with livery drivers. The Al
Jazeera news channel is prohibited inside these locations, because the
owner feels it brings about extra scrutiny from law enforcement. The café
has approximately eight tables and seats approximately twenty customers.
Downstairs has a small room with rugs where livery drivers can pray.
Cash only. ATM inside.

**Mecca Travel Agency:** 332 Bay Shore Lane
  **Business:** Travel agency specializing in trips to Mecca and Medina,
Saudi Arabia. These are Islamic holy cities.
  **Owner:** An Egyptian male named Mohamed. Has previously been
involved in identification fraud and has a record of solicitation.
  **Information of Note:** People who go on trips or "pilgrimages" to
Saudi Arabia tend to be very strict and devout in their beliefs. A female
of unknown ancestry named "Randa" works at the front desk and
recommended the "Royal Jordanian" airline for travel.

**Bay Ridge World Café:** 8690 4th Avenue
  **Business:** Traditional Arabic café; serves "Arabic coffee" and "water
pipes."
  **Owner:** Palestinian who sometimes goes by the name of "Abu Yunus"
and sometimes goes by the name of "Ahmed."
  **Information of Note:** Traditional place for young people to gather.
Underage smoking has been observed at this location. Patrons smoke
a traditional water pipe called "shisha," also sometimes referred to as
"hookah." The sale of untaxed cigarettes has also been recorded. Al Jazeera
plays nonstop from a television over the cash register. Location opens at
7:00 p.m. and stays open late.

**Muhammad Ibrahim Abdulraziq Center for Arab-American
Community Life:** 7311 5th Avenue
  **Business:** "Social services" agency. A major gathering place for new
immigrants from "Arabic" countries.

**Director:** Hisham Abbas. Born in Brooklyn. Family comes from Syria. Ran for City Council in 2008 and lost. Building donated by a wealthy retired doctor from "Palestine." Staffed mostly by volunteers.

**Information of Note:** A picture of Al-Aqsa (a mosque in Jerusalem) hangs in the lobby. No television. Suspected hub for undocumented or "illegal" immigrants. Political and inflammatory rhetoric noted here. Has a bulletin board in the lobby with flyers for local apartments for rent and jobs. Has calendar on the wall from the neighboring mosque. Caseworkers have also been observed assisting clients from Central America. It is unclear if those clients were also Islamic.

**Dunya World News:** 487 Bay Ridge Avenue
**Business:** Newsstand sells various Arabic newspapers and magazines.
**Owners:** Two brothers from Morocco named Rachid and ███████.
**Information of Note:** This location is a well-known site of criminal activity including WIC fraud, credit card fraud, and fraudulent immigration papers. Also sells phone cards. ███████ has information on criminal conspiracy in the garment district in Manhattan.

**Abu Nuwas Halal Meats:** 7148 5th Avenue
**Business:** Butcher shop and small grocery selling "halal" meat and other dry goods.
**Owner:** Egyptian male named Kareem, also sometimes referred to by the nickname "Al-Shair." Adult male son, previously known to the police, also works in the shop.
**Information of Note:** Located across the street from Islamic Center of Bay Ridge. Closes for an hour for Friday prayers. Sometimes closed on Sunday. "Halal" refers to meat that has been blessed by "shiekh" or Islamic priest.

**Holy Land Books:** 8526 4th Avenue
**Business:** Bookstore specializing in religious "Islamic" books, CDs, and tapes.
**Owner:** Jamal, possibly Kamal.
**Information of Note:** Sells Arabic books on Islamic topics, copies of the "Koran," incense, rosary beads, and sermons on tape. At least one video on jihad noted. This location has been the site of terrorist activity in the past.

**Homs Pastry Shop:** 6709 5th Avenue
**Business:** Pastry shop selling traditional "pastries" or sweets.

**Owner:** Syrian family. Surname "Haddad"

**Information of Note:** Location sells Middle Eastern pastries and nuts. Especially popular during month of "Ramadon." Foreign newspapers also observed. No Al Jazeera permitted without verbal approval from the owners. Has a "donation box" for Syrian refugees which goes to an Islamic charity with known ties to extremists.

## SECTION 4: Locations Requiring Further Examination

- Dunkin' Donuts franchise on 3rd Avenue known to employ recent Arab immigrants.
- Also Subway franchise on 5th known to hire Arabs.
- Apartment building above "Leyla Café." ████ reports that this building contains a "revolving door" apartment popular with recent, undocumented immigrants. One-bedroom apartment with two beds and three futons. Landlord Moroccan.
- "Hair Designer Wow" on Bay Ridge Avenue. Lebanese female owner. Hair salon serves women only. Specializes in women who wear the "hijab" or Islamic head scarf. Subject unable to enter.
- Sunset Park Recreation Center: Observed to be a popular place for people of ancestries of interest to pursue recreation or fitness.
- Brooklyn Public Library, Bay Ridge Branch. Known spot for locals to "browse the Internet."

## SECTION 5: Debriefings

**Mission:** To produce analytical products that specify the process by which individuals of ancestry of interest attempt to obscure criminal intent and extremist ideology and blend into general society. The products should answer the question: If an individual from _____ were to come to New York City and wished to remain "under the radar," how, specifically, would he go about doing that?

**Methodology:** The Demographics Unit will conduct interviews with subjects and confidential informants to generate answers to the questions below. The Intelligence Analysis Unit will harvest the intelligence generated to form sound analytic judgments.

**Debriefing Questions**

- If your cousin/friend/father/brother wanted to keep a "low profile," what would you suggest to him?
- What job would he get to generally fly "under the radar" of law enforcement?
- Who in the community would help him?
- What religious institution might he attend?
- Where would he work out? E.g., gym, karate, boxing, etc.
- What would he do with his leisure time, i.e., "for fun," in order to seem "low key"?
- What pool halls, cafés, bars, restaurants would he frequent?
- Where would he get his hair cut?
- How would he learn to sound "Americanized," learn English, etc.?
- Where would he eat his meals?
- Where would he drink his coffee or tea?
- Where would he hang out with "friends"?
- What music would he listen to in order to "blend in"?
- What movies or television shows would he watch in order to appear "Americanized"?
- If he needed to receive medical care, where would he go?
- How would he "play it cool" if potentially inflammatory topics came up in casual conversation? E.g., "War on terror," racism, Israel/ Palestine, 9/11, etc.
- What Web sites or social media platforms would he frequent?
- Where might he turn to obtain fraudulent ID?
- Who would he confide in?
- Where would he live?

**Findings**

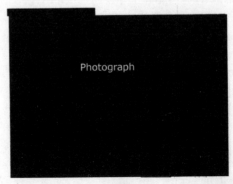

Subject interviewed identified location as ▮▮▮▮ Street between ▮▮ and ▮▮ Streets. Location where many ▮▮▮▮ frequent. Known site of ▮▮▮▮▮▮▮.

- Several interviews have pointed to in an apartment in Brooklyn, ▮▮ ▮▮ Street, known within the community as a place where recent immigrants stay. In an interview, ▮▮▮▮ and one of four roommates, ▮▮▮▮▮, described the "Lottery Visa" process. The undersigned observed four beds, three of which are futons. Upon entering the apartment, the undersigned made note of his surroundings. There is a small bathroom directly opposite the entrance and a living room immediately to the left, which contains two of the futons and an entertainment system. There are two Korans, one on top of each speaker. To the right of the entrance is a kitchen, in which hangs a calendar from Masjid Al-Madina mosque from the previous year. From the living room the undersigned noticed a doorway leading to a bedroom, which contains a twin bed and another futon. From the bedroom, there is another doorway, which may lead to a closet. Undersigned unable to confirm.
- Three recent interviews with ▮▮▮▮, ▮▮▮▮ and ▮▮▮▮▮ identified this location, ▮▮▮▮▮▮ on ▮ Avenue between ▮▮ and ▮▮ as a place where Moroccans are commonly congregating. Hashish sold from this location.
- Subject ▮▮▮▮ arrested after selling fraudulent IDs to an undercover. Subject already has a record of Forgery 2. Upon arrest, subject openly stated that he obtained forgery device from ▮▮▮▮▮, previously interviewed at ▮▮ ▮▮ Street. Subject agreed to become ▮ ▮▮▮▮▮▮▮▮▮.

- ██████████, adult male, age 21, revealed that he meets his friends at a "Muslim Student Association" (MSA) at Brooklyn College for prayer groups and study sessions and "movie nights."
- At mosque called █████████████████, located ██ Avenue and ██ Street, undersigned spoke of new "imam," or spiritual leader, who gives entertaining sermons and wears expensive sneakers. Born in New Jersey. Of unknown ancestry of interest. Encouraged congregation to donate to various charitable causes known to be anti-American.
- In an interview with ████████████████, adult male, aged 34, employee at Bay Ridge Honda dealership, identified ████████, ████ █████, and █████████ as social associates. Regularly attend Cleopatra Coffee House in the evenings and smoke, drink tea, some alcohol. Location known spot for hashish. Stays open until approximately 1:00 a.m. Serves dinner too and claims to be "halal only." According to █████, their most popular dish is the lamb "shawarma" cooked by the owner himself, █████████, of unknown origin.
- In a debriefing with confidential informant ████████, identified Paris Barbershop as popular hangout for local youths. Haircuts cost $13, more for elaborate designs typically popular with African American youth. Owner is an unidentified male of Yemeni origin. Yemen is a country known to foster extremism.
- ████████████████ ██████████████████ ██ ██ location known to █████ controversial topics and ████ unrest. Director of the ████████, as it is more commonly known, █ currently working on ████████████████████ arrest of known terrorist "████████" █████. █████████ agreed to become confidential informant after ████████████ ████████ █████████ agreed to ██████ information on local religious and political leaders. According to █████████████, █████████ of the mosque ██████████████████ is a known associate of █████████ and his sermons ██████████ pattern of radicalizing rhetoric. █████ associates ████████████████ ████████████████ the arrest of "██ █████." ████████ future protests █████ anti–law enforcement events ████ ████ unknown. █████████ informant works at █████████ ████, █████████████████ location of interest, instructed to ████████████████████████████ █ gain their trust ███████████████████████████ potential radicalizing events █████ intent █████ homegrown ██████ █████.

A T DINNER THAT NIGHT, we listened as Sami made up bogus answers to Mama's questions about the sermon. According to Sami, the sheikh spoke about how faith was like fidelity. There was a long metaphor about loyalty to a spouse and how we are all tempted sometimes, but what matters is not the temptation, but the fact that you conquer the temptation.

"Sounds interesting," Mama said.

"He came all the way from Somalia to tell you that?" Baba said.

Lina and I said nothing.

We sat outside on the fire escape that night. Even though the sun had set, the metal was still warm from baking in the heat all day. We leaned against the window and watched the neighborhood shake off the fast. If Abu Jamal's had been open, it would have been full now: men crammed in at the small tables, puffing on shisha, the water gurgling rudely inside the pipes. Families were out, walking in packs to the parks. Men were gesturing exuberantly with lit cigarettes below. Children were shrieking, chasing one another on scooters, their mouths stained red.

"What are you going to do?" Lina said.

The question made me separate from her, alone. As if she were just a spectator in my life and not one of the chief makers of it.

"What do you think we should do?" I asked, trying to pull her back in.

"You just gotta ask them straight up how they know each other and what they were doing," she said. "But start with Sami."

"Why Sami?" I asked.

"Because he's our brother. We know him. We can trust him. This other guy . . ." She trailed off, flicking her wrist as if Faraj were some sort of fly that had buzzed into our lives.

I thought about that for a minute. There were some teenagers walking on the sidewalk below us, laughing too loudly. Probably kids we knew. Both Lina and I paused to squint through the narrow grille of the fire escape, trying to make out their faces. If the kids looked up, they would see the underside of our thighs pressed against the metal slats. I had put my hijab back on before I stepped outside onto the fire escape, but I hadn't bothered trading my shorts for pants. The fire escape wasn't really public. People could see us, but only if they really knew where to look. It was the sort of thing that drove Mama nuts. "Which are you?" she would say, gesturing to my covered hair and my bare legs. But I never knew how to answer that question. "Which of what?" I would ask her, not even trying to be smart about it—just really, truly wanting to know. Are you a this or a that? I heard her voice in my head as we watched the kids pass beneath us. Maybe, if I could figure out how to fill in the blanks, it would make things easier for me.

When the roving band of kids were just a murmur in the distance, I asked Lina, "Why do you think we can trust Sami?"

Lina shrugged a little. "Doesn't he seem different to you?"

I nodded, but I wasn't sure if that should make us trust him less or more. Lina seemed to be considering this, too, because then she said, "I don't know if we can *trust* trust him, but he's blood. That Faraj guy you've been messing around with is just plain creepy, if I'm being honest with you."

I felt the heat from the metal grate rise from the backs of my thighs to my stomach and all the way up my neck.

"Like Andres is any better," I said.

"That's not what we're talking about right now," she said. "But even if we were, Andres has a good job and connections and cares about my future. And who is Faraj? No, I'm serious, Amira, who even *is* he?"

She looked at me then as if waiting for me to rattle off his life details. His birth date, the name of his mother, his favorite color.

"Whatever," I said. "I'll figure it out on my own. Thanks a lot for all the help."

I stood up and took one last look at the neighborhood, half hoping that Lina would apologize or say something to show me that I wasn't alone in figuring this out. There was an old woman sampling strawberries at Samira's Fruit Stand. She lifted a berry to her mouth decadently, like some sort of Greek god. I waited a few seconds longer, to see the woman flick the green top to the sidewalk. Lina said nothing. I climbed back through the window, and we didn't speak for the rest of the night.

Sami was in his room. I could see the light on under his door whenever I passed by to use the bathroom. I could have just knocked and asked him how he knew Faraj, what he was doing at that masjid. Lina was right—I knew him better than I knew Faraj. I knew what his mouth did when he was about to fight. I knew that he picked on the skin around his thumbnail when he was nervous. But I knew I wouldn't knock on his door. I didn't want to know Sami's secrets. I knew too many of them already.

DURING THE SUMMER of our eleventh birthday, it rained for days on end, torrential downpours that started and stopped with no warning.

We were often alone that summer. Sami was usually gone, and our parents were usually out looking for him. And so, two eleven-year-old girls alone in the apartment, we got bold. We started stealing things from Sami's room and—I don't know why—began drowning them. There must have been some little-girl logic behind it—the need to test his possessions and see if they would float or sink, as if this could reveal something essential about him. We took a single sneaker, wrapped it in duct tape, filled it with kitchen sponges, and dropped it into the bay. It appeared to float for one brief, nail-biting moment, and then it sank slowly out of sight. We stole a sock and filled it with bubble bath and hurled it off the fire escape in the middle of a tremendous gale (something about bubbles and air?). The sock soared, smacked against the side of the neighboring building, and landed on the sidewalk below, where it expanded like a slug. On a day when it did not rain, we stole a dime bag from the pockets of his jeans that had a tiny nub of weed left inside and unleashed it in the Sunset Park Pool. It floated, and Lina and I spent the rest of the afternoon eyeing it warily from across the pool. We stole a gnawed pencil from his desk and set it free in the gutter in front of the apartment. The rain whisked it away. We chased it, running along the sidewalk, shrieking, "Look at it go!" It sailed down the gutter for nearly a block before—whoosh!—down the sewer it went. Every day, we conducted an experiment—sink, swim, fly, or die—and would return home soaked and very pleased with ourselves. We had to wring out our hair and clothes in the sink.

Then Lina started coughing, these tiny, cute coughs. But then she started wheezing, her breath squeaking out between her lips. And then she got clammy as a motherfucker and started shivering like a cartoon character. It turned out that Lina had caught pneumonia in June. All those times she had flung her head back in the rain, screaming or laughing, mouth open wide to the sky. I imagined her lungs full of sloshing rainwater.

I remember Baba carrying her limp body out of our room and into his and Mama's room, where she stayed for two weeks. I wasn't allowed in, but a couple times a day I could stand in the doorway and visit her. It was the longest time we had ever been apart, and I felt unmoored without her.

So I was alone in our room when Sami appeared one night, a dark silhouette over my bed. He had been gone for a while—days, I think— and Mama and Baba were sick with worry. It was very late, and I was sleeping. I remember opening my eyes and letting them adjust to the dark, and even before I saw the shape of him standing over me, I knew he was there. I had the feeling he had been there for a while, watching me. When my eyes found him in the dark, he spoke.

"Get up," he said.

I stayed very still for a moment and closed my eyes. I thought maybe, if I didn't move, if I played dead, he would leave. But when I opened my eyes again, there he was, still waiting for me.

"Get up," he said again.

Sami had never hit me, but sometimes he looked at me like he wanted to. He had never kissed me, either, not even on the cheek or the top of my head, but sometimes he looked at me like he wanted to do that, too. Because there was always a thing, undone—an impulse not yet acted on, a violence unrealized—that lurked between us, I got up. Maybe it was because, out of the three siblings, I was the meekest. Or because I was the lightest. Or the best at school. Whatever it was, I always knew that I was some sort of important symbol for him. Like a trophy that reflected his own face back to him, distorted, but in gold. I was his to throw in the dirt or his to pick up, spit-shine, and put back up on the shelf. Sometimes I made him proud and sometimes he hated me for it. Men need something to own. And, for now, there was only me. So I got up out of bed.

When I was standing in front of him, I could smell him. Sweat and cigarettes and something else wet. He reached over to turn on the light next to my bed, and I flinched. I blinked in the light and watched as his body came into focus. His left arm was wrapped around his midsection, his palm cupping something on his side, a few inches below his right armpit. I remember thinking that there must have been a small animal there in the spot his hand covered. He kept twitching, as if trying to hold the living thing in place.

"Take this," he said, handing me a white roll of gauze.

I thought, *Something has happened to the animal. The animal needs our help.* The animal was bleeding—I could see that now—the blood under his cupped hand.

"I need you to wrap this around me really tight," he said. He was speaking gently now, as if I was the small animal. "As tight as you can."

He lifted up his white shirt with his other hand and then bit the hem, holding it up with his teeth.

"Start here," he said with the shirt between his teeth, nodding down to his left side. "And keep going around until the gauze runs out."

I unwrapped a few inches of gauze and stared at the skin on his ribs, afraid to touch him.

"Yalla," he said. "Go."

I pressed the end of the gauze to his skin and held it down with one hand while pulling the gauze across his belly with the other. I paused when I got to his cupped hand and the thing underneath.

"When I lift my hand, wrap it around quick and pull tight. Don't worry about hurting me. Just pull as tight as you can. Ready?"

I nodded. Sami grimaced and lifted his hand. There was a slit in his side like a pair of lips, an open mouth that was spitting blood. The animal was inside of him somewhere.

"Go. Fuck, Amira, go," he hissed and his eyes rolled back into his head.

I didn't want to go near those lips. Sami snatched the gauze from me and started pulling it around himself. His arms went around and around and side to side. I stood and watched as a dark red spot bloomed under the gauze. When he used up the entire roll, he held the end of the gauze in place with a finger and rooted around in his jeans pocket with the other hand until he fished out a small roll of white tape. He handed it to me.

"Rip off a piece," he said. He was panting a little, as if he had been running up the stairs.

I ripped a piece of tape and held it out to him. He taped the end of the gauze down, and then tipped his head back and sighed. He closed his eyes for a few seconds, and I could see his Adam's apple quivering. When he opened his eyes, he straightened his head and looked down at me.

"You're useless," he said.

Then he turned and walked out.

In the morning, I waited to hear Mama's shrieks when she discovered him in his bedroom. Her lost boy returned to her. Wounded. She would rewrap the gauze. She would clean the mouth on his side and close its lips. It wouldn't matter that I hadn't helped him, because Mama would make him better. But in the morning, no shrieks came. His bed was empty. My weary parents shuffled out of their room, drank coffee in silence, and then left again—another day of searching for him.

I considered the possibility that I had dreamed it all. But then I found a small roll of white tape on my nightstand. I cupped it in my palm and took it to the doorway of Mama and Baba's room. I would show Lina and tell her what had happened to me in the night. But Lina was sleeping, a slash of dark hair glued to her sweaty forehead. She tossed in her sleep. I watched her flip side to side for a few minutes. Then I turned and put the tape in the drawer on my nightstand, where it stayed for years. I spent the next few days imagining him dead, bleeding to death in an alley somewhere, knowing it was my fault.

Sami would come back. Although not until after every hospital had been called, every jail. He came back, and Lina got better, and we did normal family things like eat breakfast together and bicker over who left the refrigerator door open. We didn't talk about the time he had been gone. It was as if our parents were afraid that mentioning it, acknowledging that it had happened, would scare him off again. He was a person who could not be angered or upset. Or else he would do a thing he had not yet done. For my parents, this thing was dying.

He caught me in the stairwell to the building once, a few days after he had come back. I was coming up and he was coming down. I tried to walk right past him, but he caught my wrist.

"Do you want to know what I did to the guy who did this to me?" he asked, patting his side gently.

I said nothing, just looked down at our sneakered feet staggered across two steps.

"I broke his legs," he said. He reached down and patted my cheek as he said it. I flinched and closed my eyes. I waited for him to say more. To do more. He released me and kept going down the stairs.

After that, the visions that kept me up at night changed. It was no longer his body bleeding in an alley, but some other body. A faceless body. I pictured the legs splayed out, unrolling like ribbons from the torso, all the bones crushed until they were just two limp strips of flesh. I never told anyone what had happened between me and Sami that summer. But I kept this vision. Sometimes I see it still when I close my eyes to sleep or to catch my breath. A body out there somewhere. Proof of what Sami can do.

THE NEXT DAY, the police were back at the abandoned shell of Abu Jamal's café. They were carrying more boxes out and loading them into the trunks of cars. One man in an ill-fitting brown suit tossed a broken wicker chair out to the curb; it landed on its side in the gutter and stayed there for days, no one daring to move it.

I was getting ready for work, and I watched them from the window as I yanked my jeans on. At one point, I swear one of them looked right up at me. They kind of spooked me, the cops, dragging out filing cabinets and lumpy black trash bags filled with God knows what. It spooked me how bored they all looked. I was afraid of going outside while they were still out there, combing through the wreckage of the café, but then I got a text from Faraj.

I hadn't heard from him at all since our disastrous date, and he never replied to any of my messages from that day I saw him at our masjid. Our text-message history was embarrassing to look at, just a string of questions from me. I saw his name light up the screen and I threw myself at my phone. "Thinking of you," it said. Like a Hallmark greeting card. What was I supposed to do with that? I looked over at Lina, sleeping in her bed, her mouth wide open, one bare leg sticking out from under the blanket, a smear of something black on her calf. "Me too," I wrote, but immediately regretted it. It sounded like I had been thinking of myself. I walked to work feeling like an idiot.

But then, as I was sitting at my desk playing a game on my phone, his reply: "Iftar tonight?" I couldn't help it—I lifted my arms in the air in silent victory. A woman in the lobby looked up and smiled like she was happy for me. I told Faraj yes and waited for him to write back with the name of the restaurant.

"See you at my place at 8," he wrote. "I'll cook for you."

I swallowed and looked back at the woman who had been so happy for me a moment earlier. I wondered if she had daughters and if she talked to them about dating. If she sat them down and told them about their changing bodies. The only sex talk I had ever received was from Lina. She looked kind, this woman. Not the judgy type. Maybe she'd have some wisdom to share, some guidance. I wanted someone to tell me what to do.

The woman could sense me looking at her. She smiled and then asked in Arabic, "How much longer?"

"They'll be with you soon, inshallah," I said.

I looked back down at my phone. Of course, this woman had never had a sex talk with her daughters. This was Bay Ridge. She'd probably just tell me some story about a woman whose nose fell off moments after she had premarital sex. I told myself I had to go, because I needed to ask him what he had been doing with my brother. You're not going there for that, I told myself. You're going there for answers.

I swallowed a mouthful of saliva again. "See you then," I wrote back.

The rest of the workday was slow and boring until the Libyan's wife came in, and I had trouble looking her in the eye. She tried to sign in on the waiting list, but I just waved her in. A few minutes later, a man I had never seen before came in and told me he was Abu Jamal's business partner. He was talking into a Bluetooth, and it was difficult to tell when he was talking to me and when he was talking to the person on the phone.

"What? Yeah. I'm here to meet with the lawyer. No, I'm not talking to you. Hello, you there? Do you speak English? I'm here to meet with the lawyer."

I waved him through. I thought he had come with the wife, but, not thirty seconds after I sent him back to sit with her and the lawyer, I heard her start to yell. She was screaming in Arabic, "Get out! Get out! You traitor!" And she kept screaming that word, "traitor," as she physically shoved him back into the lobby. The man had his hands up to protect his face, but I could see through his fingers that he was laughing a little. "Okay, okay," he said in English. "I'm leaving." He was still talking to whoever it was on the phone when he left. I heard him say, "Did you hear that? The bitch is crazy."

When he was gone, the wife leaned down with her elbows on my desk, shaking it a little, and looked me straight in the eyes. She stuck her finger in my face and said to me in formal Arabic, "Don't you ever let that man in here again, do you understand me?" I nodded and said yes, yes, sure, but she didn't move. She stayed there, her index finger an inch from my nose, staring me down. I kept nodding until she finally stood, her finger now raised up, pointing to the sky. She shook it twice, and even though she didn't say anything else, I swear there was a silent curse in that finger pointing up to God. It scared the shit out of me. I thought I might try it one day when I wanted to intimidate people— I could mimic that finger, that stare. But I knew I would never get it quite right. And from that day on, I felt a sort of fearful reverence for the Libyan's wife, a woman who could put the fear of God right into my cold, teenage heart.

When my shift was over, I went to say goodbye to Laila. I peeked into her office. She was with a client so I started to back away, but Laila saw me and waved.

"Just came to say bye," I said.

The client, an old man with an elaborately carved walking stick, was hunched over some forms on her desk.

"Leaving already, habibti?" she said. She got up and walked around her desk to kiss my cheeks.

"Is Um Jamal okay?" I asked.

Laila sighed. "That poor woman."

I nodded and tried to look sympathetic. I was trying to figure out a casual way to ask Laila about Faraj.

"Do you think that protest helped at all?" I asked.

"It's hard to make people care," she said.

And then, as casually as I could, I said, "Remember that guy? The one who helped me make the copies?"

Laila squinted, looked down at the floor, and then shook her head.

"Young guy. Pakistani. His name was Faraj, I think," I said.

"Oh, him, yes, I think so," she said. "Was he with the ACLU or someone else?"

"So you haven't worked with him before? I thought maybe you knew him," I said.

She smiled at me. The old man filling out forms scowled, annoyed at me for distracting his caseworker.

"No, I never met him before that day," she said. "Why? You were hoping I could make an introduction? But, Amoora habibti, he is too old for you."

"No, no," I said, shaking my hands and backing out of her office. "I'm just thinking I should get more involved, you know, in activism stuff."

She nodded slyly at me. She would never stop teasing me about it now. I didn't even know what I was hoping she could tell me about him. That he was a good guy? For some sort of permission that I should go over to his apartment by myself, break my fast with him, and then make out on his sofa?

The old man started grumbling, and Laila returned to her desk. I waved goodbye and she made a kissy face at me and cackled.

I stood outside of the Center and looked up at our apartment across the street. If Lina was home, I could show her the text message, ask her what to do. But we hadn't made up after our fight out on the fire escape. And, besides, Lina never asked me what to do. She didn't ask me before she had sex or before she drank. She just flew off and did things. I wished I didn't always feel like I needed permission, even from her.

I turned away from our building and started to walk toward the train.


I lied to my mother. I climbed four flights of stairs. Summer was racing by, and Ramadan limped toward the finish line. It would be the end of holy days.

When Faraj opened the door to greet me, he had a dish towel slung over his shoulder. He gave me a one-armed hug and then hurried back to the stove. A pot of quinoa was boiling over.

"Can I do anything?" I asked.

"You can set the table," he said.

But there was no table, just a breakfast bar with plates and forks already on it. So I just rearranged them slightly and put napkins down.

"I didn't know Muslim men could cook. I thought it must be forbidden by God or something," I said. He was pulling a tray of roasted vegetables from the oven. He looked up at me, his face flushed from the heat, and grinned.

"I'm not most Muslim men," he said.

So everything was okay. He wasn't still mad about the last time. And I was being charming and funny and cute. I would ask him about Sami and he would explain everything. And then I could go home and tell Lina that she had been wrong.

He arranged food very carefully onto the plates, spreading the quinoa down, then topping it with the vegetables, and then spooning some sort of yogurt sauce on top. He sprinkled herbs with a flourish, and I laughed.

"It looks like restaurant food," I said.

"Better," he said. "This is a cleansing meal. Perfect for breaking the fast."

I glanced at the clock on his stovetop. It was time. He offered me the bathroom to do wudu. The bathroom was pristine, with nice-smelling hand soap. When I came back out, he was finishing up his own wudu at the kitchen sink. I felt suddenly nervous again. It was strange to pray side by side like this with a boy who wasn't family. Even though I had long complained about the barriers separating the men's section from the women's at our mosque, and now there was nothing between us. I stood next to him. He raised his hands up. I closed my eyes.

"Allahu Akhbar," he said.

I raised my hands up. "Allahu Akhbar," I said.

When we had finished praying, we sat at the breakfast bar and ate. He offered me a date first, from a blue ceramic bowl. He held it to my mouth and placed it between my lips. My cheeks burned.

The food was good. A bit bland, but healthy-tasting. It filled me but didn't make me want to clutch my stomach and go lie down in a dark room, like most iftar dinners did. For dessert, he removed a bowl of watermelon from the fridge.

We were talking about how good the watermelon is in Egypt and Pakistan when he turned to me and said abruptly, "I'm sorry about last time."

"No, I'm sorry," I said.

"I shouldn't push you to open up more than you want to," he said.

"No, I want to be open," I said.

He leaned over and kissed me on the cheek.

We piled our dishes in the sink and then went to sit on the sofa. Back home, Baba would be switching on the television for the start of his Ramadan soap opera; Salma had been killed in the last episode, but I had a feeling she wasn't really dead. From the sofa, we had a nice view out the window of the darkening sky. He sat down on the opposite end of the sofa from me, and I felt both disappointed and relieved. But then he stretched out and put his feet on my lap. I pretended they smelled and pushed them off, but, honestly, they were cleaner than mine. He laughed and sat up, this time a little closer to me.

"So what would you be doing if you were home right now? What's a night at the Emam household like?" Faraj put his chin on top of his two fists as if this were the most fascinating question in the world.

"It's pretty boring," I said.

"Nothing about you could ever be boring."

I snorted in a mortifying way and then stumbled through an answer. "Okay, well, we pray and have iftar and stuff. Then, sometimes, Lina goes out. But if she doesn't, we might watch a movie after our dad has finished his stories. Then we'll eat again and go to sleep." I didn't tell him that sometimes I went out with Lina. Or that sometimes I ruined a whole day of fasting with pineapple vodka.

Faraj nodded for a moment, as if there were a lot to consider. "You didn't mention your brother. Is he not home a lot?"

I laughed a little. "Oh. Oops. I guess, in a weird way, when you asked about the Emam family, I'm still not used to thinking of him as being there with us. But, okay, after iftar, Sami either sits out on the stoop and smokes a thousand cigarettes, or he plays basketball with some guys in the neighborhood. The other night, he stayed home and we all watched a movie together, the whole family, and it was kind of weird and kind of nice."

I glanced over at Faraj—is this what he wanted? I wasn't used to talking so much. He was looking down at his hands.

"Sorry," I said. "I told you my life was boring."

He looked up at me and smiled. "Not boring at all. I was actually just thinking that it sounded really nice. Family dinners. Family movie nights. What movie did you all watch?"

"Oh God," I said, burying my face in my hands. "It's embarrassing."

"Now you have to tell me." He reached over and elbowed my side a little, poking at my ribs until I laughed and said, "Okay. Fine. It was *Finding Nemo.*" I put one hand over my eyes and then squinted through my fingers at him.

"That's incredibly cute." He reached over and pulled my hand from my face. And then he just sort of kept my hand and held it between us on the couch.

"I just don't want you to think I'm, like, too young for you or whatever. Because I'm not."

"I don't think that."

"Good," I said. And then, to get the rest out, I had to concentrate on the feeling of his palm against mine. "I just thought maybe that was the reason you haven't answered any of my texts. Like, since that time in Central Park, you thought I was immature or something. And then I didn't hear from you again. Not even after I saw you at my masjid."

Faraj leaned back against the couch and tilted his chin up. His legs were open wide. When I finished speaking, he was quiet for a while. Then he let out a big sigh and released my hand.

"I'm sorry I ghosted you. It's not about anything you did wrong. I'm just under a lot of pressure right now."

"What kind of pressure?" I asked.

He leaned forward on the couch, held his forehead in his hands for a moment. "To fix everything this country did to my family. My parents and my brother are back in Pakistan—they gave up. And I'm supposed to stay here and put all the pieces back together by myself."

I rested my hand lightly on his shoulder. He was still leaning forward, elbows on his knees. A piece of his hair untucked itself from behind his ears and fell across his eyes.

"What do they expect you to do exactly?" I said quietly.

The question seemed to ignite him, because all of a sudden he was talking fast and loud. "That's just it," he said. "Get good grades. Get a fancy job. Make a lot of money." He started ticking off fingers on his hand. "But that's not enough. It's like they also need me to prove myself, both to white America *and* to Pakistani Americans. Like, Hey, look at how successful I am. Look at how well behaved I am. How safe I am. I'm one of you. And on top of magically getting accepted by all these people who have already rejected us, I am supposed to be perfectly happy, too. No complaints."

He stopped suddenly. I could feel that there was so much more he could say. Then he put one hand over his eyes, and glanced over at me through his fingers, mimicking me. I laughed and gave his shoulder a little shove.

"It's not funny," I said.

"No, that was a lot. Sorry."

"That sounds really hard. And I get it if you want to stop hanging out. I know I'm probably not the type of girl your parents would want you spending time with." I could see that type of girl—she was Desi, like him, of course. And she was wearing scrubs, completing her surgical residency. She had smooth black hair. She spoke Urdu and never drank pineapple vodka.

"No." He reached over and put a hand on my knee. "You're great. You're, like, the only person I feel comfortable around. When white people learn about my family, they treat me like a terrorist. And with Muslims, you know, it's like they feel bad, but they don't want to risk getting too close to all that. You're, like, the only person I've met who didn't even blink. And still wants to hang out with me."

I could feel myself blushing, but I tried to make my voice steady, to seem unfazed by being singled out like this. "It just doesn't make sense to me to blame someone for their family."

He smiled at me and then lifted his hand from my knee and draped his arm around my shoulders. He pulled me in so that I was nestled against his side, my head resting on his shoulder. I tried to relax my body, like this was no big deal, me snuggling on a couch with a boy, but my heart was pounding. I couldn't stop myself from smiling like an idiot, so I angled my face to point down toward his armpit. We stayed like that for a moment, snuggling in silence, and as I breathed in the smell of his laundry detergent, I gradually started to relax, to let my body melt into his. And then I found it easier to talk, my mouth opening against his shoulder, speaking to him without having to look at him.

"Why did you come to my mosque?" I whispered into him, felt his collarbone rise as he took a deep breath.

"It's a little embarrassing," he said.

"Tell me."

"Sometimes I go to different mosques and try to meet people. I can't go back to our old mosque. So I thought I'd try out yours, because you all seem kind of tight. Abu Jamal's family goes to your mosque. Your brother went to prison and came back. Maybe you all are more accepting than other places."

My first instinct was to roll my eyes. Bay Ridge? Accepting? There was a girl who got a nose ring once, and we talked about it for months. But it did make me wonder—did people in Bay Ridge accept Sami? I had never really considered what it might feel like for him to come back to the neighborhood. I thought about how different he looked that day I saw him laughing on the street in Flatbush with Imam Tariq. How relaxed. Like a normal boy. The only other time I saw him looking like that was at our kitchen table, wiping exploded tomato out of his eye. But most of the time, he looked so uncomfortable, like a guest standing at the corner of the party because he knew no one and no one really wanted him there.

I lifted my cheek off his shoulder and looked up at him. "So are you trying to meet my brother, then?"

"Not your brother specifically. People who have been through similar things. I just had this idea that maybe I don't want to surround myself with Muslims who are pretending like nothing is happening to us. Just studying engineering and going to Starbucks like there's no war against us. Like we can still somehow be a model minority even though everyone literally wants us dead."

He tried to pull me back into him, his arm like a hook around me, drawing me closer. I ducked out from under it and sat up on the sofa.

"What?" he said.

A moment earlier, I had been resting my cheek on his shoulder, ready to accept whatever explanation he offered me. But now I felt a heat coursing through me, rising up through my chest, and flooding my throat. "You and Sami are not similar," I said. "You always talk about him like he's some noble political prisoner. But he's literally a petty criminal. He stole shit, and he hurt people."

"Why are you mad right now?" he asked. He scrunched up his face like I was acting crazy.

"Because you went to my mosque and talked to my brother without my permission. Even when you knew how hard him coming home has been for me. And then you ignored me for weeks. And then you talked to him *again,* at that mosque in Flatbush, like you knew he would be there. You're not telling me something, and I'm starting to wonder if this"—and now I gestured between us—"is even about me. You're more interested in him than you are in me. I'm sorry your brother is gone. But you can't have mine for whatever you want him for."

Faraj laughed but in an ugly sort of way. "What is it that you think I'm doing? Stalking him? I'm an organizer, Amira. It's my job to talk to people, to get them involved."

"But organize what? Get people involved in what? You keep talking about your organizing, but I haven't seen anything."

He tilted his head to the side and looked at me for a long silent moment that seemed to stretch between us. When he finally opened his mouth, he spoke slowly, as if I needed help comprehending.

"What would you have seen, Amira? In all your movie watching and your nail painting with other teenage girls? Tell me."

I felt the shame wash over me, because, of course, I couldn't tell him anything. Over his shoulder, on an end table, I could see a framed photo of two boys in soccer jerseys, a ball under the taller one's arm. And I almost immediately started to doubt myself. I had been so sure of my anger seconds earlier. I fought the urge to apologize, be cool, nuzzle back into his shoulder. But then a thought occurred to me.

"You know Sami is on parole, right? That means he can't be involved in anything. All he can do is go to work and go home. Have you thought about that at all when you keep trying to talk to him?"

Faraj shook his head like he was considering something very sad. "I don't get you, Amira. First you're angry at me because you hate your brother, and then you're angry because you're worried about him."

He didn't wait for me to respond. He stood, and I couldn't bring myself to look up at him. "It's getting late," he said. "You should probably go home. Don't want your family to worry."

He spoke quietly, without malice. I felt like such a bitch. Why did I have to go and ruin everything? Other girls would be grateful if their sort-of boyfriends tried to befriend their brothers. I decided then that I would blame Lina. That it was her voice in my head—*There's something weird about this dude*—infiltrating my own instincts.

I nodded and rose from the couch. Faraj walked me to the door and held it open for me. I paused in the doorway for a moment, but my mind was churning too quickly for me to figure out what I actually wanted to say.

"Thanks for dinner," I mumbled.

He nodded once. I stepped out into the hallway and turned back, but he was already shutting the door. I was still standing there as I heard the dead bolt lock.

It was time to go home. Out on the street, discarded pieces of people's lives were piled on the curb. A crumpled baby stroller. Rusted beer cans. Some dresser drawers. A gnawed corncob.

When I got off the train in Bay Ridge, the neighborhood was God, and God was a vast mother the size of the sky lifting her skirt ever so slightly for me to slip under. A God like my mother, trying to figure me out: Are you a this or a that?

Aziza was restacking containers in the freezer when she heard her husband laugh and then moan. Getting everything to fit in the freezer was like a puzzle—there were so many Tupperwares and aluminum trays. Right after it happened, the neighbors had come in a steady stream, bearing dishes of home-cooked meals. Aziza didn't have the heart to tell them that her husband couldn't eat any of it, at least not now. Chewing pulled at the stitches on Yassine's cheek—he could only handle liquid foods. So, one by one, she shoved them all into the freezer. On the stovetop next to her, lentils were simmering in broth. She would blend them with a squeeze of lemon.

The most puzzling gift she had received was a box of something called "Pop-Tarts" that Imam Tariq had brought over. He'd had a sheepish grin on his face when he handed her the box, said he knew Imam Ghozzi liked this flavor—Frosted Strawberry. She didn't know how long they would keep on the shelf, so she stuck the box in the freezer along with everything else. Yassine was always a sucker for American junk food.

She closed the freezer door now and gave the soup a stir. She ought to go in there and tell him to change the channel, to watch something else, something that wouldn't make him laugh. Something serious. There was a new show about migrants crossing the Mediterranean in death boats. But she knew he would just change it back when he thought she wasn't looking—the man loved to laugh, even when it hurt him.

The show he was watching now was one of his favorites. It followed the comic adventures of the residents of an apartment building in Tunis—many of them related, because that is how people lived back home. Together. The mother on one floor, and all her grown children with their families spread out above and below her. They would barge into one another's apartments unannounced and eat one another's food. Aziza heard the creak of one of her neighbors upstairs. She looked up at the ceiling and wondered what it would be like if that was her daughter living up there and not a stranger. She closed her eyes and imagined her grandchildren hurtling down a flight of stairs, about to explode through the front door, kick off their small shoes, and run to her for a snack.

But Aziza and Yassine's daughter lived in Texas now, in a big white house on a plot of land that was as flat and dry as a piece of toast. There was a community of Muslims out there, building big houses on cheap land, somewhere outside of Dallas. Mostly Yemenis. And her daughter had married a Yemeni, a boy from right here in Bay Ridge. Was Aziza wrong to assume that they would stay here, in this place their parents had worked so hard to build a life in? But rent was so expensive here, her daughter reminded her. They could never in a million years afford to buy. In Texas, their children could ride bikes around the cul-de-sac. There was a community pool.

They talked sometimes about joining their daughter out there; she had *two* guest rooms. But Yassine didn't want to leave his congregation, even after he ceded the imam role to young Tariq. The people here needed him, he said. He visited with them when they were sick, he prayed over newborns, he laughed with them over tea. She always wondered if it was true that anyone here would miss them, especially now that they were getting old. But then someone—a stranger—walked up to her tenderhearted husband on the street, with the midday sun shining down on them, and cut his face open. And the people—*his* people—flocked to his side, brought him cuts of meat they could not afford. They sat with him and visited with him, and tried not to make him laugh, which was difficult, because Imam Yassine Ghozzi loved to laugh.

The other reason they had resisted moving to Texas was a vague feeling that they were not wanted there. They didn't mean by their daughter: she would welcome them with open arms. They meant as Muslims and Arabs. They watched the news; they saw what kind of people lived in Texas, what kind of politicians. They had grown up on the old Westerns. Did Texans—and by that, they really meant white people—really want a bunch of Muslims in head scarves building a compound in their state? Just look at what happened around the country any time some Muslims wanted to build a single mosque. And this was a whole community. This was what the white people were most afraid of—that Muslims would come and set up shop and spread sharia and plot evil against innocent Americans. Sometimes Aziza woke up in the middle of the night with this dread fear that armed men were closing in on her daughter's neighborhood in Texas. That she would wake up to headlines of a shooting rampage. Yassine told her she was exaggerating, worrying over nothing, but these things happened in America, didn't they?

Until now, however, she had never thought about them happening in New York. At least not in Bay Ridge. Bay Ridge wasn't like Tunis—families didn't live all together in a single building. Still, it was close (for America): you couldn't walk anywhere on 5th Avenue without running into at least five people that you knew. But now even this place wasn't safe. She had been blind to it before, even when they came and dragged Abu Jamal out of bed in front of his family. She thought: That would never happen to us. He must have gotten himself into some trouble. But what did Yassine do to that stranger to compel him to slice his cheek like a piece of fruit?

From somewhere below them, a door slammed. She waited for the sound of footsteps. Neither of them had been outside much since it happened. When she had to walk to the pharmacy to pick up Yassine's antibiotics, she had ended up flattened against a wall, panting for breath, unable to walk another step, because she couldn't bear the idea that someone she could not see might be sneaking up behind her. A neighbor found her like that and walked her to the pharmacist, who sat her down in the chair reserved for people getting shots and had her take deep, slow breaths in and out. She was having what he called a "panic attack," a term she had never heard before.

But now she couldn't stop thinking about the name for what had happened to her—panic attack; an attack of panic. Was this what her life would be like now? Her own imagination, her own fear, attacking her body? There were people who wanted to hurt them in Texas and people who wanted to hurt them in Brooklyn, though she couldn't see any of them. Almost as if they weren't real, as if it was all in her head. But the proof was in her husband's face.

She walked out of the kitchen and stood in the doorway of the bedroom, still gripping half a lemon in her palm. Yassine did not notice her right away. The bald-headed protagonist was making moon eyes at the woman of his dreams, who did not yet know he existed. Yassine's mouth was set in a firm line, his jaw clenched, a purple line extending from the corner of his lips up to his right cheekbone. He was determined not to laugh, she could see. But this, too, looked like it hurt him—to hold it in. She did not want to change the channel, she decided. Not now, not ever. She wanted to lie down next to him and watch the family that lived in this building love one another. She wanted to watch her husband open his mouth as wide as he could, to laugh as much as he wanted to.

Yassine finally saw her standing in the doorway, and smiled with his eyes.

She smiled back at him with her mouth. "I want to go home," she said.

WHEN I GOT HOME from Faraj's apartment, I found Sami sitting cross-legged on the living-room floor, reading the Qur'an, which was really annoying. He was staring down at the text, running his fingers along the gold-rimmed pages. I didn't even think he noticed me come in. But then he put the book down suddenly and said, "Hey, what's the best movie that's come out in the past six years?" It was like he had been waiting for me to get back, waiting for hours just to ask me this one question.

"*Fast and Furious 6*," I told him, not kidding at all.

Sami shook his head. "I saw one of those in prison. It was stupid. Not even a little bit realistic. I mean, that blond, curly-haired, pretty-boy cop stealing cars? Nah, no way."

"They let you watch movies in prison?" I asked him. Even though I had millions of questions swirling around in my mouth at any given moment, this is the one I asked.

"Sometimes," he said. "But usually really old stuff."

I slipped my shoes off at the door and threw my bag down on the coffee table. I collapsed onto the sofa like Baba. Sami smiled.

"What else did you watch?" I asked him.

"We watched this one movie with Julia Roberts. It was set in the

South. And it's just this sweet movie about ladies drinking tea and argu-ing and shit, and then, in the end, just out of nowhere, Julia Roberts *dies.*"

"*Steel Magnolias,*" I said.

And he looked up at me like this was the most meaningful con-nection we would ever make. "*Yeah.*" He continued, "At the end of the movie, you should've seen it. Old-timers, real hard dudes, straight-up crying, sniffling, and wiping their noses."

"Did you cry?" I asked him.

He looked at me, raising his eyebrows like it was the dumbest ques-tion I could ask. We were silent for a few minutes, and he picked the Qur'an back up, but now that I looked at him closer, I didn't think he was reading at all. It just gave him somewhere to put his eyes.

That night, as I was lying in bed trying to sleep, I heard a basketball hitting the pavement somewhere in the distance. I suppressed the urge to get out of bed and open the door to Sami's room to check for his sleeping body.

I turned and looked at Lina's empty bed. She was out somewhere, having told her own lie to our mother. She didn't know what I had done that day, and I didn't know what she was doing right then.

People were always saying that Lina was the sneaky one, the untrust-worthy one. But really I was opaque and Lina was transparent. I grew up watching siblings who were born with a natural talent for self-destruction. I didn't have that. I was cautious by nature, defensive, with-drawn. By watching the other two hurl themselves like grenades at the world, I learned how to erect barriers and blast walls to protect myself. But, inside, my body was my nation, where I would experiment until I figured out the best way to build myself, and damn the consequences, damn the casualties—which were, of course, parts of myself.

I woke to my cell phone crying on the nightstand. *Lina, Lina, Lina,* it sobbed and shuddered. I paused before I answered. I stared across at her empty bed. She hadn't come home. I thought, What if I don't answer? I thought, I won't answer. I thought, She needs something: money for cab fare, maybe. I thought, She wants to tell me: Don't be mad now. Be mad later. I thought, Don't answer. Be mad now.

I picked up the phone. I was lying straight as a board on my bed, holding the phone up to my right ear.

"Amoora?" Her voice was an echo. Like, at some point long ago, she had called my name down a canyon.

I knew something was wrong. But I stayed rigid on the bed.

"Where are you?" I said.

"Come get me," Lina said.

"Where are you?" I said again.

"I don't know," she said, and then she started to cry. She was telling me things that didn't make any sense.

"I'm in a motel room," she said. And, through her panicky sobs, something about how the carpets were dirty and purple. "My feet hurt," she said. "I'm alone. I don't know what happened to my purse." She was almost hyperventilating, and her breath sent loud static into the phone.

"You don't have anything?" I asked. "Money? ID? ATM card?"

"No, no, no," she moaned. "And no shoes."

"You don't have shoes?" Now I was up, on my feet, pacing the room.

"I want to come home," she cried.

I tugged some dirty sweatpants up over my wide hips. She was too afraid to leave the room—she said there had been a strange man knocking on the door.

"Describe it to me, Lina," I said. "Look out the window and describe it to me."

"I see gas stations," she said. "Exxon and BP and Shell and a Lukoil, all in a row. And lots of cars. I think it's a bridge!" she said, suddenly excited by her own ability to see and make sense of the things around her. "Or a tunnel," she said. "I think it's a tunnel."

"Great," I said. "Holland? Lincoln?"

But she wasn't listening anymore. "Oh God," she was saying, the panic stretching her voice out again. "I think I'm in Jersey."

I had moved into the living room, searching the tangle of keys hung up on a peg on the wall for keys to Baba's old Tercel, but my fingers kept fumbling. We were in different states. Somehow, we had ended up in different states.

Then I felt a hand pull the keys away from me. Sami stood in his boxer shorts, sleep dusting the corners of his eyes. It was somewhere around three o'clock in the morning. He flipped through the key ring, located the right one, and held it back out to me.

"Ask her if there's a Home Depot," he said.

"Lina, is there a Home Depot?" I asked.

"What?" she said, irritated now. "Yes, yes, there's a Home Depot right across the street. Did you even hear me? I said I'm in fucking New Jersey!"

"Holland Tunnel," Sami said. He gave me the answer I needed and let me go.

She was asleep when I arrived. The noise from the tunnel traffic outside created a sort of pleasant white-noise effect, cocooning us in the room. New York City was just thirteen dollars and ten minutes away.

Somehow, she looked weirdly at home on her Holland Plaza motel bed—sticky sheets, a scratchy polyester quilt, the pillows all yellow at the corners. When I opened the door to her room, the air conditioner was raining dust all over her glittery body.

But before all that, I had to drive over there in Baba's Tercel. I had my license but I almost never used it. I spent the entire drive there white-knuckling it in terror. When I got to the motel, I parked the car on the street, next to a tire shop and a sign that read "Welcome to Jersey City: America's Golden Door." In the motel lobby, Lina wasn't answering her phone, so I stood at a plexiglass window and pressed the bell. No one came to the counter. After standing around for a few minutes, I was about to go knocking on all the doors until I found her when I saw the reflection of a man standing suddenly behind me—a sweaty, small man who was breathing heavily and standing too close. When I turned, he said something like *Get her outta here.*

And I knew immediately that he was in that rare category of men who could not be charmed by Lina. Not like our crossing guard in high school, who let Lina direct traffic. Not even like Andres. Rather, I knew immediately that this clerk was a person who would not make any part of what was about to happen easy on us. I said something to him then, I can't remember what, and he told me to walk up a staircase along the outdoor courtyard. I did that, turning right when he said right, left when he said left, the guy following a few steps behind me the whole way. Then, at Room 206, he told me to stop. He reached across me and put a key in the lock. I could feel his breath on my neck and his eyes on my tits.

The door swung open, and my sister was in the bed. The air conditioner was on full-blast.

"Thanks," I said to the clerk.

"I can help you get her cleaned up," he said.

"That's okay."

"There's no prostitutes in my motel, you know."

I stepped inside the room, thought about responding to this, then shut the door. I slid the chain across the bolt before he had a chance to follow me. "I'll be back in a minute," he said, through the door.

Lina was fast asleep on the bed, lying straight, like a mummy. I lay down next to her and placed my hand on her stomach so I could feel it rise and fall, because this was suddenly a luxury. Once, there had been a time when I didn't need to feel her breathing to know that she was breathing. But now I felt light-headed with all her extravagant breath around me.

When I opened my eyes, it must have been four or five minutes later, and someone was banging on the door.

"Open up," the clerk called.

"We'll be out in a minute," I said.

"I need to inspect the room for damage."

I waited a second before answering, watching more dust spit itself out of the air conditioner. "Everything's fine."

I gave Lina a little shake but she didn't stir. If we'd had the whole day, I might have let her sleep. But the banging on the door had stopped suddenly, and the clerk wasn't saying anything. Somehow, this was scarier than when he was banging. I found a white washcloth in the bathroom that looked basically clean. I ran it under warm water from the sink and brought it back to sleeping, breathing Lina. I pressed the cloth to her cheek, which I had just realized was an angry purple color with a blood-crusted scratch curved around it like a parenthesis. Her eyes opened into slits, and she looked at me like a mole burrowing up into daylight for the first time. She wasn't scared, because she knew that the hand with the wet cloth was mine. "Hi," she said. I wiped the blood away from her cheek with a corner of the cloth, and I used the clean part to pat her forehead and collarbone. "Hi," I said.

The banging started again, and I yelled something; then it stopped.

I rinsed the cloth in the sink and soaked it in water again, this time rubbing it with a bar of half-used soap. I wrapped the cloth around first one of my sister's feet, then the other, wiping the dirt off and soothing the big, screaming blisters. She curled her toes toward me. I wrapped one of them, with the worst blister, in a strip of toilet paper, wishing I had thought to bring bandages. Lina was looking at me, watching me walk back and forth between the bathroom and the bed.

"I've never been to the Waldorf-Astoria before," I said as I worked.

My sister smiled. Her voice was even more swollen than her body. "This is a motel, bitch."

I pulled her up to a sitting position, slipped her dress off her head. I had brought a Fort Hamilton High hoodie and her favorite matching sweatpants. Lina was saying something about her feet as I made her lean on me, her naked breasts dangling over my forearms as I helped her into the pants. She sat back on the bed while I wedged some flip-flops between her toilet-papered toes. Last was the hoodie, which I put on her from behind so she could lean against my knees as I lifted her arms up and pulled the sweatshirt over her head, stretching the hole wide so it didn't drag against her bruised cheek. "Probably no breakfast waiting for us in the lounge," I said.

Lina smiled again. I stuffed her dress and panties into the plastic bag I had brought the sweats in and surveyed the room.

"You bring anything else?"

She shrugged and closed her eyes, so I looked under the pillows and the quilt, then under the bed. On the floor next to the air conditioner, I saw a used condom.

Then a voice from the other side of the door. "I'm calling the cops, bitch," the clerk said, in so close to a whisper that I wondered if I'd made it up.

Suddenly Lina was trying to remember. Her eyes half closed, she said something about Andres, something about music pounding on a door. She remembered fighting with him, and then being outside Lotus and trying to get a cab to take her back to Bay Ridge. Someone came up to her, started talking to her, said he'd help her get a cab. Then she remembered waking up and calling me this morning. Me, I remembered different things, more distant things. I remembered how, the previous Ramadan, she'd broken her fast with a bag of gummy bears and a half-empty bottle of Hennessy that she had copped from some boys at the park—Lina's perfect iftar meal. How I had lectured her and judged her, and how she'd just smiled sheepishly and shrugged her shoulders. How I never told her that I cheated almost every day last Ramadan, taking big, desperate gulps of water when no one was looking. I remembered some other things. I remembered when I still felt like there was a bungee cord running from my lungs, dragging along the streets of Brooklyn and up into her mouth, no matter where she was, every breath connected, my inhale dependent on her exhale. I couldn't remember when it had snapped.

"Oh God," Lina said then, noticing the condom, and she started to rock back and forth on her knees, her hands knotted over her stomach, the mattress squealing.

"Maybe it was Andres," I said, as if that would really make it any better.

"It wasn't him," she whispered, still staring at the condom, still shaking on the bed.

She got up and ran suddenly to the toilet. She hunched over the rim and started to heave. I followed her, crouched over her, and held her hair. As she heaved great shudders of nothing, I told her about my fight with Faraj, because I thought she might need someone else's story, an alternative night she could escape to before returning to the reality of this cold bathroom floor. A lesser sort of pain to feel. I made a joke about how pathetic it is when it turns out that the boy you thought might be stalking you is in fact stalking your brother.

Lina sat up and wiped nothing from her mouth. She twisted around to look at me, then stood. She held my face in her eyes and offered me her hand. She pulled me up.

The banging had resumed.

"Ready?" she asked me.

"Yes," I said. "You?"

She nodded through a yawn. The parenthesis on her cheek curved into a half-moon.

"We have to run," I said.

When we finally arrived back in Bay Ridge, we drove straight to a diner on 4th. I didn't ask Lina if she wanted to go. I just parked the car and walked inside, Lina following behind. I had a craving, although not for food. I wanted the tall booths upholstered in electric-blue pleather. The way they made us feel like we were slipping into our own private nook. They weren't curtained off, but it sort of felt like that. We sank into the seat, leaning against the button-tufted backs that rose up well above our heads. We rested and breathed out in relief, because no one except our waitress could see us sitting there. We violated the rules of Ramadan that morning, eating undercooked eggs and drinking too-hot coffee. But God made exemptions for the sick, and what were we if not sick?

"Why did we come here?" Lina asked, as she scraped gelatinous egg whites off to the side of the plate with her fork.

"The potatoes," I said, although the potatoes were not particularly good, either. But Lina pierced one with her fork, chewed on it, closed her eyes, and nodded.

With her eyes still closed, her head resting against the blue booth, I felt brave enough to speak. "Should we call someone?" I said. "Should we tell someone?"

Lina's eyes popped open. She looked at me like *Don't!* Silence was the only thing big enough to plug up the memory of that day, to smother the truth that lurked just beneath it. Her eyes softened at the corners a bit, melted into a kind of pleading. *Please don't*, they said. *Stop*, they begged.

"Let's order ice cream," I said. And she nodded, grateful. She closed her eyes, took another bite of potato. We split a bowl of chocolate ice cream. It was studded with freezer burn. We ate it all anyway.

What if I hadn't answered the phone that day? What if I had hit "decline" and gone back to sleep? But who was I if I didn't answer, if I didn't go? I was nobody, just a girl who used to sleep curled up with my cheek pressed against the cool skin of her back. If I hadn't answered, then we would never have made it to the diner that day, to the place where the booths were so tall and so forgiving.


After we got home from the diner, we crawled into our beds before Mama could see the state of Lina's face. I slept for a couple hours, but then I had to wake up to go to work. Lina didn't stir at all, even as my alarm blared. The sheet was pulled up all the way over her head, only a mess of black hair visible on the pillow. I stumbled to the bathroom, and was trying to untangle a massive knot in my hair when Mama walked by.

"What happened there?" she asked, nodding with her chin to the bird's nest at the back of my head. I was afraid she would see something in it, some proof of where we had been. I tugged the comb violently through my hair. I could feel my mother coming closer, and I thought maybe one good yank would smooth it out before she had time to ask more questions. But the comb just got stuck, and I cringed in pain.

"Here," Mama said. "Let me." And before I could even protest, Mama had the comb in her hands and was working some olive oil into the back of my head. She plunged her hand in, and I could feel her fingers massaging my scalp. I couldn't help myself—I closed my eyes. After the terror of the last few hours, it felt so good to release myself into her care.

"Did you forget to wear your bonnet last night?" she asked.

"Hmm-hmm." I nodded, eyes still closed.

She was working the comb through, plucking at sections of hair gently, when we heard a terrific crash. The mirror on the wall in front of us shook a bit, and our reflections jumped. It sounded like something had been hurled against the wall. After the initial impact, there was a brief silence. Mama and I stared at each other in the mirror. It was Sami's room on the other side of that wall. And then we heard him, his voice filled with the sort of venom I hadn't heard from him since before he went away. He was always so neutral now, like a blank. But the second I heard his voice scream, *God fucking damnit,* through the wall I knew that the rage that used to smolder just under the surface of his skin was still there. At the sound of that old voice we hadn't heard in years, Mama winced. I could see her eyes clench shut in the mirror and her hand, still buried deep in my hair, flinched, the comb ripping through the knot, pulling strands of my hair out with it.

We froze and waited for more. But nothing came. All was quiet now. We could hear a faint shuffling sound from the other side of the wall, and I imagined Sami's body hunched, as he picked up the pieces of whatever he had broken.

"I'm sorry," Mama said eventually. A sizable chunk of my hair dangled from the comb gripped in her hand.

"Don't worry about it," I said, rubbing the back of my tender head, feeling for any bald spots. "I got the rest."

She nodded and placed the comb on the counter.

"I'm sure it's nothing," I said, because I felt I had to say something.

She nodded again, and then walked out of the bathroom.

I finished getting ready for work. My hair was still tangled, but I decided to ignore it and deal with it later. I wrapped it up in my softest gray jersey scarf, but I could still feel it, the hard knot of it, at the back of my head. While I was brushing my teeth, I heard Sami open his bedroom door. I followed the sound of him, tracking his footsteps into the kitchen and then, a few minutes later, out the front door.

Before I left for work, I went into the kitchen to sneak a peach while no one was looking. We had already violated our fast at the diner, and in so many other ways. When I opened the lid of the trash can to throw away the pit, I saw the remains of a cell phone tossed in among the coffee grounds. I stared at it a while: a flip phone smashed into a dozen tiny pieces. And then I eventually covered it with sheets of paper towel that I'd crumpled up and arranged strategically over it, so Mama wouldn't see.

Later, when I had gone to work and come back, I found Sami draped across the sofa, watching Wolf Blitzer conduct an orchestra of red and blue special effects. My brother said hi, asked if I wanted to change the channel, and when I shook my head no, he turned his attention back to Wolf.

"What happened to your cell phone?" I asked him.

"I dropped it," he said.

"Did you drop it and then an elephant also sat on it?" I asked.

He smiled at me over his shoulder. "Did you hear about this earthquake in Mexico?"

Mama came out of the kitchen then to fret over him. I realized by the way she was talking to him that he was sick with something and had stayed home from the shop that day. She had made him soup and was trying to convince him to break his fast until he was feeling better. I could see it was wearing on him, the way his smile got thinner and thinner until, finally, he snapped at her. "Enough, Ma, khalas." She was holding a glass of hibiscus tea out to him, the ice cubes clanking enticingly. She pulled the glass back into her chest, wounded. And I could see the regret etched on his face. He sighed deeply. "I just need to fast, Mama, okay? I'm fine, I promise." He kissed her cheek, turned off the television, and then did something really strange. He started to clean. He just roamed around the house with a bottle of spray cleaner and paper towels, wiping down tables and even the doorknobs. I could tell Mama wanted to tell him to stop, to rest, but she was afraid and confused, so she and I spent the next couple hours just watching him warily.

Lina finally emerged from our room an hour before sunset, and he was still cleaning—this time vacuuming the rugs. I was watching TV in the living room over the droning of the vacuum. When I got up to use the bathroom, I found Lina inside, sitting on the toilet seat, with

Mama standing over her, applying some sort of ointment to the scratch on Lina's face.

"How did this happen?" Mama asked.

Lina looked at me and shrugged as if she had no more lies left inside her.

"A cat," I offered.

Then she started nodding slowly, as if the story was just coming back to her. "We found it wandering around the park." She picked up what I offered her and made a world out of it. "It was meowing like it was lost, and when I bent down to pet it—*whish.*" She made her hand into claws and swiped it across Mama's face.

Mama flinched, laughed. "You're such a softie for animals," she said, sticking a Band-Aid on Lina's cheek. And it was true—Lina was always reaching out her hand, offering herself to beasts and wild things.

We had another normal family dinner, Sami and Baba talking about Mexico. Mama tried to get us all to go to the masjid with her, but when Sami said he didn't feel like going, that let us all off the hook. She went by herself after dinner, and we were all left looking at one another like guilty, pleased children.

After dinner, Sami knocked on our bedroom door. Lina and I were inside, looking out the window and not talking about what had happened. The sky was smeared in pink and purple blobs like a Lisa Frank folder.

"Hey," he said when I opened the door. "Can I borrow some books?"

We looked up at him. Lina looked through our brother for a few seconds like she didn't even know him, then went back to staring at the sky. I pointed at the small, three-shelved bookcase in the corner. "Some over there," I said. It felt weird to have him in our room. The way he stepped in, I could tell he felt weird, too. He moved awkwardly, stepping over a pile of tangled bras on the floor. "They're mostly from school," I said. "Like from English classes and stuff." That seemed to interest him. "School?" he said. I nodded. Sami crouched in front of the bookcase and flipped through a few. He selected *The Great Gatsby* and looked at me.

"This okay?" he said.

"Fine," I said.

"I always meant to read it," he said. "Tried to get it from the library once when I was inside, but when I opened it, like sixty pages fell right out."

"Oh," I said. I had never thought of him reading in prison.

"Thanks," he said.

And then Sami was shuffling out of the room, my book tucked under his arm. For a brief moment, I saw the outlines of our father in his shoulders and I thought an impossible thought: *This boy will grow old, big-bellied, hunch-shouldered.* I wondered what this man-boy would think when he saw my annotations in the margins, if they would make me look smart or stupid. Behind me, a phone buzzed on Lina's nightstand. Mine purred in my pocket. Sami's was smashed into shards at the bottom of the trash.

That night, I dreamed about one of my second cousins in Egypt, a boy a year older than me, who I always secretly thought was cute. In the dream, he had joined ISIS. He was driving through the Holland Tunnel and suddenly put the car in park right in the middle of traffic. I knew what he was about to do and I wanted to stop him. *Don't do it!* my dream brain screamed. *You were going to be a pharmacist!* All the angry New Yorkers were honking and screaming behind him. I knew he would pray first, and then he would say the magic words and make his final disappearance, his final act of revenge. He'd press the button and the whole car would explode and open up this hole in the tunnel, and the cold, polluted waters of the river would rush in.

WHILE HER DAUGHTER DREAMED, the mother lay in bed reading. Her eyes scanned the words and her fingers turned the pages, but her mind was elsewhere. She was worrying about her children. Her daughters bruised and tangled, the way their eyes darted at each other during dinner and then quickly moved away. Her son, who was trying to smother or purge something inside of him, to sanitize it, to wipe it away. She knew it would be a sleepless night, but she was used to that. She was a mother.

When she was a new mother and a new American, she used to lie awake at night and torture herself by remembering a single, sharp detail of the life she had left behind. A life before motherhood, and a life before this enormous, cold country. She would lie awake next to her husband, who always seemed to sleep so soundly, and try to conjure the exact sound of the bell on the Al-Raml tram line. Once she could hear it dinging, she expanded out and gathered up the precise way the tram rattled and swayed like a ship from side to side around tight curves. She could hear the boys standing around the Ibrahimiya station throwing tiny firecrackers against the pavement—she always knew she was approaching that station by the chorus of miniature explosions. And then she could see herself stepping off the tram at Mahatet Al-Raml, watching its blue-and-cream-colored body rattle away from her. She could see the

tip of Saad Zaghloul's hat atop the massive stone body forever marching off toward the sea. And then, when she thought she might cry from
longing, she would close her eyes and listen to the sounds of the Brooklyn streets below and pretend they were the sounds of Alexandria, the
ancient Russian Ladas honking, the tram rumbling past her window.
And then, sometimes, she would be able to sleep.

But her sleep, if it did come, never lasted long. Because then, usually
at around 2:00 a.m., the screams would begin. Her boy, five years old
and eerily silent during the day, would awake and emit a series of blood-
curdling screams that seemed to have neither cause nor remedy. It was
hard for the mother to sleep when she knew what was coming for her.
When she heard the first screams, she was ready to jump out of bed and
rush to his room, leaving her husband sleeping blissfully in their bed.
He could sleep through anything, and as much as she tried not to, she
resented him for it more than anything else in their marriage. It was as
if God had decided that only one of them could sleep and he had taken
it from her. So, sometimes, when she was running toward her screaming son, she was also running away from a creeping rage that made her
feel crazy. After all, how could she blame him for something his body
did while he was unconscious? For the peace she was unable to muster?

She would rush to her boy's room and try to hold his body until
it quieted. But sometimes he slapped her so fiercely that she was com-
pelled to put him down. On those nights, she would sit patiently at the
foot of his bed and watch as he tore around the room, hitting the walls
and kicking his toys and screaming all the while. She sang a little as he
screamed, because sometimes this helped. A neighbor upstairs would
often stomp on the ceiling, and after twenty minutes, when he had
shrieked himself hoarse, her son would finally lie back down in his bed,
shake off his mother's palm, and fall quickly to sleep again. In her belly,
her two daughters kicked. The mother would cup her rejected palm
around her stomach and whisper, "Shh," and these children, obedient,
would stop kicking.

There was one particular night she remembered when she actually
had managed to fall asleep despite the weight of the two babies growing
inside her and despite the night terrors she knew were coming for her

boy. She had been imagining the taste of a fresh fig in her mouth, the soft pinkness of it lulling her to sleep. When she woke, many hours later, her husband was snoring lightly beside her. Besides that, it was silent in the apartment, and in the building, and in the whole city. She lay there in the dark, eyes open, waiting. Maybe a minute and a half later, it started: a high-pitched wail like a ghost's. The mother leapt out of bed. She dashed across the living room, gouging her leg on the corner of the coffee table. But when she got to Sami's room, she paused before opening the door. She listened to his cries—now shrieks, like a street cat in a fight. She took a deep breath and opened the door.

Inside, she could see his little shape moving like a feral animal through the dark. He was darting around the room. She tried to catch him, but he slipped through her fingers. Finally, she was able to corner him against his bureau. She trapped him into a tight hug, trying to pin his arms down at his sides. She knew that if she could just hold on the fit would end in a matter of minutes. If she let him continue to rampage around his room, he might keep going until he pulled the bookshelf down on himself, threw all the books, banged his head against the wall. Sami wriggled one arm out and began slapping his mother on the top of her head. She closed her eyes, winced, and held tight. Sometimes, she counted aloud or in her head. Sometimes, she sang. Sometimes, like tonight, she sat in silence and took it.

But it wasn't just the two of them crouched in the dark like that; the girls were there, too. The mother's hard belly pressed against the boy, caging him, preventing him from hurting himself. And, unable to hurt himself, the boy was left with no choice but to hurt others. And then, suddenly, as he was striking his mother repeatedly atop her head, she could feel a great wave of movement from inside of her. The girls were shifting, rolling, turning over, trading places. And with her stomach pressed against him, the boy could feel it, too. He stopped hitting her. He looked down at her belly, and together they both watched as the girls danced. His hand fell to her stomach and rode the waves. And even after the girls stopped, as suddenly as they had begun, the mother held the boy there, his hand on her belly, his moist cheek falling against her shoulder. She cupped the back of his head in her palm and waited until she felt his breathing come slow and deep before she returned him to his bed. As she walked out, on her way to return to her own bed though not to sleep, she turned back and looked at the dark shape of him. Then she placed a hand on her stomach, right where the boy's had been. She patted it twice, a thank-you to each girl inside. Because, together, they could quell terrors and tame demons.

W HATEVER SAMI HAD, we caught. Or maybe he caught it from us. We didn't have any symptoms, but we were sick, the three of us. So we stayed home. Some sort of quarantine that I didn't even realize was happening until it was over. It started when Sami didn't go to the masjid, and then we didn't go to the masjid. It continued like that for days. Sami didn't leave the building unless it was to take the trash out to the dumpster or to smoke cigarettes on the stoop after the sun set. He didn't go to play basketball or to pray at the masjid. Sami did not leave, and then we did not leave. I called out sick to the Center, told them I was suffering from something highly contagious.

We lay around in the same sweatpants and gym shorts and let our mother press her hand to our foreheads. Baba made us chicken broth, but we would not break our fast. We were sick, but the fasting was our medicine. And staying home became part of the fast—denying ourselves the world outside the apartment and the things we did in it.

Our parents liked us sick. Their three children in one place, sprawled across various pieces of furniture, watching TV, and not going anywhere. I could feel them relax over the next few days. Sometimes I'd look up from the television, and one or both of them would be standing in the doorway to the kitchen, just watching us, with these weird little smiles on their faces.

We kept the shades closed in the living room, and the only light came from the flashing television screen. At first, Sami had it tuned to C-SPAN, said it helped him sleep. But, really, I think he did it because it helped *us* sleep—me and Lina. And on the first day of our quarantine, we did sleep. Out there on the sofa, while our elected representatives debated something, we slept on and off for eleven hours.

We dozed through the rest of the day, until Baba came home from work. I remember waking to Baba's face, upside down, above me. "Yes," he said. "This is the best way to fast. This is what we do in Egypt. We sleep all day and eat all night." So that's what we would do. We would be like bats—Sami, Lina, and I. We would sleep during the day and scavenge for food at night.

We woke on the couch just in time for iftar. Mama and Sami had already prayed. We joined them at the kitchen table, where Mama was arranging dates on a tray. I thought about the date that Faraj had placed between my lips forty-eight hours earlier, then closed my eyes and swallowed the memory away. I pulled a chair out to sit down when Lina said, "Wait. I want to pray first." I could feel Mama intentionally trying not to look at us, as if she thought that if she showed any enthusiasm at all, it would scare us off. "Okay," I said.

In the bathroom, we washed our feet and elbows, the insides of our mouths, our faces and our hands. I pulled two white prayer veils out of the basket that Mama kept under the sink. We stared at each other in the mirror as we pulled them on over our heads. I was looking at her and at myself at the same time, trying to decide whether we looked more like old ladies or schoolgirls, our round faces shrouded in white. Lina adjusted her scarf, tucked it forward so it covered her hairline. "Bismillah," she said. "Bismillah," I said.

We prayed in the living room. We did all three rakat properly. We threw our salaams to the right and then the left, just as we had been taught. Then we pulled off our veils and smoothed our ruffled hair. At the table, Sami and Mama and Baba had started without us. They were eating in silence—just gulps of water and the clanging of serving spoons and chewing and labored swallows. Lina and I sat down with them. I passed her a date, and she nibbled on it slowly, chewing around in circles, until, finally, there was nothing left. Just the pit, trembling in between her index finger and thumb. She held it like that, looking at it, until Mama edged a bowl of rice toward her, gestured with her chin toward a pitcher of water. "Eat, my beautiful, sleepy girl. Eat. Drink." Lina looked at Mama and then let the date pit clatter to her plate. She plucked a single cherry tomato from the salad bowl and placed it in her mouth.

Mama and Baba went to bed not long after dinner, but we stayed up all night, watching TV with Sami. It wasn't so much that we were watching TV *with* Sami; it was more like Sami was there and so were we. We watched movies we had seen a million times before. *Sleepless in Seattle* and *Clueless* and *Ocean's Eleven,* which I had once caught Baba watching in Spanish by mistake. Occasionally, one of the three of us would disappear to the kitchen and return with a container of leftovers and three forks. We didn't talk much. We stayed like this through the night.

We were still awake, sharing a half-eaten tray of basbousa, when Mama woke up at 4:00 a.m. to pray Fajr and eat suhoor. Sami lifted himself from the couch to pray with her. We could hear the two of them splashing wudu in the bathroom in the hallway. Lina looked at me. "You want to?" she asked. "We're up," I said. "Ramadan's almost over," she said. "We're running out of chances," I said. And so we prayed Fajr with Mama and Sami.

We spent the rest of our second day of sickness dozing in front of the television, the droning voices of politicians lulling us to sleep again. It was daylight, but not in the Emam household. We were sealed away in darkness, protected from hunger and thirst.

Later that day, Sami and I were watching the news. Lina was some-where, not far away—the bathroom or the kitchen, maybe. The pundits were talking about some transit cop in Pennsylvania who had tried to join the terrorists over in Libya or Syria. The dummy thought he was chatting with a recruiter, but really he was just talking to an FBI agent the whole time. How sad, I thought. To be a cop who wants to be a ter-rorist but can't even tell the difference between a cop and a terrorist. I looked beside me, and Sami was shaking his head.

"What an idiot," Sami said.

"Yeah," I said.

"Those guys, they don't just talk to anyone online about their plans. You gotta know them. You gotta earn their trust. You have to be initiated. Just like a gang, a big global gang."

I didn't say anything for a minute. I just watched him watching the television out of the corner of my eye. He was leaning in toward the screen, shaking his head.

On the third day of our quarantine, I broke down and texted Faraj. Lina was showering, and Sami was staring out the kitchen window. I snuck into my room and plucked my phone from my bed when no one was looking, because this felt like a violation of the unspoken rules of our agreement—reaching for the outside world. But it was nagging at me, the thought that someone out there was mad at or disappointed in me. It was enough to make me forget that maybe I was the one who was mad or disappointed.

"I'm sorry," I wrote. "Are you mad at me?"

Faraj wrote back almost instantly. "It's fine. Let's just forget it." And I could almost weep with relief. "What are you all doing today? Movie night?" he wrote with a winky face.

That is, in fact, what we were doing, watching movies all day and all night. But I couldn't tell him that. I told him we were all out doing different things. And then I made up a story about some friends of Sami's that didn't exist. I thought of the soccer field in the photo in Faraj's living room. Sami had joined a soccer league. They were out there right now, kicking the ball around a lush green field, sweating into the dusk.

I watched the ellipses blinking on my screen as Faraj typed for a long time. I wanted him to hurry up so I could tuck my phone under my pillow again before Sami or Lina caught me. Then the ellipses disappeared and I panicked briefly until my phone started to buzz in my hand. He was calling me.

"Hey," I whispered when I picked up. "I can't talk."

"That's fine," he said, but then he kept going. "Did you hear about that drone strike in Kabul? All those kids playing soccer in the court-yard? They had just come back from a wedding. They were still dressed up in their nice clothes."

"No," I said.

I pulled the phone away from my ear for a minute to listen to the sounds of my siblings, to check how close they were. Faraj was still talk-ing, but I didn't want to hear any more about terrible things happening to people with names like ours. Why had I texted him? I just wanted to hang up now, to disappear back into our dark living room. I put the phone back to my ear, trying to think of a way to end the conversation.

"So I guess we're both pretty messed up by our brothers," he was saying. I had no idea how we had gotten from a drone strike in Afghani-stan to our brothers. There was laughter in his voice. But I still didn't like it—that maybe this was what we had in common, what drew us together. I made up something about my mom being on my case and said goodbye.

When I hung up, I sat alone on my bed for a minute. Then I heard the door to the bathroom open and smelled Lina's pomegranate body wash. She joined me in the bedroom, put on fresh leggings and a T-shirt, and started playing Young Thug on her computer because she had recently read somewhere that he was "misunderstood" and a "genius" and "post-language." Thugger exploded into the room with his "Ooooooeeeee!"s and his "oogachoogabaybae"s and his "GOW"s and his "uuuuhhhh"s and his "ick"s and his "eep"s. From the kitchen, Sami was narrating what he saw from the window, but we couldn't hear him because we were in a post-language world where words didn't matter anymore. Lina bounced on her bed to the beat, putting down her hairbrush every once in a while to stick her middle finger in the air.

I suddenly felt desperate to shower myself. How long had it been? I'd lost track. I would come back smelling of pomegranate, smelling like Lina, who could rinse anything away. My hair wet and dripping. I'd lotion my skin and sway back into the bedroom feeling like myself again. We'd turn the music all the way up so that we couldn't hear anything else. No car horns, no calls to prayer, no shouts, no phones, not even Sami's murmurings. In the shower, I stood with my eyes open and my mouth shut, willing myself not to let any of the water in.

Later that night, Sami, Lina, and I were posted in front of the television again, letting the movies roll on from one to the next. At some point during *True Lies,* Sami got up and disappeared. I found him in our room. Not in our room exactly, but out on the fire escape. He was sitting very still, cross-legged, staring out to the west. The sun had finally set, but it was taking its sweet time dragging itself across the horizon, leaving pink smears in its wake. Behind me, in the kitchen, I could hear a teakettle screaming.

I climbed through the window and stood next to him on the fire escape. Sami blinked up at me. He made room for me to sit next to him.

"Hey," I said.

"Hey," he said.

Then he got up and went inside, and I thought maybe he was never coming back. But he did come back, carrying two cups of black tea. We sat there watching Bay Ridge stretch after its big meal, sipping our steaming tea and waiting for one of us to say something true to the other. Inside, we could hear Baba singing gently, fragments of poems about lovers and homelands lost long ago.

One block away, a man in a white thobe stood outside of Samira's Fruit Stand. He carried a plastic bag and pulled a yellow mango from it. He took a knife from the pocket of his thobe and began to pare the mango, letting the strips of skin fall to the sidewalk. He ate it standing up, and I knew the juice was dribbling down his chin and hands. And I knew that when he got to the pit he would slurp on it loudly, because no one was around to hear him do it, and that is the very best way to eat a mango. Alone.

Sami took a sip of his tea and then cupped his hands around the mug as if it were cold outside. He turned and looked at me, his face as wide and open as the sky. "Are you okay?" he asked.

I shook my head.

"Can I do anything to help?"

I shook my head again. He was asking the wrong question. It wasn't about what Sami should or shouldn't do. Our whole lives, mine and Lina's, had been circumscribed from our very birth by those same questions.

"Whatever you do hurts," I said. "Do nothing. For a little while, could you just do nothing?" The relief was tremendous. Finally, one right question.

Sami finished his tea and set the cup down; it wobbled precariously on the steel grate. He rubbed his forehead as if trying to rearrange something in his skin.

He nodded silently for a long while. "I could try," he said finally.

"You don't sound very sure," I said.

He picked up his teacup and tipped it back into his mouth even though there was nothing left. "When did you get so smart?" he said, and tried to smile at me. But I wouldn't let him.

"But I'm not," I said. "I'm not smart."

Sami sighed. "I've gotten myself into something," he said suddenly. "Something I don't know how to get out of."

The man in the white thobe had gotten down to the pit of the mango. It was slipping in between his fingers as he sucked on it.

Sami stopped himself then, wiped the gathering beads of sweat off his brow. "Shit," he said. "It's too fucking hot out here."

Then he got up and left.


When he wasn't sleeping or praying, or showering, or watching television, or bringing us a pot of rice and three spoons, Sami was usually looking out windows. Especially when Mama and Baba weren't around. He'd stand next to a window, lift the curtain an inch, and peer sideways out onto the street. He even did this with the window in the bathroom, which was more a slit than a proper window, and only opened to an airshaft.

"There's a kid doing tricks on his scooter like it's a skateboard," he'd call out to us from the kitchen.

Lina and I would glance at each other and then turn back to the television.

"Someone's getting a parking ticket," he'd say, peeping out of his bedroom window. "The meter maid is literally sticking it on the windshield right now."

"Um Hany is doing laundry," he'd say, craning his neck up the airshaft to see our neighbor's underwear hanging off a clothesline.

Lina and I never knew what to say to these observations, so we never said anything, and that seemed to suit Sami just fine. After a few minutes, he'd seem to get his fill of spying on the outside world and he'd rejoin us in the living room, where we'd fill him in on what he'd missed in *Miss Congeniality*.

During the day, he was cloistered inside with us, doing nothing. But at night, he went down to the front stoop to smoke and he never said anything about what he saw during those excursions. I noticed that he smoked a lot all at once, as if to cut down on the number of trips he'd need to make outside. When he came back, after having smoked three or four cigarettes in a row, he'd turn the dead bolt, lock the chain, and bend to take off his shoes with shaking hands. His whole body twitched after those smoke breaks outside; it took him a long time to ease back into the rhythm and safety of our inside world.

"Have a bowl of ice cream," we'd tell him, nudging the carton toward him.

He'd twitch, hesitate, his eyes flicking all over the walls, a pack of cigarettes burning a hole in his pocket. I'd take a bite of the ice cream and Lina would take a bite, and together we'd exclaim over its excellence. Finally, Sami would lean over and scoop a huge spoonful into his mouth. Then, calm and cold, he'd lean back into the armchair and close his eyes, his head doing a sort of heroin nod.

"Good, isn't it?" we'd say.

"Yes." He'd nod. "Good."


On the fourth day of our sickness, Lina got her period. She came into our room while I was sitting on my bed, changing from one pair of sweatpants to another. She grabbed a forbidden tampon from the secret stash we kept hidden in our closet. Then she knelt down, rested her cheek on my bare knee, and cried silently and completely for thirty seconds. When she stopped, she wiped her face, and looked up at me with shining cheeks.

"Alhamdulillah," she said, clutching the tampon to her chest like a talisman.

"That's good. That's good," I said. And then—quietly, because I did not want to upset her—I asked, "Do you think you should get tested?"

She looked at me, her face like a stone.

"You don't even know who . . ." And then I trailed off, because she didn't want us to talk about that.

She got up and slipped the tampon under the elastic on her shorts, and covered it with her shirt. Then she left me sitting there with my own body.

I got my period the next day. And even though I was a virgin, I still said a little prayer of thanks as I slid my own tampon in, legs spread over the toilet.

ON THE SIXTH DAY of quarantine, the father came home with news of the outside world, and it was as if a great stone had been pushed from the opening of their cave. Light came pouring in.

Someone, according to the father, or more likely several someones, had urinated in the mosque. Piss splattered against the walls and drizzled onto the carpets. The place reeked like an animal's cage. It was as if they had walked around with buckets of the stuff, scattering it like chicken feed—a little here, a little there, a little everywhere. Whoever did this must have prepared for days in advance, hoarding all that urine in empty soda bottles, Tupperware containers, water guns? The father wondered how they felt each time they unzipped their pants to take a leak: Proud? Patriotic? Aroused?

They also left a message—spray-painted over a large glass plaque with scripture engraved into it: "now THIS is a hate crime." They were clever vandals.

The mosque was left unlocked all night long, because, during Ramadan especially, it was where people who had nowhere else to go slept. There had been a few women asleep upstairs at the time. But, when questioned, they said they had seen and heard nothing.

The police assured Imam Tariq that they took this sort of thing very seriously—there was even talk of getting the FBI involved. And they hesitated at the entrance, looking down at their shoes, wondering if they should still remove them in a time like this. Imam Tariq laughed sadly and told them it was fine to keep their shoes on: "It's already been defiled." So the cops marched in, took photos and samples of the drenched carpets. Once they departed with the evidence, Imam Tariq got on the phone and began gathering his congregants.

The people showed up with crowbars, pliers, gallon bottles of bleach, old towels, surgical masks, paint thinner, steel wool, ladders, vacuums, mops, brooms, knee pads, window cleaner, paper towels, bottles of every off-brand disinfectant sold at the dollar store, plastic tarps, and new prayer mats. They would strip the place, empty it completely, scrub it until their hands cracked and bled. But it would never really be clean again, and they all knew it.

The father watched his neighbors and customers flock to the mosque from the window of his shop. "Why would anyone want to pee on the masjid?" he asked aloud, but no one was there to answer him. He wiped down the counters, shook out the welcome mat, swept the aisles. He made sure that all the labels of all the canned goods were facing out. He stirred a vat of olives so that the red chili peppers that settled at the bottom were visible through the clear plastic lid. He wanted his customers to know what they were buying. He wanted everything to be clear, straightforward. He got a bottle of Windex and a rag and cleaned the glass case that displayed the meat. He sold only the very best meat. Everyone knew that. He wanted them to see it.

He didn't understand other people.

"And they call us barbarians," he grumbled to himself.

He went to the supply closet in the back and got an empty plastic crate and filled it with cleaning supplies. Then he locked up, closing early for the day, and went upstairs to fetch his family.

"And they call us barbarians," the father said to his family, gathered around him. His wife was shaking her head in a way he found very satisfying. For once, she was pleased with him.

For the last few days, his children had been suffering from the same strange ailment. Pale and sallow-skinned, they slept all day, yet ate heartily at night, devouring whole tubs of ice cream, scraping the last bits of rice from the bottom of pots, as if they could never possibly be full again. But now they were reinvigorated by the outrage. "That's disgusting," they said. "Who would do that?"

"Exactly!" the father said. "Who? Who? Who?"

No one could answer him.

The boy was standing in the kitchen, peering out the window, watching the people of Bay Ridge gather outside the mosque. People who had raised him, screamed at him from their porch steps, called his mother to report his whereabouts. People who had condemned him long ago, who merely shook their heads in disappointment as he passed. People who lectured him. People who ignored him. People who loved him, people who were scared of him. People who remembered the day he got sentenced, who brought his mother and father food. People who were there the day he returned, who brought his mother and father food.

Was there no end to their people's capacity for humiliation? he thought. He wouldn't go down there and help them mop up the piss of kafirs. He'd rather let the mosque rot. He would stay inside this apartment forever.

Then he had a wild thought. A thought that thrilled him. What if the vandals were Muslims? And not the self-hating variety—you know, the pornographers who peddle liberal Western fantasies of mutilated clitorises, multiple wives, and homemade bombs. No, what if they were self-loving Muslims who wanted to gather all their brothers and sisters to this spot? To unite them in a great cleansing. To keep them safe under the roof of a holy place. And then, when the people had finished scrubbing, they would step out of the mosque to find the world on fire. Burning under a black banner. Everything in ruins. Except them and that mosque.

Then he had another thought, even wilder. What if no one had pissed on the mosque? The piss was there—they could smell it; they could feel it squishing under their feet. But what if it just appeared, like a flood or a lamb, one of God's many tests? The litmus of twenty-first-century believers. What if this were a mere footnote on all their résumés come Judgment Day? When their community was under attack, what would they do? "I see," the Angel Gabriel would say, sliding his glasses down his cirrus nose, "that on the twenty-fifth day of Ramadan, in the year 1436 a.h., when a house of God was defiled, you proved yourself to be quite the pussy."

What should he do?

The father was calling him. Beckoning him. They would all go to the mosque to help clean, he said. The boy left his perch in the kitchen and joined the rest of the family in the living room. They were slipping on their shoes. The mother gestured him closer to her. She pressed a cool palm to his forehead.

"Why don't you stay here?" she said to him. "Recover."

But the father was insistent—they all had to go, the whole Emam family. "He's fine, ya Maryam. He is a grown-up man. He will come." His voice was surprisingly stern. He was issuing one of the few unilateral demands of his entire life. But then the father looked at his son, the grown-up man, his little boy, and patted him tenderly on the cheek. "Taala, ya habibi. Taala," he said.

The girls froze, their shoes half fastened, and waited to see what the boy would do. They would not go if he did not go, not because they did not want to help clean, not because they'd rather stay and watch TV than wipe up some stranger's piss, but because they could not go outside without him. They looked to him to see if the quarantine was over. Were they safe to walk outside? Had enough time elapsed? The boy shook his head—there would never be enough time. But he bent down and put his shoes on anyway. The girls did the same.

THE MASJID WAS PACKED with people. There were just too many of us there at one time. It would have been better, more efficient, if we'd organized ourselves into shifts. Mama kept trying to explain this to anyone who would listen.

"The people in each shift will have a specific task," she said. "Like, the first shift can rip up the carpet. And the second shift can vacuum and sweep up the debris. And the third shift can disinfect the floor beneath it, and so on and so on."

But no one would listen. "That just sounds like a lot of work," one woman said. Arabs preferred chaos, no lines, no shifts, no schedules. Poor Mama had always been alone in her desire for order.

And so we were all crammed in there together. I tried to kneel down to scrub a patch of wall, but my thigh pressed against Mama's ass and my arm pressed into Lina's boobs. We were up on the second floor, the women's section, which, as far as anyone could tell, had not been vandalized, but we felt the need to clean it anyway. And the men had already taken over the first floor, were prying up strips of carpet and tossing them into a big, stinking pile in the middle of the prayer hall. Rubbing up against my mother and sister, trying to find something to clean, I thought that if anyone so much as sneezed the floor might collapse beneath us and a battalion of Muslimas would fall from the sky.

Eventually, we decided that Mama would stand and scrub the wall above us and Lina and I would remain kneeling on the floor, scrubbing the baseboards. Mama's sponge sent rivulets of soapy water running down to us. Lina and I made a game of rushing to catch them before they spilled to the floor. Mama smiled down at us. But then I saw her eye catch the scratch on Lina's cheek. It was crusting over with a burgundy scab, surrounded by a yellow-tinged bruise. I had noticed Mama glancing at it a lot in the past few days.

"A cat did that?" she asked, again, pointing down with the wet sponge to Lina's face.

Lina nodded, brushed her cheek with the backs of her fingers.

I could see the cat now, an orange tabby with white stripes. I could see its claws whipping through the air, hear its hot hiss.

We scrubbed and swept and deep-cleaned the carpet. At prayer time, the crowd thinned a bit as people left to walk to another mosque, one that had not been defiled, down the street. Lina and I took a break outside to breathe some fresh air. On our way down, I spotted Sami scrubbing a spot on the floor. He was on his knees, both hands grasping the wooden handle of a scrub brush, his shoulders raised up to his ears. He was scrubbing back and forth, back and forth. I could actually see droplets of sweat flying off his body. I wanted to go in there, to stand over him, to touch his shoulder gently. To remind him that he could stop now. But there was something about the way he leaned all of his body weight onto that scrub brush, the way he rubbed himself into that floor, that told me it was too late anyway. The quarantine, the time of rest, the time of doing nothing, was over.

Outside, Lina and I sat on a bench very near the spot where Imam Ghozzi had been sliced, and watched the people coming and going. The crowds dispersed just before sunset. We went home and took turns showering the piss and the disinfectant off of us. Then we ordered pizza from Elegante and ate it in front of the television. We all looked as if we had returned from a long, tiresome journey. Mama fell asleep before nine, and Baba fell asleep with a paper plate smeared with tomato sauce resting on his belly. Sami, after smoking too many cigarettes out on the front stoop, returned inside and looked out the kitchen window.

Lina and I were rereading an old copy of *Glamour* that I'd stolen from the waiting room of the Arab Center. We sat on the sofa, reading an essay about different brands of mascara that truly lengthened your eyelashes. From the kitchen, Sami called out to us.

"They know who did it," he said. "There are cameras all over this city. Even in the sky."

Lina and I looked at each other and then at the walls and ceiling. We could smell the stench of the cigarette smoke clinging to his clothes all the way from the living room.

"If they really wanted to find them, they could."

We didn't say anything. We waited for him to come back, to sit down, to eat ice-cream sandwiches with us and watch a bad movie about people who are happy in the end.

THAT NIGHT, while his parents slept, and while his sisters typed furtively into their cell phones, the boy left home again. He slipped out the front door, as he had done countless times before in his life, and stood out on the front stoop. He thought of smoking a cigarette. Then he thought it might be better to wait. To delay gratification until the job was done. To keep him itching, to keep him hungry.

He walked across the street to the masjid. Inside, an old man sat dozing in a chair. Sami stood in the center of the prayer hall and breathed in deeply. He looked around at the walls and corners and ceilings for signs of a hidden camera. He stared at the sleeping man. He knew of at least one paid informant in this mosque, but there were probably others. It was important to do everything with intention these days, because you were always being watched. Not like when he was a kid—back then, there was so much he did that no one ever saw. He walked the perimeter of the prayer hall, listening. He drew a lighter from his pocket. Flicked it open and closed. All the chemicals. It would burn bright.

It was the sound that eventually awoke the old man, hired as a security guard for ten dollars an hour. A scratching noise. A scraping. A shushing. Shushshushshush, shushshushshush. When he touched the boy's shoulder, the boy jumped, turned, his face opening up into a snarl. The man snatched his hand back from the boy's shoulder as if he had been burned. But then the boy's face had erased itself, his features rearranging and shifting, and when they came back together, he was just a lamb. Together, the man and the lamb looked down at the floor: A spot on the linoleum scrubbed so hard that the burnt-orange color had been rubbed right out. Now just a dull beige square, an absence. The boy got up and let the scrub brush clatter to the floor. He walked outside, and out on the sidewalk, under the buzzing streetlamp and the quivering black eye of the camera beneath it, he took a cigarette from his pocket and flicked open his lighter with a shaking hand.

Back in the apartment, now that the spell had been broken, now that they were flung back out into the world, Lina and Amira lay on their beds with their backs to each other. Facing the wall, underneath the sheets, they typed invitations. "I'm here," they wrote. "Come and get me. Let's try this again."

M Y ALARM WENT OFF at five o'clock the next morning. I didn't turn it off right away—I let it ring and ring, so Lina would get up, too. She threw a pillow at me, then a hair elastic from her nightstand, then her phone charger. Still I let the alarm shriek. While I waited for her to get up, I stepped outside onto the fire escape, because I wanted to see the men of the neighborhood smoking their last cigarettes. And, sure enough, there was Abu Tamer standing under the awning of his dollar store, smoking. Two dozen inflatable animals hung above his head. I thought I could hear Baba shouting at some deliverymen at the back entrance to the shop.

When Lina finally got up, we got dressed quickly and went down-stairs for breakfast at Baba's. He had opened the shop early that morn-ing; it would be a busy few days while everyone prepared for the big feast at the end of Ramadan. When we walked into Abu Nuwas, he was wrapping a package of chicken thighs for a woman in a bright-red hijab. We hopped up on the bar stools, and Lina put her head down on the counter. "Ya banat," he said, "you knew your baba was feeling lonely down here, eh?" And then, to the woman putting her change away in her purse, he said, "Look at those beautiful girls. Can you believe they are mine?"

The woman looked at us and for a moment I was terrified she was going to say no. But she didn't. She just tilted her head, studying us, and smiled. "Mashallah," she said. "You are a lucky baba."

After the woman left, he cooked us breakfast and told us some dream he'd had about a duck. I was only half listening. I had barely set foot in the shop since Sami came home. But now, after spending a week cloistered in the apartment, I was trying to remember why it had felt so urgent to stay away. My fear was changing shape inside me. I knew I should be afraid of something, but I was no longer sure what.

"And now," Baba said, "inshallah no one come in to buy some duck for dinner, because I will be thinking about my friend." And then he told us a story we'd heard many times before, about how his little sister fell in love with all the rabbits Teta kept in a hutch on the rooftop of their house. Auntie Mona gave each of them a name and after school would come up to the roof and stroke each one between the ears and say, "Hello, Ringo," "Hello, Cher," "Hello, Mick Jagger," "Hello, Olivia Newton John." Until, one day, Teta, afraid her daughter would grow up weak and unable to perform the tasks required of a woman, forced her daughter to kill one for supper, to hold it by the ears and slice its neck open with a small, sharp knife. They recited Qur'an as Cher bled to death.

Baba opened a can of ful medames, heated it up in a small saucepan, and mashed the beans lightly with a fork, and then with a squeeze of lemon, slid a bowl over to each of us. He looked into Lina's face and saw how badly she needed sustenance. "Eat, ya malika," he said. "God does not want you to suffer."

Lina smiled shyly and began to eat. She finished the whole bowl as he stood there watching, smiling, and nodding his head.

I didn't give him enough credit, this baba, who seemed to intuit when his girls needed a man to be proud of us, to look at us and sigh, like he really couldn't believe his luck.

As we were coming back from the shop, our bellies full of Baba's food, we ran into Sami in the stairwell. He was wearing basketball shorts and a tank top, and he looked supremely normal with the basketball tucked casually under one arm.

For the past few days, we had been learning how to be together again, the three of us, but now I wondered if we were back to being separate entities. The girls and the boy.

Sami nodded at us and said, "I'm on my way to get my ass whooped by a bunch of fifteen-year-olds."

We laughed, and then, to everyone's amazement, Lina leaned over on her step and planted a kiss on his cheek.

Sami blushed up to the tips of his ears, and I thought maybe everything could be okay. There were people out there who wanted to piss in our mosques, and men who wanted to do unspeakable things to our bodies, but maybe, if we just stayed here, together in Bay Ridge, we could push it all away. Maybe I had been getting it wrong all summer. Maybe we didn't need to run away; maybe we just needed to stay.

That night, after Mama and Baba had gone to bed and Sami was staring blankly into the House of Representatives, Lina and I sat out on the fire escape, eating cherries from a plastic bag and spitting the pits out onto the street below. I had just received my orientation packet from Brooklyn College, and I was complaining about the number of walking tours listed in the organized activities for freshmen. I liked to complain about college around Lina, because I thought it might shrink the difference between us.

"And apparently between walking tour number one and walking tour number two, I have to take an Arabic exam so I can test into a more advanced class. Why can't they just take my word for it? I mean, I'm an Arab. Look around!" I gestured in a sweeping motion to Bay Ridge all around us, to all the Arabic awnings and the Arabic conversations on the street down below, and the Arabic TV shows blaring from neighboring apartments. Then I looked over at Lina and saw that she was crying silently next to me. She wasn't even moving—her body was totally still. But even in the half-dark, I could see the glisten of tears rolling down her face.

I reached out and put a hand on her shoulder, but she shrugged me off.

"Do you think we should tell someone?" I whispered.

"Tell someone about what?" she said.

"About what happened to you that night. About whoever—"

But she cut me off. "Nothing happened to me. No one was with me."

I started to protest, to say: But what about that cut on your face? And what about the bruises on your thigh, and what about the tender pain throbbing inside of you? But she stopped me by taking the bag of cherries and hurling it over the edge of the fire escape with a short, low scream.

A car with thundering bass rumbled by, and Amr Diab told us we were the light of his eye. Then Lina turned and looked at me with a weird expression, like she didn't even know me.

"Don't let me go back," she said.

I didn't know if she meant back to Lotus or back to Andres or that motel, but I nodded anyway, because I would have promised her anything.


We were women preparing for a feast that we could not yet eat. Smashing nuts, boiling sugar and orange rinds in water, battling with the sticky, papery sheets of dough. All of us looking forward to the moment when we could pour the syrup over top of the layered pastry, watching the phyllo sheets crackle and seize under the hot sugar. When Mama wasn't looking, Lina and I stole the glass bottle of rose water, meant for the dessert, and dabbed it on our wrists. We imagined that this is what Cleopatra or Nefertiti must have smelled like.

Outside, men gathered at the sidewalk cafés preparing their shisha pipes for sunset, packing in the wet tobacco, wrapping the coals, their fingers stained brown and smelling of strawberry.

Mama was bent over an old cookbook, the pages wrinkled and flecked with bits of food. She made this recipe every year for Eid, but every year she frowned over those pages like they contained the most complex mathematical equations. Long ago, our grandmother, our mother's mother, who died before we were born, had made notes in the margins, mainly to disagree with the recipe author, to suggest better ways of doing things. But those markings, made in pencil, had long since faded. And every year Mama pulled the book down from a shelf above the refrigerator and squinted at the pages. "There," Mama would say, pointing to a smear of gray. We'd lean in close, guessing what the smear might have said. This year, we decided that one particular marking said "more pistachios" in Arabic, and even though it didn't look anything like that to me, we sat there, shelling more pistachios, coughing from the dust and tiny particles of skin and shell.

When Mama consulted the book, Lina and I both raced to check our phones, which sat like hot bombs in our laps. We scrolled through photos, comments, typing replies hastily with our syrup-coated fingers. Faraj had sent me a photo. It was of me, sitting at my desk at the Center, picking at my cuticles, looking bored and chubby. He must have taken it through the glass, because there was a glare of light reflecting above my head. I didn't know when he had taken the photo. I was studying it to see what I looked like through his eyes, to the world, when Lina blew up my spot.

"Who are you texting, Amira?" she said, and Mama's head whipped up from the cookbook.

"Who are *you* texting, Lina?" I shot back.

"No one," she said. "See?" She showed me her hands, which were coated in coconut flakes and tiny green studs of pistachio. The sneaky bitch had already tucked her phone safely back between her thighs. We were engaged in an unspoken game of chicken. She didn't want me texting Faraj anymore, and I didn't want her texting Andres anymore, but neither of us could stop until the other one did first. Pretty soon, we'd crash headfirst into each other.

"Is there someone I should know about, Amira?" Mama asked. I denied it vehemently, even offering my phone up to her for inspection, a risky gamble that had Lina widening her eyes at me. But there was butter bubbling in a saucepan on the stove, and in the few seconds of our exchange, it had gone from brown to burned. Mama cursed, and then cursed herself for cursing. She told me to put my phone away and help her keep an eye on the butter, then poured the burnt stuff down the sink and plopped a new stick into the pan to melt. I tucked my phone in between the elastic waistband of my shorts and my skin. I smiled at Lina, like *Game on.*

Downstairs, the father was joking with the customers, his fingers deftly weighing, slicing, and wrapping. The boy worked in the back, occasionally emerging through the swinging metal door with a tray or box of something. The customers would eye him warily, suspicious that perhaps the meat they were holding, neatly wrapped in their hands, was not as nice as that piece on the boy's tray. The father was a sweet man. But the boy, the boy was not to be trusted.

He handed his father a full tray and took an empty one back with him, pushed open the door with his bony hip, and sighed in relief as the cool, dark storeroom greeted him. Sami started unloading a delivery from the abattoir, inspecting each squab, careful not to snap its fragile bones. Since he emerged from his self-imposed isolation in the apartment, the first thing he did was go out and get a new phone. It buzzed now in his pocket, and he dropped the small bird he was holding. It landed with a dead thump on the stainless-steel table, breast down, wings spread, as if it were trying to take flight again. His slippery fingers reached down to his phone. "Hello?" his voice called out among the dead.

"Yes," he said. "Yes, I'm ready."

Sami picked up the fallen squab with his free hand and tucked its wings neatly under its body.

He listened to the voice on the other side.

"I know," he said.

"No one," he said.

And then, suddenly, he became agitated. He ran his greasy hand back and forth across the top of his head.

"Can you see me right now?" he asked.

The voice or the voices on the other side tried to calm him, but it wasn't working.

"I know you have cameras. And drones. Why can't you use those?"

The voice or voices talked for a long time. Sami nodded his head as he listened. He kneaded his left palm with his right thumb. *"Okay,"* he said, trying to cut off the voices, but the voices would not be silenced. They went on for a while longer, and they appeared to be making sense, because he straightened up and stopped fidgeting.

"I know," he said.

"You're right."

"It has to be me."

Sami hung up the phone and slipped it back into his pocket, the black faux-leather case marred with oily fingerprints. He thought he could hear the sound of breathing all around him, but he was the only thing alive in the room. He was afraid to go upstairs and face the girl who would surely know the instant she saw him that he had failed her again. Another broken promise. *Do nothing for a while.* He had really tried. He would stop if he knew how.

He would do something special, he thought. He wouldn't squander any more time. He would give them all, the whole family, but especially her, a day they would never forget.

W HEN SAMI WALKED IN through the door, our stomachs were having a conversation. Mine grumbled loudly, and a few seconds later, Lina's did too. A hungry call and response between our guts.

"Hi, Bob," Lina said, squeezing her tiny rolls of belly fat together so it looked like a mouth.

"Hey, Frank," I said, pressing my own, more substantial rolls.

"It's hot as Hades in here, ain't it, Bob?" Lina said.

"Sure is, Frank," I said.

Sami stood in the doorway, smiling at us. He smiled like we were so much weirder than he'd ever known. Like he was pleasantly surprised, and maybe even a little proud.

"Quit standing in the doorway like a creep," my stomach said to him.

"Yeah, quit being such a creep," Lina's stomach said to him.

"Hey, Bob; hey, Frank," Sami said. "What are you doing tonight? I have an idea."

We dropped our stomachs. We looked up at him, tilted our heads.

"When's the last time you went to Coney Island?" he said.

He said it—*Coney Island*—like it was Bali or Paris. I could feel the cotton candy melting on my tongue and taste the salt in the wind and hear the shrieks of people riding the Cyclone.

He smiled. We smiled back.

It was easy to convince Mama. Sami wanted to go somewhere with the whole family. She would have gone with him to the dump if he had asked. And together the four of us convinced Baba to close the shop for the rest of the evening. "But what if somebody need meat?" Baba asked.

"There's a grocery store," Lina suggested.

Baba made a disgusted face but went across the street anyway to try and get the Tercel started. It had been having trouble ever since my trip to Jersey. Something had broken there, but I wasn't sure what.

Upstairs, Mama fretted about what to wear. It was a long time since I had seen her this excited about anything. She ended up choosing a silvery-gray abaya and the blue hijab Sami had just bought for her.

All of this was happening because Sami had found some deal online for five tickets to the Brooklyn Cyclones, a Minor League baseball team none of us had ever heard of. In fact, none of us had watched an entire baseball game in our lives, but it didn't seem to matter.

The trip was blessed from the start. We found a parking spot with a busted meter on West 19th Street and Mermaid Avenue, which was basically a miracle in the summertime. "We park for free!" Baba kept shouting. "We park for free!"

As soon as we got out of the car, we could hear screams from the roller coasters, ice-cream truck music, voices over loudspeakers. There were girls in bikini tops and cutoff shorts, and oiled bodybuilders, and old men in Speedos, and Russian grandmas in sack dresses. Lina forgot all about the baseball game; she wanted to head straight for the freak show. As we walked toward the park, we argued about what to do first. Mama wanted to ride some lame spinning-teacup thing, and Baba wanted to skip the park altogether and follow the sound of bongos to the boardwalk. And Sami just kept smiling and opening his arms wide, as if he were Willy Wonka inviting us to drink from the chocolate river. "Whatever you guys want," he said.

We stood outside the park gates and argued until Sami turned to me and said, "Amira should decide." Lina smirked, sure that I would go with her idea. Baba pantomimed drumming and Mama pointed at the twirling teacups near the entrance. I wanted to make the right decision.

To our right was the baseball stadium, and from it emanated some old-timey music, interrupted periodically by the recorded roars of fans who did not exist. "I don't want to miss the start of the game," I said, and Sami nodded at me like I had made the right choice.

Inside the stadium, we sat high up on the bleachers. The Parachute Jump Tower pulsed pink in front of us. We could see the ocean. The wind blew Lina's hair into knots, and Mama and I pounded fists—one perk of the hijab.

"That's where the gophers come out," Lina said, pointing to the mound in the center of the field. "And then all the players run around trying to whack them with their bats."

Mama said that it was like freeze tag—everyone ran around until they got to base and they were safe. Baba said that the goal of the game was to hit the mascot—a seagull flapping his wings idiotically near the dugout—as many times as you could with the ball. I said that in the fifty-seventh inning the cheerleaders would swap places and outfits with the players. Sami just tried explaining the actual rules of baseball, and we all booed him until he laughed and said, "All right. *Damn.*"

We broke our fast at 8:28 p.m. with nachos and chili fries. After we swarmed the food like carrion, we took a selfie together, all of us squishing into the frame, grinning like big, happy idiots. I realized it was the first photo of all five of us together maybe since Sami was thirteen and Lina and I were eight.

The game ended. I don't remember who won. We walked out into the night, and there was no argument this time: we headed for the beach. We strolled along the boardwalk, listening to waves we could barely see crashing gently against the sand. We came across a drum circle, seven or eight people whacking palms against bongos, and some other people dancing between them. We stood around and watched them, all of us bobbing our heads to the rhythm. I thought that pretty soon Mama or Baba would tell us that it was time to go home, head back to Bay Ridge, where our mosque still smelled of a stranger's piss, where Sami stared out windows and smashed phones, where Lina and I would glue ourselves back to our text messages, praying someone would notice us, name us, call us away, where Baba sang sad songs from a country he hadn't laid eyes on in decades. I was ready to plead: *Five more minutes? Not yet. Please. Let's stay a little while longer.*

But then Baba stepped into the circle. No one acknowledged him. The drummers didn't raise their eyebrows or smile or beckon him closer. The other dancers all had their eyes closed or were otherwise looking past us, beyond us. Baba stepped into their circle and began to dance, and it was as if he had always been there. He shimmied his shoulders and danced in the beautifully feminine way that Egyptian men dance, and the crowd, who like us had gathered around to watch, loved him. Sami, Lina, and I were standing around slack-jawed, open-mouthed, hitting each other repeatedly on the arms, as if we wanted to make sure that the others were really seeing it, too.

"Can you believe this?" I said to Mama. And she laughed and said, "Yes, yes, I can."

The moment I had been dreading finally came when Baba, his brow dotted lightly with sweat, returned to us. "It's getting late," Mama said, although she said it apologetically, not relishing the role of mother, perpetual ruiner of fun.

"Wait," Sami said. "Let's do one ride before we go."

He pointed at the magnificent Ferris wheel shining above us, spinning slowly through the hot summer air, the gondolas rocking gently back and forth. It was the god of Coney Island, the temple at which we all worshipped. Yes, we would ride the Wonder Wheel.

We lined up and didn't say much as we waited. Mama clutched Baba's hand, eyeing the topmost gondolas warily. When it was finally our turn to board, we split up without any discussion: Mama and Baba, me and Lina, and Sami on his own. I knew he'd rather be alone, spinning across the top of the city, peering out of the greatest window.

At first, Lina and I shrieked as we swayed in the wind, clutching each other and saying things like *If I go down, you go down with me, bitch.* Mama and Baba were above us, Sami below us, until we reached the top of the wheel and the order reversed. We chased each other like that, up and away, down and back, in a circle. We fell silent, gazing out to our separate corners of the universe, to other versions of ourselves, in nightclubs and motel rooms and on rooftops all across New York. Occasionally, I looked up at Mama and Baba or down at Sami. Baba had his head on her shoulder and appeared to be asleep. Mama couldn't relax; she kept trying to keep an eye on her children, her corneas stretching in opposite directions, trying to keep all three of us in her sights. She smiled nervously at me every time I caught her eye. Sami hovered below me somewhere. I looked down and tried to decipher him from between the cables and bars and flashing lights that came between us. I felt trouble creeping toward us just as our gondolas inched slowly toward the end, the earth, and I wished desperately that I could do something to forestall it.

Our gondola lurched to the bottom, and the whole machine crunched to a halt. I heard a terrible snapping noise, and then the bar was released and we were free. Back on the ground, we huddled together and began the slow march back to the car. The night was over. There was a parking ticket on the windshield of the Tercel. We stared at it silently until Baba crumpled it up into his fist and stuffed it into his pocket.

On the way back home, crammed into the car, we were all sleepy. When we were three blocks from home, we passed a goat tied up to a bicycle rack, a scrawny black-and-white goat with a big white mustache. "Tough luck, goat," Lina said as we passed him: though for a few days he'd eat like a king, soon a man would come—maybe even our father—a man who knew how to slit his throat so that the meat would be blessed.

"Do you remember when Baba had live rabbits at the shop?" I asked Lina.

"I named them all," she said. "Just like Auntie Mona did with the rabbits in Egypt. Biggie and Diddy and Ice Cube and Method Man, and some others I forget now."

Sami said, "You named a rabbit Method Man?"

"Oh, she was my favorite one." Lina smiled.

We all smiled then, remembering Baba's brief experiment selling live rabbits, before the Health Department shut it down. But suddenly there was a loud popping noise from under the hood of the car. We had rolled over a pressure cooker, a grenade, an IED shoddily assembled from bits of wire and nails and acetone. We were dead. We were flying through the air, my arm hurtling west and my leg hurtling east, and we'd end up in a tangle of Emams. Was this Lina's hand or Amira's? The father's foot or the son's? The mother's bright-blue hijab would call out from the wreckage.

The car hissed. Baba slowed down and pulled over. I looked down and found my arms were still attached to my shoulders. There was smoke billowing out from under the hood, a hot white cloud obscuring the road ahead of us. People were running out from their front stoops and yelling. Baba ignored them, scraped the car's tires against the curb, threw it into park, cut the engine, and turned around to us. "Yalla, get out, get out, get out!"

We ran away from the car and watched as it seemed to empty itself of all its rage. There were no actual flames—just a rising gray cloud coming from the Tercel's guts. Everyone stood around for a few minutes, watching the Tercel die. I looked around for Lina, wanting to mark the moment somehow, to mourn a little, the car that took us away from Bay Ridge and the car that brought us home again. But she wasn't standing with the other Arabs gathered around to witness the destruction of Kareem Emam's twenty-year-old car. I spotted her walking on the other side of the street, toward the doomed goat. I watched as she sat down on the sidewalk next to him and stroked his back. I think she whispered something into his ear as he tried to eat her hair. And then, when she thought no one else was looking, she untied the goat. He just stood there looking at her until she gave him a little kick, and then we both watched, from two different sides of the street, as he trotted away, his rope leash dragging behind him.

I thought Baba might cry. We were waiting around for the tow truck. We all smelled of oil and smoke and concession-stand grease. The tow truck arrived, and we watched the Tercel get dragged away. When it was finally gone, Baba looked across the street and said, "Hey, didn't there use to be goat over there?"

We were exhausted after our evening in Coney Island, and yet none of us seemed able to sleep that night. Each of us wandered around the apartment, sometimes sitting on the sofa to watch a few minutes of television, sometimes encountering someone in the kitchen eating leftovers out of the fridge, sometimes napping intermittently.

At two in the morning, I woke up sweating in my bed. I had dreamed that Faraj was pounding on the front door, shouting words in an incomprehensible language, a language that used to be Arabic, or that was a new Arabic I had not yet learned. I couldn't fall back asleep, so I followed the sound of the television into the living room. Sami was lying on the love seat, across from Baba on the couch. They were watching a soccer game and passing a bag of Hershey's Kisses back and forth. I sat down on a pillow on the floor and squinted at the screen.

"Who's playing?" I asked, but neither of them answered me. Sami just handed me the bag of Kisses, and I took a handful and passed it back. I watched for a while, rooting dispassionately for the green-and-yellow team. But the chocolates filled my mouth with an unbearably sweet, chalky coating. I got up to brush my teeth and try to sleep again.

I walked past my parents' bedroom toward the bathroom. A light was on inside. I could picture my mother squinting at the pages of her book, her reading glasses slipping down her nose. A floorboard creaked as I walked by.

"Amira?" she called out to me.

I pushed the door open and entered the dimly lit room. She was lying in the bed, reading a novel about women spies during World War II.

"Did you eat enough?" she asked me, putting her book down on the nightstand.

"Yes, Mama," I said.

She smiled at me and told me that she could see the effects of fasting on me, that I had the look of the faithful.

"What? Malnourished?" I asked.

She laughed. "No, you look cleansed. Your skin is glowing."

I rubbed my palm across my face, but all I felt was New York City grime. She patted the bed next to her, and I approached. I sat tentatively on the edge and wondered what she wanted—to go over the remaining chores and errands we needed to complete before Eid, to rope me into going to the masjid with her, to tell me, as she did every year, that the last few days of Ramadan were the holiest?

"Come here," she said, pulling the blanket open so I could slip inside. It was still sweltering outside, but for some reason the warmth emanating from under the blanket called to me, and I couldn't help but lie down beside her. She wrapped the blanket over us both and curled her arm around my stomach. With her other hand, she stroked my hair.

"Your hair is all Africa," she said. And didn't I know it? And didn't I pretend to love it and not to crave the silky-smooth, blows-in-the-wind European hair that Lina had inherited from her?

I didn't know what to say, so I didn't say anything at all. But it did feel nice just to lie there with her, spooning, mother and daughter. In those rare moments when my mother seemed at peace, when it felt like the frenetic, broken clock inside her had stopped ticking momentarily, all I wanted in the world was to fall into her.

Lina poked her head into the room, and Mama lifted the covers for her to join us. She skipped over and crawled in on the other side.

"Isn't this wonderful?" Mama whispered into my neck, her breath tickling my skin. "Your father and brother in the living room, watching TV with their big smelly feet on the coffee table, and me and you two in here, the girls, cuddled up."

I wanted to sink into the moment, to press myself against my mother's breast, to entangle my legs with hers and Lina's, to breathe in their hot breath under the covers. I wanted my brother to stay glued to the fake leather of the love seat, munching on bad chocolate, watching a game no one cared about.

I remembered our conversation on the fire escape. *I've gotten myself into something . . .*

But I was tired of being confused and scared. Lying there under the too-hot blankets, sticky and melting into my mother, after a day of baseball and carnivals and boardwalk beach-dancing with my perfect, all-American A-rab family—it did feel wonderful.

A METAL TABLE BOLTED to the floor. On the table, untouched: a hamburger wrapped in paper and cold coffee in a Styrofoam cup.

The boy was waiting for the man who kept calling. They had things to discuss. And here Sami was—took two train lines and a bus to get here—and the man hadn't bothered to show up yet. They were trying to make him sweat; Sami understood that. Don't panic, he told himself. They need you.

He wanted to pray, but he did not know which way was east. The room they were keeping him in was windowless, directionless. He asked the man—not his man, just another man—who came in periodically to check on him, but that man did not know, either. He said he would go and find out, but the boy didn't see him again for hours. In the end, the boy spun himself around like a top. When he was too dizzy to bear it anymore, he stopped, stumbling to a halt and catching himself on the corner of the metal table. He opened his eyes. This was the direction he would pray in. He cleaned his hands by wiping them vigorously over his shorts. But as soon as he started praying, he found he couldn't focus. He kept forgetting words, skipping over whole lines, having to start all over again. He knew that he was being watched, and it was distracting him. But the boy had always known that he was being watched, and it had never stopped him from praying before. So what was different now?

He finished, but just for show, just going through the motions. He didn't want anyone to see that they'd rattled him. He knew this was coming—the day their patience would run out—but he thought he had a little bit more time. He still had some things he'd like to do at home: help his father fix the screen door at the shop and install the new exhaust fan. The boy wanted to show his father that he respected him, his work, his commitment to doing things right. He'd had plenty of opportunities that summer to show his father some respect, but he had let them all slip by, an old vestige of childhood resentment stopping him each time. What exactly was he angry about? If he could answer that, he probably wouldn't be in this room right now. Was it some failure on his parents' part in protecting him from the world? Was it all the times they had nodded meekly under the stern gaze of judges, police officers, school administrators? Always taking advice, always following orders, never creative or confident or brave enough to come up with their own solutions. His father in particular was unbearably obedient. *Be a man,* the boy wanted to scream. But that was years ago. He'd spent the last few weeks observing the way his father talked to himself while closing up each night, the way he charmed customers with poetry and ancient love songs, the way he never cut corners, never cheated, the way he took pride in work he was never really meant for, this poet in a butcher's apron. When he saw his father next, if he saw his father, he would say to him: *I respect you.*

He wanted to tell his mother that it wasn't her fault. He wanted to admit to her that even now, as a grown man who had survived prison, he still craved the feeling of her strong arms around him. He wanted to tell her how many times he reread each and every one of the letters she sent to him while he was away. Those letters made him wish that they had always just written to each other, even sitting across from each other at the kitchen table, even when he was still just a little boy and she was still just a young woman, a new mother. Neither one of them was made for talking. But in her letters, he found traces of the divine. "The best we can hope for," she had written once, "is to die as Muslims." *To die as Muslims.* He had thought of that letter every day since—had saved it and kept it folded up in his wallet. It reminded him not just that each day could be his last, but that *if* each day could be his last, he had better make sure he was a Muslim, a real Muslim, unfailingly and unflinchingly Muslim. His mother was a Muslim, she had created him, nourished him inside of her, fed him from her breast. He wanted to tell her he was grateful. He wanted to tell her that she was the only person in the world he thought was capable of true loyalty to a cause.

And then there were the girls at home. What would he say to them if he had another day? He wasn't exactly sure. He had never really known how to feel about either of them. In those six years in prison, he had often conflated them into one person, because this is how he received news of them: "The girls are on spring break." "The girls are growing up." "The girls are fine." "The girls send their love." He had never heard directly from either of them in all that time, so when he got out he didn't know what to expect. Amira came to stand in for both of them—he could always conjure that round white face. The way she squinted her eyes when she looked at him sometimes, like she could see something he did not know he was revealing.

He thought: If he went home right now, he would find Amira and tell her that her mind was a wondrous thing. That he knew it betrayed her sometimes, turning this way and that, and that this inconsistency made her feel small and stupid. He wanted to shake her. He wanted her to turn those sharp eyes of hers inward.

She had wriggled out of his grasp in those six years. He did not know her anymore. She had used the time well, shrouding herself in layers of impenetrable shields.

Good for her, he thought.

Good girl.

WHEN SAMI LEFT the apartment the morning after our Coney Island trip, he said he was running a quick errand and would be back in time to help Baba with the midday rush. He was gone for ten hours. Ten hours, twenty-two texts, and seven missed calls later, he returned. Sami had an explanation for his absence. Not a disappearance. Just a temporary absence. He needed to check in at the parole office. But there was a delay—a long line, some bureaucratic red tape, misplaced paperwork. He should have called. His cell phone was dead. Everything was all sorted now. Don't worry.

None of us believed him, though we didn't admit it out loud. But I could tell we were all thinking it—the way we cut glances at him around the dinner table that night. Mama had been too worried to cook, so Baba took over. We ate a meal of hamburgers and frozen peas cooked in too much butter. Sami ate two burgers and three helpings of peas. His lips shone with grease. The rest of us picked at our hamburger buns, pushed our peas around our plates.

Sami went to bed early that night. I caught Baba awake in the middle of the night with his ear pressed to Sami's bedroom door, listening for his boy's soft snores. He nodded at me as I passed on my way to the bathroom as if to say, *All clear here.*

When I came out, Baba was gone and the hallway was dark. I paused outside of Sami's door. Inside, a deep and slow breathing. I nodded to no one and returned to bed.


The next day was Laylat al-Qadr, the night when something really important happened to our Prophet Muhammad, although I can never remember exactly what. On Laylat al-Qadr, families stay up all night long. They go to the masjid and listen to men take turns reciting the Qur'an, and the hours of darkness are filled with the word of God. Women bring trays of snacks and sweets. Men take cigarette breaks outside. And the children run around all night long, their honey-coated fingers sticking to everything they touch. It's a beautiful night, and everyone was excited, even the goat we could hear bleating downstairs in Baba's shop.

Someone had replaced the one that Lina freed, or maybe just caught the old goat, and I woke from a nap to the sounds of its hysterical language. Soon Baba would slaughter it at the back entrance to the shop, and when it went silent, I knew blood would flow over the concrete. He'd watch it kick its hooves, jerk, and shudder like it was doing some new dance craze, and he would recite Qur'an over its body.

He'd skin the goat, which would take him most of the day, because he wasn't used to skinning animals anymore. Then he'd gut it, clean it, and chop it up. Its meat would be parceled out to the poor of Bay Ridge.

On Laylat Al-Qadr, the whole town shoves itself inside a few mosques and stays there all night long. When we were little, I remember running around and screaming and jumping over the bodies of praying women like they were hurdles. I remember eating fistfuls of candy and throwing the wrappers off the roof. I do not remember how I used to pass out on the carpet of the women's section. I just remember how Mama used to lift me up and pass me off to Baba—I remember waking up in his arms as he carried me back home. When we became teenagers, Lina and I mostly stopped going to the masjid on Laylat Al-Qadr. It was a night for children or for the devout, not for two adolescent girls whose faith amounted to a vague hope that Allah just somehow "got" them.

But we were going this year, because Sami was going, and because he was excited about it. "You can wipe your sins out tonight," Sami told us all at suhoor that morning.

"It's not quite that simple," Mama said.

"No, he's right," Baba said. "I remember. You pray all night long, and next day you are innocent like baby."

Mama tried again to interject, but Lina spoke over her with a mouthful of eggs. "So if I do *this*"—Lina reached over and took the last piece of avocado from my plate, popped it into her mouth, chewed, and flashed a slimy, green grin—"I can just erase it later tonight?" She knew how much I had wanted that avocado, how I had waited for it to ripen in the fruit bowl for days.

Sami and Baba nodded. Mama smacked a hand to her forehead.

She launched into this long explanation that I stopped paying attention to about halfway through—she listed all these conditions, all these things we had to do, the ways we had to pray, how our intentions had to be pure, how we couldn't just recite the easy, short surahs but also the really long ones that were impossible for anyone besides her to memorize. And then, even if you did all of that, it wouldn't be like a magic eraser sent down from God to blot out all your sins. It would be more like a partially redacted file. All the praying could strike out some phrases, but that didn't erase them. They, the sins, would still be there, lurking beneath the black.

"The Qur'an says that Laylat al-Qadr is more powerful than a thousand months," Mama said. I liked the sound of that—one night to obliterate all other nights. But the way she described it made it sound like you had to be a saint to do it right, that I'd probably spend all night at the masjid, trying to pray, and still fuck it up somehow, and then it wouldn't be like a thousand nights. It would just be like any other night where things didn't quite work out as I'd planned.

There were prayer mats spread out across 5th Avenue. The street was littered with abandoned shoes. Like we all got taken, beamed up right where we were standing. The most pious, like Mama, had staked out spots inside, come prepared with water bottles and snacks to get through the night. The others wandered, prayed a little, visited friends, got some fries, prayed a little more, and so on. There were twinkly lights and little lanterns strung up from the mosque that gave the night a golden glow. Children were leapfrogging over prayer mats and bent bodies, reveling in an entire city block that had been closed to traffic. Everyone we knew was there, had excavated sins long buried, was holding them out in cupped hands, offering them to the angels, who were right now swooping down on us, invisible.

We split up almost as soon as we arrived. Baba took a mat outside, near the entrance to his own shop. We went upstairs with Mama to the women's section. And Sami melted into the crowd of white-socked, patchy-bearded boys. I tried to keep track of him, twisting back as I climbed the stairs, but I lost him almost immediately. The mosque reeked of new-carpet smell and lemon disinfectant, and maybe it was just the memory of the smell that would never leave me, but I swear, beneath all that was the faintest odor of piss.

We prayed two rakat with Mama. She recited aloud two of the longer surahs, because she knew we didn't know them. There was some stuff about being caught in a spider's web. And then setting slaves free. And then Allah building you a mansion. It was only two rakat, but, man, did she drag them out. By the time we finished, I already had to pee. Mama sat with her knees bent, her bare feet folded beneath her, and took out her Qur'an. She felt Lina and me hovering over her, and looked up at our expectant faces.

"Go," she said, nodding to our unasked question.

Lina and I started to weave our way back toward the stairs, stepping around and over the women who had raised us. Um Hany from across the hall tickled my bare foot as I passed.

"But come back!" Mama called after us.

We turned and nodded. There was a lot more we still needed to tell the angels before this night was done. We were almost to the door when someone caught Lina by the elbow. It was Imam Ghozzi's wife.

"You're not doing it right, my daughter," she said. "Your posture is all wrong. You need to be like this." She chopped her forearm down Lina's spine, straightening her. She moved her tiny hands down Lina's shoulders, repositioned her hands, folded her arms, even corrected the curl of her toes.

"Yalla, I'll show you," she said.

Lina looked at me like *Don't you dare leave me here.* I smiled back and kept moving toward the stairs. The women's bathroom was packed and nearly flooded from all the women splashing water for wudu, so I decided to go to Abu Nuwas instead. Baba had given me a key for this exact purpose. Inside, the shop was dark and still and smelled of blood and lemons. I used the bathroom in the back and then locked up again. I thought I might sit outside on the mat with Baba, but to my surprise, he was actually praying when I came out. He was sitting, his palms opened like a book, his head bowed, the chalky white heels of his callused feet poking out beneath him. Looking at him, I told myself I would try harder the next time I prayed.

I had seen some girls we went to high school with clustered around the corner, so I wandered in their direction. I slipped past the police barricades blocking off 5th and turned right onto Bay Ridge Avenue, toward the juice shop where I had seen them. A couple of the girls were headed to Brooklyn College with me in the fall, and Lina always got weird whenever I talked to them about it. Without her there, I could ask the girls about what orientation session they were going to, what they were going to wear. I would bring Lina back a juice: mango, pineapple, and ginger. But when I got there, the store lit up like a spaceship in the night, strings of coconuts dangling in the window, the girls were gone. Instead, I ran smack dab into a circle of boys. In the center, a head taller than any of them, was Faraj.

"What better night than tonight?" he was asking them.

"Yeah, I hear you, but my mom would kill me," a kid named Hamid said.

"Think about it like this," Faraj said. "Things just count more tonight. This one night equals eighty-three years of prayer. And one minute tonight is worth more than fifty-eight days. Even just one second now is worth more than twenty-three hours." He kept wagging his index finger: one, one, one.

"That's not really how it works," I said, thinking back to what Mama had said that morning. The boys all turned and looked at me. My shoes were only half on, the backs of my sneakers bent under my heels. I wished I had taken the time to put them on properly. I felt suddenly hobbled and slow.

"Oh, like you're an expert," Hamid said. And then, in the next breath, "Where's Lina?" Because he used to spend all of math class staring at the back of her neck.

"She's back there, praying," I said. I pictured her kneeling next to Imam Ghozzi's wife, her posture perfect, her hands exactly where they should be.

"Right," another boy said, and they all laughed.

I ignored them and looked right at Faraj. I was waiting for a smile, a nod, something.

"What are you doing here?" I asked.

Faraj finally dragged his eyes up to my face. "I'm sorry, sister, have we met before?" he asked.

The boys were cracking up now. A gentle breeze blew the hem of his thobe up his calf. I could see his black leg hairs, could feel the weight of him on top of me as we made out on his rooftop, remembered the smell of him as I nuzzled into his armpit on the couch in his living room.

"I'm Amira," I said, holding out my hand. I thought: Later, he'll be so proud of me for playing along. We'll joke about it, how those stupid boys had no idea.

Faraj looked down at my outstretched hand like it was a grenade. He physically stepped back away from it. I knew the gesture. He was a man who didn't shake hands with women.

The boys were gulping now, trying to swallow their laughter, choking on it.

My hand dropped to my side, my palms slick with sweat. I suddenly felt so hot I was dizzy. I looked up at the coconuts knocking into one another in the window of the juice shop, could hear the whir of the blender inside. How many sins had Lina erased while I had been standing here with a man who pretended not to know me? How far behind was I? With one second equal to twenty-three hours, she could be days ahead of me now.

"Amira." A voice I had not heard in years. I flinched.

The boys who had been circled around Faraj rushed Sami now as if he were some celebrity, a local legend. They shook and slapped hands with him, one of them even elbowing him like they were in the middle of a shared joke. But Sami would look only at me.

"Brother Sami," Faraj said, stepping past me and into the new circle that had formed around my brother. He held out his hand.

"Let's go," Sami said to me in his old voice. "Mama's looking for you."

He turned and started to walk away, leaving Faraj's hand floating in the air between us. I followed. He walked ahead of me, not speaking, until we were halfway back to the mosque. Then he turned suddenly and said, "What are you thinking, hanging out alone with guys like that?" The old voice was gone, had melted back into him.

"I was thinking I wanted some juice," I said. I pushed past him, kept walking toward the crowd gathered outside the mosque.

And then his hand around my wrist. But it was a limp chain, a gentle tug.

"Just promise me you'll stay away from the tall one—Faraj. He's asking for trouble." His voice dropped to a whisper. There were uncles and aunties and spies all around.

"Like you're not?" I shot back.

He dropped my wrist. "I'm just looking out for you," he said.

"A little late for that," I said.

I turned and walked away, following a winding path back inside, stepping over people, some in prayer, some asleep. Back up in the women's section, Lina was leaning on Mama, her cheek resting on Mama's shoulder. Their bodies ran into each other—ankle to ankle, thigh to thigh, elbow to elbow. I slipped in next to them, tried to add myself, but I couldn't quite get the angles of my body to match theirs.

"I'm here," I said. And the way Mama glanced up at me, half surprised, I could tell she hadn't been looking for me at all.

Now that I was back, Lina was desperate to leave. I tried to stop her, to convince her to stay, to tell her there was nothing out there for her. I wanted to warn her, but warn her about what?

"I just need some air," she said.

She patted my knee and stood, leaving a gap between me and Mama.

She came back thirty minutes later with a juice for each of us. I searched her face for signs of what she had seen out there, but it was blank.

Someone was reciting Ayat al-Kursi, the prayer to keep curses at bay. I joined in silently. How were you supposed to know what to wish for, what to ward against, what to say to God in your prayers? A few weeks ago, I prayed for my brother to stay away. Now I prayed for him just to stay. Back then, I prayed for a parachute that could lift me up out of Bay Ridge and drop me somewhere brand-new. Now I prayed that we would remain still, the Emams, huddled together at home.

Mama said this night was worth more than a thousand months. A thousand months of sins and prayers and good deeds and of fumblings in the dark.

We made it another three hours before we fell asleep in the corner as the mothers of Bay Ridge prayed all around us, pinching themselves to stay awake, prying their red eyes open wider, forcing themselves to keep going.

Lina and I slept through the most powerful night of all. We woke at the break of dawn to our mother's socked foot poking us gently awake.

"Next year . . ." Mama said, trailing off.

We met Baba and Sami on the front steps to our building. While we waited for Baba to open the door, we looked up at the gray sky.

There was a storm coming. Streets would flood and the lights would flicker off, on, off again. Some of the same people who had scrubbed piss out of the mosque carpets would be back again to tape the windows and pile sandbags in front of the door. The local TV news stations would come, like they did when the police took Abu Jamal. They'd stand in raincoats with umbrellas, looking just as journalists ought to, and talk about projected record-breaking rainfall and wind speeds, while behind them some women from the desert strolled down the sidewalk, their black abayas rustling in the wind, no idea what was about to hit them.

Faraj woke to the sound of the Skype ringtone—like a phone bubbling underwater somewhere. He hadn't meant to sleep so late, but staying up for Laylat al-Qadr had gotten to him. Today was his only day off all week, and he had planned to make the most of it. He was going to hit up two masjids, go to the gym, and then do some grocery shopping. But after spending all night in Bay Ridge, he just couldn't bear the thought of going out again. His arms felt weak, the muscles used up, as if he had been carrying a heavy load all day and had just now put it down. When he lay down on the sofa, he told himself it was only for a nap. But that was five hours ago. and now he felt like if he tried to bench-press he'd smash his own skull in. His phone continued to bubble from somewhere nearby.

He groped around on the sofa and finally found the phone, slipped between the cushions. He checked the screen, even though he knew who was calling. He thought about not answering, but it was 9:00 p.m. in Lahore. He ran his hand through his hair, tried to tuck the errant strands behind his ears. His mother hated his long hair, said it was the reason he wasn't married yet. Said it made him look like a Taliban. Said it made him look like a woman. Said it made him look like a gay. He conjured as much saliva as he could in his mouth and swallowed. He pressed the green button.

"Hi, Ammi. Hi, Abu," he said. His parents appeared before him—well, his mother's chin and his father's ear, at least; they never knew how to angle the camera. He could hear their TV blaring in the background; it didn't occur to them to turn it off before calling him. And behind that, the sounds of car horns blaring from the balcony doors.

"Do you know what time it is here?" his mother said.

"You called me," Faraj said.

"'You called me.' 'You called me'? Did you hear your son, Bilal? I guess he forgets he was supposed to call his parents *three hours ago*." His mother turned to face his father, so now Faraj could see her in profile. Her long, thin nose. Her hair gray at the roots, hennaed at the ends. His father was still just an ear and half of a creased forehead. It never failed to shock him—how old they looked now. He hadn't seen them in person in five years, so you'd think he'd be used to these calls. But when he thought of them while he was on his own, cooking his mother's biryani or fingering the prayer beads his father had given him before they left, he pictured the ammi and abu of his childhood. His mother's thick jet-black hair, his father's smooth brow. To watch them age across a computer screen felt like an odd sort of betrayal, like something they had decided to do without him.

"I'm sorry, Ammi," he said now. "I meant to call earlier, but it's so hot here today, I guess I just fell asleep."

"You want to talk about heat?" his mother said, and then she was off. It was ninety-nine degrees in Lahore—no, 101 actually—and the useless air conditioner was broken again, and the useless technician couldn't get the part that he needed because the useless hardware store was always closed, and how do those people make any money anyway if they're never open for business? Then she told him about his cousin's recent engagement. "The girl works at a bank," she said, as if this was supposed to impress him. And then about his aunt's always dire health problems. Sometimes it was her kidneys or her bladder. Today it was something about her pelvis being "crooked."

His father, as usual, barely spoke except to ask him, near the end of their call, "And how are your studies, beta?"

And even though school was out for the summer, Faraj answered: "Good, Abu. I got an A on my last exam." Because this is what they wanted to hear—that he was eating and praying and studying hard. Because wasn't that why he was in America on his own in the first place? In fact, these had been his father's parting words to him as they stood on the curb outside JFK, his parents' whole lives packed up into seven enormous suitcases. "Study hard," his father had said. And then they left him here, in this country that had bullied them to the point of exhaustion. Because, despite everything it had done to them, they still believed this place was golden. Faraj was expected to stay and study hard and thrive, even though they could not, though they had, in fact, abandoned their lives here, their son here, because they couldn't take the harassment for one more day. But Faraj was born here—he had something in him, surely, that would make him intrinsically more suitable. Five years later, and he was doing everything that was asked of him, but his parents were already disappointed that he was planning on law school and not a Ph.D. in engineering like his brother. But of course, his brother had never finished his doctorate. He was deported before he got the chance. He could have enrolled in school in Pakistan, but no one ever seemed to bring that up.

His brother was almost never on these calls. Sometimes Faraj caught a glimpse of him passing by in the background. He had gotten really fat and had this long, raggedy beard. Sometimes he could tell that his brother was there in the room with them. He could see his mother's eyes shifting over the top of the screen, silently pleading with him to come sit next to them on the couch and say hello to his little brother in America. Faraj didn't blame him exactly—it must be hard for Ahmed to look at him. Studying at an American college, in a place where the lights almost never cut out and the air conditioner always worked. Walking around New York, taking the subway, preparing for a future that should have been his. Just like it would have been hard for Faraj to look at Ahmed sitting next to their parents on the pink sofa in Lahore, eating their mother's food, praying next to their father at the masjid on Fridays.

"Where did you pray yesterday, beta? Beta?" He wasn't sure what his mother had just been saying. He had stopped listening somewhere around the neighbor's gaudy new chandelier: "Where does she think she is? Buckingham Palace?"

"Um, I went to a mosque in Bay Ridge. I have some friends there," he said.

"Bay Ridge? What's in Bay Ridge? Why don't you pray at Dar al-Furqan? People are asking about you. Chachi Zaynab is always saying how she saves you a plate every week but you never come."

He knew this wasn't true. No one back in the old neighborhood in Queens was asking about him. No one wanted to sit down for a Friday meal with him. He couldn't tell his mother what it felt like to go back there. To have people move around you in the mosque like you were an actual grenade. They felt bad for him, sure. But, more than that, they wanted to protect themselves. Talk too long to Ahmed's brother and you might just find yourself on a no-fly list. Or maybe your nephew's visa would get denied. Or maybe you'd wake up to find the FBI pounding at your door.

"I'll go next week. I promise, Ammi," he said. "But I have to go now. I'm meeting up with some classmates to study."

"Good. Study hard, beta," said his father.

"God keep you safe," said his mother. And then, "Oh, and, beta? Get a haircut. Please. You look like a girl."

When he put his phone down, he rubbed his forehead for a long time. Yes, he was doing everything that was asked of him. But he was also doing more—he was also standing up for his family. When everyone else had retreated, had fled and hidden, he was still here, still searching for something like justice. His parents wouldn't understand: they only knew a language of obedience. And it was easy to keep secrets from them, so easy that it made him sad. But he liked to think that they'd be proud of him one day. His mind wandered to his iftar meal; he had nothing in the fridge besides celery and some cooked lentils. If he hurried, he could still make Maghrib prayers at that mosque in Harlem. There were some people there he needed to talk to. He could break his fast with them afterward, from a halal cart he liked up there where the hot sauce was so spicy it hurt to eat.

He stood, determined that he would make the trek uptown; he could still salvage the day. But when he stood, he felt his knees almost buckle beneath him. There was a weakness coursing through him. His limbs felt useless, and he looked down at them in disgust. He could lie back down and order in for delivery. He could pray in his own living room. He could turn on the TV and rest. But Faraj couldn't abide the idea of having to regain his strength; it was unacceptable to him to let his strength leave his body in the first place. Something had slipped this week; somewhere he had made a mistake.

When he walked into the gym thirty minutes later, he felt better as soon as the ice-cold blast of the air conditioning hit him. He eyed the weight area longingly, but he knew his body would betray him there. Instead, he hopped on an open treadmill and ran for three miles, until his muscles burned.

# Part III

Say: "I seek refuge in the Lord of men, the King of men, the God of men, from the mischief of the slinking prompter who whispers in the hearts of men; from jinn and men."

—114:1–6

I T HAD BEEN a summer of almost-storms, of near misses. Every mass
of clouds spinning around Florida was the next Sandy. And this time
the weatherman was getting hysterical. I was starting to feel bad for
him. But it was raining when we woke on the 30th and last day of
Ramadan. By 5:00 a.m., Mama already had a shoulder of Baba's finest
lamb slow-roasting in the oven. The smell of it combined with the gray
drizzle outside made it feel like autumn.

It was a quiet beginning to our Eid. We broke our last fast of the
month together as a family. The food was good, and we complimented
Mama. But, otherwise, no one spoke much. I couldn't believe it was
really over. Just like that. And here I was—no different. No purer, no
clearer, no more aware of who I wanted to be than when the fast began.
I looked up at Sami, who was wiping his plate clean with a torn piece
of bread. I wondered how he felt after all those prayers. I was sure he
never cheated, never smoked when he shouldn't have, never snuck a sip
of water when no one was looking, never broke his fast with beer and
gummy bears. Did he feel cleansed now? Did he feel closer to God?
He just looked tired to me, dark circles under his eyes, a mouth full of
bread, a mouth clamped shut.

The next morning, the rain had stopped. Everyone made jokes
about the hurricane that wasn't. The weathermen were all telling us

to barricade ourselves inside, were promising an apocalypse, but we just laughed. The sun was shining, and it was a day of indulgence after thirty days of deprivation. That morning, all the masjids were packed for prayers. And then people streamed out into the sunlight and it felt like anything was possible. The parks were swarmed with families taking Eid photos in their shiny new outfits. And back at the corner of 5th and 73rd, the whole building smelled of honey. Everyone propped their doors open so we could visit one another. Small children came from nowhere to dart in and out of all the apartments and ricochet down the halls. Lina and I bounced around, sampling cookies from at least five of our neighbors. We got our cheeks kissed by friends and strangers. Whenever we stopped back at home, we'd tell Mama that her food was still the best, and she'd beam. Sami mostly hid in his room until the crowd thinned out and people went back to their own apartments.

That night, Lina and I were standing around the kitchen table, plastic forks slicing into fat slabs of macarona béchamel, when the lights began to flicker. Outside, the telephone wires were swaying wildly. And the wind was making this steady, shrill whisper. It still wasn't raining, but the sky had turned an odd grayish-purple color, and the air felt swollen and heavy.

The building and the streets were quiet now. Everyone was exhausted and ready to trade in their fancy Eid clothes for sweatpants. Mama was taking a bath. Baba had gone out to the coffee shop with some of the other dads to watch the news and argue. Sami was staying in his room, reading my copy of *The Great Gatsby*. Back in our room, I changed into pajamas and belly-flopped onto my bed. I didn't intend to fall asleep right away, but my eyelids started to droop. I looked over at Lina through half-closed eyes. She was putting on mascara, using the camera on her phone as a mirror. I remember telling myself to speak. To ask her where she was going. To tell her, *Don't*. But then I was asleep. She kissed me on the forehead before she left. When I woke later, I felt the sticky sheen of her lip gloss on my skin.

I woke up at around 2:00 a.m. to the soft chiming of my phone.

In the state between sleeping and waking, I thought that it was Sami's phone and that he was there in the room with me. I tossed and turned and pulled the sheet up over my head until I realized that I was alone. I sat up in bed and reached for my phone. Three missed calls from Lina.

My eyes still half closed, I called her back. A man's voice pulled me completely awake.

*"Finally,"* he said. "We got a situation here. Your girl is tripping."

I was confused and thought that maybe I had dialed the wrong number.

"Is Lina there?" I said.

"She's fucked up," the man said.

"Give me Lina," I said. By then, I knew it was Andres's voice on the line, and I wanted him to just reach down with those great big hands of his and scoop her up, deliver her to me here, at the foot of my bed.

"She locked herself in the bathroom," he said. "She's been in there for at least an hour now. The bar is threatening to call the cops."

"What did you do to her?" I whisper-screamed into the phone. I scrambled out of bed and tugged on a pair of ratty pajama pants.

"You should be asking what she did to herself," Andres hissed.

"I'm coming," I said. "Tell her I'm coming."

"I hope you got a car," he said, " 'cuz no cab is gonna take her like this."

Andres gave me the address of some other bar, not Lotus, up near Williamsburg. I remember thinking, *Another bar? Lina never told me about another bar.* I could be hurt by so little. We were far apart again.

After I hung up, I sprinted around the room, putting on a bra and socks, and a sweatshirt. I didn't want to bother with a scarf, so I just tucked my hair underneath the hood of my sweatshirt. But when I was ready to go, I found myself sitting back down on the bed. I wanted to scream but had nowhere to do it. So I picked up an old sock from the floor and pulled it as hard as I could. My mouth opened and twisted, but no sounds came out. *Maybe you won't go,* I thought. I got up from the bed.

The floorboards groaned as I tiptoed out into the living room. I looked longingly at the hook by the front door where the keys to the

Tercel used to hang. Baba's wallet was lying on the coffee table, so I flipped through it and removed a few bills. Then I turned the dead bolt slowly so it wouldn't click—Baba could sleep through a pack of hyenas cackling at the moon, through the bombing of Gaza and the toppling of dictators; it was really Mama that I was worried about. What would I do if she came out of her room right now and caught me sneaking out?

I made it out the door, and just as I was locking it again, I thought I heard a loud creak in the floor. I froze for a second and then decided to run. There was a gypsy cab lingering right across the street, directly underneath a streetlamp, like it had been waiting for me. The driver hit every pothole on the BQE. Twenty minutes later, we were on Union Avenue; the driver had out-crazied every other cabbie on the road. I paid him and walked across the street to the bar, pushing past drunk smokers. The wind was whipping trash down the street, and the mist seemed to come from below. When I stood outside of the bar, I could see it was very different from Lotus. This place was small and swanky. No dancing girls. No fog machine. It looked unbearably cool, and I felt like a lost little girl in her pajamas. There was a chandelier glowing inside, casting a warm orange light through the window.

The man carding at the entrance eyed my pajamas.

"No way, sweetheart," he said.

"Um," I said, "my sister's inside."

He smiled at me indulgently.

"I mean, she's the one in the bathroom."

His face transformed, and he nodded grimly at me.

"I wanted to call the police," he said. "But Andres is a friend of mine, and he convinced me not to. But if you can't get her out of here soon, I'll have no choice." He spoke sternly, yet kindly, like an older brother. I thought he might give me a talk about drinking responsibly, not mixing your liquors, staying hydrated. But he just picked up his cell phone. "Yo, Andres," he said. "There's a little Spanish chick outside, says she's here for your girl."

Then he opened the door for me. "Good luck," he called after me.

The bar was narrow but long, winding much farther back than you'd expect from outside. The walls were covered in a metallic paper that shimmered like snakeskin. The bartenders looked like models. One of them shook a cocktail shaker vigorously and poured frothy mint-green liquid into a martini glass. Another decorated the rim of a highball with a sage leaf. I felt like everyone was staring at me, like they were afraid I was about to go table to table, selling bootleg DVDs.

I looked around for Andres, but I couldn't see him, and no one was answering Lina's phone. I wandered deeper into the bar, squeezing past people sitting on stools in a narrow hallway, their faces obscured in the dim light. The hallway opened up to a slightly wider back room, even darker, with only dozens of flickering tea lights illuminating it. But even in the dark, I spotted Andres immediately. He was leaning against the bathroom door and banging continuously on it with one fist. There was only one other bathroom, and customers were lined up outside of it.

Andres groaned into the door, "Liiiiiina."

I stood behind him awkwardly for a moment. "I'm here," I said.

He whipped around, and I thought he might pull me in for a hug, that's how grateful he looked to see me. "Oh, thank Jesus, you can do something with her, right?"

Andres threw his hands up and backed away from the door. I said nothing, stood frozen. Then Andres put on this weird kiddie voice and stepped back to the door.

"Your sister is here, Lina," he said.

"Amira?" a tiny, muffled voice called from behind the door. Her voice was a twisted wind chime behind the loopy electronic music in the bar.

"Hey," I said, pressing my face to the door. "What are you doing in there? You want to let me in?"

"My heart is beating so fast, Amoora. If I move, I'll die."

I turned to Andres. "How much did you give her to drink?"

Then Andres looked like he wanted to hit me. The music changed abruptly to a nineties rap song, Ice Cube starting to tell us all about his good day, and the whole bar seemed to transform, brighten. Heads lifted from the low candlelight and started to bob. Andres wiped the sheen of sweat off his forehead.

"Not drink," he said.

"What?" I said. "What are you talking about?"

"Do you even know this girl?" Andres said. "Cocaine is not a good look on her."

I had a sudden image of my sister then, snorting white powder through a hundred-dollar bill off a glass coffee table, because this is the only way I had seen cocaine snorted—in movies.

"Is she dying?" I asked, the panic swelling in my throat.

"I fucking hope so," Andres said.

Just then, I heard the lock click open. Andres and I both stared at it for a second. Then I pushed the door open gently. Lina was sitting on the floor, her back propped up against the sink, her long doll-legs bent at weird angles in front of her. Her mascara and eyeliner were smudged across her face. She had her right hand over her heart, and she appeared to be counting.

"It slowed down," she whispered to me.

"What slowed down?"

She smiled, reached out for me. "What are you doing here? I didn't know you were going to be here."

And then that sock-destroying rage just swelled right up again.

"You didn't know I was going to be here," I said, "because I wasn't *supposed* to be here. But here I am. Again."

She didn't say anything, and I gave her arm a little shove. Her skin was clammy and hot. "Get up," I said. "We're going home."

She was wearing this ridiculously tiny dress that looked like it was made from red Ace bandage, like her whole body was a wound bound tightly underneath it. She must have borrowed it from Reina, who was several inches shorter than her. The dress looked like it was hanging on for dear life, clutching onto her ass cheeks, trying not to roll up. No one else in the bar was dressed like that—they were all wearing billowing things, asymmetrical things, things in black and gray and white. Lina looked cheap. She looked young and stupid, and I, in my cloud-print pajama pants, looked young and stupid with her.

"You're wearing *that*?" I said. She looked like nothing, a small, shivering animal. Her lower lip jutted out.

"Why are you being so mean?" she asked.

I was being mean because I thought I might hit her. Why couldn't she be fucked up like all the rest of us? Why did her fucked-up-ness have to be so much more extreme?

"Forget it," I said. I offered my hand to help pull her up, but she just stared at it.

"I'm cold," she said quietly, in a baby voice.

Finally, she took my hand and I lifted her up. Our eyes met fleetingly in the mirror. Then I turned and opened the door.

We emerged from the bathroom, Lina trailing behind me, that stupid fucking lower lip still shaking. When she saw Andres waiting for us, I thought she might bolt for the bathroom again, but instead she snuggled up to him, pressing her breasts against his chest.

"You mad at me?" she asked his armpit.

"Yes," he said. But he was smiling, and he had his arms wrapped around her.

"You gonna stop talking to me?"

"And lose my star? Never."

For a very real moment, I thought I might vomit. To distract myself from this, I tugged hard on her arm. The other people in the bathroom line were glaring.

"Say goodbye," I said.

She kissed Andres, and I could feel the people around me roll their eyes.

"You're crazy," he whispered into her ear.

I yanked her away, thinking he would follow us out, help us get a cab. But he stayed behind. When I looked back, he had rejoined a group at a table. At the exit, Lina stopped, clutched her neck, and looked around.

"I had a necklace," she said. "You don't see it anywhere, do you?"

I pulled her out the door. Once we were on the sidewalk, I shoved my sister, hard. She started to form a sentence, something with the word "fuck" in it. But I wouldn't let her talk. The anger came pouring out as I screamed at her, but I wasn't even sure what I was saying—Fuck you for always doing this to me? Fuck you for always leaving me alone?

The bouncer was walking toward us. My sister was centimeters from my face. She said something else then. "You're like my fucking shadow," she said.

The words felt true to me. My sister's shadow, yes, that was me— wherever she was, there I'd be. Then I hit her. A side-armed punch. A hammer, aimed at her nose but landing on her ear. My sister's face: a big blur of silent nothing as the concrete took her. The bouncer stopped, took one step back, and said, "Damn."


I offered a cabdriver double to take us home to Bay Ridge, but it still took three cabs rejecting us before we found one. Lina lay curled up on the back seat, crying. "You hit me," she kept repeating. She shuddered and wiped her snotty nose on her arm. I sat up front with the cabdriver, listening to the very soft Bengali music that trickled out from the radio. He didn't say anything about the girl crying in the back, but every few minutes I saw his eyes flick to his rearview mirror.

As we approached Bay Ridge, the driver slowed down as I directed him. Lina sat up in the back and looked at the window. "We're home?" she asked. I ignored her and told the driver to turn left.

Lina cowered in the back seat, gripping the door handle like we were on some wild chase. "They're going to stone me," she said. She peered up over the window, looked right and left, and then ducked back down into the seat. "Fucking Arabs, if they see me like this, they'll tie me to a pole and then they'll hurl rocks at me until I die."

"Jesus, calm down," I said. "We're not in Saudi Arabia." But then I reached over her and pressed the lock on her door, because I had a vision of her trying to make a break for it—opening the door and just rolling away.

I asked the driver to drop us off a block away from the apartment, in case someone was looking out of our kitchen window. He pulled to the curb, and the meter whirred and beeped, calculating the price we'd have to pay. I gave him the money and opened the door.

"Come on, Lina," I said.

She stepped reluctantly out of the car. The cabdriver didn't wait to see if I needed a hand carrying her. The second I helped Lina out of the car and shut the door behind her, he sped off.

I draped her arm over my shoulder so she could lean against me as we made our way slowly down the block. I paused in front of our building. I couldn't just bring her home through the front door looking like that, the tiny red dress creeping up, threatening to roll all the way to her collarbone any second now. I unlocked the door to the building and then told her to wait there in the lobby.

"Stay here," I told her, and when she didn't respond I said it again, placing her hand on the bricks of the wall. "Stay here. I'll be right back."

I started to climb the stairs to our floor, looking down every few steps to make sure that Lina hadn't run off. But she slinked to the ground and appeared to be half asleep. I thought about all the early risers who could walk out their front doors that very moment, perhaps on their way to the mosque for Fajr prayers. I tiptoed inside and all the way to our bedroom, grabbed a pair of pants and a T-shirt for Lina, and then crept back through the living room. Baba stirred on the couch. He stretched and opened his eyes. "Amoora," he said, looking right at me, his voice thick and warbling. "Ya habibti, ya hayati, ya dunyati, noor al-ayni." *My darling, my life, my world, the light of my eyes.* "Would you please bring your old baba a glass of water?"

I brought him the water and stood over him, watching. When he had emptied the glass, I bent and kissed his cheek before I took it from him. "Go back to bed, Baba," I said. But he was already asleep.

Climbing back down the stairs with the pants and shirt tucked under my arm, I thought I heard someone following me, someone stepping onto the landing. I looked up, expecting to see Sami, but there was nothing. And when I got back down to the lobby, Lina was sitting exactly where I'd left her, crying, and hiccuping softly.

Mama was waiting for us when we got back up to the apartment. She was standing in her nightgown in the dark. When she spoke— "Where have you been?"—it came out in a sort of vicious whisper. I almost screamed as my eyes searched for her in the dark. Lina, dressed in the T-shirt and sweatpants over the tiny dress, slumped against my shoulder. I had the feeling that if I stepped away she would fall like a tree to the ground. I was tempted. Mama pulled the cord on a lamp next to the couch, and the room filled with a soft patch of yellow light. Baba groaned and then shot up to a seated position.

"Girls?" he called, his eyes squinting and darting around the room.

"They're here," Mama said.

He had no memory of talking to me minutes earlier.

I waited for them to start yelling, but now Mama was staring at Lina. I tried to think of a story, but my mind was too tired. I let her look—I let her take in Lina's clammy skin, her bloodshot eyes, the quarter-sized hickey on her neck.

"Go to bed, Amira," she said. "We'll talk later."

And I let her take Lina from me. Mama pushed the hair off her face and led her by the hand to the bathroom. But it was as if I still couldn't move, like there was still a phantom Lina rooting me to the spot. It wasn't until Baba rose up from the couch and put his arm around me that I could move. And then, with his heavy arm guiding me toward my bedroom, I felt overwhelmed with relief. We had been caught. We had to be punished. We had to be stopped. Baba was patting my back and whispering as he led me to bed.

"Bad girls," he said. He repeated it softly, over and over again like a mantra. His voice was full of tenderness. But by the time he had ushered me into my bed, the mantra had changed. It became just "girls." He pulled my shoes off and arranged the sheet lightly over me, chanting the whole time. Then, as he leaned down to kiss my forehead, the chanting stopped. The whirring of the fan filled the room. And then one word whispered softly as he opened the bedroom door to leave. I was left alone with the sound of my own name echoing in my head. Sleep came quickly.

When I woke the next morning, a glass of water was waiting for me on the nightstand, and Lina was asleep in the bed across from me. She looked clean. Her hair was damp against the pillow. Someone had left a glass of water for her, too, and a wastepaper basket by her bed. I left her snoring lightly and poked my head into the kitchen. Mama was sitting at the kitchen table, shucking ears of corn over the trash can.

She saw me peering and gestured me in, her hands trailing corn silk. "Yalla, come, it's okay."

I stood in the kitchen for a moment and waited for her to begin. But she didn't say anything. She just kept shucking, her hands working so fast. There was a mountain of corncobs piled before her already.

"Cookout at the masjid tonight," she said, nodding to the corn. "A fund-raiser to get it deep-cleaned. The place still smells. They think it might be in the walls."

I nodded. I poured myself a bowl of cereal and sat down at the table across from her. I ate in silence, with only the squeaking sound of her fingers tearing back the leaves. I couldn't take it.

"So you're not mad?" I said.

She smiled, snorted, then coughed into her sleeve.

"Oh, I'm mad," she said. "I'm just not sure at who. Or what."

I had the urge to start defending Lina, make excuses for her. But then I remembered the sight of her nuzzling into Andres's armpit, the feeling of my fist bouncing off the side of her head, and I held back. I would have confessed anything to Mama in that moment, and she could sense it—the tumble of unformed words stacking up in my throat. She put a yellow-flecked hand on top of mine.

"Let's wait for your sister," she said. "I want to talk to you both."

Hours later, we were back at the kitchen table, three of us now. It had been wiped clean of corn silk. Mama made us three mugs of sahlab with cinnamon and crushed pistachios on top, like it was our birthday or something. But Lina didn't touch hers. She took small sips from a giant bottle of orange Gatorade that she had asked Sami to get her from the bodega.

"So what's my punishment?" Lina said when Mama delivered the steaming sahlab to us and sat down.

"Ya Allah, hold on," Mama said. "I never met two girls more eager to be punished. I want to tell you something first."

Lina darted her eyes quickly at me from across the table, then immediately looked back down at the wood grain of the table. Baba was home from the shop. I could hear him clattering around in the living room, but either he had no need to enter the kitchen or he had been instructed not to, because he stayed away.

"Did I ever tell you why I left Egypt?" Mama said.

"To marry Baba," I said. That's what we had always been told. That Baba came to America first to get settled and save up some money and then sent for Mama to join him. He had purchased this very apartment and then had to save enough to furnish it, because that's the way it was done in Egypt, to show that you could provide for a wife. Except, in Egypt, the bride picked out all the furniture—usually pink brocade sofas with gold trim—and the groom paid for it. But Mama and Baba were a continent apart, and there was no Internet back then, so Baba had to do his best to pick out furniture he thought she might like.

"She hated all of it," he'd say whenever he told me the story. Then he always stopped to laugh a big belly laugh. He'd sweep his hands out in front of him, as if sweeping all the furniture into the trash.

"Yes, to marry Baba. That is true," Mama said. The way she said the last bit—*That is true*—caught both my and Lina's attention. Lina's eyes flicked up from the Gatorade cap she had been palming.

"We got married at City Hall," she said. "You had to draw a number to get married. Like you were in a queue for the bank." She stopped and looked at us both like this was significant. Our faces must not have given her what she expected.

"Did you never wonder why Baba didn't come back to Egypt for a proper wedding?"

It was an obvious question, now that she mentioned it, but I had never wondered about it before. I almost never thought about my parents before they were my parents.

"I always thought it was some visa thing," Lina said, and I was surprised she had considered it at all.

Mama shook her head, waved her hand as if a visa were a trifle.

"No one would have wanted to a come to a big wedding in Egypt. It would have been too awkward with my condition."

*Condition.* I imagined my mother sick, frail, somehow physically marred.

"What was wrong with you?" I asked.

"Nothing," she said. "I got pregnant."

She leaned back in her chair and watched our faces. She wanted to shock us, and she had. Our mother, the Qur'an nut, pregnant before marriage.

"So that's why Baba hasn't been back to Egypt in so long. It's because your family is waiting there to beat him up, right? To punish him for, like, knocking you up?" Lina was animated now, as if the story had punched the last of the hangover right on out of her.

"That is a rude phrase," Mama said. "Americans have the crassest expressions. And, no, that is not why. My family is forever indebted to your father. He's like a hero to them. A fool. But also a hero. He saved them from a very embarrassing situation by marrying me when no one else would." She paused and made this circular gesture with her hand as if waiting for us to fill in the rest. Lina raised her eyebrows at me, and I shrugged back.

Mama sighed loudly. She didn't want to say the next part. "The baby wasn't his. You understand what I'm saying?"

"Someone *else* knocked you up?" Lina almost shouted.

"Lina. Stop saying that, please," Mama said. "And lower your voice. You think I want everyone in Bay Ridge to hear this story? Most of them know already anyway, but it's not exactly something I want shouted from the rooftops."

"Wait," I said. "So everyone else knows this story except for us?"

Mama shrugged.

Out in the living room, Baba raised the volume on the television. Now I was sure he had been instructed to stay out of the way.

"I don't understand," I said.

Mama took a delicate sip of her sahlab. "Okay," she said. "Let me try again."

Mama was nineteen years old when she married Baba, which, sure, always sounded young to me, but it was Egypt and the Stone Age, so I figured it was more normal back then. Baba had been in love with her since they were twelve. Mama barely knew he was alive. In the story we had always heard—told always by Baba, I now realized—she noticed him only after he came to America, when he started writing her letters. This was always supposed to make some sort of point about the power of poetry. But I knew Mama was more practical than that. I always figured that it took Baba's moving away and making it on his own in a new country to impress her. I imagined her at nineteen with a calculator and a list of pros and cons out in front of her, filling columns, adding numbers, and ending up with Baba's name at the end. But now I was learning that her marriage to my father wasn't because of poetry or practicality; it was a choice of last resort, which is really no choice at all.

"My family was furious, because I wouldn't tell them who the father was," Mama was saying. "They wanted to go bang down his door, drag him by his ear, stick a Qur'an in front of us, and marry us. But I wouldn't give them a name, and they couldn't imagine who it could be. I had always been a quiet girl. A good girl."

Mama paused then and looked right at me. I thought this talk was for Lina and I was just along for the ride, but I felt myself start to sweat under her gaze.

"You should have heard them theorizing over the dinner table. Was it this boy or that boy? Maybe it was the baker's son, who said hello to me once. But I gave them nothing."

"So who was it?" Lina asked. She was leaning in toward Mama as if waiting to receive a precious secret. But I found myself suddenly nervous about hearing the answer, scared that maybe there was no answer. How long ago was it that Lina had given silent thanks when her period arrived? A week? Two? What would Lina say if she hadn't gotten it? About the outline of a man who took her to a Jersey City motel room. A faceless man. An absence. A lack. A spirit.

"I have never told anyone but your father," Mama said.

"I bet it was someone important. Like a judge or something. Oh my God, it wasn't Mubarak, was it?" Lina whispered his name as if that drooping pile of flesh could hear us.

Mama laughed. "It was not Mubarak," she said. "It's not important

who it was. That man is"—she waved her hand as if swatting a fly—
"nothing. What matters is what happened next."

Baba heard about Mama's ruin all the way across the ocean and
wrote her a letter. "He didn't propose right then. He didn't even tell me
that he loved me. He just wrote to ask me how I was doing." She said
it like it was a marvel, shaking her head like she still couldn't believe it.
" 'How are you feeling?' he asked. 'My sister tells me that the first few
months are the hardest.' I wrote him back and told him about my nau-
sea, and *that* is how our love story began."

They began writing to each other regularly. Mama was cooped up at
home while her family tried to figure out what to do about her, how to
salvage her. Baba's letters were the only thing she had to look forward
to in those days. He told her things about his life in New York. About
the trash trucks that came twice a week to whisk the rubbish magically
away. About Chinese food, and supermarkets where everything came
wrapped in plastic.

"He talked to me like I was still myself," Mama said.

I loved hearing her talk about Baba like this. Like he was a man
among swine. But Lina was impatient. She wanted answers.

"So do we have a secret older sibling you've been hiding away all
these years?" she asked.

Mama shook her head. She took another sip of sahlab, closed her
eyes while she swallowed.

"The pregnancy failed," she said. Not *I miscarried* or *The baby died*
but *The pregnancy failed*. As if it were some sort of experiment happening to someone else. "I went into labor too early. I was only five months.
It was already dead inside me, they said."

Something in me flipped and then shuddered.

"I thought maybe it would all be over then, and I could go back to
normal. But too many people knew. My parents knew. No one could
look at me the same way. Not even myself. Only your father talked to
me like before."

I could hear the television in the living room playing the local news.
They were talking about the storm that was coming. I could hear every

other word—"sandbags," "wind speeds," "rising," "prepared." Soon my
father would board up the windows of his shop.

"Why are you telling us this now?" Lina asked. Her voice surprised
me. She sounded angry.

Mama met her eyes and held her gaze until Lina looked away. "So
we can understand each other better, habibti," she said. "People were
starting to say it was a curse that made me lose the baby. The evil eye
sent from the wife of the man who put me in that situation, things like
that. And I have to tell you that I believed them, because I felt cursed. I
could feel it in everything I touched. This cup"—she held up the mug in
front of her—"would feel somehow wrong in my hands. Like there was
something bad inside me. I felt like Hagar in the desert."

Mama had wanted to name one of us after Hagar, but Baba vetoed
it. Didn't like the way it sounded coming out of the mouths of Americans. Hagar, that slave, her womb pimped out in service of a man who,
once he got what he wanted from her, let her be cast out into the desert
to die. She wandered for days in the hot sand, her bastard son in her
arms, the two of them dying slowly. But then there was God. Then there
was grace. And the Zamzam Spring sprouted up from that life-choking
sand. She drank and became the mother of all Muslims born after the
rejected babe she held in her arms. No wonder we still believe so firmly
in things like curses. We were born out of them—slavery, rape, jealousy,
thirst.

"Sometimes I still feel that way," Mama said, fingering the handle
of her mug. "As if I still carry the badness inside. I have to work hard to
make the feeling go away."

"How?" I asked. My voice was louder than I meant it to be. My
mother's eyes jumped onto me. I held my own mug between two hands.

"By remembering how I felt when your father proposed. How it felt
to hold that letter in my hands. His love like a life raft. Like that spring
in the desert."

Maybe she could see in my face that her answer disappointed me. I
set my mug down, shook my hands out. I had no boy waiting for me,
pining for me, loving me despite or because of all of my faults. Faraj did

not make me feel like I was drinking from the spring. He made me feel like my mouth was full of sand.

"But the story doesn't quite end there," Mama said, as if pleading with me to wait, to hold on a bit longer. "The curse followed me to America. There was a brief time when no one here knew, and it felt like I could truly start over. But that didn't last forever. People talk—even across oceans, they talk. And when we started having trouble with Sami—he didn't speak for a long time, and he would have these epic tantrums; people gossiped that he was mute or dumb, said it was the evil eye that gave me a son like that—that's when I knew that I could never really escape it. And then again when you two were born," she said. Her hands slid across the table to touch us, brushing my pinkie finger, stroking Lina's wrist.

"There is an old Egyptian belief that twins are bad luck. Only idiots believe it. But people are idiots sometimes. So my first baby died. And my second baby was born angry and mute. And then I had twins, twin *girls*. Double the bad luck. Curse." She held up one finger. "Curse. Curse. Curse." Four fingers in total.

The four fingers hovered over Lina's wrist.

"Are you telling us this so we don't have sex before marriage?" Lina asked. "So we don't end up cursed like you?"

"I am not cursed," Mama said, her voice rising almost to a shout. I flinched in my seat. Her fingers wrapped back around Lina's wrist. "It's not true," she said. "That's what I figured out. That's what I remind myself of every time that bad feeling starts to creep up again. I am not cursed. I am blessed." With her other hand, the one resting next to mine, she slapped the table lightly. "When I start to feel the badness, when I begin to believe again what everyone has said about me, I close my eyes. I pray. Because I know I am being tested. If I cannot even feel God's blessings when they are all around me, what kind of Muslim am I?"

"What blessings?" Lina scoffed. She looked over her shoulder, like maybe there were some blessings she hadn't noticed lurking in our kitchen.

"I am loved by a good man," she said. She held one finger back up. "And we made a beautiful, complicated boy who feels things greatly. And then we made two beautiful girls at the same time. You two have been whispering and laughing and loving each other even before birth. You give each other double the strength of an ordinary girl." Two fingers, three fingers, four. She held her hand up for us to see.

"There is nothing bad in you," she said. "When you start to believe that, you make your own curse. That's when you have to stop. Close your eyes. Do whatever you need to do to feel God's love again."

"Come." She stood up abruptly. "I want you to pray with me. I want you to feel it." She led us out of the kitchen, past Baba in the living room, who waved at us from the couch like we were going away on a long voyage, and into the bathroom attached to her room. We cleaned ourselves, pulled soft white veils over our heads, and lined up next to our mother at the foot of her bed. She was our sheikha, reciting aloud, as if she did not trust the words we would choose for ourselves.

We were grounded, condemned to the earth. After our talk with Mama, she sent Baba into our room to deliver our punishment. We were to work in the shop, help around the house, and study Qur'an.

"I make you grounded. No fun allowed," he said, trying not to smile.

I thought maybe Lina would turn to me and complain. That we would pretend to be outraged, though actually secretly pleased by our punishment, by all the attention we were getting. But Lina was silent. She sat at the window and looked out as if waiting for something. Her skin was pallid and shiny. She looked like a wax doll in a historical exhibit from the future.

*Girl sits by window, Bay Ridge, Brooklyn, Femicidal Era.*

It was really raining now, steady sheets of it darting from a gray-and-yellow sky. I made some ginger tea for her. But Lina just shook her head from her perch at the window, her bedsheets twisted around her ankles. So I drank it myself, and my tongue burned for the rest of the night.

Mama and Baba both kept coming in to check on us, to lay hands on our foreheads as if we were sick, to bring us a small pyramid of hummus-and-cheese sandwiches, and sometimes just to look at us, to check that we were still there and hadn't flown out the window into the rain. Just before eight, I placed half a sandwich in Lina's hand. She absentmindedly took a bite and then passed the sandwich back to me. We ate it like this—slowly, passing it back and forth after each bite. She ate the last bite and then looked down at her empty hands for a long time. All I wanted was for her to look at me. But when she finally did, I couldn't handle it. Her eyes were so vacant, like she was looking right through me. I had to look away, at the windowpane above her, at the rusted curtain rod, at a corner of white wall.

At some point, I left the room and wandered around the apartment aimlessly, waiting for someone to do or say something. I took a shower and came back, and Lina had not moved from the window.

"What are you looking for?" I asked her.

"Nothing," she said.

"Are you waiting for something?"

I thought a UFO, a plane, a flying carpet. I thought a rocket launcher, a parachute, a boat. I thought a life raft.

She said, "Everything."


We worked at the shop the next day. Baba got better at punishing us as the day dragged on, eventually figuring out that he should separate us—send one girl to scrub the rust off an old metal shelf in the back and order the other girl to stack cans of ful medames in a pyramid by the window. Lina got to scrub the shelf, which meant she was back there with Sami. The whole time I stacked cans, I wondered if they were talking or working in silence.

At noon, Baba grilled four pieces of kofta, smashed them into pitas, and drizzled tahina over the top. He summoned Sami and Lina. There were only three stools at the counter. Baba tried to give them to his children, but Sami insisted on standing. We ate quietly. The sandwich was piping hot and delicious. I thought we might hang out together, might rest our full bellies and tell stories about the customers. But as soon as he was done eating, Sami washed his hands, put his apron back on, and disappeared into the back again. I wondered if it was like this every day—if Baba and Sami ever talked. Or if Sami was there, but just barely. Then some white people came in, and Baba shooed us away from the counter. Lunch was over.

It poured all day, and business was slow. Massive, hulking clouds squatted over Bay Ridge. Men in orange construction vests put sandbags down to keep Shore Road from flooding. At closing time, I swept the floors while Baba closed out the register. He kept clicking his tongue in displeasure as he counted.

Back at home that night, Lina and I sat on my bed and watched the bloated sky. The streets were empty. Arabs didn't like the rain, had all sorts of stories about what could happen to you if you got caught in it. Chilled bones. Wet lungs. A deadly cold. Baba would point to the pneumonia Lina caught that summer we were eleven. He was always telling us to bring an umbrella with us everywhere we went. So we had to be quiet when we opened the window and crept out onto the fire escape. We listened to the wind smack against street signs and push the creaking playground swings. Lina was pretending to be the weatherman. She moved her hands across the scene that was unfolding around us. "As you can see, there's rain moving in from the east," she said, gesturing robotically to her left.

"That's west," I said.

She ignored me. "From the north, we're beginning to feel those infamous Canadian winds. Hold on to your hats, folks!" I gripped the edge of my hijab and pretended that the wind was trying to rip it off.

"From the south, immigrants are creeping in to take your jobs. And from the west, or the east, or whatever, ISIS has figured out how to shoot lightning bolts at America like Zeus."

Lina had always really liked Greek mythology in school. She liked the vengeful, spiteful women, and the way those gods were always stabbing one another in the back.

"You're really smart," I said, after I stopped laughing.

"Well, I went to the Harvard of meteorology schools," she said.

"No, I'm serious," I said. "Your mind is like—I don't know how to describe it—it's like really sharp and quick. Like a knife."

"My mind is like a knife?" she said, raising an eyebrow.

I nodded.

She rolled her eyes, but I could tell she liked the comparison.

"I'm sorry I hit you," I said.

Lina nodded. Then scrunched up her face. "Wait. What? You *hit* me?"

"You don't remember?" I said, and I felt weirdly disappointed.

She shook her head. "I remember enough to know that I deserved it," she said. She reached for my hand and gave it a pat.

We came in when we really started to get wet and changed into sweats. Freda—that was what they were calling the storm on TV—was nearly manic in her fury now.

There were lots of storm-themed programs on television that night, and the whole family stayed up late to watch *Cloudy with a Chance of Meatballs.* While pancakes rained down and destroyed the schoolhouse, we were drawn back to the window. First me—I got up during a commercial break to use the bathroom, but instead of coming back to the sofa, I found myself nose-pressed against the glass, trying to see shapes in the storm. Lina joined me a few minutes later, either because she came looking for me or because she, too, felt the urge to watch the rain pelt the earth.

We were too excited to sleep that night. Every few minutes, I heard something outside snap. So I was still awake when Lina's phone began to buzz at around midnight. I rolled in bed to face her. She was lying flat on her back and holding the phone close to her face. The white light of her phone made her look pale and years older.

"It's Andres," she whispered over to me.

"Don't answer," I said. But when has Lina ever listened to me?

She picked up.

"Somebody better be dead," she said.

I sat up to look out the window. The rain was still streaming down, and there were no cars on the road now. The street was dark and empty. I watched a trash can roll down the sidewalk.

I flipped on the reading light over my bed and mouthed to her, "What does he want?" She rolled her eyes and mouthed back, "He's drunk." And then, in what I took to be a gesture of immense trust, she put the call on speaker, with the volume way down so it wouldn't wake Mama. She raised her finger to her lips and crawled over next to me. We listened to the grown man whine.

"I miss you, baby," he slurred. "I want you to be my girlfriend for real."

"Uh-huh," Lina said.

"Nah, for real this time. Straight up, I want you to be my wifey," he said.

"His wifey?" I whispered and Lina shushed me.

"No thanks," Lina said, sweetly.

"No *thanks*?" Andres said.

"I already got a new man," Lina said. "Treats me real good. And he's got this car that makes your janky old Mercedes look like child's play, okay?"

I was giggling furiously, biting my fist to keep from laughing out loud.

"You fuck better than you lie," Andres said, real quietly.

"You do both of those things equally bad," Lina said.

"Why you being so *mean* to me?" Andres said in this soft, high-pitched voice.

It was too much. I started to laugh and wave my hand in front of my face, trying to brush the sound away from the phone. But it was too late.

"Who's there?" Andres said. "You got me on fucking speakerphone?"

"Relax," Lina said. "It's just Amira."

"*Just Amira?* Fuck you. Fuck both you stuck-up A-rab bitches. Teach you to laugh at Andres." And then he hung up.

Lina and I looked at each other and laughed. We mimicked his whiny, girly voice. "My princess," I squeaked. "I need you."

She rolled into me, trying to muffle her laughter in my stomach.

"Why did you say that stuff to Andres?" I asked.

She laid her head on my stomach. I placed a hand on her forehead and ran it back through her silky hair.

"He's always nicer to me when I'm mean to him," she said to my belly button. "If I make him jealous, then he wants to be my boyfriend."

She yawned and rolled off my stomach, nuzzled herself into the nook between my armpit and my left breast. "You'll see," she said. "Tomorrow, he'll love me again."

We lay like that for a long time, listening to the wind whistling and knocking. At first, we were scared. We shone our phone flashlights, blinding each other. Then we switched the flashlights off and waited until we could see each other's shapes in the darkness. "Will the window break?" I asked. Then we both paused to watch the glass, which appeared to be trembling. "Have you ever wished you could be inside a tornado and not die?" Lina asked. And I nodded in the dark, because I had wished it.

"What would happen if we went out there?" Lina said. She had gotten out of bed and was squatting next to the window, tracing the rivulets of water with her fingers.

"We'd get wet," I said.

I slid open the window, and immediately water began to slide down the wall and drip onto the floor. I poked my head out and peered through the grate of the fire escape. Lina was breathing heavily behind me, giggling nervously every few seconds.

"What do you see?" she asked me.

"Nothing," I said.

Then the two of us climbed back out onto the fire escape, giggling and soaking our pajamas. We took turns yelling into the storm, our arms open wide in a come-and-get-it pose. We screamed obscenities. We screamed our own names. The rain slapped our cheeks, and the wind was a train through the tunnels of our ears.

Our mother appeared, with a hand towel draped over her head. She pinched the towel in at her chin and glared out at us like an angry, old-country peasant. "What on earth?" she said as we climbed back into the room. Mama slammed the window shut after us.

"What is wrong with you two?"

But we couldn't stop giggling.

Then our father and our brother emerged. They stood squinting in the light of the hallway, shivering slightly in their boxer shorts and T-shirts.

"What is it?" Baba asked. "What happened?"

But Mama didn't know how to explain to him that their girls couldn't seem to stop themselves from running out into the storm.

Eventually, the storm lulled Lina to sleep, but it kept me up. My hair was cold and wet at my neck, and the rain slapped against the window loudly. I could hear the building creaking and groaning. There was lightning, but no thunder. I turned on my reading lamp and sat up in bed. I read intermittently, picking up a novel I had started at the beginning of the summer and hardly looked at since. I had no desire to go back out there, not while Lina was asleep, but I liked watching all the vague shapes moving outside. The wind whistled against the glass, and the fire escape rattled. Every once in a while, I heard a smack or a thud somewhere in the distance.

At around 3:00 a.m., when my eyes were beginning to close and my head nodded into my book, I was jolted awake by the sound of a door creaking open. Footsteps down the hallway. I waited to hear the toilet flush or a faucet running, but there was nothing. Just a series of small creaks in the floorboards. Silence. Then I heard the unmistakable clink of the dead bolt. I could picture the chain lock swinging gently from side to side. He was gone. He was leaving.

I felt paralyzed in my bed. One Amira sprang up and followed him, no shoes, no scarf, wildly into the night. Another Amira lay there, heart pounding, palms sweating into the sheets. There was a flash of light outside, and I turned to look out the window. Two hazy cylinders of light slashed across 72nd Street. Headlights. Someone was waiting for him.

This time, I leapt out of bed. I pressed my face against the glass of the window. Lina lay motionless in her bed. It was hard to see through the sheets of rain and the moonless dark, but I could see a shape moving in the beams of the headlights. A tall, thin shape. Even through the storm, I could make out my brother's gangsta walk. He was swaggering, staggering, swaying through the night. He put it on thick. He was preparing to meet an enemy. His walk saying, *I'm not afraid of you.*

He was only a couple feet away from the car now, standing in the headlights. I thought he might lift his hands, place them behind his head, kneel on the asphalt, sink into the earth. But he just stood there for a moment, staring into the car, into the lights. Finally, a hand emerged from the passenger-side window and beckoned him. My brother disappeared into the back seat. I waited for the car to peel out, to disappear around the corner. I was already cementing the image of him standing in the rain as the last time I saw him. In the beams of the headlights, I could see distinct ribbons of rain whipping down onto the pavement. The car did not move. I wiped the glass with the hem of my T-shirt and waited.

I felt like I was watching something I shouldn't have been allowed to see. Like there was a crack in the universe that revealed the hand of God. Someone, some force, was supposed to move me away from this spot at the window. Some angel was supposed to lay me down to sleep. Because I wasn't supposed to be here, watching Sami disappear. I had spent so much time wondering where he went when he disappeared. It was the lifeblood of my imagination—how I learned to spin stories to fill the black sites of my mind. Where did Sami go and what did Sami do and how did Sami feel? These were the questions I fed on—as my brain grew from child to adolescent to near adult, this is what caused it to expand or shrink, to open new passages or to collapse others. Questions about Sami were what made me.

The back passenger-side door flung open suddenly, and Sami came roaring out of it. Even through the wind, I could hear him shouting. From the other three doors, three men followed. They were huge, these men. Through the rain and the dark, it looked like they were wearing jeans and cargo pants, T-shirts and hoodies. One of them had a baseball cap on. All of them had thick white necks. Sami was walking away from them, back toward the front entrance of our building. The three men followed. They split around him—two got in front of him and one stayed behind. One of the men in front of him put his hands out like you do to show a dog you're not a threat. Sami shoved him hard in the chest, but the man hardly moved. Now they tightened the circle around him. Sami bucked, he spun around, he tried to duck under their arms.

I thought, *I'm going to see him die.* I thought, *This is wrong.* I always imagined him dying somewhere far away from me. Bleeding out on some pavement I had never walked on. Pavement that I would have to construct in my mind later. I thought, I should scream. I thought, I should run down and hurl myself at these men, imagine I have a bomb strapped to my chest, imagine I am myself a deadly weapon. Scream *Allahu Akhbar* and watch the men dive, roll, take cover, wait for the explosion that would never come. I thought, I should take my brother's hand and run away through the rain. Run until the men who always come looking for Sami can't find him anymore.

They had Sami's arms twisted around his back. One of the men stood behind Sami—his bony wrist in the man's big, meaty hand—and appeared to be whispering in his ear. Sami snarled like a desperate beast. Another man reached behind him, rested a hand on something tucked into his waistband. I thought, They'll shoot him here, and the rain will wash away his blood, and I'll never be able to find the exact spot where life finally escaped him. But the whispering man kept whispering. And Sami stopped bucking, except for the occasional twitch, the loll of his head. The whispering man released Sami's wrist and wrapped his arm under Sami's elbow and around his chest in a sort of backward hug. I saw my brother lean back into the embrace. With his other hand, the whispering man stroked Sami's forehead and ran his palm back through his hair. The other two men looked away. The one with his hand poised at Sami's back, ready to grab, ready to shoot, slowly dropped his hands to his side. Suddenly Sami whipped around, and I thought for one horrible second that he'd go for the gun the whispering man probably had behind his back, but he was just turning for a full hug. My brother sank into the man's enormous chest, and the man wrapped his pale, glistening arms around Sami's small back. My brother disappeared into the man. He was nothing more than a pile of wet rags inside the man. My brother was just a boy, shuddering, crying on the shoulder of a big man. The other men backed away as if embarrassed. I was embarrassed. I thought, I shouldn't be seeing this.

The big man loped a big arm over my brother's shoulder and walked him slowly back to the car. All the doors of the car were still open, and I thought about how wet it must be inside. One of the other men reached inside and lifted out what appeared to be a backpack and handed it to the big man, who handed it to Sami, who took it and slung it over one shoulder. The big man patted Sami on the back, pulled him in for one more embrace. Sami rested his forehead briefly on the man's shoulder, and the man placed a large hand on the side of his face, kissed his temple, and then let him go.

My brother, who had come out to fight, thoroughly subdued now, loped back to the front door. The men slipped back into the car as Sami disappeared from view. The car pulled away from the curb and inched slowly away. I heard the front door creak open and click shut again. He was home. He had come back. Yet I felt I had watched him disappear.

I thought about waking Lina. It was as if I knew nothing and everything all at once. I wanted to bring them to Lina—the bits and scraps of my meager knowledge. I wanted to give her what I knew, and together we could make a story out of it. We'd take the bits and pieces and mold them up into a new Bay Ridge—one where we could stay and be the heroines.

I stood rooted in place. I heard the toilet flush, the sink running. I heard a door down the hallway open and shut. I imagined I could hear him dripping in his own room, peeling off his own soaked clothes, pulling a dry T-shirt and boxers out of those immaculate, desolate drawers. A T-shirt and boxers tucked between maps, maps folded and stacked, maps starred and scribbled on, maps left blank, maps to nothing. Maps I could not read. I wondered if he was climbing back into bed now. I wondered where he had put the backpack: Under the bed? In the closet? Was the backpack even real? My imagination was all I had.

"Lina," I whispered. But she wouldn't wake up.

When I woke up, I was angry at myself for falling asleep. I opened the bedroom door and listened to the sounds of my family moving around the apartment. I found my brother sitting on the sofa in the living room, looking the picture of innocence. He had a large hot circle of pita in his hands, so hot that he was tossing it back and forth from hand to hand as it singed his fingers. And I don't know why, but I thought, *This. This is the way I'll remember him.* No matter what happened next, when I thought of my brother, I wanted to think of him like this. He looked straight at me, right into my eyes. I knew he would let me sit next to him. He'd offer me a piece of hot bread. He wouldn't tell me what I wanted to know—he would never tell me, because he didn't know how, even though sometimes, I think, he wanted to. But he'd let me sit with him and listen to the words unspoken, to the steady thrum of his heart, to the sound of bread, made by Arab hands, mashed between his teeth. I thought, I'll go to him. I'll sit down next to him and we'll share bread, and maybe, for once, we'll be like me and Lina: We'll commune in silence. We'll trade telepathic messages. We'll understand better for having never spoken the words aloud at all.

I took a step toward him, one foot out into the light, one foot behind me in the bedroom. He stared steadily at me. The bread had cooled enough. He held the disk like a basketball, resting on his fingertips. I took another step, but then, from back in the darkened bedroom, I heard a gasp. Sami heard it, too. His eyes flicked away from my face and over my shoulder.

"Amira."

I could hear Lina moving. I imagined her patting down the sheets, the pillows, searching the bed for my body.

"Oh God," she said. And then it became a low, continuous moan. "OhGodohGodohGodohGod."

I took one last look at my brother. He nodded at me, and I stepped back into the bedroom. As I was closing the door, I caught a glimpse of him taking a bite out of the disk of bread, steam rising from the pocket.

Lina was rocking back and forth, her body curled around her cell phone. When she saw me coming, she reached out for me wildly, clutched my wrist in a vise grip. My first thought was that she had woken up and checked Facebook and seen that someone in Egypt had died.

"What is it?" I asked. "Is it Teta?"

Lina shook her head. "OhGodohGodohGod," she moaned.

"Just tell me," I said.

She looked at me like she was stabbing me with her eyes, and I really thought for a moment that maybe I had done something terrible to her, that she had woken up and discovered a betrayal I had forgotten all about. Then her face crumpled and she handed me her cell phone.

I was looking at a Web page, a screen full of photos. I clicked on them to expand them and started scrolling through. At first, I wasn't sure what I was looking at. I saw naked pieces of a woman's body. I thought, Why is Lina showing me porn? But as I squinted at the screen, gradually, the body parts started to look familiar to me. Lina lifting her shirt up to reveal her cleavage in a push-up bra; Lina shirtless and braless; juggling her own bare breasts; the top of Lina's head as she performed oral sex; a bare ass, flushed red from a handprint. And then there was the video. I looked up at Lina. She put her hands over her face. I clicked "play." You couldn't see much—the blurry outline of her face as the camera moved back and forth over her. The recording was jumpy, and it was hard to tell exactly what you were looking at, but you could hear her voice, clear as day, moaning his name.

I dropped the phone onto the mattress and looked down at my lap. It felt very important to say the right thing, but I didn't have the words. And then the silence stretching out felt worse than anything. When I looked up, Lina was staring at me, pleading with her eyes for me to say something that would make it better. When she saw that I had nothing, she folded herself in half, her nose pressed into her knees. I had to lean down close to her mouth to hear what she was muttering. It sounded sometimes like "He promised," and other times like "I'm sorry."


Outside, the sky was timeless, neither night nor day. The wind yanked on the trees like a high-school girl dragging some ho down the hallway by her hair.

"We have to delete them," I said.

I tapped my fingers wildly across the screen.

"Don't you think I tried that?" Lina snapped.

"Okay, well, then, we have to report them. There are rules against this kind of stuff."

Lina snatched her phone back from me and started frantically tapping on the button to report the first image.

"It's not loading," she said. "The Internet is being so fucking slow right now." She was almost shouting. I shushed her and reached for my own phone, but it was no better. The storm was slowing down time, making the air too thick for the invisible waves shooting over our heads.

"I can't do anything right now," she said, tapping desperately on the frozen screen of her phone with her index finger.

And then the room went dark. The street outside went dark. For one moment, there was complete and total silence.

"What happened?" I whispered, because I really didn't understand.

"The power went out," Lina said.

"Does the Internet work without electricity?" I asked.

"No," she said.

She was calm now, defeated. Andres had probably posted the photos right after he hung up on Lina, and that was hours ago. Who knew how many people had already seen them? It was dinnertime in Egypt. All our aunts and cousins would be scrolling through their Facebook feeds, posting the teddy bears hugging hearts and the close-ups of rose petals that were ubiquitous on the third-world Internet. I doubted there was a storm in Egypt. I bet the skies were sunny and clear. And although power outages were frequent, I imagined that everything was running smoothly over there for the first time in a long while.

"They'll take it down," I said. "Don't they have some sort of system for finding these sorts of things and deleting them right away?" I didn't really know who "they" were—I imagined a bunch of people sitting in front of rows and rows of computer monitors.

"Maybe," she said.

"I bet they're gone. I bet no one has even seen them."

For both of us, but especially for Lina, there was a constant desire to be prized by our family in Egypt. *The Americans,* they called us. The family in Egypt didn't really know us—just saw us translated through various screens, which inevitably made us brighter and sweeter. Our female cousins would sometimes crowd around the screen when we were chatting with Teta, pushing the old woman out of the frame and clamoring to ask us what kind of lip gloss we used and who we thought was cuter, Leonardo DiCaprio or Ryan Gosling. In the eyes of the family, we were special, we were wholesome, and we were thriving in a golden land.

I knew Lina was sitting there in the dark silently imagining everyone she loved scrolling through those porn-star images of her. She was just a hunched outline in the dark. But I wasn't ready to give up yet. I walked around the room, flicking all the switches as if I could magically find a single outlet that had its own private stash of electricity hidden inside. I opened our door and stepped out into the hallway. For some reason, I expected there to be more light in the hallway leading to the living room, but without any windows, it was even darker.

"Sami?" I whispered.

"Here," came a voice very close.

My eyes adjusted a little, and I saw his shape leaning against the wall only a couple feet away. Had he been listening through the wall? Or had he been on his way to the bathroom when the power went out and just froze in place like this?

"The power went out," he said.

"I know," I said. "I need it back."

I shuffled past him, flicking the hall light switch on and off. I was making my way to the hall closet, where we kept the Internet router tangled up in a pile of cords on the floor. I thought that maybe, if I shook it or kissed it or caressed it gently, it would light up for me.

I reached into my pocket and turned on the flashlight on my phone. The hallway was suddenly shot through with cold, white light.

I was on my knees, poking desperately at buttons on the router.

"That's not going to work," Sami said, standing over me.

"Help me fix it," I said.

"The power. Went. Out," he said again, slowly, as if I were dumb.

I whipped around to look up at him, my fingers still tangled in the snaking cords.

"I'm not crazy," I said.

"I never said that you were." He was frowning down at me.

"I saw you," I whispered.

"Saw *what?*"

"I'm not crazy."

He had always been good at making me doubt what was happening to me even while it was happening. Because we never talked about it. Not when he returned home after those days-long absences and was sitting across from me and eating breakfast as if everything was normal. Not when his phantom came and bled over me in my sleep. In those days, I often found myself crying. I'd be washing my hands and look up in the mirror and realize there were tears coming down. Or I'd be eating a bowl of Cheerios and suddenly I'd be crying again. And I felt disgusted with myself, like *Why are you crying right now?* Because there was nothing wrong.

I thought about launching myself up. About shoving past him, running to his room, and tearing it apart until I found the backpack. But then Lina came out of our room. She was dressed in jeans and my black hoodie. I lifted up the router to show her that I was working on it, that I would fix it. But she walked right past me.

She crossed the living room and crouched down next to the pile of shoes near the door. She started slipping on her sneakers.

"Where are you going?" I hissed.

And at this, my mother's ears must have perked up, because she appeared from the kitchen. Her eyes went first to Sami and me. Then they slid over to Lina at the door.

"And what do you think you're doing?" Mama asked as if she were bemused, as if we were messing with her.

"I have to go out," Lina said. She stood up, shoes on.

Mama's face went blank for an instant. And then she realized Lina was serious.

"You can't," she said.

"You can ground me some more when I get back," Lina pleaded.

"Absolutely not," Mama said. Now Baba had appeared behind her. He was in the pajama pants we had gotten him for Father's Day the previous year, the ones with tiny steaks printed on them.

"Please," Lina said. "I just need to find somewhere with the Internet. It's important. I'll do anything you want. I'll go to college, I'll get straight A's."

Baba put his hand on Mama's shoulder. "She wants to go out? *Now?*" he asked her. "But she can't."

"I've already told her that."

"There's a tornado outside," Baba said, meaning "hurricane." Then he stepped toward Lina, his hand outstretched. "Taali. We have candles in the kitchen. I'll teach you a card game from Egypt that your aunties and I used to play."

But when Baba stepped closer to Lina, it was like he spooked her. She snatched her house keys from the hook by the door, and made a run for it. "I'll be back soon, I promise," she yelled as she was already bounding down the stairs.

The four of us stood there, stunned. We were frozen. From outside, you could hear water flowing as if a river had erupted from the earth overnight. Then Baba went after her. I've never seen him move so fast. He ran out in his leather house slippers. I could hear them slapping against the stairs as he ran down to the street.

The way Mama looked at me then made me want to put a hand on her forehead and smooth her hair back, the way she always did with us. The way the big man, who I was beginning to doubt was real, did to Sami.

"Where is she going?" Mama asked me.

"I don't know," I said, which was the truth.

I didn't even know how to begin lying about this. "There were some pictures," I said. I had to look at my feet to finish the rest. "Of her. Online. Bad pictures. I think she went somewhere to try to get them taken down."

Mama covered her eyes with one hand, squeezing her temples. Sami went into the kitchen to look out of the window facing the street. It must have been strange for him not to be the one who ran or the one who was taken. Now he was one of the ones left behind. One of the waiting.

Baba wasn't gone long. He came back dripping. His white T-shirt was plastered to his chest. He had lost one slipper. He was shivering. Mama ran to get him a towel.

"I'm sorry," he kept saying to Mama as she helped dry him off. And I thought, What did they ever do to deserve us? God should have given them three different children, better ones, children with hearts instead of ticking alarm clocks in their chests.

They retreated into their room and were gone for a few minutes. I sat on the sofa and listened to the low murmur of their voices through the wall. I kept texting Lina, but she wasn't responding. Then Mama and Baba reappeared, wearing these flimsy rain ponchos I'd never seen before over their clothes.

"We're going out to look for her," Mama said. "If you hear from her . . ."

"I'll call you, I swear," I said.

They borrowed Um Hany's car, an old Dodge that she dutifully turned on once a week but hardly ever drove. They were going to start by checking all the local cafés, any place with Internet. I joined Sami at the kitchen window to watch them walk the three blocks to her car; they were two plastic bags being whipped violently around in the wind. I felt a familiar sort of panic from those days when they were always leaving to look for Sami. I was trying to memorize the shapes of them in case they never came back, but they were hidden beneath the rippling ponchos.

Once they were out of sight, I think it dawned on both Sami and me that we were alone together. I stepped back, away from him. The image of him resting his cheek on the big man's shoulder flashed through my mind. I blinked to get rid of it. I tried to replace the image with the boy who stood before me now, hair overgrown, a pimple on his chin. And then, for some reason, I thought about God. How God made the storm that was lashing down at us, how God kept me awake in the middle of the night, made me rise and look out the window. I'd never really felt that I was following God's plan, that everything happened for a reason, or that I was destined to do any of the things I had done. I felt more like I was on some sort of parallel path of my own making, and God was up there, watching patiently, waiting for me to step back onto the path He had made for me. But now I had seen Sami surrounded by strange men, the car headlights forming a portal to another universe. God wanted *me* to see it. It was the type of certainty I had often craved while praying or fasting, but had never experienced before this.

I made a run for it.

I bolted out of the kitchen, ran through the living room, and skidded across the hallway rug. Somewhere behind me, I could hear Sami mutter, "What the . . . ?" I opened the door to his bedroom. Inside: the crisply made little boy's bed with the denim-blue comforter, a stack of folded laundry in a basket in the corner, my high-school copy of *The Great Gatsby* on the nightstand, a single yellow Starburst candy on the dresser, and, leaning up against the wall, a black backpack. I dove for the bag, groped frantically for the zipper. I got it open and reached inside. Nothing. It was totally empty. Just a crumpled CVS receipt at the bottom. I looked up and there he was, leaning against the door frame, watching me riffle through the bag with this bemused expression on his face that made me want to scream.

"Where is it?" I asked.

"Where's *what*?" he said.

"Whatever was in this backpack." I held up the empty shell of it for him to see.

"I don't understand you," he said. The amusement had turned to a sort of weariness. He dragged a palm down the length of his face.

"I saw the men give this to you. They wouldn't have come here in the middle of the night to give you an empty backpack, so where is it?"

"Amira, habibti." He squatted down as if talking to a small child. "I've had that backpack for years. I use it when I play basketball. I put water bottles and towels in it."

"I'm not crazy," I said, but it came out a hoarse whisper. "You're doing something, I know you're doing *something*."

He stood abruptly and turned as if he was going to walk out. Then he pivoted back and pointed a finger at me. "You're the one who's doing something. I've seen you. I know what you've been doing with that piece of shit Faraj."

I felt this weird sensation then. A tingling that started in the fingertips of my right hand and shot up my arm and into my chest. Then a wave of heat. He was turning it on me. He was trying to distract me with my own shame.

When I ran at him, I kept my head down like a football player, charging straight into his stomach. I bounced off of him like I was nothing. Then I felt an arm hook around my midsection. He hoisted me into the air. I hung, folded over his arm, with my head dangling toward the floor. My hair fell down over my face. Sami turned and carried me out into the living room. His hands were a knotted lump digging into my back. He turned the corner and accidentally bumped me into the door frame. In the living room, he threw me down onto the sofa. He stood over me, shaking his head a little side to side. "Amira," he said, "what is wrong with you?"

"You're pretending that I haven't seen what I've seen."

He let out a long, frustrated sigh. "I'm sorry I fucked you up so bad," he said.

I was crying, I realized. Silent crying. Hot tears on my cheeks. I buried my face in the sofa so he wouldn't see. But he crouched down to the floor and pulled the hair back away from my face.

"Amoora, you have to let this go. You think I'm someone—like what I do matters. But, trust me, I'm no one. I'm nothing."

He patted the back of my head and stood up. I heard his knees crack like Baba's. "I'm sorry if I hurt you," he said, gesturing indistinctly to my body on the couch. He looked at me like he was trying to figure out where I was hurt. And then he waved his hand down the length of me and walked away. While I was still lying prone on the couch, I heard the door of his bedroom click shut.

In that moment on the couch—and that whole summer, in fact—I was strung up between two moons. My left arm reached toward the blurrier, bloodier of the two: Sami. And my right arm reached toward the brighter, rounder one: Lina.

Allah said: "We have ordained phases for the moon, which daily wanes and in the end appears like a bent old twig."

We were all still made of the same essential matter. We were just at different stages: Lina always full, pouring down on us her burning, bright light; Sami eclipsed, hanging, a blurry red mess in the sky that no one could bear to look at for too long.

And me? That summer, I was the twig.


Outside, on the front steps of our building, I watched a single car drive slowly down 5th Avenue. Semi-protected by the ledge above me, I held out my hand to test the rain. This isn't that bad, I thought. I took a breath, stepped out from under the ledge, and hurried down the steps.

I had an umbrella, but as I started walking toward the subway, the rain seemed to be rising up from the ground. I told myself that it felt kind of nice after such a long, hot summer. I wanted to laugh—all this fuss over some rain. But then a tree branch came at me from nowhere, like a baseball bat to the face. I ducked and it missed me by an inch, but in the process, I let go of my umbrella. I whipped around and watched it tumble down the sidewalk. I put my hood up and started to run.

I was looking for Lina, I told myself as I ran down the deserted streets. And again as I stood at the subway entrance and watched the water pour down the steps. I followed the direction of the water, both of us rushing underground. I was looking for Lina as I stood on an eerily empty subway platform, wondering if the train would ever come. I was afraid that the water was rising in the tunnel, even though I couldn't see it. That some pump down the dark hole of the tracks would fail and suddenly I'd be swallowed. But the train finally came. I was looking for Lina as I stood in the middle of an empty train car. I walked to the end and looked through the little glass window to the connecting car. There was one person in that car as well—a homeless person sleeping, sprawled out across the seats. The conductor made an announcement about all the stops we would be skipping because of flooded stations, and I imagined that wave of water again rushing through the tunnel toward us. I was looking for Lina as I stepped off the train at 45th Street. Two people came down the steps as I was walking up. I paused and waited for some recognition—we, the three people left in this underwater city of ours—for a nod, a smile, a *Crazy, right?* But not even a hurricane could thaw our stone-cold New York hearts.

I was looking for Lina as I stood gazing up at the brown-and-beige brick building, my eyes scanning the fifth-floor windows for movement. I was completely soaked by now. There were more people on the streets in this part of Brooklyn. People running, shrieking, darting from awning to awning. I took out my phone and tried to shield it from the rain while I typed.

First, I wrote to Lina. "Where are you?" I asked. I waited two minutes for a reply. When none came, I typed a second message.

"I'm outside your building," I wrote.

I looked around as I waited for a reply. There were three people huddled under the awning of a pharmacy that looked closed. One of them was a girl with long black hair. If I found Lina now, here, I thought, she could still stop me. I waited for her to appear.

My phone buzzed in my palm. A reply: "For real?"

I saw the blinds flutter in a fifth-story window above me. Lina was too late. The door to the building buzzed and clicked; I pushed it open and stepped inside.

I walked up four flights of stairs, dripping all the way. If someone wanted to find me, they could have followed the trail of water leading to his door. But no one did.

I raised my fist to knock, but then the door opened. Faraj stood there, so tall he had to hunch a little under the door frame. His face was scrunched up. "What are you *doing* here?"

"Hi, I'm Amira," I said. "Or do you know me now?"

Faraj rolled his eyes and made a gesture with his hand as if to wave my remark away. "Don't you know there's an actual hurricane happening right now?"

I stuck out my hand and then quickly retracted it. "Oh, I forgot. You don't touch women." As I moved my hand, droplets of water flew off my skin.

Faraj looked over my head and around the hallway, as if checking for neighbors. Then he grabbed my wrist, yanked me inside, and let the door slam shut behind me.

"Don't be stupid," he said.

I shivered a little under the blast of his air conditioning.

"You're soaked," he said, towering over me. "Let me get you a towel." But he made no move to go retrieve one. Instead, he placed his hands on my forearms and started to rub up and down, like I was a hypothermia victim.

I flinched and stepped back. "Do you even like me?" I asked.

"What kind of a question is that? Why would I hang out with a girl if I didn't like her?"

I shrugged and shifted my weight. My feet squelched in my wet shoes. I had made wet sneaker-prints on his floor. "Sometimes I feel like a means to an end," I said to my shoes.

"What does that mean?" And when I didn't answer right away, Faraj ducked down to force me to look at him. "Well?" he asked.

"I don't know, okay? But sometimes I wonder if you're just using me as some sort of entry point to Bay Ridge. Like you just wanted information about us. About my brother. And now that you've gotten what you can out of me, you're moving on to someone else." I was thinking about those idiot boys on Laylat al-Qadr. What had he been saying to them before I arrived? What was he urging them to do? They were assholes, those boys. But I couldn't stop myself from worrying about what they may have said to him.

"Using you for information?" Faraj scoffed. "Who even does that? I mean, what would I even do . . ." And then it dawned on him—what I was saying. His whole body hunched, coiled into itself, before springing back upright. He pointed a finger up to the ceiling, and it quivered there for a moment before he angled it down to my face.

"You think *I'm* an informant? You know what?" he said. "Fuck you."

I thought he was going to open the door and throw me out right then. But he kept going. "I'm serious. How could you even think that about me? After everything I've told you?"

He sounded genuinely wounded, and, once again, I started to doubt my own instincts. He was looking at me like I had betrayed him, like we were two characters in a Shakespeare tragedy and I had just stabbed him in the gut.

"Sami said something about you being trouble. And you're always poking around, asking questions about the police and who does what." My voice came out in a whine.

He narrowed his eyes, drew his head back. "That's because I trusted you. I told you shit I haven't told anyone. I thought—I don't know— *This girl won't judge me.*" He laughed bitterly and turned away from me.

"I'm sorry," I said. I reached forward to touch his shoulder, but he shrugged me off. "I was just trying to look out for my family."

At that, he spun back around. He had a mean little smile on his face. "Looking out for your family? Protecting them from *me*? When they are so clearly not looking out for you."

"What does *that* mean?" I spat. My voice alternated between a whine and a yell, between the one doing the hurting and the one being hurt.

"All summer," he said, "you are running around with your sister and no one is watching you. You come to my apartment by yourself. Anything could have happened to you. You're here now in a fucking hurricane. What if I was a different sort of guy?"

I opened my mouth to protest, but he kept talking right over me.

"When I first met you, I thought you had the perfect life. Your life is like an alternate ending to mine. If only things had gone a little differently, maybe I'd get my brother back and my parents wouldn't be so broken, and then I'd have a family reunited and we'd do things like go to the masjid together and watch movies, too. But then, the more time I spend with you, I realize it isn't true. You're just as fucking lonely as I am. You've got your whole family around you and you're still all alone."

"You don't know anything about me or my family. I'm not alone. They're out looking for me right now." As I said it, I pictured Mama and Baba in their rain ponchos scouring the streets yelling my name instead of Lina's.

I turned around to leave. I had my hand on the doorknob. When he spoke next his tone was softer. He stepped toward me, and I could feel him an inch from my back.

"I just think you deserve someone who's going to pay attention to you. To take care of you. It's a dangerous world out there."

I whipped around, almost bumping into his chest. "You don't think

I know that? I watched them take Abu Jamal right in front of my eyes. I saw Imam Ghozzi's blood on the sidewalk, and I scrubbed the piss out of our mosque. And everywhere I walk, I feel footsteps behind me. I can't tell who's an enemy. I can't tell if you're an enemy." Once again, I didn't even know I was crying until I felt the hot tears on my cheeks.

"I'm not your enemy," he said, his voice cracking with emotion. He put his hands on my shoulders and looked right at me. His eyes were thick with tears.

"But you're not my friend, either," I said. "You don't even know me in public. You act like I'm invisible when it suits you."

"I see you," he said. "I see you."

He kissed me there, at the doorway, as I continued to drip onto the floor.

This wasn't why I'd come, I told myself. I didn't mean to come here. I was looking for Lina. His mouth moved down my neck.

We stumbled toward the couch, and when we got there I realized that we had removed some of our clothing on the way. His shirtless stomach pressed against mine, and I remember thinking, *How did I lose my clothes?* Then he was on top of me, my hands on his shoulders, as he reached up and gently slipped my scarf off my head. It fell to the floor in a whisper. When his hands moved down to the button of my jeans, I took a long, sharp intake of breath. Faraj froze, his hand on my fly, and said, "Do you want me to stop?"

Yes, yes, I thought. I wanted us to stop a long time ago.

But I said nothing.


After, I tried to rinse myself off in his bathroom and ended up getting water all over the floor. I felt very concerned about that, the water, so I spent a long time trying to dab at it with bits of toilet paper. When there was nothing left to clean up, I finally left the bathroom. He was sitting on the sofa with his head in his hands. I stood awkwardly by the door. I was dressed, but my scarf was still lying on the floor near his feet. I had to walk over to him to get it. I walked softly, as if I didn't want to disturb him. Like I wanted to leave him with the weight of his head in his hands. I reached down and grabbed the scarf lying just a few inches from his left foot. I stood there fumbling to put it on.

He lifted his head and looked up at me. "We shouldn't have done that," he said. "This is so bad." He dragged his fingers down the length of his face.

"Why?" I asked, which made it sound like I disagreed, even though I didn't. Of course it was bad. It had been bad from the start. But I wanted to know if his bad and mine were the same.

"Because you're a Muslim," he said.

"I know I am. And so are you," I said.

"I've done it before, but never with a Muslim. Oh God," he said. He stood and started to step toward me, and then stopped. I thought he was going to start crying again.

"I'm sorry," he said. "I shouldn't have done that to you. But you should have stopped me. Now you're . . . you're . . ."

He gestured wildly at me, as if my body standing there was all that was needed to finish his sentence. He looked at me, his eyes pleading with me to absolve him, to apologize to him, to tell him that it was all my fault.

I turned from him and walked to the front door. "You should pray," I called back to him, my hand on the doorknob. I meant it as a kindness—it was all I wanted for myself in that moment, to close out the rest of the world and hear only the words of God uttered back to me in my own voice. But he took it as a punishment. His face crumpled, and I left him there, his head in his hands.

The R train wasn't running anymore—something about flooding—so I had to take the N train and then walk the rest of the way home. I waited on the platform with one other woman, in fuchsia scrubs. There was this loud gushing sound coming from somewhere, like there was a waterfall nearby. The woman in the fuchsia scrubs kept looking around, trying to find the source of the sound. This was reassuring to me. I wasn't the only one worried about drowning under there.

The train came. The woman in scrubs took one last look around her before stepping aboard. I followed behind her. Half the lights were off in our train car, but I was glad. It was soothing being in half-darkness. I sat down and pulled my phone from my pocket. No messages. I typed a message to Lina. I typed a bunch of things, and then I deleted them all. "Hi," I ended up sending. This time, her reply came almost instantly: "Hi." I smiled to myself in the dim light. I felt better about everything now that I had her back. The train was moving so slowly. It was rocking back and forth, and it felt like being on a boat. Or a submarine. The graffiti on the walls of the tunnel became long-tentacled sea creatures. I didn't need to be afraid of drowning, because we were already submerged. I looked up to check on the woman in scrubs. I hoped she was feeling better, too. But then I spotted a figure all the way down at the opposite end of the car. Black hood up. A familiar pair of sneakers. She had her phone in her hand and she was smiling down at it. I wasn't surprised at all. My first thought was: *Of course.* I stood up. One hand on the bar above me as I started to scale my way toward her. I felt the warm hand of God on my back—even after what had happened at Faraj's. When I was still a few yards away, Lina looked up.

"Hello," I said, grinning.

"Hello?" she said, as if testing whether anyone was home.

I was standing in front of her now, feeling a little bruised and a little blessed. But I was also feeling proud, like this was my life's greatest accomplishment thus far. Here she was. *I* had found her. I had been delivered to her.

"Were you looking for me?" she asked.

"Yes," I said. Because a part of me was always looking for her.

I sat down on the seat next to her. She rested her cheek on my shoulder, and for a moment, we just sat there. The train car creaked; the wheels shrieked. We were inching our way toward home.

"The pictures?" I asked.

She lifted her head, pulled at a hangnail on her thumb.

"I reported them. I went to a coffee shop in Park Slope. Nowhere in Bay Ridge had power."

"Are they gone?" I asked.

She nodded. "I stayed there refreshing my screen until they disappeared." She looked up at me then. Her eyes were the color of fog. "How many people do you think saw?" she asked. I started to open my mouth, but she immediately cut me off. "Don't answer that," she said.

So I didn't. We rattled on. We'd have to get off at the next stop and walk twenty blocks home.

"We're in deep shit," I said, thinking of Mama and Baba.

"You, too?" she said. "Good. We're the same, then."

We got off at 59th. The storm was all around us. A low wet whistle in our ears. We held hands and ran.

God was with me that day, for sure. Mama and Baba never even found out that I had left. When we got home, they were still out hunting for Lina, their search extended by false tips from well-meaning neighbors. They had called a few people, asking if they had seen Lina. And those few people called a few more, until the entire neighborhood knew. People kept calling and texting Mama and Baba—Lina was in Owl's Head Park; no, wait, Shore Road Park; no, wait, she was at the basketball courts, the library, the Starbucks; she was seen entering an apartment building on 68th and 4th with a ponytailed man; and, perhaps most improbably of all, she was at the big masjid on 6th. Baba always told me—never ask an Arab for directions, because even if they don't know they'll make up an answer just from some compulsive need to be helpful.

In the end, Lina herself called them and told them she was home. I could hear Baba yelling on the other end: "What the shit, ya Lina?"

When they got home, Mama and Baba peeled off their rain ponchos and left them dripping in a glistening pile on the floor. I wondered if the trail of water leading up the stairs of Faraj's building and into his apartment was still there. There was more yelling. Threats made—to send Lina to Egypt or maybe to Connecticut (what was in Connecticut, I'm not sure). I looked on from the kitchen. I was not part of it. I was the good one.

"Where do you go?" Baba asked. Lina was seated on the sofa, and he stood over her. She started to answer, calmly, quietly. She started to tell him about getting on the train, going to Park Slope, about how she needed the Internet. I was surprised about how honest she was being. But then Baba cut her off.

"Not just now," he said. "All summer. You are always leaving. Where do you go?" He had one hand on his head, his fingers twisting his wiry hair. Lina slumped deeper into the sofa, looked down at her knees. And then Baba found me standing in the kitchen doorway. His eyes were wet. He used to tell me about how the kids in his village would make fun of him for his eyes, big and brown with long, curly eyelashes. Aiyoon al-baqarah. Aiyoon al-nisaa. Eyes of a cow. Eyes of a woman.

"I expect this from him," Baba said, pointing over my shoulder. I turned and found Sami there behind me. "But not from you." He was speaking to Lina, but he was pointing at me. We were all implicated now. The children that kept breaking his heart.

And then there was Mama, who kept all our feelings. She took both of Lina's hands in her own and asked, "Can you tell us what's wrong?"

I looked at Lina and waited. Could we speak in words all the things that were wrong with us? Sami never could. But a boy is not taught to think and speak the way girls are. Lina opened her mouth and began.

She began with Andres. She told Mama and Baba how they had met. She told them about Lotus and how she thought she was going to be a model, how she thought maybe she was special. She told them about coming home drunk, about bleary-eyed hangovers, and cruel text messages. She jumped around in time. She went backward. She told a story about a boy who told everyone she gave him a blow job in the bathroom in the eighth grade, and how it wasn't true, but how some-times she forgot that it wasn't true. Sometimes she was the eighth-grader who gave out blow jobs in the bathroom. Baba was sitting on the edge of the sofa now, his body angled away from her, his hands rubbing his knees. She left some things out—she didn't tell them about the cocaine or about the Jersey City motel room or about the ghost who had taken her there. But her omissions were not about protecting herself. Lina had always been lousy at protecting herself. She didn't tell them the things she knew they couldn't bear to hear. And she didn't tell them about me. I barely entered her stories at all, except, occasionally, as the savior, the good one. She didn't tell them about the time she'd held *my* hair as I crouched over a toilet. Or about the time she dragged me away from a man on a rooftop. She was protecting me, but I didn't want to be protected. I wanted to be exposed. I wanted my parents to turn from Lina and see me standing in the doorway, to beckon me, to pull me down on the sofa next to them and hold my hands, too.

Behind me, Sami leaned on the kitchen counter and looked out the window. He was somewhere else. I didn't want to be like him, caged even now. I took a step toward the living room. It was time to speak. *Say something,* the voice commanded. *Do something.*

Mama was holding Lina's face in her hands, and Lina was crying. And then Lina rested her head on Mama's chest, and they were both crying, and they stayed like that for a long time, whispering to each other. I could go to them, whisper *my* secrets to my mother, and then cry into her soft, warm chest, too.

But I didn't do anything. I let Lina confess alone. I was the good one.

The rain beat on outside. After dinner, we got power back. Mama brought us large glasses of iced hibiscus tea. She placed her hand on Lina's forehead, as if checking for a fever. Lina's phone had been buzzing frantically for hours. Messages from boys—boys we grew up with, boys who lived in that very building, boys we went to high school with, boys we barely knew, boys we'd never met, men writing from other states, other countries, men old enough to be our grandfather. They wrote with invitations, some more subtle than others. They wanted Lina to purr *their* names into the camera. They wanted to yell at her, to scold and punish and threaten. They wanted to meet. They wanted more pictures. They wanted her to look up from *their* laps with her big sometimes green, sometimes gray eyes and make them feel like they were kings.

Mama looked from the phone buzzing on her nightstand to Lina and back again. She picked it up, and I expected Lina to scream, to lunge and snatch the phone away from her. But Lina just sat there. She picked up her glass with a shaking hand and took a long, slow sip of tea. Mama took one look at the phone and winced.

"I'm going to take this for a while," she said. "We have to delete your social-media accounts until this blows over, okay, habibti?"

Lina nodded silently, and Mama slipped the phone into her pocket. Then she lay down next to Lina on the bed and stayed there until she fell asleep. When Lina's deep, slow breaths filled the room, Mama lifted herself very gingerly out of the bed. She must have thought I was asleep, too, because she tiptoed over to my side of the room and peered down at me. Just then, my own phone, unconfiscated, glowed next to my pillow, illuminating my face in the dark. She saw me then, wide-eyed, looking straight up at her. She gasped a little, frightened. Maybe I reminded her of Sami in that moment, a silent, sneaking child in the dark. Maybe I reminded her of herself, a woman whose deepest feelings were known only to herself.

Mama recovered and leaned down to kiss my forehead. "Good night, my love," she said. And maybe she could sense that I wanted something more from her, because then she said, "Not all men are like that, you know. There are men out there who are better."

"Okay," I said.

She kissed me again and then left the room. She didn't pull it all the way shut, and I imagined her creeping past in the middle of the night, peering in through the crack to check that we were still there.

I could hear the water running in her bathroom. I could picture her washing her face and then patting it very gently with the thick white cream she used every night. I wanted to believe her about the better men. My father was better, I knew. But there were also men from across the globe who were writing to my sister, Lina, who only ever wanted to be loved, just to tell her that she was nothing. And then there was my own phone, still lighting up next to me. Messages from a man who had plucked me out of the crowd, chosen me out of all other girls, just to apologize, in a string of late-night texts, sincerely and from the heart, for using me up, for spoiling me, for unmaking me, for ruining my chances for love and God. I had a rash from his beard. I scratched it until the skin was raw.

. . .

The storm had squatted over us for nearly forty-eight hours, but it was finally rolling inland, losing power. The sky was still a thick, opaque gray, but the winds had died down, and it was only drizzling now. In the end, we lost power for a few hours, and some tree branches fell onto the road. We heard that Brighton Beach got kind of fucked up, and in the Rockaways, piles of rubble, which used to be houses before Sandy, sailed through the air like missiles, taking out car windows and spearing screen doors. But Bay Ridge? Bay Ridge just looked like maybe she'd had a bit too much to drink. In the morning, she smiled sheepishly, pulled down her skirt, and kept right on going.

It would take more than some bitch named Freda to bring Bay Ridge to her knees.

I woke to the sound of cumbia music blasting from a passing car. The sun was shining in a beleaguered way, stretching through a bloated layer of clouds left over from the storm. When I looked across the room at Lina, she was wide awake, staring straight up at the ceiling. Her eyes were swollen from crying. The skin on my neck burned. I jumped out of bed, feeling like maybe I would scream. I wanted to comfort her, but my hands were in fists, and I felt this choking in my throat. I had to run out of the room or I would explode. I couldn't decide what I was angry at—Andres or Faraj or the invisible man from the Jersey City motel room, or the invisible man who got Mama pregnant and left her all alone, or the invisible vandals who pissed in our mosques and slashed our imams, or my brother and his invisible secrets, or all the stupid little boys we went to school with who showed up to prayers high and fucked white girls and then told us we were too impure to marry. Or myself, for being silent when I had the chance to speak. For always being a pussy.

Sami walked through the front door as I was kicking an umbrella across the living room. He stopped at the door and looked at me but didn't say anything.

"What are you looking at?" I said.

He shrugged and bent down to untie his sneakers. He was dressed as if he had just come back from a run and was drenched in sweat.

Sami looked even thinner than when he had first shown up from prison. Even thinner now than in the month of hunger. All those cigarettes were chiseling the fat out of his face. His cheeks were sunken, his bones jutted out. He looked sick, like a cancer patient. Something terrible was happening to him, I knew. Or he was doing something terrible. Part of me pitied him, looking at his atrophied body melting away before my very eyes. But another part of me felt the rage pulsing in my chest. He kept lying to me. He told me he was no one, nothing, but when I looked at his disappearing body, it didn't feel like nothing. It felt like everything.

"Why are you always running and playing basketball when it's, like, a hundred degrees out?" I said. "What's wrong with you?"

"Beats kicking umbrellas," he said.

He stood up straight and looked right at me. "You want to tell me what's wrong?" he said.

"You want to tell *me* what's wrong?" I said.

He shook his head. "Nope," he said, and then walked off toward his bedroom.

I kicked the umbrella again and punched a pillow on the sofa. I went to check on Lina. She was curled up in bed, looking at the laptop we shared. She looked up when I came in and made this odd, cruel little laugh. "Look," she said, holding the computer out for me to see. "All my admirers." I scrolled through chat after chat from boys who had seen the photos. All boys we knew, boys who had her number. "Slut," they said. "Sexy," they said. "Want to go out sometime?" they said. "Want to blow me?" they said. "Your body is beautiful," they said. "I jerked off to your titties in the shower this morning," they said. "Nice pics," they said. Mama thought that, by taking her phone, she could contain all the hate, that she could hold it all for Lina. She had no idea.

I logged out of the chat and gave the computer back to her. She just turned back to Netflix and hit "play." Lorelai and Rory were talking a mile a minute about the most wholesome of problems, and I knew that this was yet another way Lina had devised of punishing herself. Watching this show of white childhood purity, of family values, of unbreak-able mother-daughter bonds.

I drank three cups of coffee back to back, and then I knocked on Sami's door with shaking hands. He opened it like he was expecting me.

"You want to help me commit a crime?" I asked. He stared at me for a moment. And then he followed me out the door.

Forty-five minutes later, Sami and I were standing in front of Andres's apartment building in Flatbush. His white Mercedes was parked on the street out front.

"You ready?" Sami said, handing me the bat.

I nodded but didn't move.

"Do you think we should?" I said, because now, with the car right in front of me and the sun shining down on us, I was losing my nerve.

"Do you think he deserves it?" Sami asked.

"Yes," I said.

"Will it make you feel better?" he asked.

"Maybe," I said. "Yes, I think so."

"Then I'm down if you are," he said. He flipped his hood up and I did the same. I loved the image of us, brother-sister hoodlums lurking on a tree-lined residential street in Brooklyn.

"Will you go to prison forever if we get caught?" I said.

"Probably. And you'll get the chair."

The wind rustled through the trees, and big, floppy green leaves fell down all around us.

"It's not funny," I said.

"I know," he said, "but the truth is that I'm screwed anyway. This can't make it any worse than it already is."

Just then a moped came tearing around the corner, and we both jumped. It trailed black smoke that stank up the air around us long after it had disappeared. I waited until the rumbling of its motor faded to a growl.

"And there's no one who can help you get out of whatever this mess is?" I asked.

Sami smiled a little at me and shook his head.

"Whatever it is, I can tell you don't want to do it."

He shrugged. "Doesn't matter if I want to be doing it or not. I'm stuck either way. If I do it, if I stop—the outcome is the same."

Sami's whole life felt to me then like a series of traps. But who was baiting them? Who was waiting patiently around the corner to collect him? I thought of Al-Shaytan. The devil could manifest almost anywhere, even inside you. There was an invisible hand out there somewhere. I wished there was somewhere Sami could go to rest for a little while, to lie low, to breathe freely. I closed my eyes and felt the sun on my face, heard a car honking somewhere close.

I opened my eyes. "Why don't you go to Egypt for a little while?" I said. "Just until things, you know, settle down. Maybe, after a while, they'll just forget about you."

Sami tilted his head. "Who do you think 'they' are?"

I felt embarrassed then, like a little girl playing pretend. But I liked the idea of him walking along the Mediterranean at night, smoking shisha on the sidewalk, eating our grandmother's food, the same food that had made our father.

"I don't know," I said, gesturing to the air around me, to the invisible hand that had him by the throat even now. "Whoever it is that's got you trapped."

"Egypt, huh?" he said.

"Yeah," I said, getting excited now. "It'll be great. You can ride camels in the desert and bring us back another piece of the Pyramids." I could see him riding tall on one of those great beasts, reins in hand, a kaffiyeh tied around his head. I heard Baba's voice in my head then— singing fragments from one of his favorite poems by Shánfara:

Get up the chests of your camels
and leave, sons
of my mother. I lean to a tribe
other than you . . .
In this land is a refuge for a man
from wrongs,

for one fearing scalding hatred,
a place to withdraw.

"It does sound nice," Sami said. He came toward me and took the bat back out of my hands, tucked it under one arm, and nodded. "Let's walk," he said.

I looked back at the white Mercedes. It had some bird shit on the windshield. An air freshener shaped like a pineapple hung from the rearview. Sami was moving north up the block. I hurried to catch up. He had the bat dangling from one hand now and was swinging it gently as he walked.

"Did you ever wonder why I got out of prison so suddenly?" he said. But his face was angled away from me, as if he was talking to someone else, an invisible person on the other side of him.

"You won your parole hearing," I said. "The lawyer got the date wrong."

He smiled into his shoulder. "There was no parole hearing. They just opened the doors and let me go." He swung the bat out in front of him and I pictured a giant black gate swinging open.

"Because of good behavior?" I said, remembering the way Baba had kept chanting the phrase after he hung up with the lawyer all those weeks ago.

Sami nodded. "The best behavior. I promised to do what I was told, and they promised to let me go. And here I am—their good boy. Their eyes and ears."

We walked by a barbershop, its red, white, and blue stripes spinning. A boy sat in a chair by the window, scowling into the mirror as the barber shaved the back of his head. His mother looked on from behind the chair, nodding grimly every few seconds.

We walked on in silence past a few more storefronts. A prickly feeling started at my chest and rolled up my neck. I rubbed my skin, trying to wipe it away.

"I don't understand," I said.

"Yes, you do," he said. "You saw. You already know."

I wanted him to look at me, but he kept his eyes straight ahead. I tugged on the bat dangling from his fingertips and pulled him to a stop. I stepped in front of him, looked right up into his face. It was brown and shining with sweat. The sharp angles of his face looked like they had been chiseled from stone, as if he were some dusty pharaoh from thousands of years ago carved into a tomb. I reached up and patted his cheek the way our mother would have if she had been there with us.

The lines of his face crumpled into a silent sob. "I just wanted to go home so badly," he whispered into my palm. "I didn't think I'd actually have to do anything."

"It's not your fault," I said. But then he shook my hand away, wiped his face roughly with the crook of his elbow, because if there was one thing Sami couldn't abide, it was empathy. He had to be alone with his feelings. I imagined them ricocheting inside his closed body like a pinball. He started walking again abruptly.

I followed a few steps behind him. I watched his skeletal frame, the hard lines that made him. Our mother had been trying to soften those lines, to weigh him down, to root him. All these weeks, I had been wondering what it was like for Sami to be home. But now I knew he had never come home. He had been released, but not freed. Returned to Bay Ridge, to his childhood bed, to his mother's cooking, his father's singing, his sisters' whispers, but not to home. What was it I had said to Faraj? It's hard to know who your enemies are? Did the man who attacked Imam Ghozzi get to go home? Or the people who desecrated our mosque? What about the men in suits who tore through Abu Jamal's café? Were they sleeping soundly in their beds right now? Or eating food that would fill them, that would make their footsteps even louder? Those people could go anywhere, belonged everywhere. Sami only belonged inside the frame of an LCD monitor, through the scope of a camera's lens or the sights of a rifle. We were the enemies. Those kids playing soccer in Afghanistan. Sami lurking around Bay Ridge. Me and Lina conspiring on the subway. I didn't need to look behind me when I felt footsteps a little too close. The men who followed us out of jail cells and into mosques and to motel rooms and schools, who chased us down city streets, who played us like a video game in the Nevada desert, who played us against one another—they were all home.

I thought about giving up then, about taking Sami home and telling him to lock his bedroom door and never come out again. I'd bring him food and tell him about the world. But then I pictured opening the door to my and Lina's bedroom and her asking me where I'd been and what I'd been doing and me saying the same thing I always said: *Nowhere. Nothing.* I didn't want to play by the rules anymore, to try to be good. I was an enemy. I looked up and realized we had walked in a circle around the block and were right back where we had started, in front of Andres's car. My empty hands twitched. I grabbed the bat from Sami's hands.

"Okay, count to three," I said.

"Are you sure?" he said. "Maybe we should just go home."

"Just do it," I snapped.

Sami counted to three and nothing happened. He tried again, in Arabic this time.

"You want me to take the first shot?" he asked.

"No," I said, feeling more ashamed by the second.

"We can just go home," he said.

And then, like jumping into cold water, I lifted my arm and swung the bat down on the windshield. Sami made a little yelp of surprise. And then he whispered, "Keep going, Amira, you can do it, hit it again." The windshield was only a little chipped, but I kept hitting it, harder and harder, and then I was running all around the car, hitting it with the bat and yelling, "This is for Lina, you piece of shit."

I swung and swung until my palms were sweaty and the bat slipped right out of my hands. It clattered to the ground, and Sami picked it up. He smashed it against the back windshield, which made a terrific crunching noise. He hit it again, and the glass shattered completely and caved inward. I laughed and clapped my hands. "Do the front one," I said. And Sami ran around to the front of the car and swung the bat down with such force—the bat was like an extension of his bony arm. He was so skinny and shrunken and gaunt, and it was like he was saving up the last of his great power all for this Mercedes owned by a guy whose name he did not know. He didn't know anything about what Andres had done. He just knew that I needed him to help me make someone hurt. He stood on the hood and he was this terrible, beautiful monster and I felt for the first time ever that his power, his anger, his pain, was mine, too. That the bat was a link, funneling unspeakable thoughts and feelings between us. "Fuck you," he screamed to the car. "Fuck you," I screamed to the car. "Fuck you, fuck you, fuck you." And the bat came down again and again.

We heard someone yelling at us from a window up above. Sami leapt down from the hood, let the bat clatter to the pavement, and grabbed my hand. "Run," he said. He pulled me so hard it felt like my feet were barely touching the ground. I twisted around just before we turned the corner. I wanted to snap a photo for Lina. But Sami hooked an arm around my waist and hoisted me up. "Run, Amira," he said. "You gotta run."

We ran until my sides felt as if they had split right open. We ran all the way to the subway, down the stairs, through the turnstiles, and into the first train that pulled into the station. We rode five stops going the wrong way before we got off and switched sides and got on another train, headed in the right direction. Sami slipped the hood off his head, and I did the same. "Shake the glass off your shoulders," he said. I did as I was told, surprised to feel tiny shards fall down onto the ground.

We were quiet for most of the way home. I was jumpy, waiting for a SWAT team to swarm the train car we were sitting in. I felt like everyone was staring at us.

"Relax," Sami said finally. "No one is coming for us."

"How can you be sure?" I said. But he didn't answer.

From the advertisement above our heads, Dr. Zizmor looked down on me from a rainbow spray of stars. His downward-slanted eyes smiled and told me that I'd done the right thing. When the train paused at Church Avenue, the conductor said something unintelligible through the loudspeaker. "Pardon the interruption," I imagined him saying. "But Amira Emam finally manned the fuck up and did something. The train will be moving again shortly."

At Parkside Avenue, Sami nudged me. "How you feeling?" he asked. "You feeling bad?"

"No," I said. "I'm all right. I think maybe I even feel kinda good."

He nodded, and I wondered if he had felt this way the first time he smashed something.

"You were whaling on that car like a boss," he said.

"I was?" I said.

"Yeah. I was a little scared."

"You were?" I said, feeling flushed with pride.

"Uh-huh. I thought, What's stopping her from turning that bat on me?" he said. He was pushing the skin of his left palm with his right thumb. "I'd deserve it," he said.

"No, you wouldn't," I said, but we could both hear how hollow the words sounded, how false.

"So what happens now?" I ask.

"Nothing," he said. "We go home, shower, and never speak about it again."

I wasn't sure if he was talking about the car or about the thick white hands that were wrapped around him even now.

"I won't say anything," I said. But then, in the next breath: "What do they want, anyway?"

Sami looked up at the ceiling of the subway and along the railings as if he could find the answer there. "They want to prove that we are what they say we are."

"And what's that?" I said.

He turned to me and grinned. "Scheming barbarians," he said. "The type of people who can't control their anger. Who plot revenge on innocent people. Who smash up cars. Who wear hijabs and beards." He pointed to my head and then to his own chin.

"Stop making jokes," I said. But I couldn't stop myself from smiling. I reached my hand up to my head, patted my hijab.

"I don't want you to worry. It's all over now. I won't do it anymore," he said.

"But won't they be mad?" I asked.

He didn't answer the question. He just looked down at his hands in his lap, which were dotted with little red scratches.

At Atlantic Avenue, we switched from the Q to the R. Sami got up without a word, and I followed behind him out of the train and through the station. Our next train was packed. We had to squeeze ourselves into a corner. There were bodies pressed all around us, arms crisscrossing over our heads. We were caged in by limbs.

"Are you leaving us?" I asked then. It came out in a whisper. This was the question permanently lodged in my throat. It felt strange to finally spit it out. I felt like there was an empty space inside me now. I took a deep breath in. I could smell the perfume of the woman next to me. Sweat from the armpits stretched over our heads. From somewhere down the train car: a teenage rapper that Lina loved, his auto-tuned voice warbling out from someone's phone.

"Hell no," Sami said. "I'd be happy if I never left Bay Ridge again. Besides, someone needs to keep an eye on your crazy ass."

I could tell he was trying to lighten the mood. He wanted me to forget that he had ever cried into my palm, even if it was only for a second. I could never forget, but I decided to let him slip into jokes, to leave the truth back on that sidewalk in Flatbush, among the smashed glass and the wounded pride of some petty boy. I preferred this—the two of us riding the subway home toward Bay Ridge, our hands red and raw, having just created something brand-new together.

And I think he did, too, because then he said, "But I hope you're not thinking about a life in crime. Because you're straight-up terrible at it. Taking a photo of the crime scene. Ya Allah."

I laughed. "I guess that was pretty stupid," I said. "I just wanted to show Lina."

"She'll know," he said. "She'll know something's up the second she sees you. You can tell Lina, but keep your mouth shut around other people, okay?"

I did have visions of all the boys of Bay Ridge, all those boys who had texted Lina, who had been clicking their tongues at her and calling her a whore behind her back for years, hearing the story of her twin sister who took a baseball bat to a Mercedes. I imagined Faraj opening the door to his apartment to find me standing there, bloody palms clenching a bat. But I just rolled my eyes at Sami and said, "I'm not *that* stupid."

Finally, we rolled into Bay Ridge. We were walking down 5th, brother and sister Emam, waving to our neighbors and salaaming the shopkeepers. Some boys driving by in a Ford Explorer with a sticker on the window that said "RIP Paul Walker" rolled down the windows to shout at Sami. "You gonna be at the courts later?" they asked. "Probably," he shouted back, and they nodded and kept driving, Drake whining loudly from their speakers.

We saw Baba sitting out on the steps, talking to one of his friends. The other guy was waving his hands wildly in the air, and Baba was shaking his head so hard I thought it might roll right off. "What do you think? Arguing politics?" Sami asked, gesturing toward them.

"For sure. Stupid Egyptians," I said in my best Baba accent.

"Stupid Libyans," Sami said in his.

"Stupid Americans," I said.

Baba could see us coming now, and his face lit up in a smile. His children walking toward him. He would call out soon. Say, *Ahlan, ahlan, ahlan, ya habaibi. Taalu hina and hear what this crazy guy is saying.*

"That was fun," Sami said. "Next time if you want to key up a Lexus, let me know."

We were ten feet away from Baba now. He was lifting himself slowly up from the stairs and opening his arms, greeting us. "Ahlan, ahlan, ahlan, ya ibni, ya binti," he said. *My son, my daughter.*

We stayed outside with Baba for a while, sitting on the stoop and listening to him argue with his friend about who was worse—the Saudis or the Qataris. When we arrived, he had unclipped his phone from his belt and called up to Mama. "They are here," we heard him tell her. "Yes, together. And they even dress alike today. They look so cute," he said, winking at us. I hoped Baba wouldn't notice the matching cuts we had on our hands.

I couldn't see her, but I felt Mama peering down at us from the kitchen window. Poor Mama—always watching. It would never be enough.

It was a Sunday—Baba's day off—but he had already spent hours doing the books with Mama in the morning, and even now he'd occasionally unlock the door if a customer ambled along, pleading with him that he just needed one quick thing.

"You see this guy," Baba's friend, a Tunisian named Khalid, said to us as Baba was returning from helping a customer at the shop. "Always working."

Sami and I turned to watch Baba lock the door once again and walk back to us on the stoop. He had a lopsided walk—not quite a limp, more like one of his shoulders dipped down lower than the other, like years of carrying heavy loads had dragged the shoulder to a permanent collapse.

"This is American way," Baba said as he returned. "Americans work hard."

"Yes," Khalid said. "They work all the way to their graves."

This started a new debate between them, Baba arguing that Americans weren't lazy like other cultures, that Americans didn't wait for other people to take care of their problems, and Khalid arguing that Americans had no balance, no time for family or faith or even for a good meal.

To everyone's surprise, I jumped in.

"I agree with Uncle Khalid," I said. "Sometimes, when I'm about to fall asleep, I wish I could find a way to do something else while I sleep. Like to make sleep a more productive use of my time."

Sami smiled at me and bumped my arm a little with his. A tiny flake of glass fell from a fold in the fabric of my shirt.

"Bezzubt!" Khalid said in our Egyptian dialect, nodding his head vigorously at me. "The problem with your father is that he has not been back to Egypt in so long. He doesn't remember the way of life there. He needs a vacation from American work-all-the-time life. If he go back to Egypt, he will see how his country take care of him. In the balad, the heart is at ease."

Baba shook his head gently and looked down at the cracked concrete step he was sitting on. Some kids tore by on bikes, screaming and knocking a trash can over as they passed. At the masjid across the street, Imam Ghozzi was sweeping the sidewalk near the very spot where his cheek had been sliced open by a stranger's knife.

"Egypt is where we come from," Baba said after a long silence. "But it is not our mother. It does not love us any more than this land." He gestured out toward the sidewalk with the fallen trash can. "I know here in Bay Ridge all everyone talk about is 'fee balad,' 'fee balad' this, 'fee balad' that, but let me tell you, habaibi," he said, looking straight at Sami and me. "There is no magic fee balad. And there is no magic in America. Everywhere the same."

Khalid couldn't really find anything to argue with in that, so he changed the subject to a rumor he had heard that all Muslims in America were going to be microchipped. Baba took the bait. I sat and listened to them argue for a while longer. But then my palms ached, and I wanted to go inside and check on Lina, and to see if Sami was right—if I really looked different now. I got up and shook Uncle Khalid's hand, kissed Baba, and fist-pounded Sami.

When I was upstairs in the apartment, I immediately made my way to the kitchen window. I peered down at the stoop below, and just as I expected, I saw Baba and Khalid still there, still waving their arms around. But Sami was gone. I couldn't crane my neck enough to see in which direction he had gone. He was walking on a sidewalk somewhere. Somewhere, his palms burned.


It was dim in our bedroom. Lina had the curtains closed. I stood over her in her bed and grinned wildly.

"Where have you been?" she asked, and I grinned some more.

I held up my hands for her to see. They were checkered with a thousand tiny cuts.

"Flatbush," I said.

She narrowed her eyes at me, glanced from my palms to my big happy mouth.

"Oh no," she said. "What did you—"

But I reached into the pouch of my sweatshirt and then held out my hand to her.

"I have a gift for you," I said.

In my hand, a shard of glass, a small jagged star.

.   .   .

I showered to rinse off the rest of the glass, and afterward stood in front of the mirror in our room, admiring the pink scratches on my hands. The rash from Faraj's beard had faded, and now there was a small X-shaped cut behind my left ear. I pressed it, winced, and smiled. Lina had placed the small star of glass the size of a thumbnail against the windowsill near her bed. It had a bluish tint and looked like a piece of sea glass we might have picked up from a faraway beach. It shone like a jewel in the sunlight.

When I got dressed and came out into the living room, there was a baby trying to cram one of my shoes in its mouth. It had the thick black curls of a twenty-year-old on its tiny head, and arms coated in a layer of black fuzz. It was fat and wearing a Mickey Mouse onesie. It was an Arab baby.

Mama and Lina were standing over the baby, and I wished one of them would rescue my shoe.

"Oh no," Lina was saying.

"I hope you don't mind . . ." Mama said.

"Please," Lina said.

". . . I volunteered you to watch little Mahmoud here."

"That baby hates me," Lina said.

Mama scoffed. Then, finally, she scooped the baby up and handed him to Lina. I could see a trail of slobber running down my Jordan. During the transfer, I noticed he had what appeared to be a Cheerio stuck in a roll of fat on his thigh.

"It's just for a little while. Um Hany had a doctor's appointment, and she said you did such a good job watching him the last time."

Lina rolled her eyes. Mahmoud clenched a fistful of her hair.

"I'm busy today," Lina said.

"No, you're not," Mama said. "You're just going to sit around crying all day over a boy who's not worth the dirt at the bottom of that shoe," she said, pointing to my discarded sneaker.

Lina looked up sharply. She winced as Mahmoud yanked more of her hair and began stuffing it into his mouth. She glanced from me to Mama and back to me. Then she looked down at the baby munching on her hair. "Never fall in love," she told him. Mahmoud looked up at her with big, brown cow-eyes and grabbed her earlobe.

As I finished getting ready for work, I could hear Lina talking to Mahmoud. She was just outside the bedroom, following him as he crawled up and down the hallway.

"Never trust anyone who wears cologne every day," she said. "Wait until you're forty to have sex. Never let anyone take photos of you, like, ever." She gave him other advice, such as "Shave your arms" and "Take a bath."

When I came out of our room, she was sitting on the floor, using my phone to snap a photo of herself with Mahmoud in her lap.

"I thought you told him never to let anyone take photos of him," I said.

"He doesn't listen to me," Lina said.

"Are you going to be okay while I'm at work?" I asked.

"Yeah, I'm fine," she said, handing me my phone.

Baby Mahmoud was nuzzling into her neck, trying to get comfortable.

"I hate babies," she said.

Mahmoud's cheek slipped down from her neck and rested on her breast. He yawned and closed his eyes.

"I can see that," I said.

"I'll never have kids," she said.

At the front door, I turned back to look at them. Mahmoud was already fast asleep, curled against Lina's body, her breast a soft pillow for his head. I saw her smile at him. I saw her twist one of his black curls around her finger.

Baba cooked dinner that night. He shooed Mama out of the kitchen, swatting at her with a kitchen towel until she sat down on the love seat in the living room.

"Go watch television with your children," he said as he ejected her from the kitchen. "Make your brain like a mush."

Lina, Sami, and I were watching an action film. I don't remember which one. Though it wasn't scary, Mama kept jumping and gripping

Sami's forearm. I waited for him to get annoyed, but he didn't. He just gave her a gentle pat each time until she released him. She also asked a lot of questions—about the feasibility of the stunts, about the emotional growth of the characters, about the moral arc of the story. The woman was incapable of just sinking back into the love seat and watching a movie that made absolutely zero sense. She couldn't make her brain like a mush. She was a mother. There was no "off" switch. Lina answered all her questions thoughtfully, posing increasingly complex hypotheticals that had me doubting what I was seeing. Maybe this movie was deep? Maybe it *was* really a metaphor for deportation?

Baba made a casserole of potatoes and meat in a tomato sauce. It was delicious. We ate in silence, watching the end of a movie that was suddenly profound.

There's a chapter of the Qur'an called "Comfort," sometimes translated as "Consolation" or "Solace." And in it, a verse: "With every hardship there is ease. With every hardship there is ease." The same line repeated twice, in case we have trouble believing it the first time. In case we have a hard time recognizing ease even when it is offered to us, even when it is served to us on a white plate. In case we are drowning in our hardship and cannot see those tiny life rafts of ease—soft potatoes, meat slow-roasted to velvet, your mother's laugh trilling gently in your ear.

THE BOY COULDN'T SLEEP. As he tossed and turned in his child-sized twin bed, he kept hearing the sound of someone slipping a note under his door. He sat up and turned on his bedside lamp and stared at the door, but no one and nothing was there. A few times, he fell into fitful sleep—a brief flash of vivid color, of shapes and figures blurring together—before waking up again moments later, his breath wet and heavy.

It was very important to him to be brave, although he had never articulated this to himself. It was more a struggle his body waged on behalf of his unconscious—the need to be brave, to be hard and unflinching and still. So he pushed himself out of bed, disgusted with himself, determined not to sleep if sleeping meant this gasping dance. He pushed his hair out of his face—it had grown long in the two months since he arrived home—curls tufting unevenly in a black mass around his head. In prison, he had always kept it shaved close to the scalp. He had developed an absentminded tic of outlining the jagged white scar that split the back of his skull into two warring halves with his middle and index fingers. He had gotten it in prison, but it felt like it had always been a part of him. He reached for the scar now, but found the over-grown curls in his way. Strangers wouldn't even know the scar was there now—they wouldn't be able to see that easy marker of a barbarous life. How had he let his hair grow so long?

He walked out into the living room, thinking he would watch some television in order to keep his mind and body still until morning. But when he turned the corner, he saw the other girl—not Amira, Lina—sitting on the sofa watching Al Jazeera on mute. He was immediately and acutely aware of their aloneness, and realized that they were rarely ever alone together. He racked his brain for childhood memories of the two of them alone, but his mind was blank. He always found it difficult to look at her for too long—her face was always transforming, trying to find the expression desired by the beholder. Her expressions faded in and out like images replacing one another on a screen. Not like Amira, his prized girl, who had mastered a certain emptiness in her expression that he always thought, perhaps vainly, she had learned from him.

"Couldn't sleep," said the girl with too much emotion in her mouth. "Me, either," said Sami.

He half sat, half stood on the arm of the love seat, hovering awkwardly across from her. She stretched out her glowing legs across the couch, making it clear he shouldn't sit there. On the television, pilgrims were swarming Mecca. The boy scratched his scalp through his thick, unruly hair.

Muslims all around the world were wrapping themselves in white cloth and flying east or west, north or south, to that glorious Black Box, the Ka'ba in Mecca. The boy could not believe how much time had passed. The entire summer had slipped away while he snuck around Bay Ridge. He was like a boy in a fairy tale who fled the castle and left a trail from the dungeon to the woods. He kept stopping to cover his tracks, to erase the trail, and so he never got very far from where he started.

On TV, men draped in white and women cloaked in black, some carrying black umbrellas, circled the Black Box like water down a drain. Sami watched and waited for the pilgrims to get sucked down into the center of the earth. He felt the pull of gravity at his own feet. He closed his eyes and waited, but nothing happened. He longed to be inside that crowd, to jostle, to touch the gold-and-glass casing that protected the

306 Aisha Abdel Gawad

footprints of Ibrahim, to press his feet into the rock where everything began.

Sami had been thinking of the prophets a lot recently. Of Ibrahim and Muhammad, Yaqub and Isa. And of virtuous Yusuf, especially him. The prince's wife tried to seduce him, but he would not be tempted! He let himself be dragged to prison instead, where he interpreted the dreams of his jailers and brought God into that dark place. And eventually, of course, because he was steadfast and brave, the truth of the temptress's lies came to light, and Yusuf was released from prison, a man made even more righteous by the fact that he had been wronged.

*O my Lord! Prison is more to my liking than that to which they invite me.*

There was something that appealed to Sami about being the tragic hero—the boy who wouldn't accept what the world dangled in front of him. It was so easy for Yusuf to choose prison; in fact, for him, it wasn't really a choice at all. Sami had been trying to convince himself that he, too, had only one path in front him, the moral path, which led straight back to a cage. But now, as he watched the pilgrims with their shaved heads circle the Ka'ba, he knew this was a lie—to prefer prison to life. His sister shifted on the sofa and yawned with a little squeak. He wanted to run to her, clutch her shining legs, stare into that shifting face, and ask her to tell him what to feel.

It's said that if you make the great pilgrimage your previous sins will be erased and it will be like you are reborn a stranger to yourself. So the pilgrims flock, hundreds of thousands of them, to the place where the first prophet, Ibrahim, smashed the pagan idols, and from where the last prophet, Muhammad, ascended on his Night Journey, traveling from Mecca to the Dome of the Rock in Jerusalem and thence to the Throne of God. They circle and pray and cry because they will miss their sins. The Saudi police stand guard, watching out for signs of a stampede, with all those people pushing and pushing to get closer to forgiveness.

While Sami thought of Yusuf, Lina thought of Hagar as she watched the pilgrims crowd the television screen. Hagar, a whore on the verge of death who birthed a tribe of two million.

Now this sacred place in the desert has been repaved in marble. It is air-conditioned, and there are vending machines and bathrooms inside. After the pilgrims have been purified and forgiven, they can go to the Mecca Mall and buy lattes from Starbucks.

Sami couldn't help but wonder what it would feel like to wrap himself in white, to circle the holiest spot on earth, to return home to his family an elevated man. He watched the masses writhe. He longed to be inside of them, just a white speck tucked among endless bodies. What it must feel like to be both holy and nobody—to be blessed and anonymous, just a man, just a Muslim, and nothing else.

Lina, on the other hand, was thinking just the opposite. How awful, she thought, to be crushed in among all those bodies, not knowing whose limbs were pressed against your own, losing your body to the crowd. And to have to compete with so many others for the grace of God. How would He be able to see her down there, how would He know her? She wanted to stand alone in a room, to look down at her breasts and hands and feet, to feel her body rooted in the ground, and then she might be ready to lift her head upward.

Sami was ashamed, and ashamed of himself for being ashamed. He was a sneak, a thief, a snitch. He was a survivor, a fighter. He was a traitor and a coward. He was a martyr and a hero. He wanted to stay home and eat his mother's cooking. He wanted the peace of a locked cell.

Lina was defiant, her heart a pumping rebellion. She dreamed herself a warrior princess, a supremely bad-bitch goddess-divine. But there were photos of her on the Internet, preserved for all time, kneeling at the feet of a man who wanted to plant a flag in her body.

The boy turned away from the pilgrims and from the girl with her magic eight-ball eyes. *It is certain. It is decidedly so. Without a doubt. Yes, definitely. You may rely on it. As I see it, yes. Most likely. Outlook good. Yes. Signs point to yes. Reply hazy, try again. Ask again later. Better not tell you now. Cannot predict now. Concentrate and ask again. Don't count on it. My reply is no. My sources say no. Outlook not so good. Very doubtful.*

He found himself rummaging under the bathroom sink for his father's electric razor. The low buzzing noise it made soothed him as he watched curls of his black hair fall into the sink. He moved the razor back and forth across his scalp until it was bare and red and he had nowhere to hide anymore.

Out in the living room, the girl was gone. The oil from her body lotion had left ghostly outlines of her calves on the fake leather of the sofa.

Birds kept flying into the windows. The sun had risen, and the sky was bleached. The birds can't see, I told myself behind the screen of my closed eyelids. That's why they keep flying into the windows, one after another. The sound of them colliding into glass all around me. An assault of beaks and feathers, their bodies landing with a gruesome thud, thud, thud. Relentless. A holocaust must be waiting for us on the fire escape, I thought. And on the sidewalks down below. My mother and my sister and I will take turns with the dustpan, sweeping the small crushed bodies off the streets. Lina will want to say a prayer for each bird, to whisper blessings over broken wings, to bury each creature, one by one, in the earth. My mother and I will prefer a mass grave, an unceremonious pile in the dumpster.

*Thud, thud, thud.*

The Prophet Suleiman once said that we Muslims have been taught the tongue of birds. With my eyes still closed, the sheets of my bed twisted around my ankle like a rope, I tried speaking to them. "It's a window," I said. "The sky stops here. Fly upward, birds." But, apparently, I did not inherit from Suleiman the gift of communing with animals. That magic died with him. Not that I didn't try. After I learned the story of Suleiman and the lapwing bird in Qur'an school, I remember crouching down to earthworms on the playground and whispering into where I thought their ears might be.

The lapwing once delivered a wondrous and frightful message to Suleiman. "I have just seen things unknown to you. With truthful news I come to you from Sheba, where I found a woman reigning over the people. She is possessed of every virtue and has a splendid throne. I found that she and her subjects worship the sun instead of God." All anyone else in the room would have heard was the lapwing's melodious whistle, like a woodwind instrument. But Suleiman heard the lapwing's words clearly. Eventually, he won over the Queen of Sheba. She abandoned her sun and worshipped the one true God. She gathered her people, and they joined the battle array of men and jinn and birds.

After Qur'an class, Lina and I used to take turns pretending we were the Queen of Sheba. Except, in our games, we never stopped worshipping the sun. And in our world, it wasn't sacrilege, because God made the sun. Because, when we raised our browned arms up to the sky, there was God sending His rays of light down to us.

The thuds were louder now. I could hear that the birds were inside the apartment, swarming, flying into lamps and walls and tables. They were colliding with our belongings, smashing the artifacts of our little world, the relics of our tribe. I crawled out of bed, staying low to avoid the assault. I dodged and ducked my way to the door and reached for the handle just as it came flying open, knocking me hard in the shoulder, so that I went flying backward and landed on my tailbone, my feet splayed out in front of me.

Boots pounded against the hardwood. There were so many of them, and they were all screaming. "Down!" they screamed. "Get the fuck down." Even though we were all already down. There were Mama and Baba lying on their bellies like slaughtered animals in the hallway. Lina was next to me somehow, huddled into a ball, her arms crossed over her head like a helmet. I was lying on my side as if taking a nap. I could see the rise and fall of my father's back as he breathed. I could hear the pleas of my mother as she shouted. "Don't hurt him," she kept saying. There was a boot by her head. He reached his black wing down to her face and screamed, "Stay the fuck down." I realized I could understand every word the birds were saying.

The winged man shook his head at my mother, and spittle flew out of his mouth. He and his brothers were crashing around as if they had forgotten how to fly. As if panic degraded their basic instincts. They were afraid, I realized. They were terrified of the huddling bodies on the floor. As if under my T-shirt, under the skin of my bare legs, hidden in the tangle of my hair, I had a slingshot and stones that could pierce their small, beating hearts. They had guns and armor, and they were everywhere, and we were on the floor, but they were afraid of *us*. A scared animal is a dangerous animal, and suddenly I joined my mother's chorus. "Don't hurt him," I called out. I lifted myself up off the ground. I was crouching, I was reaching for the door handle to pull myself up. I was going to come at them real slow, with my palms lowered and outstretched. I was going to offer myself to them, to whisper soothing words, to calm their fears. But it was too late. They had my brother. They surrounded him in a cage of their own bodies. Once they had him, once they felt his beating heart thudding against their own chests, they were calmer. They remembered how to fly straight again, how to inhale and exhale, how to balance and chew and swallow. They hugged him close. My brother the earthworm, now jostled and torn, tossed from beak to beak. The birds swept him out.

We could hear their many feet pounding down the stairs. Somewhere, a neighbor screamed. But in the apartment, it was quiet. Lina was shuddering into the floorboards, her arms still crossed over her head. My parents were lifting themselves up, but they were too slow.

"Hurry!" I yelled, running over to help them up. "They're taking him."

I kept repeating that as we ran down the stairs after him: "They're taking him. Mama, they took him. They're going to take him. They are about to take him. Baba, Baba, hurry, he's been taken." I would have gone on forever. I would still be repeating the words now, a story that never ended. But at the bottom of the stairs, just as Baba was pushing open the front door, Mama whipped around. I collided into her chest. She held my face firmly, so firmly it hurt, between her two palms, and said, "I know." Her voice was clear and steady. Her eyes did not flick about nervously. She didn't wring her hands or tug at the ends of her gray-black hair. My mother knew exactly what was happening. It had all happened before. There was always only one end for her boy.

Then she turned and stepped out into the early-morning sunlight.


Out on the street, my father was talking to two policemen. He was using the voice he reserved for white Americans, even though both cops were vaguely brown. Excessively polite, verging on obsequious. Every word a big, toothy smile. His English suddenly impeccable, as if he had it on reserve for emergencies.

"Forgive me, sir, maybe it is my misunderstanding, but what is the charge here? When I studied to become an American citizen, one of the great honors of my life, I learned that you must charge someone if you are going to arrest them. So, if you wouldn't mind, could you please tell me what you are charging him with?"

My mother stood off to the side, half in sunlight and half in shade from the awning over the Abu Nuwas storefront. Her body was angled away from my father, away from the policemen who had been sent over to deal with him. She was watching the other spectacle, the main event.

I felt eyes all over me. I looked upward and around. Some of our neighbors had come out of their apartments, and more were poking their heads out of windows. Someone was frozen across the street with his hand on the door handle of his car, as if he had been about to get in when the police dragged Sami out but had been transfixed by the sight of this boy in a cage of human bodies. There was a camera, one of the black eyes, affixed to the streetlamp in front of me. Another camera, this one more old-fashioned, like a miniature camcorder, pointed at the front door of Abu Nuwas. But I knew, and Baba knew, and Sami and Mama and Lina knew, that this camera led to nothing. It was a joke to pretend that we could watch, too, could threaten people with our watching.

I wanted to run away from all the eyes, to turn back into the safety of our dark stairwell and into our apartment, the one that had just been invaded and just as quickly abandoned, a worthless conquest, to rejoin my sister, who was still curled into tornado-drill position, head between her knees, eyes shut, the hard shell of her body pressed into the floor. I thought I could get on the floor and cover my neck with my hands, too, and wait for the storm to pass. But then I looked at my mother again. And, finally, I forced myself to follow her gaze, to see what I had been trying to blot out. My brother's body pressed against the side of a boxy black van. His arms and legs spread wide like a star. Two police officers, a man and a woman, were patting him down, and others just stood around watching, ready to form the human cage again. I could see these officers, but it was also like they weren't there. Like it was just my brother alone against that van, wincing at nothing. His wrist twisting all on its own. He was shirtless, wearing only a pair of faded blue basketball shorts. The bruise the shape of an eye in the middle of his forehead blinked into the sunlight.

Suddenly his arms were folding themselves behind his back, his wrists pressed together. I saw the gleam of handcuffs, and that is when I made my confession. I ran into the cluster of officers, made visible again by the clank of metal, and started telling them everything. How the whole thing had been my idea, Andres, the bat, the car, the broken glass.

"I did it all myself," I said. "Sami wasn't even there. And I know I shouldn't have, but you don't know what he did to our sister. And I'll pay for the car to get fixed, I swear."

One cop, a small man but surprisingly strong, caught me in his arms. I would like to say that he was rough, that he tackled me and threw me to the ground. But he didn't. He merely caught the seventeen-year-old girl who had hurled herself toward him and wrapped his strong, thin arms around me, pinning my own arms to my sides. He was like a gentle straitjacket, and I poured the whole summer into his chest.

I told him about how sometimes I dreamed about the motel room in Jersey. How I was back there, except that I was Lina and the man who brought me there was in the bathroom and I was on the bed and I knew he'd be back any minute, except it didn't occur to me to run. I told him about the sofa in Faraj's living room. About the stranger who had plucked me out of the crowd. About the days Sami and Lina and I spent hiding in the apartment, where it was safe, eating the rice our mother made, impossibly soft and silky and salty, straight out of the pot. Picking pieces of meat off the bones of an animal our father had cleaned and sliced. I sobbed into this man's chest and told him that it was all my fault. I had been running all summer, running and bringing trouble back home with me. I could see now that I had been wrong. That feeling of disaster I felt when I first saw my brother in the living room, surrounded by our neighbors and our sheikh and our parents, it wasn't coming from him. It was coming from me.

"Please," I begged. "It was all me. He didn't do anything wrong. It was me. It was us." I tried to gesture to the invisible girl next to me, the one my family and my neighbors always saw when they looked at me, even when she wasn't there. But my arms were still pinned under his arms.

"Shhh," the man said, squeezing me even tighter. "We're not here for any of that."

From somewhere in front of me, someone was calling my name, but I did not recognize the voice. I still thought maybe I could stop this. If I just kept talking, if I finally said all the things I had kept secret inside my body. I did not admit it was over, not when I saw the officers opening the door to the van or when I saw them walking on either side of my brother, their hands at his elbows like two prom dates escorting him to the black box that would whisk him away. And even when I saw the cursed one, the precious one, that miraculous Zamzam baby, my brother, Sami, following tamely, even when I saw his tattooed wrists handcuffed behind his back, I still wouldn't admit it. They wouldn't come now, I thought, not when the holiest of all months was behind us and the holiest of all days ahead of us. More neighbors tumbled out of the buildings surrounding us.

They pushed Sami toward the black van but he was walking on his own, placing one foot in front of the other, and he had his chin lifted in the air. They turned him around so that they could push him into the open mouth of the van. Suddenly he was facing me and looking straight at me, like he'd always known I would be there, like I had been there all the time. He smiled, and he was the twelve-year-old bringing me a snapping turtle again. There wasn't anything scary in that flash of crooked white teeth or in the one small dimple in his right cheek—it was the smile of a boy who still thinks he can save the world.

They shut the doors. The female cop patted the side of the van like it was a good beast before she hopped into the passenger side. Someone was already in the driver's seat, had always been there probably, waiting for this day to come. The man whose arms were around me was gone—in the van, or perhaps he had just rejoined the cluster of police left standing on the sidewalk. It was just us and them now. The van drove away, headed north on 5th Avenue. The boy was gone.

The boy was gone, but people kept tumbling out onto the streets, our neighbors approaching from every corner, circling us. My mother had sunk into a crouch, one hand braced against the sidewalk. There were women around her, hands on her shoulders, stroking the top of her bare head. In a matter of minutes after the van had pulled away, I lost sight of my mother. She had been absorbed into a circle of women—women who had always kept her at arm's length, women she had never tried to win over. But here they were, shielding her with their bodies.

I could hear my father behind me, his voice getting louder and less controlled. His careful English was unraveling, his accent slipping out of his mouth.

"Where did you take him?" he shouted at the remaining cops. But they were done with him, done with us. They started to disperse, walking in clumps of three or four to various cars parked nearby, as if they were headed home after a summer barbecue that had dragged on for too long, as if they had consumed too much sun and too much beer and too much cake, as if they were going home to lie down in a cool, dark room and sleep it all off, this whole day, our whole lives.

"He ask you a question," one of our neighbors shouted. "Answer him."

There were maybe thirty people gathered around us now. The crowd started to murmur and shift. Some of them stepped off the curb and began sort of pacing around in the middle of the street. The police—there were maybe seven or eight of them—seemed to notice our tribespeople for the first time.

"Where is the boy?" a woman screamed from her window four stories above us.

"Feyn al-walad?" another woman, with her hand on my mother's back, echoed in Arabic. The question started to swirl around us. Our neighbors began to repeat it softly at first, the words tossed like a few pebbles at the backs of the retreating police officers. But then the chant swelled, and pretty soon we were all shouting in unison, alternating back and forth between Arabic and English: "Feyn al-walad?" "Where is the boy?" "Feyn al-walad?" "Where is the boy?"

We were milling about in the middle of 5th Avenue, walking in circles, asking the same question over and over again. A man with a cane began jabbing the end of it into the sky as if poking God for answers. The police were retreating even faster to their cars, some of them talking into radios. We followed them. I found myself sandwiched between two big women as we slapped our hands down on the trunk of an unmarked Crown Vic. The sun was on top of us now, the white sky of the morning replaced by an unblinking, cloudless blue. The cop cars were pulling away. I remember thinking, You can't get away from us now. Look how many of us there are. All these Arabs and not a one of them *moderate,* the way they like us. Mild, tepid, drained of all that foreign flavor. We were mad. We were desert people, our brains steaming in the heat. I could feel the ghost of the baseball bat clenched in my hand, and I could hear the sound of glass cracking and then shattering, the satisfying *thwack* of the bat against the windshield. I ran after the Crown Vic as it was pulling away. I chased it and kept slamming my hands down on the trunk. I felt my people all around me. We were forming a human barricade, we were blocking the streets. The cops would be trapped inside the cage of *our* bodies now, and then they would have to answer us. But the Crown Vic kept going—faster and faster, it accelerated down 5th Avenue. It slowed momentarily to dodge a cluster of three Arabs in the middle of the street, but then the road ahead was free and clear. It sped off as I chased it, my hands slapping the air in front of me. "Feyn al-walad?" I shouted. But the chant had died down. My tribespeople were slumped over and panting now. The cops were gone. There was no one to listen to our screams now, no one to whom we could point our canes and fingers and say, *If you see something, say something.*

There was a man bent over next to me, his hands on his knees, panting into the asphalt. I loved this man then, and I have loved him ever since. He was having trouble catching his breath. He was heaving like he might never get it back. That is how hard he had run after my brother.

Over the heaving back of that beloved man, I saw the figure of a girl in the doorway of our building. She was barefoot and wearing pink terry-cloth shorts and a neon-yellow T-shirt. Her eyes were gray, or maybe green. She stood sequestered in the doorway, safe from the panting ruins of our almost-riot. She held out her hand to me, and there was nowhere for me to go but toward her.

# Acknowledgments

I'd like to thank my editors, Margo Shickmanter and Cara Reilly, for asking all the hard questions and reading with such wisdom and empathy. I'm grateful to the whole team at Doubleday for ushering my book into the world. Where would I be without my agent, Claudia Ballard, who read a hot mess of a draft many years ago and stuck with me through countless revisions and three babies (mine, hers, mine again)? Thank you for your unwavering support and guidance. I am indebted to the Creative Writing Department at Cornell, especially to Ernesto Quiñonez and Helena Maria Viramontes, who pushed me to take myself seriously. Thank you to my fellow writers who read early drafts of this novel, but especially to Daniel Peña, Kimberly Williams, and Sally Wen Mao. Thanks to Shawkat Toorawa for introducing me to a world of Arabic and Muslim literature I did not know existed and which still nourishes me. Thanks to the MacDowell Colony and the Blue Mountain Center for the gift of time. Thanks to the *Kenyon Review* and *The Muslim World* for publishing early excerpts of this book.

I'm grateful to the Associated Press for their incredible reporting on the NYPD's surveillance of the Muslim community. It is thanks to the AP that I was able to read so many NYPD reports documenting their surveillance of Muslims across the five boroughs and even beyond. The

"Demographics Report" in this book is a fictionalized report inspired by those documents (although the NYPD originals are even stranger than fiction).

Shout out to the Arab American Association of New York and to all the AAANY homies I was in the trenches with. Thank you for all the incredible work you do. You introduced me to a community that continues to inspire me with its warmth, strength, and humor. And thank you to all the amazing people I met in Bay Ridge.

Thank you to my students, past and present—I am in awe of you always. And to the entire GA community for all the support. Locker Room 119—you always have my back.

I'd be nowhere without all of my "sisters," whose love lives in this book. Kelly, your light shines brightly still. Naty, my twin through the ages, thank you for a sisterhood that transcends time and geography. Thank you to Karen Yi, Sara Elghobashy, Sandhya Nakasi, Courtney Ferguson, Reem Hassan, Savannah Strong, and to Molly, Chloe, and Darcy. Your friendship buoys me. Emily, I'm so grateful you "Meislered" your way into my life all those years ago; I can't remember how I functioned before I met you.

Finally, I have to thank my big, beautiful family. First, my parents: Fiona Macintyre and Atef Abdel Gawad. Mama, thank you for giving me your love of books and for carrying our family on your back. You're my rock. Baba, you're still the best storyteller I know. Thank you for never letting me settle for second best. Shout out to my brothers. Neal, thank you for always making me feel like maybe I could do something special one day. Zack, from séances in your room to the long-distance phone calls of adulthood, you are still my best friend. Jake, James, and Jason—I'm lucky I got to add you all as big brothers. Thanks to my stepfather, Stan, for all his love and support, and to my nephew Landen (my first baby). Thank you, Cristina (and Theo and Alice!). I'm so lucky to have the Shortsleeve crew in my corner—John, Susan, Joe, and Bani—thank you for everything. I'm grateful to the entire Adler family for loving me like a fourth daughter. Thank you to the Macintyres and the Abdel Gawads—I'm proud to be a member of your clans. Lastly, to Chris and our two beautiful babies. Chris—thank you for kissing me outside of that Walgreens in Times Square and telling me to quit messing around and be a writer already. I wouldn't have done any of this without you. Ayan and Zain, you are the two lights of my eye.

Alhamdulillah.

## ABOUT THE AUTHOR

AISHA ABDEL GAWAD has been published in *The Kenyon Review,*
*American Short Fiction,* and the scholarly journal *The Muslim*
*World,* in a special issue on Anglophone Muslim women writ-
ers. She won a 2015 Pushcart Prize for her short story "Waking
Luna." After graduating from college, Gawad worked at the Arab
American Association of New York, a community center and
social services agency serving the immigrant community in Bay
Ridge, Brooklyn. She is currently a high school English teacher
in Connecticut.